For A New Life

Timothy A. Esser

ISBN-13: 978-0984874309

"Snowing at the Lake"
Cover Image by CSCredon
www.Istockphoto.com

For A New Life is dedicated to:

Craig A. Birkholz, who served tours in Afghanistan and Iraq, rising to rank of Sergeant in the U.S. Army 10th Mountain Division, and as a police officer for the city of Fond du Lac, Wisconsin, until he was killed in the line of duty at the age of twenty-eight trying to save another. My nephew, my hero.

Jerry McBrayer, who knocked three times on my desk that fateful night at work a long time ago, and psychologically, emotionally, if not physically, saved my life over those next two months.

Mary, my wife, who supportively and lovingly endured many years and hours of me writing in vain, steadfastly encouraging me to continue, to finally see success with me. It took thirteen years to get it right. Thank you—I love you, too.

Raymond Esser, who encouraged and showed me ways to pursue my writing. Cancer took him before he realized his own dream of becoming an author.

Johua K. Hill, who looked over my shoulder that one slow day at work and insisted on reading what I wrote and that I write more, not knowing it had once been my dream, to reignite that dream into this novel.

Lynn Gregg, almost a long lost cousin, who asked to read and gave a pivotal, critical, essentially independent review of my book that gave me additional strength to carry on.

Ms. Corrigan, my fourth grade teacher, who first told me to become a writer. Thank you.

To my many friends and family who lent their names and some of their personality to this story at the time it was originally written; Gay, Bill, Paul, and Craig Birkholz; Rick, Paula, Michelle, and Brian Smith; Mark Schultz; Ron Sebetic; John Stancato; Doug, Sandy, and John Sorensen; Michael Angelo; Dean and Wendy Langer; Craig, Lynn, and Brad Kewenig; Joe Fosbinder; Sarah and Kelly Warner; Ben, Jami, and Kerri Miller; Todd Heyden; Big and Little John James Melesky the 1st and 2nd. I hope I did not forget any real people because all other named characters in this novel are completely fictional, though Franklin is based off an actual one-time meeting of an inmate whose name I never learned.

To my parents; Arnold and Sally Esser for their lasting support and encouragement.

And thank you, for reading my story.

For A New Life

1

In 1977 the Wisconsin State Employees Union went on strike.
The Army National Guard was called up to staff the prison
system.
(Sunday)

Bright blue skies carrying patches of flat gray bottomed white clouds, drifting by, can be seen through the windows. A sight that begs us to go outside to enjoy this late autumn day. Turning instead within, being pulled in, by the clatter and chatter of this busy prison mess hall, I look across the table with a questioning face. John's posture answers we have to go. I take two quick bites of food and a gulp of my drink as we rise. John moves his head to indicate a side door to the outside, between this building and the next; "It'll be quicker."

I follow only to bump into him outside the door for he suddenly stops as he looks to our left and quietly says; "Wow."

What caught his eye? I repeat his quiet word as I see, as the door closes off the mess hall noise behind us. Unseen from where we sat in the mess hall, to our left stands an expansive white canvass tent about a hundred feet away, and a wide strip of asphalt runs in front of it. Five rows of inmates, three inmates to each row, and each row spaced every ten feet or so, each monitored by one of our fellow National Guards, are lined on our side of the asphalt opposite that tent.

"What's going on?" I ask John as we hear the mess hall door open behind us.

Someone else answers for him; "Closest thing ta sex visits we got here. Women visit third Sunday every month."

We turn to see an inmate, food slop staining his sleeveless A-shirt, trying to show off shoulder muscles that just are not there on this unshaven potbellied man with a hairy chest.

"I cook here," he says on seeing our questioning faces. "All like ta show when da women come strut their stuff ta take their man ta the tent. Got fifteen, twenty minutes with their man, maybe a half hour—I dunno—whoa, I see what you two sissies been lookin' at—whoa, she's hot."

John and I return our gaze to the asphalt and to the women who are crossing it, to the one who immediately re-catches and holds our attentions.

My mind strains for the term the cook has described before it comes to me. "Conjugal visits?"

John glances at me. "Is that legal?"

"The women strut—nobody 'ficial calls it, but all like it," the cook explains.

"No. Sex. They have sex in the tent?" I ask.

"Why'dya go find out?" replies the cook. "Only those claimin' ta be married git to go in there…"

"Wisconsin doesn't have conjugal visitation," I quietly answer John.

"Seems like they do now," John replies.

"Look at her, man, ain't she somethin'?" demands the cook.

The woman is taking her sweet time coming near, as if for our pleasure. Her ebony legs flow forward and back, tantalizing us with the mesmerizing sight of her hips rising and falling under a thin silken red dress slit open to expose nearly the entire length and smooth glistening skin of those long graceful legs from the tips of her black string high heels on up. The dress comes tight around her waist by a black belt with a gold buckle at her midline. It teases of what lays underneath and rises in a V-split to both isolate and expose bountiful cleavage held in check by the same thin revealing silk spread just wide enough to keep her breasts inside, as they bounce from her runway model-like exaggerated yet slow movements. A thin long gold necklace dances joyfully within her cleavage. Her shoulder length dark hair, tightly bound in many thin red beaded braids, waves back and forth and bounces off the collar of her white full length velvet coat which she holds wide open to catch the day's considerable chill. Her purposeful exposure to this cold makes her more captivating, more enticing, more appreciated—she not only invites but also will want the touch of her man's warm hands. Her smile appears as wide as her coat is open yet is also tentative; she knows she looks good but her expression asks her man if she looks good enough. An expression I don't quite understand. Her almond brown eyes should captivate anyone, especially her man, but her eyes speak of too many worldly experiences at too young an age, and that current concern of not being good enough, which I cannot put a finger on as to why, is a curious thing. Something isn't right, and it isn't the coolness of this late November day.

John and I keep staring as our breaths crystallize in the cold air. She is strutting towards the closest line, about eight or nine yards away, when she notices us. John reacts just enough for me to know he, too, feels uncomfortable getting caught looking. For me, it's not that I want her, I don't, but I do appreciate her beauty, the show she is purposely putting on, and I'm curious to see the interaction between her and her man, because of the way her eyes talked.

"Shit. Her man is Franklin. Lucky bastard," says the cook.

Franklin wonders why her eyes broke from his and turns to find and to glare at us. He too wears a sleeveless white A-shirt, but he fills this shirt extremely well. A large solidly built black man; six foot and probably two-hundred-thirty pounds or more, he is powerful, and powerfully mean in the eyes. His lips pull into a silent snarl. He holds little tolerance for our distraction. Her soft words and beauty turn him quickly from us, however, to our relief.

"Wow," John says again.

"Yeah, he be a lucky man today," adds the cook.

"Yeah," I echo. "Gotta get going though, John." John takes a step but does not really move, and neither do I, instead, we continue to stare. I don't know why, but then I do.

"She's a beauty, ain't she?" asks the cook.

Franklin glances at us again. Though unseen, I sense the cook just gave acknowledgement to this man, and maybe something more.

John agrees; "Yes. She sure is a beauty."

She is next to him now. She stands so close but purposely does not touch—does not press herself against him. Her hands are on his breasts to hold him at bay while her fingers caress. His arms have gone hidden under her coat and must be resting on, enjoying, the curves of her hips. She purrs words softly into his ear with her face hidden on the far side of his, her neck shows nicely as a long gold teardrop earring, matching her necklace in style, shifts gently on her neck as she speaks.

"Yeah, we gotta go," John interrupts my thoughts as he finally answers me.

"Naw, enjoy her sight. She be gone in a minute. Take her candy in," entices the cook.

"We gotta go," John repeats, and we begin to move as the cook speaks up again.

"Heard he oft her back door lover in front ta her, snapped dude's neck as he begged—as she cried. Near did her, too, some wicked things to her. Crazy jealous mean son-of-a-bitch he is ... gotcha, I just kiddin', he ain't jealous, he's just mean. He shot the man between the legs before he shot him in the head. Ha-ha, had ya goin' there befo', didn't I? He ain't told me, though, exactly what he did to her."

We can't help but to look harder at her, trying to see the damage done by him when we realize this would have been done and healed long ago. It is too easy to stare at her. She has not taken his hand yet, not led him across to the tent as the others have and who are already entering there. She demurely glances our way and smiles.

We stare—difficult not to—she wants us to, as she gives the slightest jiggle to her breasts along with a rise to her chest—a sight we cannot easily look away from.

Trouble is Franklin is not watching her—he is watching us, and he looks inflamed with anger.

"Whoa, she likes ya—smile back," the cook encourages.

"We gotta go," John says apprehensively.

"Yeah," I agree as we begin to move, this time for real, turning toward the cook.

"Naw-naw, man, smile back at her or Franklin will take insult," warns the cook with an open smile as he stands to block us and as he nods past us towards Franklin.

John and I look at each other, give a quick look back and smile at the woman, and turn to go. The cook moves to block our way again.

"Hey, we gotta go, man," John says firmly to the cook as we hesitate in front of him.

"Naw I think ya done too much already—wanta see how ya get out of this," the cook replies with a devilish smile. We recognize his bad intent too late. Some preceding noise is put quickly into the background, overwhelmed by the deep threatening voice of a man close beside my ear.

"Fuckin' white boys dreamin' o' mah woman? Rapin' her wit' yo eyes? You ain't shit."

Franklin's hands are suddenly resting on, and firmly gripping, both my own and John's shoulders, causing John and I to look up together at him.

"No, man," John says.

"No—we just ... haven't seen this before," I answer.

Franklin bares his teeth and gives a slight shake to his head; "I hate liars."

"No. man, we mean the tent, the women ..." John begins to explain.

"Mah woman," Franklin interrupts, "Ya two ain't been lookin' at no other woman but mine. I don't be likin' dat."

"Ah," I say, as his hand slowly hardens its grip on my shoulder as he turns his face to watch me speak, and his look intimidates me, "Um, you, ah, your woman, ah, makes the other women here jealous."

His eyes tighten so I hurriedly add; "And, ah, she picked the right man with you."

Franklin keeps staring at me as he squeezes John's and my shoulders with an easy strength that makes us both hurt. "You're a freakin' pussy—I ain't got time for you, but if I see ya lookin' again I'll make time. I don't care who ya are. Don't mess with mah woman or me again," Franklin warns as he releases us and starts to step away, until a quiet thoughtless reactive word escapes my mouth; "Asshole."

A thrust of power comes hard against my shoulder so quick I cannot avoid it, and I see John as he falls across from me as I fall, stumbling, trying hard to stay upright and only my right hand bracing the ground saves me from a complete sprawl.

Franklin towers above between us, flexing his powerful arms with his fists clenched almost touching each other in front of him. His voice snarls and he looks like an enraged great ape as he exposes his teeth and widens his eyes, cocking his head slowly side to side.

My feet clumsily find footing below me as I pause and struggle against the fear and confusion Franklin has put into me. What just happened—I do not want to rise in challenge to this man, in a show of foolish pride, yet I do not want to stay low in shame.

"Stay down twinks. Ya uniforms mean nothin' ta me." His sneer widens as he warns us. He seems to drool in anticipation of more physical action. He wants us to take his challenge and stand up, to take a stand.

"Ones with guns comin' Franklin," warns the amused cook. "They 'bout half a minute away."

Franklin grunts as his eyes take a swift look around.

My eyes and ears now catch the commotion that surrounds us; whistles blowing, men shouting, men hurrying toward us, that I had not noticed during the seconds before. I slowly, humbly, gain my feet. Franklin's eyes set on me.

"I'll remember you," Franklin threatens just to me as he begins again to back away—but I'm stupid, as more quiet thoughtless words escape my mouth; "Fuck you."

Despite the increased distance between us he hears my whisper and comes with fury towards me. His hands impact my chest, expell my breath, to send me flying backwards into the mess hall door, its handle gouges the small of my back and catches my clothes to keep me on the glass. Franklin keeps coming. His fists slam into me and take my breath away again. He grips my uniform and draws it tight, so tight I cannot capture enough air. I feel my heart race. I feel a heat rush through me as fear fills me, as he slides my body up the door glass, off the latch, until our eyes meet. There exists no soul within his brown eyes, within the coldness of him, only a hint of enjoyment shows in them, from the fear my eyes display for him. A shiver runs down my back. I have not met such evil before.

"I kill you someday twink—apologize."

He gives an unexpected yet humiliating chance to get away but I want nothing to do with that; "Fuck you."

Am I crazy! Did I say that? My head bounces hard against the glass as Franklin jostles me. "No—I'm sorry, man," I blurt out but he doesn't care as I feel his power as he pulls me off the door and into the air. As he begins to throw me my left arm lashes out and my fist hits hard and square on his jaw, but this only angers him more. He tries to catch me, stop his throw, to pull me back to do more damage, but too late. I fall free and scrape the ground. My pants tear open at the knee and skin cuts send sharp pains up my leg as I see him launch himself at me.

"Ya dead white shit."

I roll to my back and my feet greet his face solidly to slow him, but this does not stop him. Some child-like sound utters from my mouth as I realize I will die. He slaps my legs aside as I roll again and struggle to rise. I see the men about me; inmates cheering, guards trying to restrain them, a single guard stands watching. I hear John shouting for someone to help me, as Franklin's weight slams me into the walkway and blood spurts from my lips. Franklin growls as I block one of his arms from grabbing my head but he finds success with the other, grabbing hair and savagely twisting my head from side to side, trying to snap my neck. A whimpering sound escapes my mouth as I resist, fearing my end is near.

Then I see boots. Shiny black boots of a guard standing only inches away in front of me. I feel Franklin quickly stop his efforts and reluctantly release his grip.

"You get up. Slowly," says the guard above me, but not said to me.

Franklin first puts his elbow and then a knee painfully into my back as he does so.

My head comes to rest face first on the pavement. Silent tears fall from my eyes as quick waves of emotions rush through me; relief, anger, fear, confusion, and others. I quietly gasp and regain my breath. I will live another day—how did this happen ... what just happened? My forehead rises from the pavement and then gently drops to it again. Why did I say what I did? Where did those words come from? I don't care, I'm just grateful I have the chance to keep living—thank God.

"Put your arms behind your back," I hear the guard order Franklin.

The heat that flushes my face, from the anger I feel within, from the fear Franklin has instilled in me, and from the public embarrassment I have just been given; these feelings start to lessen as I remain laying on the pavement and on knowing Franklin is being held captive. Yet I realize this event isn't over—I need to pay attention to what is going on now with a clear mind.

With a soft tap of his boot against my shoulder the guard asks; "Hey, you need medical attention?"

"No." I hold my voice steady and my tears back as this is my public cue to rise to my feet.

"How's your neck?"

"Too painful to know yet."

Two guardsmen hold Franklin's arms behind his back readying to handcuff him—he will allow them to because my guard, with an additional two guards watching his back, points a shotgun at his belly. There is no doubt this gun is loaded for my guard purposely ejects an unused shell to prove this point as Franklin thinks about resisting. The guard will have five or six more shells in the gun.

"Your name," my guard demands of the inmate.

Franklin turns his head to look more at me than the guard, and sneers at both of us. His eyes narrow as he watches me. "Franklin," he spits out.

"You just got yourself in a shit load of trouble, Franklin," my guard replies.

"Kiss my...." Franklin's words are stopped short by the quick rise of the shotgun toward his face.

"And you," my guard says as he glances at me, "You're in trouble, too. How'd this start?"

"Damn right dat white twink started dis," Franklin quickly voices.

The guard shows both irritation and restraint but before he can retort John steps near and answers; "Sir, we just finished mess hall, came outside and saw the women a-and the lines. We were just wonderin' and watchin' a while..."

"My woman..." Franklin interjects.

"...When we turned to leave the cook got in our way..."

"Damn right dey started it—see?" Franklin again. "Dey admittin' it."

"Franklin, you the cook?" my guard asks.

"Hell no, saw dem beatin' on him and ah came to help mah man. Dat's right. Dat's what I did."

"They what?" asks my guard.

"Beatin' on ta cook, man."

"He's lyin'," John asserts.

"Ain't so. Dem twinks thought dey could push dem uniforms 'round..."

"He's lying," I state, as I feel a sharp pain from my bloodied lip.

"He got mad 'cause we were lookin' at his woman," explains John.

"So you were lookin'. Why were you lookin' at her?" my guard asks. John hesitates and looks at me.

"Sir," I also hesitate, stopping from another sharp pain from my split lip and the renewed flow of blood trickling down from it, "They were closest to us, that's all."

Franklin scoffs; "Bull. Dey eye rape my woman. Couldn't have her so dey started beatin' ta cook."

"And where is this cook?" asks my guard.

We look around. The cook is not in the crowd.

"Any cooks here? Step forward," announces my guard, who I notice has a sergeant's rank. No one steps up.

"Who is this cook?" my sergeant guard sternly asks.

"He ain't here," answers Franklin.

"Why ain't he?" the increasingly frustrated sergeant demands.

With a casual shrug of his shoulder Franklin replies; "Don't know. Bigger trouble if he stay. I want you ta arrest dese twinks for beatin' on ta guy."

The sergeant looks around again. "My ... I don't see no guy ... you see a guy?" The sergeant asks John and I.

"No sir."

"No sir."

"Ain't no guy here Franklin. What all are you talkin' about? Looks like you got charges coming against you," the sergeant states.

Franklin shifts his body in anger and glares at the three of us. "Dey'd be eye raping and insultin' mah woman and beat on ta cook. You ain't puttin' no charges 'gainst me—them—them deserve it—them do."

"What woman is he talkin' about, guys?" asks the sergeant.

"His woman," admits John, "She's a looker."

"A hook—I meant which woman, see her?"

"Go on twinks, put charges 'gainst me—c'mon," challenges Franklin.

"You shut up," the sergeant orders Franklin, then asks us; "She's a hooker you said?"

"No, no, a looker—she's hot looking," John replies.

"Is she here?"

We don't see her. Franklin becomes more frustrated as he also searches for her.

"Press charges against me twink—see how far you get," Franklin challenges again.

"Yeah," comes a chorus of inmate responses from the surrounding crowd. "Do it. Do it."

"Get this crowd dispersed—now," the sergeant loudly commands to the other guards. "Now." The other guards go to work moving the other inmates away. The sergeant shakes his head. "I can't believe the amount of paperwork I gotta do because of this. I can't believe you guys got into this. I'm pissed. You two lucky you ain't carrying arms. Well are you or aren't you pressin' charges?"

He looks at John first.

John looks at Franklin, me, then the sergeant. "He ain't worth my time, man, I don't want to cause more trouble—no, no sir."

Franklin gives a knowing condescending smirk as he nods his head.

"And you?" the sergeant asks me.

"C'mon twink, do it," goads Franklin.

I pause a moment, feel my lip, feel the fear again ....

"Dis is gonna be fun, twink, c'mon," Franklin goads some more.

"Man, you don't wanna press charges. That's months of coming back and forth here. Time. It's just messed up. Say no, man," John advises.

"Yeah, I'll press charges," I answer.

John clenches his fists and tightens his face. "Take it back."

"You doin' it then?" asks the sergeant.

"Yeah, I said yes," I answer.

John lets out a disgusted sigh. "No, man, take it back. You don't want this."

"Yeah, John, I do. I do. I'm pressin' charges."

Franklin stares at me—I believe with some inner-felt evil satisfaction. "Twink, I'm here for another twelve years, you ain't puttin' more time on me, I'll kill you first ...."

"Franklin," sharply calls the sergeant. "Shut up."

Franklin mouths the words repeating his intent to kill me.

I feel the fear he instills—I believe him … if he ever has the chance he will try to kill me. He will try … and somewhere within me comes an answer that he had better succeed the first time, because I will kill him if he misses—a thought, a feeling, that I really mean, to my surprise, to my discovery, that some part of me I did not believe really existed before does … and I like it—I like it a whole lot. I make eye contact with Franklin and hold steady.

The sergeant looks at me closely. "You sure?"

I take a moment, keeping Franklin's eyes on mine; "Yes."

Franklin resists as his guards take him away, resists long enough to give a final furious glare back at me and another snarl.

"Shit," the sergeant says in monotone, "The work I gotta do now."

"Um, Sarg?" John politely interrupts, "We gotta get to our posts. We're probably late already—can we go?"

The sergeant looks up into the sky in disgust, letting out another sigh as he thinks a moment. "You need medical attention?"

"I'll go after my shift," I answer.

"Good, because you two will get under my skin if I take you with me now, anyway. Shit. Where you two at?"

"Cottage two," John answers.

"The tower above three," I answer.

My reply catches the sergeant's attention; "So you shot expert, huh? We only put experts up there. Must have been a long time ago, way you look—fifteen-twenty years? You still current?"

I look down. With Franklin so publicly overpowering me, embarrassing me—I feel a large measure of humility ... having shot expert, and that a long time ago, doesn't seem something I should be anything proud of at this moment. "Yeah," I say simply. "Can we go?"

"Fill out reports and have them on my desk at the end of your shifts—before you do anything else. You know where to find me?"

"Yes."

"Yes."

"I expect you two there then. Give that man over there your names and info, then get out of my sight."

We choose to walk across the grounds heading for the gate in the fence close to where they park the jeeps. The transporters there will take us around and between the two perimeter fences of this medium security prison to our posts. Meanwhile we have our chance to talk to each other with no one else near and John opens up with stern emotion the first moment he can.

"We've been friends," he says as he shakes his head, "What—all our lives? Grade school. Junior high—high school, technical school, this National Guard—I know you sometimes are an idiot, walk yourself right back into a corner you can't get out of just 'cause you do that kind of idiotic thing for whatever idiotic reason you do it for but don't you think that what you did here is the most idiotic thing you ever did—are you crazy?"

"John ..."

"Don't freakin' John me—say yes, this is the most IDIOTIC thing I have ever done—say that to me, you idiot."

"John ..."

"I could kick your ass. You know by filing charges you draw me into it, too. I gotta stand as witness—and I don't want ta do it. Not that the inmate didn't assault us, doesn't deserve punishment, but we're punishing ourselves for what—for what?"

"Principle."

John stares at me. And he stares some more. Long enough for me to think he wants more of an explanation, but he doesn't give me the chance.

"I understand principle. Do you understand not all principles have to stand? Not all are worth following through—to do—some just hide as stubbornness—do ya—do ya?"

I don't know what to say.

"Well, do ya?"

"Yeah, I understand but ..."

"But you're gonna do it anyway?"

"Um, well, yeah, John ..."

John jumps ahead of me and puts his hands up in front of my chest to stop my walk. He doesn't say anything as he begins to back away. He shakes his head, and his hands act as if they are pushing me back. He shakes his head again, turns and starts walking off fast before me.

He is several feet away when I ask; "John?"

Without looking back he shows me his middle finger over his shoulder.

"John?"

Still not looking back he straightens this arm and holds it as high as he can, his third finger pointing to the sky.

2

(Four days later, Thursday evening)

"So, the story is your fight at the prison, huh," Doug says as our caravan of vehicles merge with the I-94 traffic. Bill and Gay, Paula and Mary, are in the truck following us, and Tom and Roy follow them in their car. "You're gonna tell us about it now—aren't ya?"

"Ah-man, no, I …"

"Naw—you're gonna tell us, none of this no crap," interrupts Rick, who is driving but takes a quick look back over his shoulder at me. I'm sitting behind him, Mark is next to me. Doug is up front with Rick.

"Yeah, this trip isn't gonna be any fun if you don't share an experience like that—it won't be fun for you," Mark adds.

"Yeah," the other two chime agreement.

"Guys…" I sigh.

"Tell us," they reply.

Well, seems I have little choice, so I tell them and in detail—why not, they asked for it.

"You know, somehow it reminds me of when the three of us, Rick, were playing two on one basketball and he got mad," Doug says right after I finish, "Mad at you, Rick, and told you to go home. You laughed. I laughed. He got madder. We laughed more. He got even more mad and told me to go home, too—remember that?"

Rick lifts his head up in his characteristic wide open mouth non-verbalized horse laugh of a smile, then brings his head down and says; "Sure do."

"You know where to stick it, guys," I respond. This only makes the three of them grin.

"What's the catch?" Mark asks—he doesn't know the story.

Rick chuckles. "Well he sure was mad and tellin' us to go home, trouble was we were at Doug's place. It was something to see his face when we told him that and he realized where he was—ah, we busted a gut laughin'."

Mark is looking at me long and hard.

"What?" I ask.

He shakes his head. "There's one of you everywhere, isn't there?"

"Uh?"

"Ah-nothing," he replies.

"We're gonna be going near there," Rick says.

"Near where?" Doug asks.

"Near Plymouth. Kettle Moraine medium security prison is just outside Plymouth and we're gonna be driving kinda close by. There's road work on I-43 and I want ta miss that so we'll take highway 57 going by Plymouth instead. I figure it might just be faster 'cause on 43 there'll be traffic backed up for miles at the overpass they're repairing—was the last time I came through anyway."

Doug and Mark are both looking at me.

"What?" I ask.

They smile.

"Okay what?" I say. "You figure I'm scared to get that close to the prison again or somethin'—what gives?"

Rick chuckles as he glances at the other two. "He got the message."

"Oh screw you," I answer.

3

(The same Thursday evening, as seen through Franklin's eyes)

Tonight's the time, man—about time, as my feet find the floor beside this stinking prison bed. There ain't no turnin' back, ain't none at all, as I dress, put on my winter coat and inside it go the things they don't know nothing about, 'cause I'm about to leave this stinking cell forever, feels good—real damn good. Then this stinking cottage hallway I'm walking in ... a sight I refuse to see again. The cool but humid sweaty smells of the commons area almost puts a smile on my face, except I see Beckley sitting in my seat at the left end of the couch facing the set of glass double doors which overlook the outside yard. That's my place. Nobody sits there—nobody but me sits there, especially tonight. He sees my reflection off the glass too late—I'm coming at him from behind.

My hands grab his upper arms as he rises. I lift him easily and bring his thin petite short waxy body back up and almost against mine. His feet rapidly search for footing against the couch below, and I smile over that. I hold his arms too hard for his hands to reach mine, but he tries. He squirms without hope.

"Girly boy outta know better," I growl into his left ear.

His white pimpled face turns ghostly as he pulls his head away from me and turns it the best he can to face me. "S-sorry Franklin."

The cottage guard taps his baton against the bullet-proof window glass of his protected room twenty feet away behind us but I take my time whispering to Beckley; "I ain't want no man-ho like you. Ya fag otta know'd not ta sat here—mine fer weeks, yo."

"I-I know Franklin—I know, but after a few days you know, you know you might be wantin' somethin' since you ain't get it from your woman Sunday."

The guard taps his baton loud and hard this time. I can hear his warning.

All this just pisses me off. I toss Beckley toward the doors. He falls onto the tile and bounces into the ceiling-to-floor windows that complete this common's wall overlook of the prison yard and he runs off, not looking back. The cottage guard still yells at me, so I turn round to face the jerk with my hands open in offering. "Wha? A-hole wanted mah dick. Girly boy don't got what ah need—you do?"

The guard stares angrily back, gives me the finger, then turns away to other duties.

Freak.

I want to pace—my habit, but I know better. I need to sit and look calm now. It's less than thirty minutes and I can't blow this being angry. Tonight is our chance for a new life.

Drew Jackson sits down at the other end of the couch. He stares straight ahead, but I do hear his whispered voice. "What the fuck nigger, you're dead if you screw us. You cool now bro?"

Jackson, ha, calling me a nigger when he is one—a bit educated but no matter. He's here for murder. He, myself, three others in this cottage of seventy, are here for that. His pimpin' and heroin dealin' got him here. He and me planned this escape. I call him lots of names but none get to him. In a few minutes I ain't about to care. He'll be going his way and me, mine.

"I'm cool, man, I'm cool," I quietly answer.

"Better be."

"I'm ... cool."

"Where's the cutter?" His quiet question is pointed, and we ain't been looking at each other yet.

"Up my sleeve."

"It didn't fall out?" he gives a whispered surprise. "You lucky ass."

I now realize the chance I had taken. I *am* a lucky ass. Getting that wire cutter in from the outside before work release was taken away by the strike, from the few prisoners who were then allowed again to work outside the prison, who worked so hard getting the cutter in, and keeping it hidden from several weekly searches, was not easy. I am a lucky ass.

"Beckley would've snitched ..."

"With his life," I retort.

Drew nods. "They fixed the heat fifteen minutes ago. They're not gonna let us keep our coats on much longer."

"Bit more dan a half hour ta lock down, Drew, dey don't give crap," I answer. I watch Drew's eyes search out the window reflections before he gives another slight nod. The reflections do show the guard is back looking at me, studying us. Time for Jackson to go and he knows it. He leaves to make the rounds with the others who are going.

They started fixing the rusty inside perimeter fence before the strike, slowly replacing it with a taller stronger one. Three sets of coiled razor wire on and along the new fencing will replace the simple three barbed wires that are only strung along the top of the old fence, these coils making escape so much harder. The second, outer, perimeter fence will be replaced after they finish the inner one, so it carries those three barbed wires, like our inner fence section still does. Tomorrow, however, they will work our inner fence and final section of this prison to change all that, the razor coils will then be here, and our chance at escape will then be gone.

They're stupid though. Thirteen-fourteen days ago when the State went on strike, the regular guards who know us so well left us and these naive great social heroes in green, the National Guard, came here—and them contractors just kept on working the fence. This is what my cutter is for—those two sets of three barbed wires on those two fences. I'm the man. Every other man going tonight depends on me, even Drew Jackson. My job is to cut those damn barbed wires as quickly as I can or all will be lost. I got no trouble with that.

Drew returns.

"Four backed out," he whispers.

"What four?" I ask, hoping that two would be the idiots who could not figure why we broke the heating system earlier today—they had to be explained to why we needed to be wearing our coats tonight.

"The old man Deuce, the old Jackson ..."

"The old dudes," I say.

"Yeah, the four old ones."

"Damn," I reply. The idiots remain. None of the four old dudes are in my group but I want as many men escaping as we can make go. More numbers, more chance for me to make it, but I know why. The old dudes ain't sure the security locks are shorted, the glass double doors mechanically being already open, not sure of climbing the fences in time, making the woods in time, under gunfire.

"Miller sure 'bout them alarms?" I ask. "And them doors?"

"Yeah. Yeah he is. They ain't workin'. These doors are open. Asked him again myself after the third old man backed off," Drew replies.

"Wished ah'd knew how Miller did that," I say.

"Me too. Gettin' him all those times to work that stuff over these last two days right in front a the man, man, was hard, man. Can't believe myself it'll work," Drew says. "And no guard noticed."

"Dem ain't guards. Ta real guards ain't here—dats why this is gonna work."

"Better, with the four backin' out, though, it makes nineteen going," Drew states.

"Whatever," I say, looking at the wall clock to the right of me; it is across the room but large enough to easily see. Sixteen minutes before the guard tower shift change outside. Twenty minutes before they start pushing us into our rooms, six minutes later it's lock-down.

Somehow they screwed that up, too, these men in green. Tower shift change should happen ten minutes after lock down, not ten before. Someone made a mistake, didn't do their job, and no one noticed—except us. Now we depend on this mistake happenin' again tonight.

"Garcia's boys cool?" I ask.

"Yeah, soon as you give the signal."

"Nineteen betta not get obvious."

"Your turn, this time," Drew replies.

After my rounds I end up standing against a urinal and my mind races on; when the jeep driver, and whoever else, do see us, they won't know what the heck to do. They'll be afraid. We outnumber them. They know we know they drive up unarmed to the tower. They'll stay hiding on the far side of the tower, banging the door, desperate to get inside, or even drive away. If the tower guard is already at the door he may take a step out to see why and the door may close behind him ... that would be too lucky. How reluctant the tower guard will be to shoot us is more important, every second of hesitation is another second for me to fly this coop.

Tobias Grant puts himself in the next urinal. He is not here just to piss.

"Franklin," he whispers, though no one else is here, "Take me with your group. The ones I'm with are dumb-shits."

"Can't man, you know dat. Plans set. Numbers set. You'd be too many. Good luck to ya, man."

"C'mon Franklin," he quietly pleads.

I return a stern gaze. "Yo, git out on yer own once you're clear, but you ain't comin' with us. Keep dis friendly, Grant, cause I respect ya."

Grant wants to say more. Instead he gives a bitter look, zips his pants, flushes the urinal by pounding its old-style handle in anger, and stomps out.

"We each take our chances," I say to myself as I hit the flusher and leave.

The tower three guard also got in a nasty habit—our tower, the one overlooking this cottage so well that guard can see us undress in our rooms—that faggot, to leave his post early, usually half a minute, to get downstairs, that takes twelve seconds, to wait blindly by the door hidden from our escape path by the tower itself. He has every night since that first night's rain—found out the twink guard I fought on Sunday was up there, but he ain't no more. He got his replacement to do the same though—crazy luck. We count on the habit of the jeep driver to pull behind the tower also, hidden to us, to exchange tower guards, also set that first rainy night they were here. They do this so wrong, but them doing it gives us time. We give the guard twenty-four seconds to go down and up those stairs, and we take six seconds off to make sure he is on his way down. So we have from six to eighteen seconds to make the best of our break—that's a freaking lot of time to give us.

4

"... So Joe and I see these two girls thumbing for a ride. They're not dressed right. Somethin' was odd. It was a cold night and they didn't have no coats on. Anyway, they weren't bad lookin', one was pretty good, so we stop and pick them up in Joe's van ..."

Rick is telling his story. One Doug and I have heard before, but Mark hasn't.

"...Turns out they just escaped from one of those detention centers or jail or someplace close by where they're held for a while and they wanted to get the heck away. We drove some before we found this out and by then we were gettin' kinda friendly with them—these girls were horny ..."

"Oh—of course that's where this is going," Mark sighs. "I should have known."

Rick chuckles. "Yeah. I did the pretty one and Joe got the other. He was rather mad at me for awhile after 'cause the pretty one seemed to warm up to him first."

"Yeah, there it is," Mark responds. "The Smith conquest of yet another woman. What else can we talk about?"

"Oh—want ta know her number?"

"No Rick, we don't," I quickly reply.

Rick gives another chuckle. "Alright, I'll keep the number to myself, but it's only double digit and comes right after ..."

"NO!" The three of us harmonize in one way or another.

"We know you beat us. Let's talk about somethin' else," I say.

Rick looks to the other two and realizes we do want to move on. He resigns; "Okay."

"What do you do, Doug?" Mark asks.

"Air traffic controller—head guy at Yuma's airport," Doug answers.

"Wow. Cool. See anything?"

"Believe me, you don't want to see anything. It's scary just to see a tire blow or a thrust reverser panel tear off a plane, or a bird strike. That's scary, too, but nothing serious—nobody hurt," Doug replies. "How 'bout you?"

Rick answers before Mark; "Remember those construction machines parked at his house growin' up? Well, Mark inherited his dad's business. He owns the place up in Chippewa."

"Hey great," we say.

"How long has that been?" I ask. "I remember you movin' right after high school."

"Yeah … we did move about then. Oh, uh, owned the place, well, going on four years now."

"Wife's name?" begins Doug in a growling interrogating voice, "Got children? How many? What car you drive? Where were you on the night of April 14th last year? What was your dinner? Why'd you kill him for? Where's his body?"

We start shaking our heads and giving out sighs as Mark growls an answer; "You ain't gettin' nothin' otta me man. My wife Jenny will beat the crap out a ya as Tom, twenty, and Michael, eighteen, come to my rescue first before ah say a word. We'll throw ya in the trunk of our Cadillac and take ya body ta Rice Lake, like we did with that other guy last April 14th, who tried ta get in my wife, and we'll have a steak dinner ta celebrate gettin' rid a ya, just like we did him—how's that?"

Doug is tongue-tied and we laugh.

"You, Doug?" Mark asks.

"That was good, Mark. Quick thinkin'. No, not of my own. Sandy, my wife, has a son John. I raised him. I consider him my son. Though he knows I'm not his biological father, he calls me dad. We're close."

"How about you?" Mark turns and asks me.

"Um … I'm estranged from my four going on ten years now."

"Oh," Mark replies. "I guess we better leave that alone, huh?"

"Unless you provide plenty to drink," I answer.

"Rick's told me some about that," Doug says, "If we can find the time I'll buy you those drinks, just out of sympathy."

"I-I don't need no ..."

"I might sympathize but I ain't gonna pity you, you jerk, just buy you some blasted drinks—that you are gonna accept—got it?" Doug insists.

He surprised me; "Got it, man—thanks."

He shakes his head; "Yeah."

"What about Mary?" Mark asks. "Any children?"

"She has three; Ben, Jami, and Kerri. None between us," I answer.

"What you do?" he asks.

"I'm a design engineer—design lawn tractors."

"No big heavy equipment like my construction company uses?"

"No. Almost a completely different science that stuff is."

"Too bad, we'd have a lot to talk about otherwise," Mark responds and asks; "So where's this place you got, Rick, that you just recently bought?"

"Yeah. Remember I shared some land with Fosbinder?"

"No, you're not going back to those prison girls," Mark states.

"Yeah—naw. Our land got bought up by the mining company up there. They gave us pretty good dollar for it. Paula and I looked around—we've wanted to move up north when we retire anyway, and we found this place nearly smack in the middle of Nicolet National Forest. This trailer I'm pulling is gonna stay up there as our home until our real home is built."

"But in a National Forest? They allow that?" Doug asks.

"Yeah, how do they allow that?" I add.

"There was a scattering of privately owned lands that managed not to be bought up, or was simply not bought—maybe if there was a homestead they let the people stay, um, like a, like a grandfather clause, I guess. I don't know—back when they first made it a National Forest, whenever that was, but I do know I own the land," Rick asserts. "And I do know there are a number of fingers of land that are like mine that extend deep into the preserve. There are at least a half dozen small towns inside Nicolet. We'll be somewhat near Tipler, Wisconsin."

"How deep we going in?" Doug asks.

"About three miles by the way we drive. Don't know how far straight in, but it's a ways, I tell ya."

"What about power—electricity and water and, um, plumbing?" I ask.

"They'll run a power line. In the spring we'll be installing a septic system, digging a well. I arranged to have some people meet us over that stuff tomorrow. I'm anxious to show you guys the land when we get there."

5
(Franklin)

Drew and I stand in front of the glass double doors, ready.

"Jeep's coming," whispers Drew.

"I ain't blind, nigger," I quietly reply.

I know Drew glances at me but I'm watching the tower guard, wanting him to go down those tower stairs and out of our sight. He's slow tonight. He's looking at me—that twerp. "Glad to see ya," I whisper but with large mouth movements, hoping the guard can read what I say as I make arm movements in pointing at him.

"What are ya doin'?" Drew almost screams, yet speaks in a whisper, as he hears me and sees my reflection off the door glass. "Don't make him stay up there you fool."

I turn to face Drew, realizing he is right—angry that he is. I stay looking at Drew, hoping my new pose relaxes the twerp so he goes down them tower stairs. Drew is boiling mad. He looks back inside to the cottage guard, at me, then outside to the jeep that is now at the foot of the tower and all but disappeared behind it. Drew's eyes fall on me to stay and I can't help looking back into his. That tower guard better disappear or I'm about to fight for my life. Drew is a big enough man not to hesitate about taking me on.

The tower guard twerp disappears down the stairs.

I give a nod to Garcia. His men walk over to the guard's station twenty feet behind us and break out in an argument right in front of the bullet proof window the cottage guard is looking through, to block his sight of us. They begin showing signs of getting physical to increase the guard's attention, but not enough to make the guard push any buttons for help or to sound an alarm, just enough to keep him busy.

"Three one-thousand, four one-thousand ...," Drew is quietly counting the planned time.

At six seconds my body slams against the left glass door handle as Drew slams his body against the right. The supposedly secured doors bang loud against their stops behind us as we're already halfway across the thirty yard distance to the first fence as the alarms begin to blare. The wire cutter slips into my hand as I run and jump high onto the twelve-foot fence.

I see the tiny gritty details of the aluminized wire fencing like I have never seen anything before. Real—every motion, every sight, every smell, any touch. The high tower beacons shine yellow-white against the night sky before me to put the gray metallic braces carrying the barbed wires above me in a surreal light. I watch my hand grab hold of this brace as the fence sways from the climbing loads of the other men as my mind separates from the sounds and events around me that fill my senses, and I feel like I am in someone else's body. My feet push. I reach higher. I rapidly cut through the first two strands and watch as the rusty wires part and tiny puffs of metallic dust appear in their place and drift off into the cold night air, the two wires twanging as they disappear from sight.

The alarms blare, loud enough to hurt. Below me I hear Miller's voice rise in a weird laugh—rejoicing over his success in short circuiting the electronics and mechanisms of the glass doors. Someone else to the right of me is counting seconds of time. Many are cursing, telling others to hurry, telling me to hurry—I am! Against the glare of the lights I watch the continued upward reach of my hand and the slow motion action of the cutter snipping the last wire in half, it's gone with another high pitched twang and dust puff.

The fence sways as the men climb, jump, and some fall over it. Someone slaps my back leg as I begin to swing it over and I lose my grip as I fall forward. My back slams hard into the ground below, jarring me, taking my breath away, yet I smell the ground's musty odor as I wince from the hurt.

"Franklin's down—get the cutter—get the cutter!"

I suck a painful breath into my lungs—no way—no way is anyone taking over for me.

"Git away!" I say as loudly as I can as I roll over and quickly find the cutter in the grass. I rise and begin sprinting for the second fence, waving off those who started for me.

I glance quick over to the tower as I cross the perimeter road to see the jeep driver's head slink back behind the tower's protection.

The men part just before I jump onto the second fence and climb.

"S-Stop! S-Stop what you're doing! G-Go back!" yells the tower guard high above us in a frightened, unsteady, and youthful voice—too soon!

Men swear. Men curse. Some have already reached the top of the fence before me and are trying to slip underneath the wires, over the wires, trying to pull the wires down, insanely working against one another in their efforts to escape.

Crack! The tower guard's rifle spits out a warning shot as I snip the first wire.

The second wire's gone. Men are slipping through.

The third wire is gone and I drop the cutter.

Crack! A second warning shot that only shoots more energy into us.

This time my foot finds someone's shoulder as I make it over the fence top and I hear that someone curse from the other side of the fence behind me—who gives a damn who that is?

My feet hit the ground and I begin to run like I've never run before.

6

Rick is telling Mark and Doug about his experiences at the Post Office, stories I've heard before, so I watch the city of Milwaukee pass by as we drive over the high rise bridge that gives an expansive view of the city's downtown skyline, the river, and the parts of the harbor that can be seen. Milwaukee was once known for its beer producers, foundries, and heavy machinery manufacturers, but all have been hit by hard times—not as many are here as before. Still, we catch the distinct yeasty smell of fermenting hops and barley which go into making the beer.

I glance at Mark. It's been a long time since we played sandlot ball. He is a barrel-chested man just a touch shorter than Rick but heavily muscled and blond haired. As German looking as his name of Schultz suggests. His gray eyes hold a hint of arrogance—also shown in the way he spoke to me, where a feeling he has done better than us seems to come out, but I'm not sure of that yet—his quick witted response to Doug's interrogation earlier showed a sense of humor I didn't recall him having. He was always on the more serious side, like me. If he does feel superior he doesn't know we don't care. Back when, he had the strength to hit the baseball over the centerfield fence two hundred some feet away, like Rick—for kids of our age that was something. Doug and I competed for singles and doubles. Mark hunted. Rick hunted. Doug and I sometimes hunted—I did not like doing it. They did.

Doug contrasts us all by being almost as tall as Rick yet being the thinnest. He has weathered skin, just as you would expect of a cowboy who spends a lot of his free time outside. His brown eyes are still penetrating, always seemingly able to see more than he would let on. His lanky appearance is deceiving; he has good strength. Just like I'd be called respectable when compared to Rick or Mark. Rick once said I'd be more than what they bargained for in a bar fight if someone who doesn't know me got me into such a fight. I would chicken out before then, but, hey, I appreciated the compliment.

Rick is the tallest and strongest of us four here. Six foot two inches and two hundred twenty, maybe two hundred thirty pounds, he is a force to be reckoned with. He liked to fight in his younger days, our younger days, and he could fight. Never knew nor heard him losing a fight—except once, over in Italy while in the Army. Maybe I can drag that story out of him later. Now, like me, he has graying hair and a matching mustache-goatee. He carries a hint of a belly, but just a hint. Like the rest of us, he keeps in shape. It is his size and air of confidence that strike you the first time you meet him. He likes to laugh, has an easy smile, but he also has those wolf-like warrior eyes that give men pause and which seem to mesmerize a certain type of woman. They and Rick know each other instinctively—opportunistically? He simply likes women too much. He had an affair during his first marriage. Paula came about from that, but it was not her that caused the break-up. She came about when Rick and his first wife already began to divorce. I don't fault Rick at all for divorcing his first wife; she liked to play drama queen; liked long drawn out arguments. It bothers me, though, for Paula, that Rick's eyes still wander and linger too long too often. We others might get caught staring at a good looking woman—I'm guilty, and there are too many women who want to be looked at that way. We see enough of them around revealing themselves knowingly in the way they dress; buttons unbuttoned lower than needed at the bust line or skirts higher than needed for their legs to look good. We may look, but Rick drools. Rick also doesn't like getting messed with; smells and goes for blood quick. It's good he knows how to fight ... and is our friend.

"When's the last time you did any huntin'?" Doug asks me.

"Oh, man, years ago. Many years ago."

"You never liked it much from what I remember," Mark says.

"No it didn't catch on with me, but I went out deer huntin' a few times."

"Yeah," Rick adds, "I heard one of those times he got lost, accordin' to Bill."

"Whoa," calls out Doug, "We got ourselves another story—let's hear it mister."

7

(Franklin)

Crack! Crack! Crack!

A spray of debris erupts before me in the pebbled grass as I run by the point of impact. I push myself so hard I lose awareness of anyone and anything not directly in my line of sight or hearing—again feeling like I'm in someone else's body. Two quicker men sprint out ahead of me, spreading from each other as they bound through into taller grass and brush. I follow one of them, running, slanting, to my left and keep running for all that I am.

Crack! Crack! Crack! Crack! ... Crack!

I hear a scream cut short. From somewhere right of me I hear someone cry out, uncontrollably, Jenkin's name.

I force a glance there, to my right, as I run. As I hear more shots I see, further over, the soil kick up in front of three men as bullets impact twigs, earth, and stones, sending these up into the air but the men do not stop. Nearer I see bark blast away from the center trunk of a young tree, causing the whole tree to shudder. I hear an odd noise, closer to me, and look right again to watch a familiar outline of a man going down without a face, blood spewing, pieces of bone and flesh fanning out before and below him like a ball of liquid red and yellow vomit as his lifeless body collapses unnaturally into the dirt at the base of another young tree. Repulsed I jerk to the left and immediately see the effects of a bullet rip the side of an oak tree just ahead of me, bits of its bark spraying me, as I run past this same tree. A bullet meant for me. I feel my legs straining, can see my knees pumping wildly in and out of my peripheral sight, as I continue deeper into the darkness.

Two more shots and this rain of gunfire is over. The guard's twenty rounds in his magazine are all used, and I cannot tell if any of the other tower guards have fired on us from their distances. We, who survive, are safe for the moment, but none of us slow our run into the woods and for the covering darkness of night.

8

"C'mon, we gotta hear this famous lost in the woods deer huntin' story, stop wasting our time and get on with it," chides Doug.

"No."

"Yes."

"Man, everybody's got a lost in the woods or I got my first deer story—what's the big deal?"

"Uh, man, what a dead pan type of guy here," remarks Doug. "C'mon, when we hear that you had some kind of life experience, Mr. Excitement, you can't get by with 'no'. You have to tell us, you boring son-of-a-bitch."

"Wow, Doug, don't hold back none, now, ya hear?" I reply as I hear Rick chuckle and see his horse smile through the mirror. Mark has an amused look on his face but is courteously holding his thoughts to himself.

"C'mon Perfesser, instruct us on how to get lost in the woods or we'll make sure you do once we get up there."

"Thanks, Rick, mighty friendly of ya," I answer.

"We're all against you, if you can't tell," Mark says.

"I failed to notice. Thanks," I answer.

"So get on with it," Mark replies.

Well, maybe I can tell it in an amusing way. I don't know. It's embarrassing. "There was Bill, Michael Angelo, Big John and his father Little John ..."

"Ah," Mark interrupts, "This is a real story—right? I mean Michael Angelo the painter, Big John and Little John from, ah, Robin Hood? C'mon, tell it right."

I grin. "Mark, I am. Remember Angelo florists in town? Mike's dad. Big John is a big guy and junior to his little dad Little John, who has no teeth." They sneer, not believing me—yet. "Ask Bill when we stop, he'll tell ya. Anyway we are up in Nicolet somewhere. They're tellin' me the lay of the land the night before. We will post up to hunt in the morning on a hillside overlooking a crescent shaped bog or swamp that follows the hill's base. Two logging roads are on the hill. One along the top, where we will post, the other goes down and stops somewhere along the swamp. We're posting because they figure other hunters in the area, on this first weekend, will be too impatient to post and instead organize a drive of the deer. They will be yelling 'hello'.

Angelo becomes concerned when he sees my hunting clothes, feels I'm not properly dressed, so they give me better boots and a few other items. Angelo senses something else, though, and tells me not to wander off tomorrow, not to shoot all my shells—slugs in the shotgun they give me, not to take off all my clothes as I run and get sweaty, because I'll freeze during the next night and have no shells to protect me or signal with. He looked sincerely into my eyes, but I thought he was nuts. I won't do anything like that ..."

"No," Rick interrupts. "Not him—but he will."

"Smart-ass," I reply. "Yeah, well, the next morning they sit me on a stump and tell me not to move 'cause deer can see the slightest movement. So I sit so still when the snow falls it covers the barrel of my gun. The snow stops—it hasn't covered the ground but that's when I hear the snort of a deer from behind some tall bushes about twenty feet to the side in front of me. I wait. I turn my gun slowly to point. Nothing happens. So, after a time, I get up and move quietly to get behind those bushes and what do I see? Fresh deer droppings and a clear trail. I take a look around, decide to follow the trail, get myself a deer ..."

"Can't get lost by following a trail," Rick says. "As the story goes ..."

"You want to tell this? Because I don't," I retort.

"No, go on—Hansel."

"Yeah, you shit ... well, I lose the trail down by the swamp where the dirt path turns into a crease in the grass. I look around, feel I know where I am and follow the crease—until I can't go any further. Yep there comes a wind blowing and now the path I took has been combed into the other grass—can't see where I came from, from shit. No panic. I go back straight away but see nothing familiar. I'm just getting nervous when my boot breaks through the ground into the marsh water. While I don't get wet I go into a panic. I'm not sure which way to turn, which way to go. I start running and luckily find harder ground. I yell for help, except I did not yell the word help, I yelled the word hello. I thought I was yelling for help. Maybe I thought one of the guys would answer me without me getting embarrassed if I said hello instead of help. I don't know. All I know is from this point on I was yelling at the top of my voice and I was later told I yelled only hello. I yelled it as I ran by a thick bush and a large grayish brown creature bolted from it so close I could almost touch it. Blam went the shotgun towards that deer. I'm in real panic now—creatures are after me. Hello! Blam. Hello! Blam. I stumbled—blam! Hello! Hello! A real emphatic hello! A panic-stricken real terror filled insanity hello! Blam—I've clipped the top of an evergreen tree with that shot and even I, seeing it, don't believe it! I've run all through this from one side of the swamp to the other and I am sweating a river. I begin taking my clothes off and that's when Angelo's words come back to me and I pull my jacket and clothes back on. I check my gun—all the shells have been spent. I realize what I've just done and lean against a thin trunked tree and begin to cry when I hear the old man Little John call from the slight hill above me in his toothless way; 'You lost mother-fucker?'

'John!' I cry and shout; 'Yeah, yeah I am.' And I start running to him. As I near he says; 'Don't kiss me mother-fucker—I'll have ta kill ya.'

Wonderful words.

Turns out I'm only about thirty feet away from the stump they first put me on. When Little John takes me to the others they laugh so hard two of them can't stand up. One goes against a tree, the other to the ground. Just blaring in their laughter. Bellowing from Bill. I'm so glad to be found, however, all I can do is to look radish red embarrassed and be glad of it. They heard someone yelling hello from here, then there, over there, over here, along with the gunshots they all thought a party of hunters were driving deer all across the swamp except old man John, who thought he recognized my voice and went looking for me. Rescued me. There, that's the story—you like it?"

They chorus agreement.

Good.

Though this experience did not make me fear the forest, it made me realize how easy it is to get lost, to panic, to lose one's mind in the moment—and that is something I deeply fear.

9
(Franklin)

The prison alarms blare loudly behind us. Searchlights scan the forest, and while these lights sometimes still reach us, they cannot find us, but cast confusing shadows instead. The nearly full moon in the almost cloudless sky above gives barely enough light through the trees to see the larger debris that clutters the ground everywhere; bushes, tree branches, stumps, weeds, clumps of clingy weeds—damn stringy clinging weeds, pulling on my feet, trying to trip my feet, distracting me.

Men shout. I shout. We are trying to gather into our groups as planned; Malone's group of three is to head south, I guess they want Memphis by way of Chicago. I don't care as long as they go south. Wakowski should be leading four men west, where they'll later split into two groups, but I don't think he has three other men anymore, or that he is alive. If he is dead the rest of his men will get confused and the law will find them. They didn't plan well. Nothing I can do about that. Heck, their failure might help me complete my own escape. I don't care about the rest of them—I am heading for Canada—for a new life.

"Rad!"

"Meirs!

"Meirs?"

"Yeah, over this way, man. C'mon!"

"Guys?"

"Franklin?"

"That's Franklin, man."

"It's me! Meirs, you're between us—stay there. We're comin' to ya!"

"I ain't stayin' nowhere dammit! You hurry up while I'm runnin' and get here! We've gotta move!"

A few scattered dark-edged silver clouds drift here and there across the indigo sky to blot out the stars. A misty halo is cast about the moon, giving light that seems to be getting brighter through the sinewy and bared blackened haunted trees now that we have gotten past those confusing, shadow throwing, prison lights. I actually see better in the moon's lesser but steadier light, can go faster now. We begin making our way through this gloom, but the glaring lights and the blaring sirens of the prison still feel much too close for us to consider catching our breaths.

I'm glad Radwell and Meirs made it through. They're in great shape, better than most others, except myself. That, by itself, is good reason to go with them instead of anyone else, even if they are both whiteys.

Trouble won't come from Radwell. People told me he goes crazy when given power, but I haven't seen it, or believe it. He's a cool headed guy. He also has the all important connections to Canada. Meirs, though, is often a little off in his head, but he's a good thief, a good team player, and stealing cars is something the cops never learned about him, from what he said. Radwell doesn't know, I don't know, how to take a car. We have an ace up our sleeve if Meirs is as good at stealing one as he claims.

Another minute or so goes by. We are moving along well. The shouts of others are fading fast, being put in the distance, except for one. A familiar yet remote voice is shouting loud to our right. The prison is now off to our left as we make a wide turn north to nearly circle around the east side of the prison and leave it, and those others who escaped, behind. This voice is slightly further east of us, behind us, is insistent and getting more desperate.

"That Jackson?" Radwell asks between breaths.

The voice does sound like Jackson. He was supposed to go west with his men. What? Why? If this really is Jackson he is way off his mark. The three of us slow to a jog and try to listen as we gather our breath.

Drew—and it is Drew, calls for what sounds like his last time. I answer. We direct him in as we start moving with speed again, faster the more he nears.

"What happened, man?" Meirs asks Drew.

"Someone fell on me. Knocked me ... off my feet," he says between breaths, "Think he dead, man. I kept runnin'... didn't know my way after … couldn't hear my men ... heard you."

"Heard us?" Radwell questions. We hadn't realized we were being that noisy.

"You talk too much," Jackson explains in one quick breath.

"Shit, we gotta get quiet. We ain't planned for this, man," Radwell states. "How we gonna do it with four?"

"Shuddup!" I bark. "We'll find a way."

"Hey, I ain't sayin' we get rid a him or nothin'," Radwell replies.

I answer, with humor in my voice; "Good, cause we'd get rid a you 'fore him."

"You can't you idiot—I got the connections," Radwell mocks.

"Shit," I sigh humorously.

Radwell laughs. I'm glad I hadn't expressed anger.

"Cut it," interrupts Jackson. "I'm bustin' your plans. We'll work it. I'll git later."

"Fine," Meirs closes the subject. "Quiet now n' move faster, huh?"

We cross Forest Drive quickly, the main road to the prison, without incident. We know with the moon to our backs, to the south, or on our left, to the west, because the moon is at least an hour past its peak, we'd be able to track west to north from now on. We want to go straight north for our first plan, but if we wander, going west is okay. We have a backup plan for that. The stars and moon are rough checks for direction, but not much good. We depend on our memory of the local maps; the road maps, the topographical maps, the city maps. Meirs, Radwell, and I each know the routes needed to get us reasonably close to the town of St. Cloud, our main goal, nearly six miles away—straight north, to a car service center there on its outskirts. We need to get there quick—so quick the law will not have expanded their search there by the time we reach that point. And we are in good enough physical condition to do it. Hopefully Jackson is, too. I believe he is.

"God—we did it!" laughs Meirs as we run. We have been silent since crossing Forest Drive.

Radwell laughs through his breaths and I can't help but give out a short laugh of relief, too. "Nobody hurt, right?" Radwell blurts out in his excitement—a little late to ask, but still important.

"Not me," answers Meirs, to my relief. With Radwell asking I know he's not hurt. I give my answer. We three made it through okay. Drew is good, too. Meirs starts laughing again.

"Shut-up Meirs," I command, half laughing, "Save it. Long way ta go. We need ta hear."

I can barely see Meirs's outline shaking in agreement ahead of me as I hear him grunt out another laugh. This great feeling of gaining a new chance at freedom fills us, squashes our fears and concerns, pushes us to stay on our very quick pace. Still, we measure ourselves carefully as we hurry and we take turns leading the way through the often tall, always stiff and dry, underbrush, making decent time despite the darkness that too frequently keeps us from outright sprinting. The land is much harder to pass through than expected—grabbing and tearing at our clothes, the footing is often more uncertain than hoped for. The land, though, remains much as we have seen it from the prison during the day and from the maps; a patchwork of tree stands, small open fields, and small marshes, though we can't see any of it that well in this dark, and we are all concerned about twisting an ankle, or worse.

For a while, after we quit laughing, there are only the sounds of our movements, our breathing, the rare needed word, but then comes another sound, first noticed when it was my turn to run last in line. Someone is following us … again. How? Who? The Guard, the Law, they can't be this swift to find us. Another inmate—has to be—and that is a problem which can be taken care of—permanently.

We've passed three farms already and our first landmark appears through the openings in the woods; the radio tower standing east of County Road U against the night sky, its red warning lights blinking on its dark skeletal steel structure. We have planned to stay well off the roads we have to follow by using landmarks like these so we don't have to see the road, be that close to any of them, because the police will search every road—a lot. We change course per plan and pick up our pace even more. An east-west road called Hilltop will be next, and we'll follow it west. If we hit a southwest to northeast road, County Road T, we'll follow it north. They meet at Division Road—our next goal. This junction is our mile and a quarter mark and Division keeps us off the main roads yet shoots almost straight north for most of its length. If we set our pace right, nine minutes will have passed when we reach that junction. Not more than ten. None of us carries anything like a watch to check—we had not been allowed to have them, but we know from our map work.

Though I'm sweating my legs feel fine, my lungs feel just a hint of strain. Miles and miles of running and heavy workouts give me these benefits. Radwell and Meirs had trained, too. I don't know how Drew trained, didn't think I had to. He had better keep up.

"Can't we outrun 'em?" Meirs asks.

"If they see us—no. Too close. We could try," Radwell responds.

"Can't we take 'em with?" Drew asks.

"Too many," replies Radwell. "Too hard to do."

"Gotta be an inmate," Drew says.

"Don't care," Meirs replies.

"I can kill 'em," I offer.

Radwell coughs with surprise. "Huh, Franklin, you're nuts."

"We got 'nother choice, huh?" I chide.

Radwell utters syllables of disgust then says; "Do what you freakin' want. We ain't waitin'."

Finally the sirens of the prison are behind us, cannot be heard, or have been stopped. We are making good time. As we come to a clearing Meirs takes the lead, though it is my turn to be in front. Hilltop road appears beyond as a grayish-black ribbon and the next and thin stand of trees is on the other side of it. After we cross the road and enter the gloom of these trees I quickly hide behind some brush and look back to see the emerging dark silhouettes of a large man and a second smaller man behind him begin their crossing of Hilltop—and a third behind him, come running along the path we had taken, the large man moving in a stumbling, desperate sort of way, towards me.

Damn. How freaking special is this? This first man is Cal, a white-honky-trash sour smelling murdering rapist—a disgusting sight to see. Damn. He is one of Wakowski's men.

My anger boils as he comes off the road and nears. I explode out from hiding and charge into him, hitting him squarely with my right elbow across his chest and my arm feels his flab as I knock him off his feet. He tumbles into the brush while I maintain my stance. The two startled smaller men give brief hollers and stop well short of me: Tollin—a twentieth man! How many more inmates opted to go on impulse? Perez is the other, another of Wakowski's men. What am I going to do with these three? They give us far too many in numbers to move about unseen. Cal is too dumb, too out of shape. Tollin too old. I know Perez but he's a spic—and I hate spics—spics once put a bullet into me. I hate Hispanics. I even hated Garcia.

I thought I'd be offing one inmate. I can't oft three. Radwell, Meirs, and Drew will not wait for me. Damn. I didn't think this out.

"What the …?" Cal exclaims from his place in the brush below me. Lucky, for him, he keeps his voice quiet and does not attempt to stand, though he does ready himself for whatever might come next.

"Fuck you, Cal," I rasp as I approach him out of the shadows. "Why ta fuck ya follow us for?"

"Franklin? You shit. I almost thought I hit a tree or somethin'," Cal responds, breathing heavily from his running. "Why ta heck you pounce on me like that fer, man?"

"Answer ta fuckin' question, shit-head, or I'll screw yer fuckin' head off."

"Answer?" he retorts, bewildered for a moment, "Answer? … asshole, they were fuckin' shootin' at us. I had to fuckin' jump over Jenkin's body as he went down, me and Schneider. You think I'm goin' to care where I run after that? Huh? Kiss off. I ran—the only guys I followed, the only guys I saw," Cal takes a quick deep breath, coughs, and continues; "You guys. Truth man. It's the truth! (Cough). C'mon, Franklin, I'm stuck with ya now."

"Shit if I'm stuck with you—any of ya. You shit-ass dull brained mother fuckin' whitey. Ya ain't prepared ta go our way. Dere ain't no room for ya. Take off! Take dat fat white lard ass a yours and get ta heck outta my sight."

Cal carefully rises to his feet before me, coughing lightly. I'm eager to fight him—both of us knowing he is too winded to fight for long but, with two others nearby and not knowing for sure what they'd do, I have to wait for him to make that first move. Instead, with panting breaths, he says;

“We’re wastin’ time. There are more of ya. Your guys … leaving ya behind. Take me some distance, Franklin?” he pleads as he coughs, trying to catch more breath, and I allow him to continue. “C’mon! We knew things weren’t goin’ ta work perfect. This is one. Me. Tollin here, too. Perez. We’re losing your guys. We’ve got ta get movin’ ... (cough) ... C’mon Franklin, take us along.”

“Hey, just get me outta this area, man, and I’ll do the rest,” Tollin adds. “We can split later—and we can’t stand here this long, we gotta get away from this road.”

Damn. I know all this already. Heck. If I fight them now I’ll never catch up to Radwell and Meirs. Nothing like getting totally damn frustrated by a white ass ... asshole. I say nothing as I look from Cal to Tollin, to Perez, and back again. Tollin offers me nothing more as he stands hands on knees, panting, watching me from a few short feet away. Perez is quiet and apprehensive—he knows I hate him not just because he is a spic, because he is not just any spic—he is a member of that gang who shot me on the outside, and we’ve already had a couple clashes inside.

“Fuck,” I expel the word as I turn and start after Radwell, hoping to lose these three who now straggle behind. I hope Radwell, Drew, and Meirs have not traveled so far ahead that I cannot catch them.

10

Rick is looking at me through the rear view mirror and winks his eye. We just came off I-43 maybe two miles back and are on highway 57. He is pulling the truck into a gas station and restaurant. I don't know why he winked his eye, usually our visual communication is so intuitive I typically have a good idea what his wink means, often a good looking woman to see, or he is about to take some action he needs my back-up on; be on this side of the court or go seven yards cut right not left and expect the football immediately, but I spy no woman standing out by the buildings and there is no action to take, and it's been awhile for sports. I think he just says hi.

Rick moves to begin fueling his vehicle, as does Roy and Bill, as I and the others begin walking away. Mary comes towards me from Bill's truck, while Gay and Paula part from her and head for the restaurant.

"Hey," Mary says as she nears.

"Hey," I reply, "Having a good time?"

"Yeah we are. Bill is quiet though."

"Well," I chuckle, "he is out numbered by three women."

"Yeah. You havin' fun?"

I nod my head; "Interesting time. Some moments it's like no years have past, others I don't know them at all."

"I'm sure they're thinking the same."

"Oh, I'm sure."

"I was thinking we needed to stop pretty soon."

"Why's that?"

"Your small bladder," she answers with a smile.

I smirk in return.

She gives a quick sweet giggle, and I love to hear her laugh. "Well, we figure we haven't forgotten anything, you know, like toothbrushes and stuff," she says, "Food—Bill joined us in that talk."

"Good. I know we didn't talk at all about those things. Glad somebody did."

"So, we going to eat here, too?"

"Yeah."

"We going to ride together after?"

"We could. I know we've planned on it—uh, well, us guys kinda understood it 'cause Tom and Roy have met Doug and Mark only once before, I think, like me—with Tom and Roy, so we talked about mixing it up. Why, you want to stay with the girls?"

"Yeah, a little longer anyways, but if not, that's okay, too. I love my man."

My eyebrows raise and I smile and, while I don't say anything, I like what I heard.

Mary begins to walk toward the restaurant.

"Hey," I say, stopping her.

She grins, turns back. "What?"

I step forward to grab her, pull her back to me, and give her a kiss. She waits to leave with me, smiling. "That was nice."

As I move to go with her I see Bill signal for both Rick and myself to come over to him. "Oh, I can't, Bill wants me over there for something."

"Mmm, I'll save you a seat."

"Thanks."

The other guys gather near Bill, too.

"While I was fueling I heard the weather on the radio," Bill begins, "There's a major storm moving in from the west. Eighteen to twenty-four inches of snow is expected by Saturday morning."

"No way, that's a lot, even for northern Wisconsin," Mark states.

"No. C'mon. That's not what they said earlier today. That sucks," Rick replies. "For Wisconsin—you sure?"

"Yep. And upper Michigan."

"We're gonna be able to get out on Sunday—won't we?" Roy is asking Rick. Standing behind Roy, Mark nods his agreement with the question.

"You sure?" Rick asks Bill again.

"Yeah, I'm sure. Heard it twice. The women will want to turn around on hearing this."

"No. No. How are we gonna do that?" Rick asks.

"We could take 'em back," Roy offers as he lights a cigarette.

"Yeah but they gave us such grief in wanting to go with us. I know Paula won't care—she's lived up there. What about Gay?" Rick asks Bill, then turns to me and asks; "What about Mary?"

"I'll leave it up to Gay, but we have a cabin on the other side of the State. She's been snowed in before, so I don't know. She didn't like it then, but it was her idea for the women to go with us here in the first place ... I don't know."

"Mary won't want to stay. Going out in the woods on a good day is hard for her to do. She's about as interested in this stuff as someone is in getting an enema," I answer. "It still surprises me she's along."

"Well, let's eat first," Rick suggests, "Then decide after and we'll talk to the women after we eat. We may have to send them back with you, Roy."

"Hey," Roy wonders. "You ain't got no phone up there yet, do ya Rick?"

"No," Rick answers as we all pause our movement.

"Then, then I am worried about being there. I got to go to work on Monday."

Rick looks at Roy and nods his head, then looks over at Tom. "What about you Tom?"

Tom shifts his stance and begins rocking back and forth slightly with his hands in his pockets and grimaces as he lowers his eyes as he begins talking, then raises them as he continues; "Ya see ... I got the whole week off but got kinda of a insane family back home, truly, and if ya can give me a excuse for not being there on Thanksgiving, I'd kinda appreciate it, ya know?"

We either shake our heads, smile, chuckle, or laugh on hearing Tom say this.

Rick's smile is wide; "We'll see what we can do for ya, Tom. C'mon everybody, let's go eat. We'll figure out somethin' over dinner. I'm hungry."

We agree and begin walking to the restaurant when we see our women walking back out into the parking lot toward us and in a hurry.

"You guys," Gay says with urgency while she is still yards away, "We just saw the weather on the TV in there and there's a big storm coming our way this weekend."

"Yeah," Paula adds, "It's supposed to be real bad. Like twenty-four inches bad. Like, you know, we had to pick this weekend."

Mary gives me a quiet worried look before she speaks. "I just want to know we can get out. We have plenty of food, but I don't want to stay cooped up in a cabin all week either. Can us women stay in a motel up there?"

Rick gives his horse smile; "Staying in a motel won't be much better than the trailer. Bill just heard about this on the radio while he was fueling up. He told us."

"Well, what are we going to do, Rick?" Paula asks. "Like we need to make a decision now, don't you think?"

"We thought we'd eat first, work things out over dinner," Doug answers before Rick can.

"No, I want us to work this out now. I want to know if I'm going home tonight or not," Mary demands.

"If we get snowed in, Rick, we don't have no phone and what if our trucks get stuck?" Paula adds.

"Yeah, Bill," Gay adds, "I don't even like the thought of you staying up there if us women stay back. It's supposed to be some storm."

Bill raises his hands and then moves them downward in wave-like fashion to calm the women as he reacts. "How often is the weatherman right? Just, take it easy, we got time to figure things out. So let's do that."

Everyone is quiet, no one knowing what to say. I break the silence with a suggestion; "What if we rent a snowmobile? Can we do that up there?"

"Hey," Doug says, "That works for me—who said you were good for nothin'?" He grins at me.

My look to him tells him to shut up. He grins again.

"You know," Rick says, "That should be easily arranged. They got plenty of them up there. We might be able to do that."

"And what if we can't," Roy asks. "How do we get out?"

"Maybe, if we can't rent one or two, we can have a couple riders come in on Sunday, or Saturday, and take you three out, or anybody else. It'll cost us some, but it will be worth it, and we'll park Roy's car out by a motel, a gas station, or wherever the snowmobiles are coming from—how's that?"

"Oh I don't know, Rick," Paula answers.

"Yeah, me too, I don't know," Gay adds. "That doesn't sound too easy to arrange."

"If you're sure you can do this, then maybe. I don't know—I'd rather go home," Mary states.

"Oh no you don't," Paula replies. "We had a hard enough time gettin' you to agree to come with us and the men to agree we're coming along. Whatever we're doing—Gay and I, you're doin' too, okay—you said so."

Mary looks perplexed, not liking all of what Paula said. She wants to resist the command—the demand she do what the other two women do but, at the same time, feels the friendship in Paula's voice. I smile at her. She's stuck between a rock and a hard place. An experience is not the same if there isn't someone there to go through it with you, and Paula clearly wants Mary to be with us in whatever our group chooses to do, whatever the women choose to do.

"Didn't you tell me you have the whole week off?" Paula asks Mary.

"Well, yes I do," Mary answers, "but I don't want to be snowbound when I can spend Thanksgiving with my family."

"I doubt if we'd be snowbound that long. At worst a day or two, that's all," Rick replies.

"Tell you what," Mark begins, "Let's at least drive up there. The snow isn't supposed to start until tomorrow evening, so let Tom, Roy, myself, and maybe the women stay in a motel tomorrow night. If it's not bad we come in Saturday morning. If it is, we say goodbye, nice try, leave the rest of you snowbound—how's that?"

"Sounds good to me," Rick replies. "I'll still arrange the snowmobiles—just in case—for us, if not you guys."

"Me too," answers Paula. "I'm good with it."

"Uh-well," Gay says slowly, "Okay, I can give that a try."

"Well, obviously, there's no one to take me home now," sighs Mary, looking at me as if I should have foreseen this problem and provide a different answer for her—I give her an amused yet pleading smile back. "So I have no choice," she sighs again, mouthing a pleasant but worried kiss to me, "So, okay."

"Done," Doug states. "Good. Let's go eat. I'm hungry."

11
(Franklin)

Any trail Radwell, Meirs, and Drew make is lost in this night, to no surprise. I got no concern 'cause I know where we—I want to go, but hope to catch them soon to avoid being separated long. Together; Meirs, Radwell, and I—and Drew, have a better chance to solidify our escape. We can rid ourselves of Cal, send Cal on his way, cripple him—or leave him dead—I don't care. Tollin is something to be talked over. Perez goes the way of Cal. Drew earned his keep with us because he helped plan all this. Radwell might not be keen concerning Drew, but he accepts him. Drew will earn his keep a second time if he helps put Cal away—and he will enjoy putting Cal away. I know that. Perez will be the trouble.

Hilltop is quickly put behind as we enter more open land. It seems every one of the lonely homes we've seen, and we've stayed as far from their sight as possible, has a barking dog kept outside tonight. Every one of those mutts sense us and howl a warning to any who will hear. Don't matter, we're not interested in getting into any home so soon. The dogs can bark all they want.

The land makes it hard to keep the pace I want, denies me hope to distance these three worms. They stay within sight. I break path for them. It's frustrating. The normal sounds of the night are broken time and again by Cal's coughing and wheezing. He ain't doing well. He blindly follows, it seems, but still finds his way. I can't be sure—I don't care. I don't want to take the effort to look back at him, or Tollin, certainly not Perez, but I have to because of Perez—I cannot trust him. I'm frustrated.

I climb over a barbed wire fence, cross a field, cross another barbed fence, up and over the side of a small hill, then through two more small stands of woods before I come to the edge of a large farmed clearing, and still they manage to keep me in sight. I want to run faster just to lose them but it is dangerous enough how fast I go. I fear if I go faster I'll lose sense of direction and, if Drew, Meirs, and Radwell do come within hearing range, or sight, I'll not notice them. I'm caught by events to lead these three scum along—I hate it.

Just a little ways within this farmland a sound stops me … not from Cal or the other worms, but from another noise in the air that Cal cannot smother. A disturbing yet familiar noise in a night already so filled with them and their disturbing endings. As I turn I see Cal and Tollin and Perez have also stopped, all four of us looking back almost together.

"Shit!" I hear Tollin quietly exclaim.

Cal mutters in despair. Perez looks at me, is reluctant to keep looking for the noise. He will not be taken off guard. He knows I don't trust him. He doesn't trust me.

The reverberating sound makes us too curious and concerned to stay hidden, so I find myself, and them, walking carefully out away from the tree line and into the open. I stand on a small finger of undisturbed stony ground extending out from the darkened woods and several feet above the rest of the surrounding farmland and they, a little ways back from me, stand out below in this turned farmed field.

From this rise I see the tiny image of a distant spotlight shining down from the sky, moving to and fro, sweeping the area it is over, back near where the prison would be. We can't always hear the chomping slapping sounds that quietly arrive over this distance but the momentary sights of this machine carrying that light appearing, disappearing, then reappearing, behind the black edge of the small hill we passed only seconds ago, in and out of the dark ragged line of treetops silhouetted against the moonlit sky, places real fear into me, into us.

At present the helicopter is too far away, and looks to be headed in some other direction to worry us, but we know eventually it will come our way. This must also mean the dogs are out and running, so I let Cal and Tollin and the spic catch some more breath as they approach me now as I begin to speak; "If dat chopper … we don't got much chance when it comes our way, and you know it will soon. You know dat."

Cal silently nods his head from where he stands on the edge of the rise, refusing to close any more of the space between us, as does the spic. Tollin stands closer, within arm's reach beside me.

"Dogs gotta be out. Know anythin' 'bout dogs?" I ask.

Cal only shakes his head no, as does Tollin.

"They need horses to keep with the dogs, man," Perez says without accent. "If they don't we can lose them any other way with the distance we already got."

I don't listen to no spic. "I figure … if ta dogs just got our scent—the way dey run, they'll be here in 'bout just less than a half hour maybe—movin' faster the more dey smell us. Hill we passed I think is our two-and-a-half-mile mark. Dat chopper got here mighty quick. Trouble ta someone, hope not us. Chopper, dogs, we gotta keep runnin'—better if we do. If ya can't keep up, I leave ya."

"I'll keep up," Cal spits out hoarsely, his throat sounding raw from exertion.

Tollin is still panting, too. While he is older, grey-haired, he is a well-toned man with an average build, somewhere in his fifties, yet his breathing is sounding better than Cal's, who is somewhere near thirty years younger. I seem to catch Tollin saying things under his breath but he doesn't say anything, which doesn't make sense to me, but I ask nothing of him. Tollin is generally known to keep to himself. I know little else about him.

"Too quick," breathes Tollin, surprising me by his sudden speak, especially after I just thought he is the lone silent type.

"Huh?" I question. "Just said dat."

"Too quick for cops," he says rapidly between breaths. "Milwaukee—too far for a cop (breath) chopper to get here now," Tollin pauses for breath again. "Has to be Fond du Lac. Traffic. News maybe. Private."

Tollin could be right, and if he is that helps us a lot.

"Where're we goin'?" Tollin asks.

"Yeah," gasps Cal.

The two scum suddenly think it is their business to know where we are going, to know what my—our plans are for freedom? Drew has earned that right—them, they have not. Screw them.

"Ain't you goin' to tell us?" Tollin asks.

"Heck no."

Tollin stares at my face through the darkness. I don't know what he can see in my face in this deep gloom but if he can see it, my look is not good. In the background Cal jerks his arms and shoulders in resentment as they both realize they overplayed their hands. Their question was too loaded. They inquired too early. Their effort showed them as the freeloaders they are. Scum.

None of us say more as we begin to hurry again.

12

We just passed the last road signs to turn off to Plymouth when we see flashing lights coming our way, heading south. Highway 57 is a two lane road here, so we pull over before the police car passes.

"Another one's comin'," Tom says a moment later. Tom's driving.

We pull over again.

"I feel surrounded by postal workers in this car," I state from the back seat. Roy and Tom are rather new to me, being Rick's friends. I only met them briefly once before as I realize I've said something awkward.

Paula, sitting next to me, looks over and gives that sort of understanding smile; "We've worked together, what, almost ten years with you, Tom, isn't it? And Roy, hasn't it been like five or seven?"

"Almost ten for me, yeah," replies Tom.

"Four and a half abouts," Roy answers.

Paula smiles again as she looks at me; "So yeah, you are surrounded."

I shrug my shoulders. "Hey, just thought I'd say something. We've been pretty quiet since the restaurant."

"Do you own a gun?" Tom asks me.

"No."

"Then when's the last time you hunted?"

"Many years ago, almost twenty-five now. The third season out for me I got a deer, a female with horns—one of two registered in that county, and I quit after that."

Tom and Roy look at each other before Roy asks; "Why?"

"I never liked huntin' enough. I guess when I proved I could do it that was enough," I answer as we see a third set of police lights flashing in the distance and coming toward us.

"Somethin's going on," remarks Paula. Roy reaches to turn on the radio as the police car races by.

"Roy, what do you do at the Post Office?" I ask.

He shakes his head. "Ahh, I'm just a mail carrier. I like it most of the year. It's fine with me."

"Tom?" I ask.

"I work in the back loading the mail trucks, unloading the big delivery trucks mostly."

Another set of police lights come into view.

"Holy crap," exclaims Roy. "There sure is enough of them comin' out of the weeds. What the heck happened?" He searches the radio more actively for a local station.

Paula looks over at me with a worried look.

"What's the matter?" I ask her.

"Like it's just, just a lot of cops. A big accident or something."

"Not an accident," Roy says, "No ambulances, fire trucks—yet—too many cops, somethin's different."

"Hey," Tom says, "There is—these were all city cops I saw, or town cops and from different places—whatever, but none were sheriff or State police cars, but we're out in the county—where're they comin' from?"

"Ahh, man, you know maybe 'cause the State is on strike, remember?" Roy answers him. "They're probably comin' from other towns in this area because of that, would be my guess."

"What strike? Can that happen—the State go on strike I mean?"

"Haven't you been watchin' the news Tom?" Paula responds.

"I guess not," he answers. "So the State's been on strike—over what?"

"Over a week now," Roy answers. "Wages and benefits, working conditions, supposedly they are so bad, ya know."

"Today is the thirteenth day," I add. "The Governor activated us the day before the strike came. I was here at the Kettle Moraine medium prison back outside Plymouth until Monday this week when my term of active duty came to an end."

"What, you were in the National Guard?" Roy asks.

"Till Monday," I reply. "You sounded surprised about that."

"Well you said you didn't handle a gun in like twenty years."

"I really haven't. I was a cook."

"And you were at the place we just passed—and they let you out while this was going on?" Tom asks.

"Um, yeah, I was sort of surprised, too," I answer.

"Did that fight with the inmate have somethin' to do with you gettin' out?" Paula asks.

I look at her. "Yeah, Paula, it did. My term of duty was up like four days earlier and they were going to keep me until after this strike was done but, with the fight, they made sure I was out before any further trouble came of it."

"Another cop," Tom announces. "How many does that make?"

"Five," answers Roy, and then Roy finds the news on the radio. There has been a large scale breakout of inmates from the Kettle Moraine prison.

13
(Franklin)

Time is our enemy. Enough has passed for the panic to settle out at the prison, allowing the various law agencies to stop arguing with one another, realize how big our break is, to come together as a team to hunt us down. Everything we do will soon become dangerous with the dragnet they will set in place.

"C'mon, man, we can do better if we know what's goin' on," Perez says to me, as we overlook a road that's ahead of us from on top a small hill, where I had to wait for them because of a car driving by below—these scum are so lucky.

"Fuck you Perez," I respond. Perez is not standing close enough for me to go after him.

"He's right," Tollin adds, who is close enough. "He is. If we know where we're goin' and why, we'll know what ta look for and help you."

"Ah ain't needin' yer help," I answer.

"If we know, there's less chance of us gettin' seen," Tollin replies.

"Ya don't get seen, man, 'cause ya don't want ta get caught—you an idiot?"

"You might be," Tollin retorts, daring my anger. "You stupid? Together we got more eyes, more hands, ears, to make our way to, to where, Franklin—where are we headed?"

"Yeah Franklin, hope ya break a leg if ya go it alone. No one ta carry ya to ya buddies," Perez's sarcasm cuts deep.

I sigh. Tollin's right. Perez is right. I hate spics. I hate 'em. Cal chooses not to speak but tilts his head to show he agrees with the others. I sigh again and decide to tell them. "If we don't cross Highway 23 in twenty minutes, man, we be in serious trouble."

"Highway 23?" Cal rasps.

"It's da first east-west big road dat is first choice ta guard for a north border," I answer.

"What's between us and that?" Tollin asks.

"Marsh," I reply, "Mullet River, a few roads, man—what'ya see? More of dis crap we run through. We ain't doin' good."

"What road is this?" Perez asks.

"Perez ..." I begin to say.

"Hey, man, truce," Perez quickly states.

"Fuck you," I reply.

"Hey, kids," Tollin says. "Meet after school if ya want ta fight. Right now, let's get our butts to a safe place—together—first—understand?"

Perez and I stare at each other. I know Tollin is right, again. I know Perez wants what Tollin said. I know it is the right way to go, but I hate spics ... I hate this spic, but it seems Perez will work with us ... "Keep ya distance from me, Perez, or I take your balls off."

"Si—yes, distance. You come at me—your balls come off."

Glad we understand each other, for now ... spic.

"Dis road must be ...," I answer as I look at the sky, trying to figure which way is north—I can't tell. I lift my hand to place the moon and shift my body. I'm getting a bad feeling. "Dis runs north-south. Dey will have crossed it already ..."

"No it don't," Tollin says. "It runs on a slant. See the tree lines over there? See how they square off but the ones on this road don't? This road runs on a slant."

"Yeah I see dat ol' man," I snap back as I look at the trees' dark outlines. My stomach is churning with that bad feeling—Tollin is right. We—I forgot to follow Hilltop west until it met Division after these three scum became baggage to us—to me. Now I think we went east and have no idea how far off we are. I'm just not going back—no way. We head north. We slant west. We don't go back. I sigh; "Dis is County T—only slantin' road around, so we ain't lost. We gotta cross it and start going left."

"Sure?" he dares.

My left hand extends quickly to feel his sweaty throat and tightens around it. I look at him. He makes no effort to resist. Ah, ... he is too old for me to make such effort. I release my grip. "I'm sure. North n left."

"What're we tryin' to get to, to get ourselves from here…" Perez asks.

"Yeah, where we tryin' to get to?" Cal asks.

"What?" I ask. "Ya hard a hearin'?"

"Not highway twenty—all this effort leads us where after that, Franklin?" Tollin tries to explain with a question.

"Ya tried dis before, ta know my plans. I ain't got no need ta tell ya."

"We can help you get there…"

"I ain't needin' ya help."

"Yeah, just now you did, we almost got lost, so yeah you do…"

My hand is on Tollin's throat again and this time with pressure. His hands grip mine, trying to pull it away from him. My hand isn't moving.

"You got a choice," Perez calmly says. "We give you more sets of eyes and ears to make your plans happen, or you go it alone thinking you can handle it all your own. If you break a leg, no one carries you. Make your choice, Franklin, but if you choose us, let us know what we're doin'."

"Forty-second street Crusaders, huh, Perez—sounds like ass-lickers ta me," I taunt.

Perez's eyes narrow as anger fills them. "Ya bullet didn't learn ya none, did it Franklin? This ain't the time."

"How is it, Perez, that ya speak so damn well when ya want to—you educated or somethin'?"

"Me? With the education you 'sposed got book learnin' in prison why don't you speak better—huh? Street don't leave ya that easy does it, nigger? I wonder if ya think betta than ya speak. What's it matter to you, nigger, how I speak—you tryin' not ta make a choice?"

"Crusaders sound like some Christian God-lovin' I do what my mamma says boy group."

"That bullet *sure* didn't learn ya none at all—and ya doin' a shit job of tryin' to insult me. I've been better insulted by a toy doll."

I scoff. "Spic perv, doin' it with a doll."

"Franklin," Tollin forces out his words from his clamped throat. "Get outta grade school. What're tryin' ta say, Franklin—can't find words or reasons, huh? Are ya too stupid ..."

"Watch ya mouth old man—I crush it," I snarl as I apply more pressure.

"Make a choice," Tollin daringly squeaks back, "Tell us."

"I told ya already—gotta get north of twenty-three."

"We're talkin' after and you know it."

I can do this all alone. I don't need them. My chances are better without them. I can do this. I can … without them. I can. Yet … yet, if Radwell, Meirs and Drew have already gone when I get there, what do I do? Then I will need help … damn. I get it; "A car shop on ta outskirts of St. Cloud. We be takin' a car north ta Michigan—dat's all ya need ta know fer now."

14

"You okay?" Paula asks.

I'm leaning both as much against the car door as against the seat, my head doing the same, watching the dark landscape rush by through the window, the land dimly lit by the nearly full moon overhead. "John Stancato is still at the prison—long time friend. I hope he's not involved, or hurt. I'm worried. Some of those guys in there shouldn't be in this prison. They should be in Waupun's maximum security. Makes me wish I was there, but I'm glad I'm not—know what I mean?"

Paula doesn't say anything, just nods her head.

"What's it like in there?" Roy asks.

"Ah, well … ah, surprising," I answer. "What struck me was, well, there are several cottages and in each cottage is about fifty small walk-in closet-sized rooms. They put about seventy-some inmates to a cottage. I guess the logistics prevent more than that. So some of the inmates have their own room. Free to walk around the cottage and this large room they call the commons and able to go outside on the grounds, with permission—I don't get it, they're supposed to be in prison, but they got so much. They get to use a up to date gymnasium and library, and take courses to the piled higher and deeper level. They got opportunities in there we don't get out here, yet they think they're in shit-land …"

"Good—they should," Paula interjects.

"What did the radio just say?" I ask.

"There's been shots, reports of serious injuries. At least one fatality," Tom answers. "It happened about thirty-five, forty-five minutes ago. The news says the police will be holding a conference in about ten minutes. Everything so far has been hearsay."

"What time is it now?" I asked.

Tom answers; "Ten-thirty-eight."

The break seemed synchronized with the shift change at the towers, but I don't understand why that timing would have given any advantage to these inmates.

15
(Franklin)

Three lights edge this gravel pit we've come upon. I remember this pit from the maps and it gives me a good sense of where we are and where to go. Son-of-a-bitch, I was beginning to think we were lost … and we've lost so much time already. Two of the lights break the night air like tiny bright stars shining from across the pits large expanse, but neither light reaches into the pit itself; a deep black emptiness between the two lights and us. The yellow light shining close by comes from the third lamp perched high on a makeshift post by the pits edge. It shows the rocky barren ground quickly slanting down from the dirt roadway to disappear at a stark, ragged, and eerie drop-off into the blackness below. The light falls on nothing else, causing the pit to look bottomless and, though I don't stand near its edge, I feel the dizziness caused by the pits unseen depth. The earth-moving equipment used by the gravel company is in our sight through the remaining thin barrier of trees and brush that separate us from that dirt roadway we need to use, which should circle the rim of the pit and then turn northwest—should turn northwest.

"Which way?" Tollin asks.

"Dat way. It should turn left," I answer. "Den goes down hill to ta north, man. We need ta follow dis road n keep goin'."

Cal grimaces as he suddenly holds his left thigh. "Cramps," he explains.

"Feet blistered," Tollin states. "I think my feet are getting blistered."

I nod my head. "Tough shit."

Perez remains wise, refusing to give a clue to how he feels. We want to rest, except we know we can't have it. We are not safe—not anywhere near safe.

Tollin mutters something. I think he is just complaining.

The night air gets colder as we leave the pit behind. The air is more penetrating—humid—we are getting closer to the main marshes. There are no other guiding lights nearby. The darkness has become more eerie with only the moonlight, which thankfully allows us to see some feet ahead.

I never liked the woods, never liked the outdoors. I was city born and raised. The bustling never-ending background of sound and movement making up a big city's character twenty-four hours a day, seven days a week, is for me.

This stillness surrounding us, this darkness, this chill, makes me uneasy and I'm not the only one. We slow our movements more and together to look about, searching the night—something out there is making us do this. We find ourselves standing still on our path, peering around into the darkness, trying to make out what has caused us to stop, but it turns out to be nothing else but critters, and we drudge on.

16

"Dean Langer came walking up when we were playing baseball and blew off a pipe bomb that scared the heck out of all of us. Dean, he comes laughing like a crazy man. Big smile on his face, eyes wide with excitement, and he's lighting the fuse, throws the bomb up in the air as he runs off that low hill on the first base side. Scatters all of us. My sister screams his name. Dean laughs louder. Most run for the backstop. Me and somebody, I can't remember who—Craig Kewenig or maybe his brother Brad—maybe even Dean—we dive behind one of the park's green steel garbage cans and just in time. Boom! Part of that pipe hits the can we are hiding behind, going clear through the far side and putting a big dent into the can on our side—right between our heads. You want crazy? Dean is crazy."

"I remember that. I was runnin' for my life in the outfield, dived to the ground. Heck, I thought he was insane. Didn't want nothin' to do with him, but you still see him?" Doug asks.

"Yeah. Dean and his wife Wendy are good friends. Rick and Bill hang out with them, too, once in a while," I answer.

Bill snickers; "Yeah, but Dean never leaves my sight."

Mary's head has been resting heavily against my shoulder since we rotated car assignments from the latest stop, but she is not asleep.

"You know, I got another friend like that, like Dean, crazy. His name is Mike Angelo. Back in high school we'd race motorcycles. Mike would be insane with a car," Bill says. "I'd do about anything with the guy except get in his car with him—I, ah, I wanted my life, ya know?"

"I had Angelo drive my car," I add, "He was driving back from my getting lost hunting trip and we were in Green Bay, on a two lane highway, in the wrong lane. Mike didn't care. I wanted to poop my pants, man, as the cars veered away before us but I was clenching so tight, ya know …?"

Some laughter from the others as I see Doug nod his head. "Don't know Angelo—I've been hearin' about him, though," he admits, as he gives a point of his thumb towards me that Bill could see. "But this crazy guy I raced after leaving Rick's one winter night when I took off to go somewhere. Home I think, but we immediately started racing instead. We took off towards Forest Park school; me in my subcompact wagon and him chasing in his sports car. This being the middle of winter, you know, snow packed hard on the streets and piled high along where the curbs should be, three-four feet high, maybe in places a bit more, ya know?"

"Yeah, I live here year 'round, ya know," smartly answers Bill, "I know what snow is. I ain't no wuss who lives in the warm dry south like some guys I've heard of, hey."

Doug pauses, knowing Bill means him, and we see Bill turn to face Doug, and give a wide smile.

"You wanna hear this story or not?" Doug challenges.

"Go on, man," Bill answers.

"Alright, don't get pushy, don't make me deal with you later—'cause I will," Doug promises, offering a serious face, but Bill doesn't take any of it as he tilts his head towards him and opens his eyes wide with a pose asking as if he did not hear Doug correctly, yet letting Doug know he has and is thinking *him* to be a crazy man, like Dean. A wide smile breaks on Doug's face before he continues, and Bill once again turns back to his driving.

"We come to the end of Rick's road, you know, and we hav'ta turn. Well my car slides out across the joining road and bang, I find myself up on top of the snow bank before I practically know what is going on. So I make my way down the road but on top of the snow bank. My car just couldn't seem to get off the top of it—and I dared not stop to get stuck up there. Pedal to the metal I finally manage to get myself off this hill of white stuff and quickly wonder where he is, you know, because I've been so busy. I find him right behind me coming off the same banks of snow. I thought he's an insane bastard. I did this because I had no choice—he had to been doing it on purpose just to do what I was doing. It's like, well, it's like he had lost his mind."

Bill nods in exaggerated agreement and glances back at me as he leans over to Doug. "I got news for ya," he says as he nods his head again then shakes his head, as if to double up on his agreement, "he's never had a mind."

"Who they talkin' about?" Mary quietly asks, "You?"

I reluctantly whisper; "Yep."

"You did that, um, too?"

"Yep, but don't ask me how."

Mary went on, "You've been tellin' me I would not have liked you in high school."

"Been tellin' ya that for years," I quietly chuckle.

"Well, again, you're right," she answers. "Every time I think I heard all your stories something else comes up. And I've seen you and Dean get wild …"

"Uh-uh," I interrupt and answer her in a quick whisper because Bill is asking me something, "Getting wild with Dean is not setting off firecrackers with a fifty pound barbell, shooting crows out his upstairs window with a pellet gun—in the city, or putting firecrackers in one-half of a pop can to blow the other half up into the air, just for fun."

Mary's eyes look scrunched as she looks back at me. "That was wild enough," she replies.

"What you have to say about that?" Bill has asked me.

"It's true. It's true," I reply as I squeeze Mary's hand lovingly. She squeezes back. "Except I didn't have much choice about going on top the snow bank either. The road was way too slick at the intersection."

Doug gives out a laugh. "Rick told me once you were chasing Kewenig down French drive on wet roads. Neither of you could stop as you reached highway fifty—true?"

"True."

All of us fall silent a moment.

"Well you gonna say something or sit there like a stump in the ground?" Bill asks as he puts it to me.

I heave a sigh. "Kewenig couldn't make the stop and knew it well in advance, so he tried to turn into the service station lot that was there on the corner at the time, nearly hitting a pump before he swung back onto French drive again, and winded up spinning across the first two lanes of highway fifty. We watched all that as I find out we aren't going to be able to stop in time either, but I keep my car straight. That is, until we got into the first two lanes of fifty ourselves when my car begins to spin, too. We end up side by side heading the same way—the right way, if you were interested in going down the far two lanes, ending up right in the middle of the boulevard that stands between the four lanes of traffic. Somehow Craig had made it through between a two-car set and a three-car set as he spun through to the boulevard. I have no idea how we made it through untouched. I understand there were cars around us, too. Rick's girlfriend, however, bumped her head against my window and had been so scared she would never get in my car again."

"Who would blame her, you … idiot," Mary blurts out.

Bill and Doug shake their heads in laughter, as they agree with Mary, like I am. Live and learn—sometimes you are even given the chance to do that, after doing something stupid.

Bill pulls the truck to the side of the road as the oncoming lights rapidly advance before two late arriving local police cars speed past.

"You're lucky your death wish wasn't granted that day," Bill seriously says. "Real lucky."

"I kno-ow," I answer solemnly, as we notice another set of flashing lights approaching in the distance, causing Bill to pull to the side of the road again.

"What happened to Craig? Know anything about Kewenig?" Doug asks.

"What I know is Craig has been married over fourteen years to a woman named Lynn. Never met her. They live in Toledo, Ohio area. He has a stepson. They have some grandkids and a bunch of cats. Craig has kept his interest in cars and other things that go fast, I hear, but I don't know much else other than that. Brad, his brother, is a butcher back in town, and has four kids. I don't know much else there either."

"Ya know, why do the cops keep comin'?" Bill asks. "You'd think they got enough by now."

"Hey, 'cause a breakout from a prison is a serious thing, man—duh," replies Doug.

Bill rolls his head and smirks, glaring at Doug. "I know that, dipwad, but we're quite a ways away from there now yet they keep comin'..."

"Tryin' ta throw a dragnet down, stoppin' all cars within a certain radius from the prison would be my guess—and we're far enough away not to be stopped," I say.

"Hope they don't get away," Mary adds.

"Yeah, well, most of the time they got help waitin' for them outside. I read true crime books a lot," Doug says.

"Well, do ya now?" comments Bill, "Never guess that 'bout ya. You being able to read, I mean."

Doug smiles. "Considerin' you sign your name with an 'X', that's a compliment."

Bill smiles. "It is. It is. Hope none of 'em ride this a-way."

17
(Franklin)

The trees hide me as I peer down the highway's lengths. The road stays clear. No road sounds and only an indistinct rectangle of a speed sign can be seen in the murky darkness. The lack of other highway markers pisses me off. I want to know what road this is. Then, to my right, a vague dark line of a waterway appears if I tilt my head, use my side vision. Beginnings of a bridge can be seen, too, and must be the Mullet River. They are both not too far away.

"See that?" I question, pointing to the waterway.

"See what?" they wheeze. Tollin speaks unclearly, adding something that sounds like; "should we run for it?" but I'm not sure and don't care to ask.

"We're going dere. When ya follow me now ya step in my tracks best ya can—not in da mud, especially near da waterway. We'll leave enough tracks—don't need ta make 'em big enough ta be seen from da road—got it? We walk on hard a ground as we find—got dat?" Cal nods his head in the darkness and whispers yes. I don't bother to look at Tollin, but measure where Perez is.

The road remains clear as we hurriedly make our s-shaped path through the dry grassy slope from the trees down to the cemented structure of the bridge and step within its hollows.

"Keep yer feet outta da water," I command them, "We too far from where we need ta go. Ya get your feet dat wet, you kiss dem good-bye." They listen, though within the deeper darkness under this bridge I cannot see their faces at all, but I know Tollin and Cal follow me before Perez does, so any fancy sound will be Perez coming for me—I don't trust him.

"My feet are blistered bad," Cal coarsely announces and his voice faintly echoes off the bridge's understructure, "Water ain't gonna matter much."

"Well, shit, dick-head, dat's what ya get for not stayin' in shape. Ya try dragging me down, I'll kill ya. Ya feet already bleedin'? I don't care—don't get 'em wet. Water will rip dem apart within ya shoes. C'mon, we need ta get deeper into dis thing." I grope along the cold wall until I feel I'm midway. Then I rest, but not because I need to. The others stop, too.

I pull out a book of matches and feel for the photocopies of the maps I made. After the match's light breaks the darkness I see Cal looking surprised. He is also looking pale, for a white guy, weakly resting his body against the cold wall of the bridge's understructure as he leans there a few feet from me. He is bent over, hands on his knees, head hanging heavy, his chest heaving in and out, his butt against the wall. Tollin has the same posture as he rests on the far side of Cal. Their weary eyes again show surprise on seeing the maps I open. Screw them—they didn't think of this? Stupid idiots.

Perez, he stands on the far side of them facing me, studying me with his cold black eyes. I know why. He is biding his time, measuring me.

"They'll," Tollin squeaks between breaths, "check ... this ... out. Post here?"

"Yeah, time's short." I respond, and seeing them nervous, I explain; "Have ta know where we are. Get some idea. Dat road above is kept up, must be Division on ta map. Dis water must be Mullet River. I gotta check on where we go from here 'cause I don't wanna make no mistake 'bout where we go next. Division is what we want, but we took too long, man. Gotta see different ways. Get your breath back. Dis ain't gonna take but a minute."

Cal silently watches me after I light another match. Some critter scurries away somewhere in the darkness as this match bursts to life. A third match is needed to finish.

"Dis Division. The road above us is Division. We can go straight north. Highway 23 is 'bout a mile. Follow me."

Using the bridge's structure we cross this water without getting our feet wet. I lead them away to the west side of Division like we entered; going quick to hard ground, up to the thin line of brush and small trees, through the barbed wires fencing a narrow strip of farm field, hopefully the beginning of more farmland—hard ground, hard and worked enough for us to move quickly on, maybe even run on. This harvested corn field is maybe twenty yards wide that, for some reason, has not yet been cut down—I don't care. It gives me firm soil and confidence to run again, and I do—intent to lose the scum, despite my earlier agreement with them—I think I can do this alone. I want to do this alone.

18
(Franklin)

Cal runs like a bull in a china shop, crashing through dried upright stalks of corn making all kinds of noise, leaving a freakin' easy trail to follow. His clumsiness enrages me.

"Asshole. Turn sideways," I hiss back at him.

"Huh?" Cal says.

I stop and turn suddenly around causing Cal to jam into me as I grip his sweaty throat. His momentum, my strength, our impact lifts him clear off the ground. Our eyes meet in the murky light as I stand below him, holding him above me for that fraction of a second before his heavy weight overcomes my strength.

"I said," I growl into his face as his feet reach the ground; "Turn ya-self fuckin' sideways. Less noise. Less trail. Git it, white-ass?"

Gasping, Cal simply nods yes as his hands rapidly search for a grip on my sweating, partially exposed forearms, finally grabbing hold of the sleeves to my jacket, before I let him go. I soon realize, as I start running again, that my hands now carry his disgusting soured flesh smell, as his sweat landed on me from his neck and hands.

As we near another stand of woods we hear approaching road noise on Division drive to the right of us. Looking that way I see a pile of cleared trees near the edge of this field bulldozed together and I climb them until I see the road.

Coming fast, heading toward the prison, a local police car zooms out of the darkness with its lights flashing but without siren. Moving from my left to my right, it is speeding south past the bridge we crossed under without the slightest change in speed.

"Pig," I tell the scum, who all stand hands on knees below me, two gasping for breath, none bothering to lift their head to look at me, except Perez, who watches me with those ratty black eyes of his. "Zoomin'," I continue, "We're safe."

I begin to climb down when the road noise renews. It is another police car, traveling in the same direction as the first, but this one slows to a crawl quickly. Lights flashing but with no siren this car's driver begins searching the woods and the roadway on both sides with a powerful light.

"Second pig," I whisper, "Trouble. Goin' slow. Searchin'. Looking at ta other side of ta road. Get ready, if this one stops...."

Cal tries to take in a deeper breath but he goes into a coughing, gasping rage instead.

"Shut-up!" I command in a whisper as I glance down at him, but Cal can't stop. Tollin looks to me as he quietly reaches for a thick short length of wood lying near him on the pile of trees below and moves to stand behind Cal, waiting for my signal to knock Cal out. Tollin is thinking, but Cal's head is so thick it's probably also hollow, the brainless shit, and Tollin hitting him will make more noise than what Cal is making now. Perez takes a step toward Cal and looks ready to do something, but he doesn't reveal what—and that tells me he has a blade. That stinking spic is carrying a blade. I'm not.

"No," I softly command to Tollin as I shake my head, and he backs off. Cal does not catch on. My attention returns to the second police car. Its windows are open and it has pulled to a stop on the bridge. The cop shines the spotlight all over the waterway leading into the underpass as the car begins inching along the bridge's edge. Damn if they find our tracks—damn if they hear Cal, now coughing into the ground on his hands and knees, muffling his sounds the best he can with cupped hands. The squad stops. My lips tighten. I take in a deep breath, ready to run, but the squad begins moving slowly once more and continues on down the road, turning its searchlight off as it gains speed.

I'm worried, though. Warning bells ring in my head. "Stay here," I say to the others.

"No way," Tollin answers. "You're our best shot. We ain't lettin' you outta our sight."

"I'm goin' to ta road to take a look, freak," I answer in disgust. "Watch me."

Easily seen, even a mile away, are headlights shining down the road our way. Cop cars parked side by side blocking Division by Highway 23. We have to find some other way.

"C'mon," I command as I return to the scum.

"Where we goin'?" Tollin asks.

"West," I answer. "Cops block our way, gotta get around dem somehow. C'mon, let's get out of here."

19
(Franklin)

I forget any time goal as I, we—these freaking scum stick to me, come within sight of County G. Pigs stand by their cars with lots of lights flashing at the crossing of G and Hwy 23, don't got the headlights pointed our way yet, and are too far to see us cross this road in this dark.

The traffic on Highway 23 can be heard, seen a lot, as we move along, but the cops are seen too often too and we're too open in these farm fields, so I head back south into the marshes again before going west. The marsh's tall grasses give cover, but these same stuff; tall brown grasses, reeds, and cattails, lay broken behind, leaving clear sign, too easy seen if looked for, so we walk behind each other to cut the damage. The ground is moist, slippery, getting our shoes, soaking our feet with cold smelly waters; never know what we step into or on next; water, mud, grass, fallen trees, life sucking bog growth—if we break through it, don't knowing how deep it can be.

Hillview Road is in sight now, going north—south, with pigs there, too. Somewhere on the other side this road is a small waterway we need that takes us past the north-south barrier the east-west road of Highway 23 is, now only several hundred yards to the north of us—and get us past the law. We pause, hidden in the weeds at the edge of Hillview Road, to study the cops.

"They can't see us cross here, let's go," Cal weakly says and begins to do so.

"No," I command. Bells ring in my head and I do know why. "Look again."

This stops Cal in time and he pulls back. "What?"

"Look, man" I answer, pointing to the two cop cars parked under the highway overpass on Hillview.

"What about 'em?" Tollin asks.

"Dey parked side by side, man, lights pointin' ta same way. Why dat be, man?"

Tollin grasps the idea and looks south. Perez's cold eyes study me before he too looks south. There are four lights shining our way from far down the south end of this road, so far that those lights seem merged together. With both Perez and Tollin looking, Cal looks south, too. Cal shakes his head, not understanding.

"Pigs point two cars one way, two da opposite down there, man. Somethin' passin' between them two sets a car lights breaks them lights. They'd know it's us, man. We have ta find a way under them lights."

"Can't go around them, Cal," Tollin adds. "The land won't let us."

"Crawl on our bellies across the road then," Cal suggests.

"Dat don't work, man, with you. Fat ass. Da only one would be Meirs ..."

"You're with Meirs?" Tollin asks. "Who else?"

"Shit. None a your fuckin' business ol' man. Business now is gettin' across this damn road."

My eyes settle on Perez for some reason. He accepts my gaze and nods, as if I asked him something—I didn't.

"The road cuts through the swamp ...," Perez begins to say.

"Oh, we didn't know dat, spic," I say.

"Franklin," Tollin scolds.

Perez hesitates, looking at me, then continues; "Means the swamp's water levels have to be maintained both sides—they got a bridge or water passage we possibly could use ..." Perez pauses as he points south, away from the overpass, "... our only choice is that way."

Some kind of change, a commotion, makes us look toward the Hwy 23 cops. The police there at Hillview are walking about, looking over the land with hand held flashlights and others use car mounted searchlights. They talk on the radio even though we cannot hear what they say, and that's when we hear the first baying call of a tracking dog, quickly joined by a chorus of other dogs. The police are now walking down this road. We move quickly south into the swamp.

The dogs are closing the distance, enough to unsettle us, but not enough to panic as we reluctantly slide shoulder deep into the icy waters of the marsh. We found a rodent infested, muck filled, corrugated steel drain tunnel beneath the road, just large enough for us to pass through one at a time, that does maintain marsh water levels across each side of the road. With the slippery muck underneath my hands, feet, and knees, the smell, the buggy debris within, knowing we just scared away wet rodents, the cold waters that cover everything but our eyes, nose, and mouth as we move through this tight tunnel—is a punishment for someone I hate. I shudder as I leave the tunnel to a place where I can stand on what I now call ground. I want to vomit, but I'm too cold, too wet.

As we put the worst of the marsh behind, our movements become rabbit-like; a five maybe ten-yard rush for the next cover, a safety check and to where we run next, doing this until Highway 23 comes back into view, doing this as the dogs follow our trail over on the other side of the road as those animals head toward the middle of the swamp we are going away from. The police on Hillview are no longer in sight as we follow the stream, but we can see their lights sweeping the fields.

On the raised Highway 23 before us semi-trailer trucks and cars pass by.

"How we gonna do this?" Tollin whispers as he looks over the darkened land between us and the highway overpass and back to the waterway below that is our path. "One at a time or in a rush all together?"

"One at a time," Perez quickly answers.

Cal grunts; "Me first ... or you guys'll run off on me ..."

"Yeah," I answer, "Dat be a good thing, man, to leave ya behind. Told ya, ya don't keep up, we leave ya."

Cal grunts again, harder; "Me first."

"He goes last," Perez states.

"No," Cal protests, "No, man, first—you ain't leavin' me."

"We get stuck between the highway and marsh if someone sees your clumsy ass," Perez retorts. "We go first. The other side of the highway gives us a chance—you're last."

Cal looks at Tollin for support.

"Ya last, Cal," Tollin answers firmly. "But Franklin goes third—I don't want ya runnin' off on the other side," he finishes as he looks at me.

"Kiss my ass," I reply, knowing he was dead-on right in his thinking—I would run for my life if I got to the other side first.

20

The highway is running very dark and the trees bordering the road obscure the hazy near-full moon that is setting low on the horizon to our left. Our headlights frequently illuminate the eyes of various creatures peering from the roadside, or catch them crossing the road ahead of us. We are well inside Nicolet National Forest on Highway 139, just past Newald, and headed for some logging road turn-in past Long Lake, somewhere near Tipler, at a point roughly ten miles from the Michigan border.

Then, straight ahead, appears a bright light, slowly separating into a set of headlights but these lights seem to be in our lane and seem also not to be approaching at a closing speed toward us. The car must be parked in our lane? Cops?

"What the heck is that?" Bill asks quietly, so not to waken either Gay or Mary, who are sleeping in the back seat.

"I was thinkin' cops," I reply. "But then there should be more lights."

"I ain't sure what it is."

"Aliens."

"Shuddup."

Bill continues to slow. The lights aren't spreading apart any more. They remain spaced close together, making us more curious. It's like the car is travelling backwards at the same speed we are going—but how could that be, and how can the two headlights look to get larger in size and yet not spread apart more?

"Is this an optical illusion, man, am I seeing things right? They seem ta be gettin' closer, don't they?" I say.

Bill chuckles. "Weird ain't it? It's got to be somethin'. We're gonna find out here in just a few."

"Tellin' ya it's aliens."

"You wish your space family would come back and take you away—ain't gonna happen, man. They dropped you off here for a reason," Bill replies. "Ta get rid of ya."

We start to laugh. Staring mesmerized into our headlights the cow's eyes glow bright as the sight of its body, standing broadside to us in the middle of our lane of the road, emerges into view.

Bill puts the truck into park, climbs out, and walks ahead to shoo the cow away, flapping his arms and roaring with laughter so loud I feel sure he will wake Gay and Mary, even though he is a good thirty feet away. I give a nudge to my sister but she is deep asleep. Mary cannot be gently wakened either. We think they will not believe us on this one.

Now that we're stopped Rick moves his fifth wheeler ahead to take the lead for this final distance. Mark, Doug, and Paula ride with him. I stay with Bill, up front in his cab, while our wives continue sleeping heavily in the back. Tom and Roy follow behind.

The cow gave Bill and I a reason to renew conversation, for this trip has become long and tiring, though we soon fall silent again. Few vehicles of any kind are on the road at this time of night. I watch the road lines pass by and allow my attentions to turn inward, to anticipate my being out among these woods again after a long twenty-some year absence. I hold a quiet eagerness for it. I hope to experience it again the way I remember; times I just sat out in the woods alone and listened to the sounds, felt the breezes, seeing animals I would not normally see, and the silent thrill of doing this so near to them—hearing things I would not bother to take the time to listen for, or appreciate elsewhere; critters scampering, sounds of wings flapping, breezes rustling the woods—a reminder to notice the often-subtle smells of the earth. After this supposedly hard day of hunting; of sitting on a tree stump, branch, or hillside, to then come back and rest, relax, and enjoy each evening with friends around a campfire; all will make this week a fine time.

A small white-breasted bird with black wings landed on my shoulder those many years ago. I talked to that bird, turning my head slightly to face it, the small bird flying off only after I made a quick physical motion a couple of minutes later. The attitude of a kid survives inside me, for I yearn to have another experience like that one again. I am not here to hunt, and I believe the others know this, though I will go out with them.

"When was the last time Doug hunted, you know?" Bill inquires, breaking my thoughts.

"Don't know for sure," I answer. "I believe I heard his wife doesn't like him being out alone in the Arizona heat, if anything goes wrong. I think it's been some time for him, too."

"Wonder if he can still shoot straight," Bill remarks.

He is just making conversation. He believes Doug can shoot. Bill must be feeling more than just tired. He must feel sleep coming on strong and wants the talk to keep alert. I have seen this before. I have been there before, many times. "Oh, I'm sure he can shoot as good as he used to. He was a pretty good shot back in high school, you know."

"Now how am I supposed to know that?" Bill wearily wisecracks with barely a smile.

"Got me there," I answer, smiling back.

"You figure you can still shoot?"

"A rifle—probably; a handgun—probably not," I answer. "I got thicker glasses now and my eyes aren't as good—the lenses in my eyeballs themselves aren't that good."

"Oh?" Bill questioned with a rising voice, "With them thicker glasses I wonder if I'll be safe standing beside ya."

I am slow to smile as I cock my head; "Ahhhhh….."

Bill smiles slowly, too.

We see Rick's truck decelerate and pull left across the highway and head into a wide entrance of dirt that looks like a logging road, to disappear before us into the woods. Rick's truck and trailer bounce ahead of us as he comes back into view after we also slow, cross the road, and enter the woods.

Our swift turn and the rough and bouncy trail, the noises of the trucks getting jolted about, rudely shake up our waking women.

"What's goin' on?" Gay sleepily asks.

"Yeah," adds Mary.

"We're here," Bill answers. "Just whatever it takes to get to camp now."

"Gosh I hope it ain't too far or I'll piss my pants—my bladder's full and you're bouncin' me all over back here," Mary says.

Bill and I smile to each other.

"Just let me know if you really gotta go, I'll stop," Bill replies.

"Yeah, as if I'm gonna do that out here—in the dark."

We watch as the woods close in quickly as we travel this logging road. The various trees cast eerie shadows about as their trunks, brightened by our pale yellow headlights, pass starkly by before slipping back into the darkness in a silent rush. Evergreens do the same, except they appear like scattered dark conical sentinels in the midst of these other trees, as we move and bounce about.

"Kind of reminds me of the time in Ladysmith when Rick was accused of shining deer," I say aloud.

"Yeah," Bill answers, "Was he?"

"Not exactly," I reply. "We were looking for a dirt road intersection, and Rick pulled a million candle powered lamp out and swept it partly across a field—full of deer, to find the crossing. A DNR guy was parked at the corner."

"Ooops." Bill exclaims. "Gotcha."

"Yeah," I answered. "The DNR guy took Rick's lamp and his gun. Rick eventually got the gun back, though."

"He was lucky," Bill replies. "They're pretty tough enforcing stuff. They take their jobs a bit too seriously mostly. Coulda taken his truck."

"Yeah, tell me about it. We split a hefty fine. I was the reason we were out there. We were heading home, taking a short cut, from some bar up there."

"Figures. DNR guys gotta justify their own existence sometimes, you know, and shinin' ain't hard to do. Deer are accustomed to the logging operations up here, ya know. They won't run all that easy unless we get right on top of 'em. Happens all the time," Bill turns briefly to me and the women. "Keep your eye out. It's really something to see how many there are when you catch them in the lights, and it's common, we should see some."

The women murmur back, unimpressed, yet agree to keep a look out.

"How far into this stuff are we going?" Mary asks a moment or so later.

"Your guess is as good as mine," replies Bill. "Rick said it's three miles by the way the truck travels, remember? To me the further in the better, you know."

"Oh, I know that," Mary flatly answers. "I don't like it but I know you would."

"Well, you know guys." Gay adds, "They fantasize they're mountain men, if they can."

"Uh-yeah but why? Why do guys like that, like this?" Mary asks.

"Because they want to feel they are as rough and tough as woodpecker lips in wintertime, I hear," Gay answers and persists; "Don't you guys?"

"Yeah, I do this every year, Gay," I reply stiffly, though smiling as I look back at her.

"I guess I referred only to my husband," Gay responds, "My brother isn't so daring."

"Ooh, watch out there, man, you're earning more Mr. Excitement points," Bill warns me.

"Ahh, I sense that," I sigh. "Thanks for sticking up for me."

"No problem."

21
(Franklin)

Beyond Highway 23 we move fast, driven by thoughts of dogs and helped by the return to solid farmed ground. We've gone east after sighting the second radio tower landmark, crossing Hillview again—with no cops in sight, then northeast onto higher land, leaving the marshes, the dogs, and the cops well behind. We are following a mostly dry creek up a long gentle hill where it should start near a second gravel pit, the five-mile marker north of the prison.

"Five miles," I say to myself.

"What?" Tollin asks.

I surprised myself, saying the words out loud. "Nothin', man, just talkin' ta maself." Five miles, just a mile to go, but feels like I've gone ten to get this far—fatigue gots its grips over my body. We've lost much time. A big amount of time. Any motivating joy from the break left me in the marsh, with the barking of the dogs. I hurt. I smell like marsh. My clothing is damp from its waters. I feel its greasy slime in my clothes, on my skin, its taste in my mouth. Its raunchy smell mixes with the stink of my sweat. A skunk might envy me. Cal has the same trouble as he puts his finger to his nose, closes one side, and weakly blows.

"Smell ain't in yer nose Cal," Tollin says.

"Stink's disgustin' man—what'd we go through back there?" Cal replies.

"Mucky shit," answers Perez, "Rat turds, worms, dead bugs, your mamma's tampons …"

Cal gives Perez the finger as he asks; "Why we ain't hearin' dogs?"

We all wonder except Perez. "We bought time with the water, man, the tunnel, the water again. Be glad we ain't hearin' 'em. If we don't get where we're goin', we'll hear 'em soon 'nuff."

Some time ago the moon dropped below the horizon and deepened the night, making our way difficult and slowing us as we approach this second gravel pit. There are five guiding lights around this pit this time. We reach the perimeter road easily.

"Which way?" Tollin asks.

"Left," I answer. "It goes down hill to ta north, man. At ta bottom we leave ta road n keep goin' north. We'd be climbing another hill soon after dat, following County G, ta road being on our right. We follow dat right to ta car shop, pretty much. We in trouble though, man. With this moon going down we can't go fast but we gotta get there by mornin'."

22

We watch the path ahead twist and turn, rise and fall, as we bounce our way deeper into the woods, passing more than one intersection of logging trails, until we reach and stop at a large clearing. Rick pulls his truck off to one side as much as he can and sticks his arm out of his truck's window and slowly waves us alongside. Bill moves little by little as he pulls up, since half of our truck is off the other side of the logging road and crunching the unsteady underbrush. Rick has since closed his window, which takes our attentions elsewhere.

"Okay, guys, so you were right," Gay acknowledges.

"What'dya mean ...?" I ask but they don't need to answer as I sight many, often vague yet remarkable images, of deer grazing out in the brown grassy field, starting, maybe, forty yards from us. A few of the deer stand completely mesmerized by our headlights, though our lights do not shine directly over the entire group. Some of their eyes glow in reflection to our light, but most do not. There are two large and well-horned bucks, one near and clear to see and one on the other side of this herd, barely visible. Both had been, until our arrival, apparently more interested in the charms of the two-dozen or so females that separate them than they were in fighting each other. Some begin to shift and prod the ground. One or two begin walking leisurely toward the covering forest behind them as Rick starts to slowly move his truck again. The rest of the animals begin to turn from our lights and we see a few of their white triangular tails go stiffly upright before all suddenly bound swiftly into the darkness, their numbers disappearing in a blink of an eye.

The logging road divides again and we take the less used path that continues in the northwest direction we had generally been going in. Maybe a quarter mile further the road rises slightly and ends in a large semicircle of gravel and dirt. Rick pulls to a stop and waves us to pull alongside him once more. Bill pulls my side of the truck beside Rick and we roll our windows down to let the cold night air in to frost our breath as we speak.

"Who put the gravel out here?" I ask.

"I did," Rick answers. "I'm going to use it for a bunch of stuff come spring. I had them dump it here. This is where our land starts. There's gonna be a drop-off at the edge. It's not that steep but enough to worry ya at first—okay? Later on, when the path gets worn in, I'll use the gravel for traction up the incline along with some railroad ties. Right now, though, it's important for you to follow my tracks 'cause I know where it's good ground—okay? Our place is about a third of a mile away but it's more like a half-mile by how the trucks gotta do it—ready? Okay, let's get there, so we can sleep. Oh, wait a minute … I need to do something, and say some more, before we go…"

23

"…I need to do something, and say some more, before we go…"

"You own this part of this logging road we're on, then?" I ask.

"Yep, kinda, belongs to one of the paper mills up here. I got to pay them a user fee for it, but it ain't much. Stay put." Rick finishes as he places his truck into park and slides out the door to stand in the headlights before us.

"You can stay in the trucks where it's warm," Rick says loudly, "I just want everybody to hear me … and, and I gotta take a quick leak after this," he states with a broad sheepish smile. "This is where our land starts, over to the right here." (It is to our right as we face Rick). "We're going in another third of a mile to a clearing with a small rise on the right side of it. That's where the trailer will go. It's a nice area somewhat protected from the wind. I want to point the ends of the trailer north and south, hoping this will catch a lot of sun during the morning and evening to help keep the trailer warm longer, but not get it too hot at midday. So I still lead when I get back," He pauses and sees Bill acknowledge him.

"When we get there I will need you to watch the back end and make sure the entire trailer is on the higher ground. I need it there 'cause I'm going to skirt the trailer sometime or another, leavin' it here year-round." Rick waits for Bill to acknowledge again.

"We have to go down this ledge a certain way, too," Rick points before us to a spot on the perimeter where the grass and gravel meet, "'Cause it's no good going straight over the edge—I tried before with just the truck. It will catch the bottom of the trailer if I go straight," Rick explains. "There is a landing of sorts wide enough for our trucks that slants down off the edge over there," Rick points left of us to a location on the rim of grass bordering this graveled semi-circle. I don't see any opening, only the grass fading off from our headlights disappearing into the night. "We're gonna swing around and go down that way. I'll be back in a minute," Rick finishes with another sheepish smile and hurries off out of sight of our lights.

"This really is way out in the middle of nowhere, ain't it?" I say across the gap between the trucks to Doug, as the women plead behind me to close my window.

"No kiddin'," Doug replies.

"It's the best kind of place to be if you want to hunt," Mark explains loudly from further inside Rick's truck, making sure he will be heard. I can hear Paula, who is sitting beside Mark, tell him he doesn't have to speak so loud.

"Close the window!" demand the women behind me. I smile across to those in the other truck as I do so, leaving it slightly open to hear if they call to us from the other truck.

Rick returns and exclaims; "Whoa, chilly out here. You guys are going to enjoy this."

Rick backs his vehicle up until the trailer's end is into the logging road. Bill has moved us around to watch where he goes. Rick drives to a far point on the semicircle and gently takes his truck over the edge. Our headlights shine the area and we see those inside Rick's truck brace themselves as his vehicle suddenly dips steeply downward onto the hidden slope. Rick guides his truck slowly along as the lengthy trailer reaches the edge of the circle and comes onto the slope. We can see Rick's truck, as it disappears below the ledge, resist the trailer's pull to tip it over as the trailer bucks, pushes, and pulls at the truck until both come onto flatter, smoother ground.

Our headlights flash about the fields and show three small leafless trees set close together off to the left side but near the bottom of the short slope as Bill begins to follow in a likewise precarious way. Rick has not waited but continues slowly through the fields and the sparsely wooded sections he chooses to go through. Twice we watch as Rick and Doug climb out of their truck ahead of us to move either fallen branches or brush out of the way, before we finally reach our campsite. There, after making sure the trailer is positioned correctly, Rick has Bill pull up and park left of his truck somewhat parallel to his own, and positioned so Bill's camper door is easily accessible and facing the main trailer's door. Roy and Tom park to the left of Bill.

24

All headlights and engines remain on as we gather around between the vehicles and shiver from the chill we feel on leaving the warm comfort of our truck's cabins or car, yet we smile as our breaths crystallize in the crisp night air, glad to finally be here and the thought of sleep being not too far away.

"As the crow flies," Rick begins, "Just to give you guys some idea which direction is which here, uh, so none of us get lost, the highway we were on is about two miles that a way." Rick is standing facing all of us; his back is to and his right arm is laying across the top side panel to his truck bed, his right hand begins to play with the lid to the metal tool box spanning across the truck's bed next to the cab, opening and closing it slightly, as if he needed something to do, as he speaks. His left hand points almost ninety degrees away from his truck and out into the darkness of the night directly behind where we stand. "The trucks and the trailer are roughly pointing south, and we're parked, ah, about parallel to the highway, so we will be seeing the sun coming up from this same direction," he says. "That makes it east for you women," he finishes with a smile.

"Oh, that was not called for," Gay replies resentfully. "Why do men always think women can't figure these things out?" she asks the other females.

"Yeah, I was gonna say; like duh," adds Paula, "I mean, like, if we're facing south, then that's got to be east to our left."

Rick's eyes squint with pleasure as he leans forward and says; "But you're facing west right now—south is to your left." The women give out loud gasps of exasperation, realizing he is correct, but knowing his statement matters little to the general understanding.

"He's a lost cause, isn't he?" says Mary.

"No, he's an asshole, and I'm married to him," Paula remarks. "Love him, but I know what he is."

"Any civilization closer to us than that road?" Tom asks.

Rick still smiles from Paula's comment. "Love you, too. Ah-yeah, 'bout a half mile west and south, but I'm not sure exactly where, and the paper companies move about tearing down trees so they could be anywhere, but you can't count on anyone being at their sites," Rick replies. "Tomorrow I'll show everyone around. We'll cover the whole place to lessen the chance of anybody losing their way." Rick winks at me as a reminder to my past. "And to show the place where I'd like us to hunt. A couple of things that Bill and I talked about, just to let you guys know, is we're going to be leaving the propane and the guns outside against his trailer...."

"That's fine with me," Mary interrupts, "I don't want them inside."

"Why?" Gay asks, "Is that safe?"

"I told you why," Bill gently reminds her.

"I know, for cleaning, but leaving them outside, they'll still get dirty. Why not inside the other trailer?"

"Yeah," acknowledges Rick. "We'll do that at night." Rick sees puzzlement on some of our faces and explains; "The guns won't get dirty. We put a small piece of tape over the barrel tip but we want them outside because we don't want condensation to get moisture inside the guns, you know, bringing cold guns in and out of a warm trailer every night will force us to clean them every time when we don't have to—not as often, anyway, if we haven't shot them and we leave them out here. I think we got ten guns, ya know, ah—what, Bill, you brought your semi-auto, Mark is borrowing my other semi, I got my semi …"

"Tom and I brought our bolt actions," adds Roy.

"I brought two bolts—one for Doug, the other for you know who," Bill says.

"I brought a shotgun, too," Roy says.

"So did I," Rick replies, "So I guess that's ten guns—maybe you're right, Gay, we'll put them in a cab of one of the trucks. That'll help protect them, too. We might have to take them out during the day tomorrow, though, because we'll be doing a lot of work, going in and out of everything."

Mary shakes her head with understanding.

"I want the women to take a couple of practice shots sometime tomorrow too, okay?" Rick says, and he waits for each woman to acknowledge. "We'll keep my handgun inside the main trailer tonight with us, though—alright?"

Paula shrugs her shoulders with indifference, she is much more comfortable around guns than either Gay or Mary. "Hey, that's fine with me," she says. "I mean, just in case a bear comes snoopin' around we can scare him off with somethin', you know?"

The other two women's eyes widen, mine too, for just a moment. We hope she is kidding.

Rick catches my expression. "Paula's right, that can happen," he says to reinforce her. "There are black bear up here."

"Bill!" Gay quietly yells at her husband. "You said I didn't have to worry about things like that!"

Bill raises his hands in the air amidst our chuckles and answers; "Hey, I said nothing of the kind—really. And, if I did, well, there's nothin' to worry about," he continues, more soothingly towards his wife, "They are as afraid of you as you are of them. They won't come near this place. I'm tellin' ya. Relax." His hands and arms spread out before her in a silent plea as Gay's eyes stay wide in disbelief as she turns and looks around at us. She is trying hard to believe him. "Besides," Bill adds, "They should be hibernating by now, anyways."

"I hope so," she sternly replies, "One sight of them and I'm outta here."

"Oh me too," Mary adds. "I'm gone."

There's a moment of silence before Rick talks again.

"Sometime tomorrow I'm gonna need help diggin' two pits; one to bury some of our garbage, the other for a shitter. I'm gonna put the shitter in a place where us guys can use it with some privacy so as not to tax our water supply inside the trailer—got it, guys?" Rick announces authoritatively. "We need the water for drinking and cooking, not for flushing."

"Aw, man," I exclaim, "We'll be freezin' our butts off. Did we bring enough toilet paper?"

"Each of us guys agreed to bring our own—didn't nobody tell you?" Bill chides. I return a resentful look.

"No. No one told me, but I did bring my own figuring you guys wouldn't tell me—I know you."

"Bill and I are gonna dig the pits," Rick said, "But I have other work for you. Maybe for Tom or Roy—they might help you, too."

"Okay."

"Brave man," Doug states.

"Huh?" I ask.

"Well, you agreed and you don't know what work he's got for ya yet."

"Oh, yeah, shit, what is it, Rick?"

Rick smiles. "Cuttin' wood."

I turn back to Doug. "Ain't so bad."

Doug smirks as he nods his head. "Okay, if you say so."

"And I thought," Bill interrupts cautiously, for he does not know them well, "That you, Mark and Doug, maybe Roy and maybe Tom, would go 'round and gather up freestanding firewood, you know, fallen branches and twigs and stuff like that, for a few nights of fires, unhitch and stake down the trailer. Maybe walk the women through handling their guns once more. What do ya say?"

"Alright with me," Mark agrees.

"Me, too," Doug says. "Sounds easier than digging pits."

"We have to be sure to show Mr. Excitement here how to use a rifle again—and where the safety is and what it is used for—alright?" Rick prods me as he watches my expression change to one of weariness. He sees but ignores my reaction, speaks up again and changes the subject. "There are large water jugs in back of the trailer. I'm gonna need help to move them around before we can sleep there tonight, alright? Are we gonna try to do this—sleep all of us inside this trailer?" Everyone nods yes. "Then we gotta do some work. It's gonna be really tight."

"Hey," interjects Tom, "I don't want ta try ta sleep in the main trailer. I'd rather sleep in the camper if what you say means I'll be sleeping on the floor."

"I'll sleep in the backseat of one of the trucks. I-I don't wanna get stepped on, ya know," Roy adds. "So, me too."

"Yeah, that's what I meant. Someone will have to sleep on the floor. I figured that would be me, so what you say is okay by me—it gets me off the floor," Rick says. "But you guys don't have to. We should have room, both of you on a bed or a cot."

"Thanks but I won't rest easy if there's too many people around. I'll take a truck," Roy answers.

Tom cocks his head. "I agree with him."

"Whatever people, let's get it done, then," states Doug, shrugging his shoulders. "'cause I'm tired, bet the rest of ya are, too."

"We gonna set the generator up tonight?" Bill asks Rick.

"No. We don't really have to until tomorrow evening. Let's not worry about that now. It's work better done in daylight anyway with all that electrical stuff. The trailer batteries will be plenty good until then."

"Alright."

We move much of our supplies over to Bill's camper, clearing the main trailer of them, push out and secure the main trailer's extendable sections and open the sleeper sofas. Then Rick discovers one of the water jugs has cracked open from the travel and has soaked the one cot he used to brace them during transport, so the jugs would not roll about. The cot, though, had been intended to sleep one of the guys and this soaking stops that. Rick gathers us around him again.

"Sorry, guys," he announces, "Even with Tom and Roy sleepin' elsewhere I don't think we can sleep all the rest of us in this main trailer now, so maybe someone can draw straws as to who wants to sleep in the cab of one of the trucks. Tom and Roy figured a way to both sleep in Bill's camper even crowded in with all those supplies—I don't know how you guys are gonna move around in there, so sleepin' in the back seat of one of the trucks is the only choice left. The weather should be in the upper twenties, maybe, I heard the radio say. That's for tonight only though. I think we can get the stuff arranged enough tomorrow so all of us can sleep in the main trailer, I don't know. It's too much for us to do that rearranging now—unless you guys want to? Otherwise; who's gonna be 'the man'."

"What a wordy welcome," Doug states.

"Well, hey, I'm sorry, don't know what else to do—you could sleep on the floor? But you can see, with the two sleeper sofas out and the way we arranged the stuff, you'll get stepped on if anyone needs the bathroom during the night," Rick answers as he leans forward and smiles, slightly shaking his shoulders and opening his hands in offering. "You got any ideas?"

"Ain't no problem, Doug," Mark interrupts before Doug can reply, "I'm so tired from the long day I've had—I've been up since four-thirty this morning, and I worked extra long all week, that I can just about sleep anywhere. I'll take the truck—Rick's truck. You got plenty of blankets to spare, don't ya?"

"Oh, yeah," responds Paula, shaking her head in disbelief. "Rick, really, how 'bout you sleepin' there? It ain't right having a friend sleep out in the truck when you tied the jugs up."

Rick nods his head. "Yeah, I really should..."

"That's okay, Smith," Mark says, "I snore loud. Ain't no problem, I've done this a whole bunch of times with my kids and back when I was a kid camping. I'll take the handgun, though. Don't want to be surprised by anything lurking out there when I got my pants down during the night, ya know—okay?"

As Rick gives the weapon to Mark, Mary says; "That's a big gun."

Rick smiles and says laughingly; "Thanks."

"O-oh—I didn't mean it that way," Mary replies, rolling her eyes.

"I know," Rick laughs. "Couldn't resist. We'll give you a chance to fire it tomorrow, if you want."

"No, I don't."

"Sure?"

"Yes."

"Ah, maybe that's best. A semi-auto like this is too big for your hands. It'll kick your hands back too much and might jam."

"Why?" Gay asks. "Break your hand you mean?"

"No, no, I mean jam. The first bullet's gas pushes the slider back to load up the next one. If you don't hold the gun rigid enough the gas might not get enough force to push the slider, it'll just rotate the gun in your hand instead, and a bullet shell sometimes gets stuck when that happens," Rick answers, then addresses Mark; "There's one in the chamber now so be careful, keep the safety on."

"Gotcha."

"You sure you're okay sleepin' outside Mark?" asks Paula again.

"Yeah, I'm fine with it," Mark replies.

"Oh, no sympathy for us, I see," remarks Roy. "Tom and I in the camper and no one cares. I understand. I understand."

Rick smiles as he shrugs and lifts his hands in offering. "Ya got each other—ain't that enough?"

"Don't go there. I'm way too tired," Roy answers. "Forget about it. Let's get to sleep."

"Well Mark, what a bummer when you're on vacation, huh? I'll get you plenty of blankets," Paula says. "You think that jug broke loose when you went over the ledge back there, Rick?"

"Yeah, likely, a lot more water would have leaked out had it happened earlier," Rick answers her. "It's just a small crack near the top of one bottle, ya know. I'm surprised at just how much did come out. Sorry, Mark, sleepin' out in a truck ain't my idea of a good time, you know? But thanks for letting me stay inside."

"Yeah, well, you're really a wuss," Mark smiles.

25
(Franklin)

The eastern sky brightens as we study the road below. Down this gentle hill, across this road, the six-mile goal is finally in sight. I should've gotten here in the darkness long ago. How could I have misjudged so bad, planned so poor? How could the difficulties in crossing six miles in the night not been more expected?

We manage worried smiles as we study the lights and the sign for the dealership in the distance. It's our hope. We can't keep running much longer. We *have* to take a car from there.

"You three," I begin, wishing again they weren't by my side, pissed because they are—still angry with myself for stopping to deal with them. "We've gotta cross ta road and find ta service area. A lotta open area—yo gotta be quick—ya think you can make it?"

Cal rasps painfully—defiantly, sneering, hearing the disdain in my words. "You think I'm a fuckin' pussy? You've been wantin' to leave us behind all along. Ain't gonna happen. I'll make it, nigger."

"You fool enough to believe you can leave me behind—after what I've chanced—huh?" sharply challenges Tollin, his voice raw but surprisingly strong.

I smile, because we both know I can do just that—easily.

Perez silently gives me the finger. Ask me if I care.

"Just wait," Cal rasps further, coughing, "On a better day I'll kick your black ass—stick your head in it."

"You fuckin' wish," I scoff.

Tollin sighs. "Guys, let's get this done."

Cal and I go quiet, understanding Tollin's intent. I give our next moves; "S-shaped path ta the road again, man, like befo'. We find ta repair car side, find one ready ta be picked up ..."

"How're we goin' to know?" Cal snaps.

I keep my patience. "Tickets in ta windows, man."

"And if none?" Tollin asks me.

"Then we get what we can, man … don't make me think I'm doin' all ta thinkin' here—you'll piss me off."

I begin my way to the road, being forced to lay down twice in the tall grass of the hill as lone cars go by. When the way clears I start my run across the road and Cal attempts to bolt with me. I cross easily to dive behind the brush seconds before a staggering, gasping Cal does, enough time for me to look back and see Tollin's pained expression, his shared concern that Cal is too slow and will be seen. Moments after Cal hits the ground beside me a semi trailer truck cruises on by. The timing of this truck increases our worry. Tollin and Perez quickly cross after the truck disappears from view.

The sky brightens more over every minute. The road will become busier. We need to hurry. We can see hundreds of yards ahead now, or further. It's becoming a dangerous time, and not much time before the workers arrive, little time before full light.

The auto center front faces south, towards the corner of G and CCC. We got lucky, the service area is on our side of the building facing west, facing us. The cars needing work are parked on the cement side strip extending out from the building towards us until this strip stops at a narrow ribbon of grass lined by barren oak and maple trees, and this ribbon separates the center's grounds from the farmer's field we are in, defined by a foot high drop-off from the grass ribbon into the farmed land. The vehicles are in two lines; one along the wall of the building, where possible, and the second, nearer to us, lined up parked along the grass ribbon. I count twenty-two cars. This is a busy place.

To the right of me is a thin line of tall barren bushes beside a water drainage ditch next to the highway. These give little cover to hide behind, but the open flat farm field to my left gives none. Time is short—I think again about the owners, the workers, who will be at this center soon, and how tired I feel as I say; "C'mon, we got ta run. Little time ta work with."

I hug the brush as I hurry towards the service center. I can see more of the new car area in front and the service side of the building. The new car section is too open to view from the roads, too in front of the building, for any of us to be there. Whatever stands on the other side of the building ain't no use and I don't want to waste time going there to find out otherwise—for now.

"Yo ever take a car, Cal?" I ask.

"Naw."

"You?"

"No," Tollin replies.

I hate to, but I turn and ask Perez.

His sneer is big and wide; "I ain't needin' you no more, black ass."

I stop my run. The others do, too.

Slimy spic ... I know he's got a blade so his words alarm me—only he don't know if I carry. He bets I don't—and I don't. I glare back at him—I can't ignore his challenge, can't give him leadership, can't let him know I don't carry until it has to be. "In ya mind a-hole. C'mon, spic, let's do this."

Tollin moves in quickly between us. "Damn idiots. Think. Dammit. Let's get ourselves otta here first. What've we done all this for if ya just want ta kill each other now?"

From inside the building a dog begins barking wildly and distracts Perez and I cautiously away from each other. The dog is big, angry, frantic, and we see the effects of its pounding and jumping against the one large service door facing us near the rear corner of the building, its nose and sometimes its entire pit bull head shows in one of the many windows of the door as it jumps. It does not seem to be barking at us but at something else—and that something catches our eyes; someone moving alongside one of the vehicles on our side of the building ....

"Who's that?" Tollin asks.

"Lookin' like Meirs—it is 'im. Man, they're here—I still have a chance," I exclaim. Cal gives me an annoyed look. I don't care.

Meirs is crouched beside an older two door tan colored pickup—an extended cab, big enough to fit most of us in. He is working its door lock. It is the fourth vehicle away from the door where the dog barks. Radwell or Drew, however, ain't seen. We're still a ways back in the farm field so I turn to the scum; "Stay here, by ta bushes, man, we'll come get ya. I gotta tell Meirs we're here. I be back, man."

Halfway there I glance back at them. Cal and Tollin are slow in moving but are creeping forward, against my orders, Perez too. My anger passes fast—I know I would be doing the same.

"Franklin."

The sudden whispered call sounds from my right as I hurry hunkered down between two cars. I stop on hearing my name to find who said it. Radwell! Only his head can be seen above the trunk of the vehicle two cars over. I reply, turn around, and head along the grass side of the cars to meet him.

"Freakin' good to see ya," I say quietly, and meaning every word. "Any trouble?"

"Same," he replies. "Trouble in gettin' here—don't get me started. We crossed triple-C twice. Man, after we split, Meirs and I must have started making one big wide loop. Just lucky we caught the road a second time. Even luckier it had a sign, so we knew we were going the wrong way. Way out of our way, man. Got me freakin' nervous as a fire for a while. Thought we'd do plan 'B' and go Mount Calvary way but we didn't know which way that was anymore till the sign, then we knew we were closer to this. We got here, maybe, fifteen minutes ago. You?"

"It was Cal."

"Damn!" he whispers, "Where is he?"

"Tollin, too."

"Tollin?" Radwell quietly exclaims in surprise and confusion. "What the…" Radwell curses softly as he looks around for them. "How many others left on impulse?"

"Perez, too."

"What the ...?" he exclaims as he sees them heading our way. Radwell continues in a sarcastic whisper, quickly speaking; "Well now, we couldn't ta done no better gettin' all five killers together."

Radwell's right. He, myself, Drew, Cal, and Perez—the five out of the seventy in the cottage who were in for murder. It's not good luck. The goal was to spread us around to force the cops to spread out, too, them would be more worried about us murderers than the common-folk inmate. We figured someone would get caught, like Cal, and tell them we're spread. Now the pigs will figure out we're together—it's not good luck.

Radwell continues; "We hoped for Tyler. You know, his way with words and women and all. Thought he'd help some, but Cal? Blast. How you and Perez not kill each other yet, huh?"

"We're gettin' ready."

Radwell laughs quietly. "Franklin relax, we'll keep him from ya. Perez can help us. What was Tollin thinkin' about? He's crazier than I thought."

"Keep Perez far away—far away," I order. "What'ya mean Tollin crazy?"

"Nothing," Radwell says to me, "Nothing serious as I know him, anyway, his age and wasn't he s'posed to get out sometime next year?" Radwell's answer relaxes me. "Oh, and he's a mumbler—he has some form of Torrente's syndrome, I guess."

"What?"

"He blurts out insulting stuff, most times nonsensical, and he can't help it. Sometimes he's kinda loud too."

"Ahh," I reflect, "Makes no sense. Mumbles some. He don't curse none. And I'd want Tyler, too. Much. How long Meirs been at it?" I ask as the three scum join us.

"Damn dog got us nervous. Had to check for cameras, too, you know?"

"Don't see none."

"We don't either. He's on his third car or fourth. I've checked every car in this row except these last three. So far nothing. All keys are inside the place. Damn you guys smell—what the heck you guys get yourselves into, huh?"

"Swamp," Tollin answers. "Didn't you?"

"Heck no, man, we just ran along Division. No cops—but they got you into the water, huh, man, that's funny."

"Fuck you Rad," I answer. "You get dogs chasin' ya, you'd get in ta water, too. Came across Hillview. Drew with us?"

"Yeah, he's on the backside—or front side, takin' a quick look. Hillview, huh? Damn sure hope you lost them dogs." As Radwell finishes we hear the slowing approach of a car coming unseen from behind us and to our right, from the road I and the scum had crossed.

Police! The squad swiftly glides by the front of the building and disappears from our view as it enters the lot but surely it will come around to here.

26

A harsh snore, the typical overpowering man type of snore, emanates from my brother-in-law over in the other pullout bed. From what I can tell, everyone else is asleep. In a way I envy them, for the warmth of the fresh bedcovers so comfortable against my skin and the coolness of the air inside the trailer combine to make me want to stay right here in bed too, and relax all day next to Mary's warm soft body. She is also snoring. Yet the day calls me to leave this soothing comfort and explore the world outside.

My feet slip quietly out from under the sheets and I sit up without disturbing Mary. Though the trailer floor is handsomely carpeted and insulated, it is not enough to stop the coldness from seeping in and chilling my bared feet. This invigorating chill quickens the search for my gym bag, which is filled for easy and ready clothes, as I planned for this. I quietly hurry into the bathroom and close the door to change.

Everyone's still sleeping as I place the gym bag back beside the bed and lean over to give Mary a soft kiss on her cheek. My kiss doesn't disturb her. Gay and Bill, in the other pullout sleeper sofa bed, are oblivious to my movements. I leave them all as I quietly step outside the trailer and into the gaining morning light.

Sparkling silver frost covers nearly everything in sight; trees, weeds, grass, the evergreens, even the sides of the trailer itself and on the three black metal stairs underneath my feet. Thin white wisps of ground fog hang about and above the winding trail we made with the trucks during the night coming here. Elsewhere I can see this silky fog lofted up among the trees, and I take in their frail beauties, knowing these whiffs of clouds will quickly disappear with the rising sun. The morning is becoming bright though quiet, not even the birds seem awake and when one does call out from somewhere, its sound is so sharp and clear—and remote.

I wonder about Mark and how he slept through the night, though it appears he must have slept well, for the windows of Rick's truck show signs of frost from the inside as well as outside. The driver's side window is cranked open just enough to see the inside of the windshield, but there is no sign of movement within. Bill's camper is much the same way. I can faintly hear Roy and Tom snoring away through that camper's partially opened side windows.

I head down along the truck path stepping as quietly as I can and taking my time as I look about, just to take the scenery in and enjoy it. There's nothing majestic or breathtaking here, it's just an everyday sort of scene with slow and gentle rolling fields and barren trees, ready for winter, yet this sight is magnificent compared to my dark, poorly ventilated and isolated office cubicle, that has no windows to see out nearby. I stop every five steps or so, because I was once told much more than this is an unnatural sound in the wild; animals, unless on the run, stop frequently to listen and look around, so I will do the same. Step by step I ease my feet down on the tire-flattened grass to keep things quiet. The grasses rustle and collapse further under my feet, but these sounds do not carry far. I feel like a mischievous kid, sneaking around, getting away with something, and I carry a touch of a child's smile.

After walking far enough, I turn around and face south toward our camp. I face the point where Rick stood last night by the back of his truck to tell us which way is which, and I see that our camp is nestled within a shallow pocket of land as Rick said it would be. The trailer and trucks stand near the right side of this pocket on a raised step-like portion of earth, before the ground gradually rises away from them, continuing to my right to the west. Following along this rise to the west is the southern borderline of woods standing many yards further away and behind our trailer camp. These woods are thick with trees of various kinds and continue on in a rough line beyond the crest of this gentle hill to the west, eventually disappearing behind the land. The crest of this western hill rises to a height about fifteen feet above my head maybe a quarter mile distant. From this crest back down to me is open field of tall browned grasses and scattered brush. I turn more to my right following the crest line, until the next island of woods, a hundred yards distant, appears before me. The tree line of these northern woods runs roughly parallel to the southern woods but are more open, at least at first, for I can see well into their coverage. I follow the sight of these north woods as I go on with my turn around until I directly face them. The woods stretch to my right, to the east, maybe two hundred yards before they end abruptly as the sea of brown and golden grass sweeps down the hill and in and around this corner of north woods to stretch out for some distance beyond toward the north and east. The path of our trucks wanders through this sea of grass as I turn more and face directly east. A thin finger of trees appears extending out into this grassy sea before widening into the next stand of woods about four hundred yards away. These woods meander in and out of the grassland for as far as I can see east and south as I turn until my sight is hampered by a blunt rise of ground coming to about half the height of our main trailer, as our camp comes back into view. There is only open field between the meandering tree line to the east and this blunt rise. There is enough level ground between this blunt rise and our trucks to turn Rick's trailer around if ever need be. Only two young evergreens, standing at the top of the blunt rise on the left and nearly directly across from the trailer's door, have enough substance to them to block my view of what lay between them and the southern borderline of woods that once again appears behind our trailer camp. I can understand why the far side of these two evergreens is the chosen spot which Rick plans on having our, ah-hem, outhouse and, a bit further away, our temporary garbage pit—this pair of evergreens gives some privacy.

I turn away from the sight of our camp and walk on north along the truck path and follow it east among the open lands. The grasses are in a variety of colors ranging from gold and browns to burnt deep reds flowing among the large islands of gray and black and barren trees—all adorned with a sparkling wetness from the quickly melting frost. Dark pillars of evergreens are scattered here and there among these island woodlands. I continue along the truck path, making my way through the eastern meandering woods. I keep on walking until I reach the foot of the semicircle of pebbles and stones where the logging road begins, or ends, before I head back. The sun is above the horizon now and I know I will have stayed away a bit too long for the others liking, but this walk has been worth it and I promise myself I will work hard when I get back.

27
(Franklin)

"Meirs!" Radwell calls just loud enough for him to hear. Across the way Meirs pokes his head up over the bed of the pickup to look at us, shows surprise to see me and the scum. "Cops!" Radwell says, as he spins his finger in the air to show which way they are coming around the building. Meirs' eyes widen as he stiffens, abruptly looks toward the rear of the building, and then out towards the field. He knows he can't make that distance, and we don't know what he's going to do as we turn and run back several yards to where Cal, Perez, and Tollin are now. We make it in time, diving behind the foot drop-off that starts the farm field as Cal motions for us to do so, and we lay still. Only Cal has positioned himself to see.

I hate not knowing what's going on as I lay there, having to trust white trash, but any more moves in such little cover will certainly cost us … and what about Drew …?

We hear the cop's engine running as the vehicle slowly advances through the parking lot. The dog goes angry with barking and bangs against the service door, and we hear the cop's radio cackle, but can't make what is being said. The car slows more and then stops. We hear the pig getting out.

"He's checking the shop," Cal daringly whispers.

Long minutes go by until we hear him re-enter his car, which he then drives slowly along to pass before us on the other side of the parked cars.

"I can't see him," whispers Cal as he lifts himself, pushing up with his shaking arms.

"Get your head down," Radwell quietly commands but Cal ignores him.

"Ahh—highway entrance," Cal tells us as his arms shake more. The cop waits there for what seems too long a time, with no traffic forcing him to, before finally pulling out and accelerating down the cross road. "He's gone now—whoa, too close," Cal gasps as he drops to the ground.

Another minute passes before we dare to stand up, but Cal can't. Radwell and I hesitate as we rise over him, watching him struggle. He lacks the strength. His skin is ghostly. The whites of his eyes are lined pinkish-red in stark contrast to the rest of him, as he turns his sweaty face to look up at us. His eyes plead, but he dares not say a thing. My look to Radwell tells my wish to leave Cal behind, but Radwell doesn't agree.

"Cal will say everything he can if we leave him here this way," Radwell explains.

"Not if he's dead," I reply, glaring down at Cal. His eyes show both hatred and fear in response.

"No dead bodies to mark our trail, Franklin. We can't afford that. We take him. Our trail has to be as thin as possible. Help me get him up."

Cal is one with the ground, gasping. Tollin looks at us without expression before weakly helping us get Cal up. Perez wisely does not get near.

"How'd you not get seen Meirs?" Radwell asks as we approach him.

"Lifted myself up against the driveshaft and frame under the truck, man. A long thin guy like me can do that kind a thing, man."

"Huh," Radwell smiles. "Lucky the cop didn't look there."

"Yeah, well, it worked," Meirs replies. His nose crunches as he gives us a prolonged look as we stand near; "Man, you guys smell like shit."

"Lick me," I reply as I give him the finger.

Meirs smiles before jumping into the trucks bed and moving to the rear of the cab to begin work on the small sliding window centered in the larger rear window. I watch him repeatedly scratch a line down the center of the glass with a stone. He places a small chunk of scrap board along this scratched edge and pounds this board with a brick he'd found. By the third hit this window snaps in two main pieces and a sliver breaks off as a third main piece, leaving a slotted hole. Through this slot he slips a scrap piece of rusting metal, a one by one-eighth inch thick by several foot long bar, into the cab and against the door lock and unlatches that lock with what is practiced swiftness.

"Why ya just not break ta whole damn window, Meirs?" I ask, amused by all his efforts.

"Hey nigger, broken glass would be everywhere and a broken window is a curious thing to any cop—don't ya know?"

"Ya ugly white wise-ass. Ta window is broke."

"Yep—not shattered—looks work related—this is a construction truck, or looks to be one. And I got us in, so you can walk if you want to."

He quickly opens the driver's door and slides under the steering column to hotwire the vehicle. He is so quick he starts the engine while we are shoving Cal into the back bench seat, where Cal ends up between Tollin and Radwell. Meirs sets himself up to be the driver. I make sure I sit up front for a quick escape. Tollin is behind me. Perez is still standing outside, not wanting to sit between me and Meirs. Perez is about to say something when fear strikes us all as we see a white crew cab pickup truck driving toward us in this service parking lot, coming in the opposite way the cop left us.

"Shit," whispers Meirs.

"Don't move," Radwell orders everyone. "I don't think he's seen us yet."

Perez happens to be standing enough toward the building to be hidden from this driver's sight by the pillar of the next truck over, but if this driver continues and glances this way Perez will be seen. Perez is looking at us, at me, with a tightness in his face, a fierceness in his eyes.

"Shit, man," Meirs says, "He'll see the exhaust smoke—hear the engine running."

All of us shift to see the driver, who has already driven past behind us and is turning in to park only two slots over and facing the farmland opposite us, his back to us. Perez is running, crouched over, the knife in his left hand, rushing toward the man who is now opening the truck's door.

"Get out!" Radwell yells to us, hitting the back of the seat. "Get-out, get-out, get-out!"

We pour out of our truck and run to help Perez.

The driver is halfway out the door when he sees Perez coming at him and manages to jump back in the seat and begins slamming the door shut when Perez gets there—Perez jams his closed right fist between the door and the truck frame in time to keep the door open and the door bounces off his right hand. This gives me just enough time to get there and grab the door itself and pull it wide open with the help of Radwell and Meirs. Perez can't contain his pain and falls back onto the ground, clutching his right hand.

"Help!" the confused, frightened driver screams as Meirs and Radwell deflect his kicks and grab his legs. The driver's hands latch onto the steering wheel and the upright side of the seat as he struggles. There is an opening for me to step between Radwell and the door and the man's crotch appears before and below me. I punch down at his balls as hard as I can, my right fist burying itself past the flesh of his legs and I rake it back out. The man screams and lets go of the wheel in a vain attempt to stop me. I grab his arm and pull him as we drag him out and he falls onto the ground, hard enough to throw the back of his head against the cement with a thud, to stun him unconscious.

"Now what'da we do?" Meirs asks rapidly as Perez gets himself up behind us and walks away, holding his hand, rocking up and down, hiding his face, as he quietly cries in pain.

"Shuddup. Shuddup," Radwell responds as he looks away from Perez. "Gotta think. Keep him down."

Meirs has the man's legs, I grab his arms, but the man isn't going anywhere—he's out for the count. Drew shows up, looks at us, looks at Perez, then goes to attend to Perez.

"Perez's knife—where is it?" I ask, searching the ground around the truck. Radwell has it in his hand.

"We should kill him. Throw his body in ta field and get ta hell outta here," I tell Radwell.

"No. No. Not here," Radwell responds impatiently. "Throw this guy in the back seat. Meirs you take the other truck with Cal—and Perez and Tollin. You two come with me. Hurry. We gotta get outta here now."

The guard dog is crazy barking behind the large service door as we leave—and as we leave west on CCC coming over the hill as we pass it, the one the scum and I came down from, appear the tracking dogs.

28

"About time, slacker," Gay calls to me as she places two of the water soaked cot cushions into the sunlight, balancing them on top of two folding chairs someone brought along, off to one side of the trailer's door.

"Yeah, well," I explain as I walk off the truck trail to the central area of our campsite and head toward her. "I had to take a walk like that, been a long time, you know."

"Did you take a compass along?"

"No—oh, that hurt, coming from you."

"Ah-huh, twenty years of kidding and you haven't learned a darn thing," she responds with a knowing nod of her head, "My brother. Darn, you made it back. I can't get any insurance money that way."

"Yeah, funny—you're not a beneficiary—any longer."

"You're just lucky the rest of us slept in or you'd be doing all this work alone."

"Hey, I haven't been gone that long," I respond, "How long have you guys been awake?"

"About twenty minutes, well, maybe forty now ... it's been, well, awhile. Long enough to just have finished breakfast without ya. You can have what's left if you hurry inside. Mark, Roy, and Tom worked up an appetite sleepin' out in the trucks and Paula and Mary didn't want us pigging out so soon, so they're not making any seconds."

"Ahh, I'd better be getting in there quick then."

"Bet you'll go hungry," Gay says behind me.

"Probably," I answer as I place my foot on the first trailer step, turn to take the next step, only to find the trailer's doorway blocked by Mary standing above me.

"Good morning," she smiles, her eyes meeting mine as she dries her hands with a dishtowel. I hear my sister softly laugh behind me as I allow myself to be enthralled by the penetrating and loving stare of my wife's eyes.

"Love birds," my sister murmurs as I hear her work to squeeze out the remaining water in the cushions. "How long you been married?"

My sister does not expect a reply.

"Four years," I answer without looking back. I can see only Bill's head inside the trailer, who must be sitting down at the near end of the folded up sofa, that I cannot see, that had been his bed during the night. He is leaning over past the short hallway partition to look at me and he is shaking his head from side to side, rolling his eyes, stretching out his one hand as if to present me to others unseen.

"Well, speaking of the boy," Bill calls out, "I see he's arrived. Where have you been gallivanting about, dare I ask? And, tsk-tsk, not kissing your wife hello when you get back—when she obviously wants a kiss—what kind of a man are ya, anyway?" A broad teasing digging smile spreads across his face, and he gives another shake of both his head and finger, both directed at me. "What's ya gonna do, I say," he continues, "with a boy like this? I dunno. I dunno."

I hear the others, the low chuckles of the men as they offer additional comments I cannot discern, and the higher pitched giggle of Paula agreeing with one or all of them coming from within the trailer.

I ignore them, grab Mary and kiss her.

"Hey now look at this, the boy is kissing a woman," Bill tells the others inside, causing them to coo and make fun of us as I see their heads appear at the windows or poke their head into the hallway to see. Mary, who could have refused my kiss under these circumstances, releases me and smiles instead, then blurts out a giggle. I try to give another and more passionate kiss—resulting in more comments from the peanut gallery because Mary giggles again and now does refuse me.

"Give it up, mister," Mary says.

"Ah-man, this ain't fair," I reply, then say to the others; "And don't you guys have better things to do?"

After finishing a breakfast of scraps left behind by the others I help them move supplies into and out of both the main trailer and Bill's camper, until we are satisfied with the arrangements. Much of the food and other supplies that were first stored for the trip in the kitchen area and within the second bedroom are now inside Bill's camper and cab, the water jugs being the major exception; these will stay in various places inside the trailer because they are so heavy and we do not want them to freeze if placed outside.

During all this re-arranging we place our guns; three semi-automatic and five bolt action rifles, and two shotguns, leaning upright and outside alongside Bill's camper, between the rear wheel well and the back end of the truck on the driver's side. Several of the extra propane tanks form a line about ten feet away from the rear of Bill's camper, like a fence from one side over to the other. No reason why the tanks ended up that way, someone just put them all in a loose row. We want these tanks outside in case they leak, the outside air will carry their fumes away safely and we will save propane by heating only the main trailer, if we can. We hope to find enough room for all of us to sleep inside the main trailer tonight and not have anyone sleep inside Bill's camper, but that does not look likely. We want the guns to go in the camper too and last, at the end of the day, so we could get to them first tomorrow morning when we set out to hunt.

After this is done Rick and Roy leave for a quick trip into town.

29
(Franklin)

Radwell's driving. Drew is up front across from him. I'm in the back seat behind Drew looking through the groaning man's wallet. "Edward, Edward Williamson, fifty-six. He got one-hundred-twenty-two freakin' dollars in his wallet he gave ta us—sure a nice old dude," I say. "He's waking up, too, what're we do now, man?"

"Anything to tie him up with?"

Drew looks around, as I do. "No," Drew says.

"Give me ta knife, Rad, he ain't a small guy and it ain't easy ta fight inside a truck."

"Franklin, we can't kill him—especially inside this truck."

"No ... I didn't realize dat, man. Want me ta push him out?"

"Franklin."

"Then how 'bout you-n-me tradin' places, man—see what you can do?"

Radwell sighs, shakes his head, hands me Perez's knife—it's three plastic knives glued and taped together, worked to a sharp point. It'll break off in you—and it will get in you.

"He big enough for ya to take his clothes?" Drew asks.

I look the guy over. "No."

"Then what're we goin' to do with him, Rad?" Drew asks. "He's wakin' up. We can't dump him on the side of the road—he'd wave somebody down too quick. Can't spend the time driving somewhere ta hide him. Rad? How long're we gonna keep him—do we want to?"

"I know-I know." Radwell is irritated. "I don't want a exposed path a murder. The cops don't give up on that stuff. I don't wanta give it to 'em, ya know?"

"Yeah," Drew answers, "But we got a problem."

"Got 'bout a minute before he comes to, man," I add.

"Fuck," Radwell exclaims, shaking his head side to side, his mouth clenched tight. His hand hits the steering wheel in disgust.

#

"Sit up slow, keep yer hands on yer knees," I command Mr. Edward Williamson. I have the point of the knife pressing against his throat as he awakens beside me. "Ya got a problem with dat?"

He clears his throat and swallows as he looks up at me. “No.”

“Den do it,” I say impatiently.

He rises slowly into position as I follow him, keeping the knife at his throat.

“Good. Ya try anythin’, ya die,” I state. “N stay quiet.”

He slowly nods, wincing as he stretches his head wound and feeling the point of the knife. I pull the knife away, fearing someone else driving by might see.

“Guys got any money?” I quietly ask. "I got thirteen.”

“Thirty-four,” Radwell answers.

“Twenty-seven,” Drew replies.

I look at Mr. Edward Williamson and smile. “Ya gave us a hundred-twenty-two—proud a ya support, dude.”

He looks me up and down with scorn but says nothing, like a good boy should.

“A hundred-n-ninety-six n all,” I say, “Should be ‘nuff ta get us dere, huh?”

“Should be,” answers Radwell. “For us. Hope the others got enough.”

I glance out the back window to see them following behind. “How we gonna separate Meirs from ‘em?”

“Damn man, you just told this guy one of our names,” Radwell flatly states.

“Well ah figure he knows already, don’t ya Mr. Edward Williamson—don’t ya?”

He looks at me, says nothing.

Radwell monotones; “Ya can answer him. He ain’t gonna kill ya if he’s askin’ ya a question.”

Mr. Edward Williamson nods his head; “Yeah, ain’t hard to figure who you are. The break is all over the news. You gonna kill me?”

I smile. “Well now, Mr. Edward Williamson, I had ta best chance and easiest death fer ya just a time ago, but ta driver here, he says no, so here ya are—fer now.”

Drew reaches and turns on the radio. “What station you hear that on?”

Mr. Edward Williamson does not respond.

“Hey,” Drew says forcefully, “What station you hear that on?”

Mr. Edward Williamson answers; “1450 AM out of Fond du Lac.”

“What they say ‘bout us?” Drew asks as he finds the station. Mr. Edward Williamson is slow in answering again. “Hey. I’ll tell my friend to slice ya if you don’t answer when I speak.”

"Said, last time I heard, twenty-eight of ya broke out last night. Three of ya are dead. One in the hospital—shot I gather. Another broke his leg. They got every cop in the State lookin' for ya. You're not getting far, don't know how you think you can."

Drew and Radwell pass glances to each other and to me. We don't like his words but know he feels he speaks the truth, which is what we asked for.

30

"Paula and I own forty acres—okay, and we just seen most of it," Rick says as we gather by him, near the point in the trail where I stood and did my turn-around look at the land much earlier in the morning.

Rick continues, "Now, after lunch and after the septic and power companies get here in about an hour so ..."

"When do they ever run on time?" Tom asks.

"Yeah, well, I talked with them enough. They should be, even said they might hook up power lines to the trailer sometime next week while we're here. That'd be nice, wouldn't it?"

"Power lines from the highway to here, man, that's costly," Bill states. "And get it done so soon."

"Yeah, a nice paycheck or two, but the lines aren't that far away. I've been talkin' and arrangin' and payin' for this awhile. The line comes from the south side a half mile or so, not two from the highway. I'll be finding out what they can do," Rick concedes. "We'll be running on generator and battery power until then, but the septic system won't be installed until spring."

"Then what happens to our … um, shit?" Mary asks. "Not you men, I know what you're doing. Us women?"

"The trailer collects it in a basin we can empty. Don't worry—I'll take care of emptying it," Rick answers her. "I was getting to that."

"Oh good. Good," she replies.

Rick continues; "Anyway, the four stands of forest you see; the ones we're gonna hunt in, which is the one close behind us here—we'll call it the north forest, is entirely on our land. The one over there to the east we're not going to get into, isn't our land, and the south one our camp sits next to—some of it is on our land. Only this north one we're gonna hunt in. The west woods we can't see from here and is too far away, anyway, to drag anything back, and any others you see are either part of Nicolet or controlled by the paper mills."

We are looking around in each direction as he speaks.

"You guys look a little confused," Rick explains further; "Our trucks and trailer sit close to one edge of our property. About halfway through the south stand of trees behind the trailer our land ends. About a hundred feet into the trees in the woods to the east is another border, and then it runs on in an angle over to where we came in last night by the semicircle. Don't worry if you guys find yourselves off the property—none of it's fenced or posted. No trespassing signs, no no-hunting signs. I don't have any of that posted 'cause nobody around here cares much, as long as you got a valid hunting permit, all right? And, if it's a DNR guy who stops you, you better have that hunting permit with you if you're carrying a gun, or he'll sure take the gun away, give ya a big fine. He may also want to know if you know which county you're in, because we're somewhat close to Florence, but we're in Forest—okay?"

"Not Nicolet?" Mary asks.

"No Nicolet," Rick answers, "No such thing. Nicolet forest extends across Oneida, Vilas, Florence and Forest counties."

"Did they join the other State workers on strike?" Doug asks.

"You know, I don't know," Smith answers, "And as far as I know the strike could be over with. If it is and they get a worse deal, they'll be mad as hornets in summertime if they meet ya—heck I don't know. Just carry the permit with you—C-Y-A."

We acknowledge him. We're too foot weary to want to disagree or make long conversation, for Rick hiked us all around his land and it has been a workout. During the hike we learned where each of us are going to post tomorrow, agreed when to meet for lunch, and again where we should try not to go. This hike took a couple of hours and we are more than ready for a break. Our camp looks so inviting from where we are. Rick, though, says one more thing.

"Since we're so close," he says, tapping me on the shoulder, "We're gonna let the others go on in. C'mon, I'll show you and Tom where I want you to haul in some wood for our pit."

"Now?" I ask in mild complaint. I had not anticipated some long and hard work, instead of the lunch I'm hungry for. "Can we do it after lunch?"

"Hey, I'm hungry, too. I just want to show you two where it's at so I don't have to come all the way out here again after lunch, you know?" Rick grins, as he gives a quick look at Bill.

"Now you're talkin'," Bill answers, as he returns a head nod and a smile.

"When I was scouting for where to hunt, the last time I was here, I found a tall birch tree that fell six-seven weeks ago. The tree should be pretty dry by now. My plan is for you two to cut it up into four to five foot lengths. Trim it nice, it'll be our toilet seat," Rick informs us.

"Trim it nice," I echo.

"Yeah man, 'cause in the middle of the night, out in the cold, when the wolf howls, I don't want no piece of my clothing catching the tree and holding me back from gettin' back inside the trailer," Tom matter-of-factly says.

"Gee, I just didn't want anything stickin' in my ass," I say. "I didn't think about somethin' bitin' it."

"Take a gun—and I'm serious," Rick says and continues, "Best to trim the tree where it falls, too. You'll have enough work carrying the pieces back."

"How far is it?" Tom asks.

"Almost the other side of these north woods, a little west of center in our property."

I look at him as if he is crazy. "Why that far, man, can't we cut somethin' closer? Won't spook the deer as much, you know."

Rick gives an understanding look. "Yeah, but the deer are used to the sounds. The birch, this birch, is a clean tree. A pretty smooth trunk. I hope it's stayed that way, anyway. The trees closer here are mostly oak, maple, or hickory, as you'll see. You don't want ta be sittin' on that bark, compared to a birch."

"Well, I catch the bottom line to what you're sayin'."

"Yeah, I bet your ass you do."

"So you got a chain saw?" Tom asks.

"Yeah, and a long armed axe," Rick replies. "Better take both, the saw hasn't been used in a while, didn't have a chance to get it ready."

"Oh thanks," Tom says.

"I'd better go, too," Roy says.

"Why?" Rick asks.

"Ah, because I'm gonna end up there anyway, I guess," Roy answers. "Because I know Tom will come back asking for help, and I might as well know the way if, for nothing else, to be a runner back and forth."

31

(Franklin)

The truck suddenly slowing and shuddering wakes me. Any haziness in my mind leaves when Radwell gives an alarming, disgruntled, groan. I follow his tense stare forward to see a cop car parked a mile up along the roads shoulder on my side, his radar unit looking like it's clocking us. Radwell had been speeding.

A shiver straightens my back as I suddenly realize Mr. Edward Williamson is still beside me and clench my hands and find Perez's knife is not there. Drew clears his throat in front of me, shows the knife, then gives it back to me. "I've been watching. Slept twenty minutes."

I nod in thanks. I think Mr. Edward Williamson could have grabbed the knife from me before Drew could have done anything. Ha, Mr. Ed, you coward, that was your chance.

"Yo don't slow no more Rad," I carefully tell him, "And don't freakin' stare at him, either."

"What?" Radwell exclaims, "I'm still speeding."

"I know," I calmly answer, "But not much. If ya slow more—quickly, it'll look bad."

"Dammit Franklin, you better be freakin' right," Radwell warns anxiously.

"Slow more but don't do it fast," I tell him.

Radwell groans again.

I don't stare at the cop as we approach. I look instead at Mr. Edward Williamson to appear to the cop as if I'm talking to him, and I am. "Ya move like you try ta warn 'im an' ya die—ya got dat Mister Edward Williamson?"

"Yes."

Out of the corner of my eye I watch the cop until we zip past it. I feel the officer's gaze as we go by. I turn and catch an image of him, through the side mirror, looking down at his radar gun one last time before we round a bend and lose sight of him.

I sense Radwell never took his eyes off the cop and this worries me. Things like that stay in the minds of these guys—these cops, and Radwell had not listened to me.

After twenty seconds of watching our mirrors, silently, for a chasing police car, we realize he is not coming. After rounding another bend, Radwell sighs, relaxing; "Shit."

"Shit yeah," I answer, equally relieved. "Keep dis speed now, man, okay? Let's not get noticed ya know, man?"

Radwell quietly nods. "Yeah. They've mentioned us on the radio a few times now."

"And?" I ask anxiously as I turn round to look at Mr. Edward Williamson again.

"Said now thirty of us broke out last night and they're still looking for us."

"All of us?"

"Yeah."

"Thirty—Mister Edward Williamson said twenty-eight—don't they know?" I scoff, "Man, dey not caught none a us since—how can dat be?"

"I agree," Radwell says, "Don't sound right. Those choppers seemed really freaking busy last night. Tell me they weren't on the heels of some of our guys. Don't sound right."

"No mention of this truck or the dealership either," Drew adds. "They must be missing Mister Ed by now, know his truck."

"And that cop back there didn't know?" I ask, "How could he not by now, man?"

Drew and Radwell look at each other. Drew speaks first. "It's been two hours abouts. They probably just learnin' now—confirming him not showin' fer work, maybe. We could got lucky."

"We've been gettin' lucky a lot," Radwell adds.

"'Cause it's meant, man, 'cause we get a new life," I answer. "Fate is on our side—right Mr. Edward Williamson, ain't I right, man?"

He looks at me in disgust. "Fate is a word that gets delivered by a series of choices. You better hope you make the right ones if you want to live."

I stare at him. I wasn't quite sure what he said, but it didn't sound all that good. Drew is looking at him the same way. Radwell seems confused, too. "He tell us ta kiss off?" I ask.

"Naw, no, he didn't," answers Drew. "He just don't like bein' here."

"Ha," I reply. "I don't like ya bein' here too, Mister *Edward* Williamson, you bastard."

32
(Franklin)

"Where we at?" I ask as I wake up again. This time I felt the sleep coming on and had given Drew the knife. "Got any idea?"

"Ah, we just passed Briarton," Radwell answers.

"Briarton?" I ask.

"We're on fifty-five north of Briarton," Radwell replies.

"Ah, geez," sighes Drew.

"What?" both Radwell and I ask.

"I wasn't payin' enough attention, man, I'm sorry."

"'Bout what, shit head?" Radwell asks.

"Well," Drew replies, "Check that map you got, Franklin, you'll see why."

"Marsh killed 'em. Got yours?"

"Mine don't cover north, man, I was supposed ta go west, remember?"

"Yeah," Radwell snaps as he takes his maps from Drew and hands me them, "Here's mine, man. What'dya tell me wrong, Drew? Where are we—Franklin?"

"Hey freak, give me some time," I retort. I see, though, as soon as I open the map. We are going north, okay, but we travelled west needlessly. "Aw, woman," I say.

Radwell looks disgruntled. "Alright, what screwed up?"

"Not bad, man, we're 'bout sixteen miles west slant as we should be dat much freakin' straight north," I reply. "We need ta go east ten miles ta catch the right road."

"Fuck," Radwell says as he hits the steering wheel with his hand. He is irritated, but not that angry. "What's the next town?"

"Cecil, on ta map anyway," I reply.

"We'll stop in Cecil for fuel and to go to the can, see if we can get food. Can you see how Meirs is doin'?" Radwell asks.

I twist to look back at the other truck. I hand signal the best I can to get them knowing we'll stop soon.

33

After going over several small rises and bends in these north woods, filled with difficult brush, we find the place. It is hidden and a good distance away from our camp, far enough that our sawing, or chopping, may not be noticed by anyone, though we'd probably hear them if they practiced shooting.

The birch tree had toppled off a ledge overlooking a small brook. This ledge, a narrow short strip of open ground, has three other trees still standing; two close together to my left as we face the brook, and one tree to my right—all birch. The ledge stands only a foot or two above the brook and the fallen tree spans across this trickle of water. Much of the surrounding earth at the base of the fallen tree has eroded away to form this sheared ledge during past heavy rains and caused the tree to fall almost directly perpendicular from it. Exposed roots still cling to the ledge's black earth, by our feet, but some of the root system of this tree touches a singular finger of water off the main run of the shallow waterway, the ground is otherwise moist and strewn with stones. The sheared edge shows roots from the other three trees as well. The creek runs from west to east, left to right, as we stand facing it.

I look at Smith as my hand sweeps back and forth, pointing to the destruction of the ground, the edge of the ledge.

Smith nods his head. "Yeah some heavy rains early in the fall. A couple a storms later the exposed roots couldn't take no more and the tree came over. What do you think of the size, though? The upper parts of the trunk seem small enough to carry with one arm, yet plenty strong to hold our weights. I figure a four foot cut length will be light enough for ya to carry two or three of 'em alone, and smooth enough to sit on, especially if a little clean up is done on the wood. What do you think?"

"I don't know about the carryin' part," Tom answers Rick. "We're gonna be carrying quite a ways."

"That's why I chose two of ya."

"Yeah, yeah, glad you're keepin' me outta this, Rick, because, looking at this, I'm glad these two are doing it, not me," Roy says.

"Thanks Roy," I respond.

"Yeah, thanks buddy," Tom adds.

"C'mon, let's get closer," Rick suggests.

We jump down into the creek bed and begin looking the tree over.

Rick points, "The trunk is clean—that's good—I didn't take a real good look when I was here before. You won't have too much trimming to do."

"The tree does not look dry," Tom states.

"Ah, you know you might be right," Rick acknowledges, "I forgot to consider the roots here."

"Pick another tree—closer?" I ask after I step next to the birch's trunk and spread my hand across it. Its diameter spans from the tip of my thumb over to the tip of my pinky finger at the point where I stand more than halfway up its length. I give a look to Smith as I ask the question. He takes a moment before he answers.

"Good try. Maybe if this one's too wet. Won't know until you start sawin'."

Rick notices my studying the ledge and the way in which we came. The one to two foot high wall of sheared earth rises from the creek bed and then the land slopes higher still, reaching the height of my shoulder. It will be an effort to carry a burden up and over this initial elevation, going through the tall underbrush, standing thick and looking impenetrable everywhere, except at the point where Rick, Tom, Roy, and I had come through. After getting through that we will have to battle the unfriendly underbrush that follows—carrying cumbersome loads—that will not be easy.

"Did I say this was going to be easy?" Rick asks, as if reading my mind. "But you're in real good shape. You can do it."

"Oh thanks."

"Yeah, thanks, considerin' I don't work out none," Tom snipes.

"You want me to send Mark or Doug here to help?"

Roy grins. "You're sure helping me, Smith. I'm standing right here and you offer Mark and Doug and not me, but don't get me wrong, I'm glad you're doing it."

"You wuus," I say.

"No," Tom answers.

"No, he's not a wuus?" I ask.

"No-no. I meant answering Rick. No, we don't need Mark or Doug, or Roy the wuus, either," Tom replies. "You and I will do this."

"Well," Roy responds. "Thanks buddy, back at ya, buddy."

"No, I'm serious. This will be tough work," Rick states. "You don't hesitate about asking for help, you hear?"

"Naw, we'll be alright. Maybe after our first time back we'll grab one of them to help. We'll be okay," Tom answers.

Rick looks at both of us a moment before he nods his head and shakes his shoulders. "Okay."

34
(Franklin)

The self-help gas station is on the outskirts of town, not much else nearby. We pull in on the far side of the pumps, to partly hide us from sight of the cashier in the store.

"Who's gonna pay?" Drew asks after we've wrenched our pained bodies out of our trucks to gather where the trucks meet.

"Needs ta be one a the drivers," Perez answers, holding and hiding his swollen right hand as casually as he can. "It's the most normal thing."

Radwell looks at Meirs. "You and I then. You get somethin' for us ta drink, eat, and you pay. I get the key to the men's room. Rest of ya wait here 'till I come out."

The station is old style, it's got the customer rest rooms on the outside of the building, forcing us to ask for a key. We watch Radwell and Meirs enter the station as the rest of us either fuel the trucks up or stand beside them, including Cal, who still looks very weak, and Mr. Ed—because I ain't trusting him out of my sight, or reach.

"Mister Ed," I say, for he stands between me and Drew, as Drew fills our truck with gas and I'm more by the engine. Mr. Ed looks silently back at me with his continuing look of scorn. "Don't think of it, okay?"

"Don't have to—they got video cameras." He nods his head towards one.

I don't take the bait and look. I've heard of these cameras coming on the scene over the last few years and don't believe a place like this would have them, so I just smile. "We know," I answer, though I know we didn't. "We'll be long gone."

Mr. Ed smiles back. It's an unnerving smile.

Tollin comes up to me. "Well, we know why this truck was in the shop."

I cock my head—I really don't care but know Tollin will tell me why anyway.

"The front end shudders when we brake. Meirs says this is brake rotor warp, but nothin' will fall apart anytime soon. Makes all kinds of noise though, and from the back of the truck, too. The spare tire someone threw in the bed bounces around, and the chain for this tire, hanging underneath the truck, clangs loud, very attention getting."

I study Tollin. I once thought him a quiet guy. He's anything but. I don't say a thing more, 'cause I don't want him sayin' anything more.

Cal had the hardest time shuffling off to the restroom and back on his own, but to help him would make a scene. Meirs brought us chocolate bars and a couple of gallons of chocolate milk. We're too hungry to complain. By the time Radwell returns the restroom key the rest of us are back in the truck, anxious to move on, and glad the attendant took no special note of us here. Because he didn't, I'm not worried about the cameras; I did later see them tucked under the roof corners above the pump island.

Radwell has returned, climbed in, and is putting the key in the ignition when a car pulls in the station lot, coming toward us, driven by a pretty young blonde-haired white woman. Our eyes get pulled to her sight. Somehow this brings her looking to us in the first truck.

We hear Meirs start his motor behind us as she stops her car on the other side of the pump across from us. She gets out of her car and looks at us again as Radwell starts our truck, he forces himself to look away from her. She glances our way twice more, each time her glance holds a bit longer.

Radwell pulls us away and stops at the road to let other cars go by. Meirs is right behind us. Drew is looking back and says; "She just left the pump in place, hurryin' to the store. She made us, man."

"No she didn't," Radwell contests.

"Yeah, she has," asserts Drew.

We turn to look back. She hesitates at the store door as she stares once more at us. There is the look of alarm in her face.

35

"Tom plays cribbage," Rick remarks as we make our way back.

"Oh, no kiddin'? Do you Roy?" I ask.

"Yeah, he does," Tom answers before Roy does.

"Better than Tom, anyway. Tryin' to mess with me by answering for me?" Roy replies.

Rick and I smile.

Tom replies; "Uh-huh. What?"

"What?" mocks Roy.

"We know what we're doing tonight," I state. "With you and Roy able to play that means everyone knows—tournament time. How much money you got?"

Tom shakes his head and sighs. "Not enough. I've played with Rick. He counts cards. Knows what you're goin' ta play. Unless I can be your partner, Rick."

"Paula's here."

"Oh you wimp. Just 'cause your wife's here you gotta smooch up and be her partner, huh?"

"Yep."

"Roy don't want me as his partner, you know," Tom states.

"Couldn't tell. He won't be," smiles Rick. "We'll probably match ya up with Doug or Mark."

I'm enjoying this and I have to add to this talk; "I never play poker against Rick. He gets serious then."

Tom's turn; "I learned that lesson a while back, too, when I ended up owing him almost half a paycheck. Man I'm gullible. He led me on so well. How long you guys known each other again?"

"Long time," answers Rick, who gives a look to me.

"Since we were thirteen," I add.

"'Bout thirty years abouts, then," Tom remarks as he shakes his head. "Can't let you two be partners either, you'll have too much silent talk."

Rick and I smile to each other.

"Yep, we will," admits Rick. "He won't play poker against me, I only play chess against him when I have suicidal thoughts."

"Chess?"

"Yeah, he's good. Not that you can't beat him," Rick says, glancing at me. "It's just hard, painfully hard, and when he beats you, you feel like he tortured ya."

"How good are you?" Tom asks me.

"Good enough to beat chess masters," I reply. "But I don't play or enjoy the game much anymore and I never bothered getting rated or cared when I did."

"Okay. Well, no chess with you," Roy states. "Rick and I met at the post office. How'd you guys meet?"

"Baseball field at Forest Park," I answer.

"Good, because I didn't remember," Rick says.

"Rick and I did a lot together during those years. Sports and more sports. Walking the street at night. Raiding gardens. Rick getting into fights. Remember Akers at Forest Park school one summer?"

"Um … yeah, sort of. I don't remember you being with me."

"I was."

"And what was it about?"

"You know, I don't remember that too well. Something like we come walking around the school building and there is Akers finishing up beating some kid enough smaller than him to get you going enough to ridicule him for beating on smaller guys. Akers was about your size then and challenged you, the fool."

"Really? I know I fought him. Maybe I fought him more than once. He'd be that kind of guy. Did I get him in a head lock and he almost went unconscious—right?"

"Yeah, that's right, and all I did was stand around and watch."

"Well, that's expected of ya."

"No it's not," I exclaim. "I'm supposed to fight with ya."

"It was one on one, man. You just watched my back, which you did."

"Yeah, I guess so."

"Ah-yeah, no partnering up with you two—way too much understanding going on between you two guys," Roy says.

"Yeah," agrees Tom. "Sounds like Rick though."

"Definitely Rick. You'll hunt 'em down if they run away, have less mercy on those than if they stay, knowing you," Roy adds.

Rick returns his horse smile, his eyes showing solemn agreement.

36
(Franklin)

Meirs impatiently revs his engine behind us. We know he's asking; what's up? There's a clear road in front of us yet Radwell hasn't moved. It's been maybe five seconds since the woman disappeared into the station behind us.

"Rad?" Drew asks.

"I know," he answers solemnly.

"Either we go or we go back but do it quick-huh?"

"Damn it," Radwell spits out, hits the steering wheel with his fist, "We won't get far with her talking. Franklin watch the man. Drew you got the attendant. I get the girl." He spins the truck around and rapidly drives to the stations door.

He and Drew spring out from the truck and enter the station before Meirs comes to a stop behind us. Meirs and the others, though, don't need to be told what's going on—they instinctively know and all are in the station in a flash except Cal, who hobbles in as quickly as he can.

My attentions are split between Mr. Ed and what I can see within the station. We hear the woman scream. I see the attendant pull a handgun up from behind the counter but he is slow to use it and it fires once into the ceiling as Drew knocks his arm up and wrestles with the man long enough for Perez and Meirs to bring the man down.

Mr. Ed opens his door to escape, but I'm much too quick. I hold him, drag him back in by his belt, and the door latches loosely as he still holds onto it. He kicks me as I pull him up then his right arm flies at me, his elbow hits square in the center of my chest, his withdrawing fist finds my chin, but these impacts do no harm except anger me. My right hand swings hard to hit just below his chest and Mr. Ed gasps and stiffens suddenly, quits struggling, looks down at the knife as I snap the plastic handle off as blood flows from the wound. I watch him try to grasp what shows of the blade but the blood makes his fingers slip away from the plastic. He looks at me with a sweating flushed face, fear and pain in his eyes, as he gasps for breath and tries again to remove the blade.

I smile at him. "Told ya; don't try it, but ya did ya fool—so long *Mister* Edward Williamson. You die now, go whimper and cry now mother-fucker," I finish as I get out of the truck to join the others. Mr. Edward Williamson gives a gasping cough as I slam the door closed behind me.

I hear the woman's muffled screams coming from the back room as I enter the station. Drew is standing behind the counter, putting things back in their places.

"They doin' her, I want a part a dat," I say to Drew as I start for the back room.

He shakes his head; "No you don't. They are but ya don't want a part a that now. Both Perez and Cal have the clap, herpes, or something you don't want ta get. One of 'em's gotten her by now."

"How ta hell you know?"

"Saw 'em each in ta shower with Beckley."

"Shit, dat diseased mouthed twink. Can't believe they'd do dat, man."

"Hey," Drew continues, "Help me clean up around here the best ya can. I'm shutting the place down. Where's Mister Ed?"

"Dead."

"Fuck. We're making this a slaughter house. Meirs, Perez killed the attendant," Drew says. "We'll all get life for this."

"We all got life last night when we broke out, man. We ain't goin' back." I reply.

Drew gets distracted and looks outside. "Shit, customer's been fuelin' up—how the hell long he's been doin' that? Tell the others quick ta be quiet."

I open the back room door to see the woman's clothes ripped off her waist, her legs spread and dangling down from the edges of a large wooden shipping crate, her mouth bloody, her chest heaving in pain, her face smeared wet with tears, make-up, and blood, her left arm hangs down the side of the crate at an angle that just ain't right. Cal is in her.

"Customer coming. Get her quiet."

Cal glares at me as he thrusts again. Perez, who is holding her down by her shoulders, looks around the room.

"Meirs," Perez says with a point of his head; "The box cutter—that rag."

Meirs, who was unbuckling his pants and had been giving me a disgusted look as I told them, follows Perez's point and sees the cutter hanging on a hook off the nearby wall, the rag on a shelf, takes and hands them to him.

Perez puts the rag and his swollen, purple and red colored right hand over her mouth, winces from the pain he feels as he controls her face, and quickly cuts her left jugular vein, drops the cutter and puts his left hand over the site to keep the blood from spraying all over while Meirs covers her neck with a second rag he found to help contain the blood. Her muffled, crying, screams rapidly end.

I'm back peeking out the door to watch Drew. The others behind me fall quiet and just in time. The customer comes in.

"Good mornin'" Drew says.

"Hey," the customer answers as he looks at the scattered cans and snack bags on the floor. "What happened here?"

"I was clumsy. My foot caught the edge of the stand. Had to jump myself over to the chair here to see how bad I hurt my foot, ya know?"

"Oh," the customer replies with polite disinterest. "Sorry to hear that. Fifteen on pump four."

The customer hands Drew a twenty. Drew punches the cash register and it opens. He takes out a five and hands it to the man.

"Hey, I haven't seen you in here before, where's Chuck?"

"Oh," Drew looks at the man, "Just started a couple a days ago. I was called in 'cause some guy called in sick. Don't know everybody yet. Could a been Chuck. I don't know. You need anything else?"

The customer shakes his head. "No. Where you live?"

"Oh, ah, south a here 'bout ten miles. Sure you don't want nothin'?"

"Yeah."

"You have a good day now, okay?"

"Sure," the customer replies, thinks about saying more but decides not to, and turns to leave, "You too."

Once the customer is out the door Drew comes around and starts to pick up the scattered debris but he keeps an eye on the departing man, as I do as I come out of the back to help him.

"Ya get lucky workin' dat cash machine or ya know what ya doin'?" I ask him.

"Both. Soon as that guy gets out of sight I'm shuttin' the pumps down, the lights off, takin' the cash. Tell the others we're switching cars, too. See if that attendant has a car in the back. Find his keys. See if his car needs gas. Someone has ta put ours behind the buildin' fast. Hurry."

"Yeah man."

"And see if ya can find where they video this place. We gotta take that tape, put another in its place."

37

"Hey, man, you're so full of stories one could think you're full of, ah, … shit, too," Tom says to me. I'm not sure to smile, laugh, or be offended. Rick laughs, which makes me do so, too.

"And you thought he was a quiet guy I bet, too—right?" Rick replies.

"Well, I, I don't know this guy well enough for any of that, but, hey, you warned us," Tom answers.

"Warned you? What's he mean by that, Rick?" I demand.

Rick gives his horse smile. "Some one puts a nickel in ya, you'll talk, that's all."

"Uh-uh, sure," I answer.

"Well, you say there's a story about Sir Rick, here? What he do?" Roy asks.

"Yeah, this time, what he do?" adds Tom.

I look to each of them as we walk through the grove of hickory and oaks—the last of the north woods before we come out on the western slope across but out of sight of our camp. I'm hesitant to say anything. I like telling stories but I don't like being played with.

"Yeah, I'm curious, too, what did I do when, ya know?" Rick asks with a smile and a push of his hand against my shoulder. "You can lie if you want to."

"What fun is that?" I respond, "Can't out do the truth when you're involved."

"Uh. The time Brian's underwear was thrown and stuck to the basement wall?" Rick asks, referring to one of his younger brothers.

"No," I answer.

"The time we climbed the water tower and Todd Heyden got caught on top spotlighted by the fire station next door?"

"And you halfway up—no."

"The time you got frustrated and knocked me down when we played one on one basketball at your house?"

"Heck no. Still regret that."

"Yeah, for some reason I let you live. What's the story?"

"The time we met up in Columbia, South Carolina on base …"

"Geez, you remember the time that homosexual puts his hands on my shoulders when I was at the urinal?" Rick exclaims.

Tom and Roy are fully attentive as they look wide-eyed at Rick.

"Well, okay, let's take that one," I say. "You tell it."

Rick's smiles wide; "Who was with us—wasn't it John Stancato?"

"Yeah."

"Us three were off base in our uniforms enjoying the Saturday—had to be Saturday …"

"It was—*it was a hot summer afternoon in downtown Columbia. And there she was just a walkin' down the street singing do-wa-ditty-…"* Tom sings.

"There was no girl involved in this one—WTF, you know."

"I know," I answer, smiling. "How about we sing Jive Talkin'?"

I quietly laugh as Rick shakes his head at me and continues; "And we decide to stop at this bar to have a beer. A few minutes later I go to the men's room to take a leak and I'm standing there at the urinal when this other guy comes in. He starts rubbing my shoulders, man, and my eyes practically pop out of my head …" Rick pauses as Tom and Roy chuckle, knowing Rick the way we do we expect fireworks next.

"I want to stop pissing but I can't, so he's talking to me, rubbing my shoulders—I can't do nothing till I'm done. He's tellin' me how big and strong I am and shit like that—what brings me to town—as if he can't tell by my uniform. Finally I finish, zip up, say I'm with the guys out front—they'd be jealous, thanks but no thanks, and got the heck out of the restroom, went to the table to get John and this jive turkey and we took out of there and *ran* down the street about two blocks before I told them what went on."

"What I want to know, now," Tom says, "Any dates with this bar guy, Rick?"

38
(Franklin)

Meirs is driving the woman's four-door compact car. I'm in the back, behind him. I don't like it but Perez sits up front. Cal is beside me. I hate this arrangement but there was no room in the station attendant's small pickup that Radwell, Tollin, and Drew are riding in ahead of us. Perez is looking at me with scorn for some reason.

"Ya got a problem, Perez?"

"You."

I sigh. "I don't got ta problem with ya," I say to him. "Ya bustin' up your hand gives my respect ta ya. Besides, I'd get disrespected if we fight now."

Perez is quiet a moment, then says; "Ain't makin' no long term difference nigger."

I shake my head disbelieving, actually wishing he'd answered differently, but any truce we have here won't last anyway, like he said. "Understood, spic, we find ta time later—when things are even, man."

He nods his head slightly and relaxes, sensing I may have been straight with him. "Later, then."

I look down at the map and give Meirs directions. "We keep goin' north on county R then hit county M, then highway 32, ta get inta n through Ni-co-let National Forest."

"Nic-oh-lay," says Perez. "It's said Nic-oh-lay."

"Whatever spic, shuddup," I reply calmly. "We're freakin' goin' through there ta get ta Iron River, Michigan."

"What's there?" Meirs asks.

"I dunno," I reply. "I don't. I just know Rad needs us ta get dere."

#

The radio says they caught Steward and Rogers in the Kettle Moraine, and this makes me happy. Not for Steward and Rogers, but for the distraction they gave the law. Meirs catches my smile in the mirror as he drives.

"What you smilin' for, Franklin?"

"Glad fer them makin' the law look dat way instead a our way, man."

"That's freakin' weird ta me, Franklin."

"Yeah, not surprised, man, over ya head like."

He laughs—and says a strange thing to me. "And where ya goin' with that Franklin—think ya goin' somewhere, Franklin?" And he laughs again. "Tryin' ta tell me I ain't smart? My momma told me that. Longer nobody gets caught, the better—I don't know how you think it's good."

I watch the landscape go by as I re-hear his strange laughing response in my head.

"And where do you think you're going with that?" he laughs again and, as I hear his words, they awaken the old haunting voices in my head; *"You go somewhere, Franklin?"* the old Hispanic voices ask. *"We know where you go, Franklin. We play with you, Franklin, because you a joke, Señor Franklin. You nothing but joke,"* the voices taunt laughingly. "W*e get you ... you dead!"*

I stare at Perez. He was in that gang that day. He was there. I made the mistake of looking back to the tall cyclone fence I scurried over moments before to see his gang slam against it and begin to taunt me, knowing they could not catch me. He might have been the one who said those words as the bullet entered my leg as I dived for my life off the retaining wall and into the dirty river, swept out of their sight, out of their reach. He could have been the one who shot me. My emotions erupt; "Stick it," I snarl as I lean towards Meirs, my eyes tightening with intent.

"Kiss my ass," he responds as his eyes meet mine through the mirror. "What's the matter with y…."

My right fist flies around the driver's seat and lands hard against his right shoulder causing the car to swerve across the centerline as he gives a pained yell. Perez rapidly reacts and catches my retreating arm with his good left hand while Cal hits my face with his right fist, landing it squarely against my jaw, jolting me, surprising me, as Meirs gets control of the car.

"Fuck you all white trash!" I shout as I easily break Perez's hold and sit back away from Cal, glaring at him. "Fuck you!"

"Cram it down your own ass, black-ass," Perez harshly responds, "We don't need you to make this work anymore—you need us. So, shut the fuck up and control your flamin' temper, Franklin."

His words threaten but speak the truth. They needed me for the breakout, but not now. I have been put in my place and resent it, have to accept it, its bitter taste. In silence I look away to watch the land grow thick with evergreens, holding a more subtle wilder look, still open and farmed, yet filling out with stands of mature trees and other woods on lands which increasingly can't be easily farmed. Nicolet National Forest starts here.

At eleven-fifty-seven the radio tells that we are the ones who stole trucks, kidnapped a man, where we did this, and the vehicles we are no longer in. All other inmates are caught, enjoying less than a half-day of freedom. The seven of us remain and the law believes we travel together. They don't seem to know about the gas station yet. The Law will concentrate their efforts with roadblocks north of Green Bay and at the state line. They caught the others in the south, the west, the east, so it don't take rocket science to figure we're heading north. The thing is many on the radio say we've already left the State. I wish we could say that is true.

"They ain't got enough men ta block every road north of the Bay, man, who they kiddin'?" Meirs scoffs at the radio.

"No," agrees Perez, "but enough to search the main roads, like the one we're on."

"Shit, we're not on a main road," Meirs comes back, "Heck, are we?" he asks, and then looks at me and Cal through the mirror. "This thing—it's a main road?"

The road we are on is simple two-lane, opposed traffic, and paved. I nod my head; "Yeah, being where we are, man, it's a main a road as any like."

Meirs gives a groan.

The radio says heavy snow is expected by nightfall as county road R becomes M and we head towards our first major intersection after hearing the law's intent to block roads north of Green Bay. The Bay, however, is at least an hour east of us and we don't care what they do there. Our plan now is to pass the town of Hayes before meeting up with Highway 32 and this happens with no incident.

We later exit the town of Mountain. Still no police sightings, but this gives little comfort. The radio remains busy with reports of our breakout and repeatedly gives accurate descriptions of who we are. The law has asked for, and received, the help of local civilian pilots; people going up in their own planes and of the use of two more police helicopters to search for us—just us, the only ones left to catch. The aircraft, though, won't be up in the air long with the approaching storm, but that's no comfort to us.

Now well into Nicolet Forest, I realize how few roads pass through its vastness, making us easy to find from the air, or ground, when looked for and a sickening tension develops inside me—foreboding, not helped by the dark thick expanse of the tall trees we zip by which fill this land around us and makes the early afternoon sun seem, at road level, like evening's twilight.

Of the ways we could have gone, this forest gives the fewest options and risky covers if we have to run on foot—not a good trade, to me—I wish for a big city, wish we went a different way. I was stupid not to realize this. Yet another mistake, like moving through the night, but this one is Radwell's—he chose this route. Looking at the map, had we chose to try for Iron Mountain or Menominee, instead of Iron River, there seems hundreds of roads in which to get to and beyond either of those places compared to the way we're taking. Or, again, had we chosen a western way through Rhinelander things would look much better than the way we're going.

Radwell's truck ahead of us scares up some crows off the road. The birds are slow taking off, fly near, and squawk loud enough to hear through the car glass as we go zipping by. The old voices inside my head speak again as I hear the birds caw and watch the brief sights of their pure blackness pass against the forest; *"We know where you are, Franklin,"* the old voices say. *"We know where you are."* I shift my body against the pain of the words, resisting the urge to yell out. *"Franklin, you can't go anywhere without us knowing,"* the voices taunt in their familiar Hispanic tones, *"You can't go anywhere at all."*

A crow had given me away that day, the day the spics shot me. I knew the warehouse and train station well enough to know when to fake a path and ditch the other way—twice, so even if they explored some they wouldn't have thought of going as far as I did in the time I had to do it—down each alleyway, around the corners of several buildings. But a squawking loud mouthed crow went wild as I made my reach for the fire ladder that would've taken me up to the roof to the sheltered structure providing a way over the trains without being seen. It cawed loud enough for them to hear and to know where I'd gone. I had no time to climb, had to run again.

I shift my body as anger rises inside me, trying to keep this emotion in check. I killed two of you slime-back Mexicans—so what? Did it and does it matter now they were the wrong two—huh—tough that all you spics got hot over it, so what—so what?

"Cool it, Franklin," Cal softly yet firmly says, breaking my pain. "It's just fuckin' crows."

I look at Cal. "Hate 'em."

"I know," he says, "Heard why ya hate 'em, too. Don't let 'em get ta ya."

He quiets me. I don't know what to say. This is unexpected empathy. It confuses me about him. I don't like that. And how the ... how did he learn about the crows? But I won't ask.

Another car pulling a small trailer zooms by and gets between Radwell and us, carrying bright orange clothes, seen through the back window of the car. Trucks with campers on the back of them … trucks pulling trailers … cars loaded with men and orange clothing ... orange clothing everywhere … incredible, more and more of them on the road—we've seen them often and everywhere—and I just realize why; they're deer hunters—what has been my problem?

I've been in jail too long—much too long.

"Deer season," I say, startling the others, as we have been quiet for a time; "Ye-ah, deer season—time ah many guns n many people in ta woods, man." I begin to smile as my mind races and I look to the others, who look back as if I'm talking strange. "Don't ya get it? Luck again knocks on our door. This is meant ta be. How can ta law follow—know who is who outtin these woods? Too many hunters for dat," I state, stressing my last words by working my hands. "Tomorrow must start ta season. Plenty shots be fired—and at who? These dirt things—these logging roads we see n pass—we pull inta one a them, any one a them, n see what's down at ta other end, don't you think?" I search the faces of the others and see now they understand. "We find somebody—don't matta who—we get ta hole up a time—ya know?"

"There'll be food and drink—and I'm plenty hungry," Cal adds.

"Ah—a cabin maybe, to hole up for a while like you say. A different way outta here 'cause we'll take their truck," Meirs envisions correctly.

"They'll have money."

"Yeah-hey-yes they will."

We are becoming eager when Perez calms us down. "Wait a minute," he says. "What does this lead to? ...."

"Freedom," Cal responds with his rasping, scraping voice. "A life. Vanishing inta thin air so ta law can't find us." Cal coughs repeatedly into his sleeve, his face reddening from the strain and the pain.

We clamor in agreement before Perez silences us; "Killing ... They be hunters and won't have a mindset ta go with what we say. Only if ta punishment is painfully clear—demonstrated. We're not goin' to be able to avoid it, we're just not. Don't tell me we tie them up n leave them behind. They're not going ta let us do that easy, only under the point of a gun. We ain't gonna resist pullin' that trigger, after what we did back at that station. C'mon, assholes, if we're gonna try somethin' like this, we gotta be on ta same page. How we approach them; what story to give; what job each a us has ta do—before we control them. Huh? You guys with me on this? Agree up front as ta what we each do, so they don't split us apart with words or whatever—so we know what to do. Are we gonna agree up front on this?"

"Mexican momma, ya hen-pecker," Meirs blurts out, "We be good little boys—who do ya think we are, ya spic, you think we're fools?"

"I don't give crap if we have ta kill some sucker to gain our freedom," Cal interjects, "But yeah, okay, Perez."

"Ya think I do?" Perez responds. "Ya think I give a crap?"

"I ain't goin' back to prison," I say, as I face Perez, "And you say you ain't either. They either do what we say or they dead meat, man."

"But they are gonna be, um, on guard when they see us—we gotta know, gotta be a team ta first take control, follow?" Perez asserts.

We each nod our head in understanding.

"Where are we now?" Meirs asks.

I look over the maps. "We're through Newald, passed by that 'bout five minutes ago. I think we're halfway ta Long Lake, man."

Meirs asks; "How far is Long Lake from the border, again?"

"Mmm, roughly ten miles," I answer. "Why?"

"They be puttin' road blocks off ta border, not on it—gotta get Rad ta pull over and talk this with him real quick."

39

"… Someone else can't hold their liquor, either," I say defensively. "Gay and Mary went one night to the Chinese restaurant at the end of our street. Had some plum wine. Pulled into our neighbor's driveway at the end of the evening out—okay?"

"Sure, that qualifies," Doug says with a nod of his head.

"It was good wine," proudly explains Gay, nodding her head as her hands raise in a mock plea for forgiveness.

"Yeah," quickly adds Mary, her voice dancing; "It's gotta be the best."

"Mr. Excitement," Rick begins once a moment passes, "After his divorce. I got him up by Ladysmith at Joe's and my place. Let him go huntin'… I know this is something you had to be there for to really appreciate …"

"What? Him going huntin' or drinkin'?" Bill teases.

"Ha-yeah, no drinkin' in this one," Rick acknowledges. "You know what a gray squirrel looks like. It's about this big," Rick pauses as his hands show how large a gray squirrel is. "But he brings home a red squirrel," Rick accents his voice, making it grow higher in pitch and squeaky sounding, his hands illustrating the contrast he wants to describe; "Tiny little thing no bigger than my hand. He comes carrying it, holding it out, by the hairs of its tail," Rick's voice falls back to normal; "He walks in with a swagger like he's some mighty hunter, ya know? He was so proud of himself."

Bill and Mark smile while Doug shakes his head. The women look annoyed, not fully appreciating the playful mocking Rick just gave me. Tom and Roy, well, they smile as they keep eating. I suppose they like it that I'm back being the brunt of the jokes and not them, after they both got razed for several minutes just a little while ago. I, now, have nothing to say about Rick's overblown demonstration. I just take this friendly ridicule and agree this was how it happened by giving a quick nod of my own, rolling my eyes.

For the next minute or so everyone falls silent, eating their hamburgers, corn on the cob, and chips. Our breaths faintly frost in the cool air. Doug sits back in his chair and quietly looks around. I don't know why I watch him as he leans over and opens the cooler to grab a beer, but he quietly inquires as he sits forward and offers me that beer; "Um, ah, this is one of those drinks I said I'd buy ya when ya agreed to talk about ya divorce," Doug carefully says. "I'm pretty curious, really, if you don't mind."

Doug's inquiry gives an immediate headache. I frown as I take a glance toward Mary, wondering how I should answer. She has only a bite or two left on her plate, but she has stopped her eating. She looks back searching for a clue to my demeanor but offers nothing in guidance; it's up to me. "Uh, Doug, some of us here have heard so much of this. I dunno," I answer.

"I was about done," Mary begins, "I see Paula and Gay are too. We got work inside the trailer to do, so go ahead and tell him."

I'm surprised. It is unusual for Mary to encourage me to talk about this, so I wonder if Doug approached her first. "Oh, man, I don't know," I reply.

"Go ahead," interjects Rick. "Take the beer and talk. Bill and I are about done. We'll start digging the pits. Tell Doug—and Mark. Heck, Roy and Tom might be curious too, who knows."

I'm confused. Why would any of them be that interested? "What's goin' on?"

Rick's eyes meet mine a moment, before he continues; "Think Doug and Mark want to know. Roy and Tom, well, I know it's a bit unusual, but if you tell them, they'll understand you better—you're not always that easy to know, ya know—it takes a little time with you, ya know? Thought I'd speed that up a bit for ya."

Mary and the women have stopped their walk and Mary is looking back, nodding her head in agreement—so they did talk. Why and when and what for? Yet, that's where we're at.

Roy answers; "Heard it really gets sick, so, like a car crash, we're interested."

"Oh, well, yeah," I moan. "It certainly is that."

Doug smiles. "Give us the quick run-down. Spare the little details, if you want. Rick told us some about it. Says you say it better than he can. Some mighty traumatic stuff. It's personal, we know, so we understand if you'd wanna keep it to yourself."

I smile politely at Doug. "I don't know," I answer. "Most people can't wait to talk about a traumatic incident in their life over and over again, especially a prolonged one like my divorce was, but I've come to where I kinda hate relivin' it."

"Well, then, you don't say anything. Heck, I was being intrusive," Doug states, and pulls back the beer with a smile on his face.

"That's okay, Doug. It's not like I don't understand the curiosity. It's happened before."

I believe the subject is behind us when I hear my sister say; "Let's just say his ex-wife threatened him with death several times during the years. She also thoroughly alienated his children against him—and us, to the point where two of his children promised him the same fate of death—when they become old enough to do it. She's a witch."

Like everyone else I'm looking at Gay who suddenly realizes she said quite a lot in a few words. She returns a look of apology for furthering the subject as she comprehends this.

"Seriously?" Mark asks.

Doug has decided to be quiet, believing I will still close the subject out. I want to … I sure want to, but feel my situation needs more explanation now. Being silent might give the impression of my having done something very wrong or terrible to my ex-wife for her to threaten my life, or to my children, for her to alienate them from me when that was not the case.

"Unfortunately," I answer him, as I wave Doug to give me that beer.

"What did you do to her, for Pete's sake?" Mark inquires.

"Everyone always asks me that. I've asked myself that a lot, too, because I'm not perfect. I find no matter how hard I try, however, to twist or construe my mistakes or actions I still cannot—could not see how my errors warranted such magnified and unrelenting abusive responses from my ex-wife. The professionals I had seen supported this—my side, in their results. And I went to them not caring so much about fault. I just wanted answers and understanding. If I was at fault I hoped for a way to change—a way to change and solve this war she and I were having that I did not want to be involved in. Actual evidence, the overwhelming majority in fact, pointed to my ex-wife as having done much of what she was claiming against me. I'm talking independent evidence, too. Like police records and charges, social service report findings, psych reports—stuff like that, showed her to be doing these things, but none of it mattered 'cause you can't tell young kids about it." I take a breath and then a big swig of beer.

"Wow. And your kids … they have nothing to do with you?" This time Doug is asking.

"Nothing. They might view me as someone completely evil and worthless to know—I don't know. They almost always accept the money and birthday gifts I send them, never returning them. My money is good enough but not me, you know."

"Okay, sorry to have brought this shit up, man. I see it gets pretty deep. This ain't the time, anyway," Doug concludes. "I was wrong ta ask. Smitty kinda put us up to it, ya know."

"Thanks," Rick replies over his shoulder as he and Bill had waited through this discussion and are about to start walking away again.

"But why would she do that?" Mark persists, unable to resist curiosity.

I'm not surprised at this—it is a pretty natural follow-up, but I still sigh from the mental pain. "I, uh, feel she put the focus on me as being evil in her teachings with the children. If she didn't, she would face the truth about herself and all what she had so intentionally done as being wrong, both morally and frequently lawfully—the great majority being her fault. She has never accepted accountability or responsibility for her actions, her affair—and I suspect she had several, her gambling, extensive denials of visitation, except over those actions she feels she can twist to put her in a favorable light, or a justifiable one—she'll pretend to take accountability and responsibility for those. Twisted justifiability. Too often this means her stories change by the minute in a five minute, ah, in any talk with her. You don't have real conversations with her. You got the time someday, Mark, I'll sit down and talk about it at length."

"Fair enough," he acknowledges.

Doug, however, cannot help but ask one more question; "So it makes you angry?"

I gaze out into space, my mind full of memories. "Incredibly, at times, Doug, at her and at the system. The system always seems so full of hope and promise—to me—I should know better. You put your trust in it so desperately. The system tries to do right, but it's not God. I'm not angry with my kids, just frustrated and disappointed they can't see through her bullshit. Most times I knew when my parents were bull-shitting me—why can't they with their mom?"

"Okay," Doug resigns, waving his hands, "I'll sit down with you over something stronger someday, okay?"

"Okay," I say with a shake of my head.

Mark and Doug fall silent while, from their distance, Rick's eyes meet mine and they stay for a long moment. Rick knows my story well, he and I discussing it many times as things developed over the years, for Rick has experienced several rough times himself with his own divorce. We also knew our two ex-wives kept in contact with each other. Rick has one child; a daughter named Michele. She is a bright young teen with an easy smile. For all of Michele's promise I see an often-frustrating emotional future for her, as I do for my own four children, who are also very bright and alert, because of the long-term trauma of the fighting between their respective parents—between my children's mother and me. I acknowledge Rick to let him know I'm okay with what he did and watch him turn to continue after Bill.

Gay and Bill, everyone in my family, know the intimate details of my divorce and the concerns dealing with my children. They had lived it. They, for the most part, no longer want to discuss this for they correctly want me to move on with my life and not have me dwell in the cesspool of despair and anger over something they feel I can never now change. I have to agree, but I hold out a parent's hope.

"Hey Smith," I call after him, causing Bill and him to stop and look back. I wave my hand to bring them, and the women, back. "I got somethin' ta ask ya, Rick. Think it's better I do it with everyone around."

Rick and Bill exchange glances. Bill gives a shrug of his shoulders and they start their return.

40
(Franklin)

"Man, this betta be massively 'portant 'cause I don't like pullin' ta the side of such a busy road, man," Radwell states after quickly walking over to us, his arms straight out, his hands on top of our roof as he leans against the car, glaring at Meirs through the driver's opened window.

Meirs holds his hands up as he looks up at Radwell and bobs his head once in agreement. "Rad, we're figurin' there's road blocks not too far ahead. Radio says they would. Franklin noticed all the orange clothin' and we're in ta forest, man—hunters—cabins, trailers, guns, food, different cars ..."

"I'm with ya," Radwell says with a wave of his hand. "What's the plan?" he asks as he shifts his body against Meirs door to look forward toward his truck, putting his back to the cars that continue to pass by with frequency.

"See these paths off the road? They're loggin' roads or ways to a cabin. Figure we explore one, any one."

"What if we don't find nothin'?" Radwell asks.

Meirs shakes his head, gives us glances. "Ah, Rad, we didn't figure that far ahead I guess."

Radwell looks a little annoyed but then relaxes. "You're right, though, it's certain they got blocks up ahead. They'd block this road. In a hurry they'd do that before lookin' for us. Makes sense. Makes sense we have ta take a look or two, 'cause we can't cross the State lines now. Next good one I see we're goin' in."

Cal speaks with rasping urgency. He is talking away from us, facing the back window, and speaking towards it. "Make sure you do. I swear I just saw a cop turn inta the woods (cough) about a mile back. They're lookin' for us dat way too."

"Fuck!" shouts Meirs, shaking his head once violently. Radwell is running to his truck. I have turned with the others to peer through the rear window searching for this car that we can't see as we hear Radwell's truck spin dirt onto our car and Meirs spins the wheels to our car, too, leaving clear tracks behind us as we leave.

#

"He's goin' in there," I call out, pointing to a wide gray clay entrance, much wider than many of the other logging entrances we'd seen, and watch as Radwell's truck kicks some of its moist gray clay up in the air as he enters the path. It's on the left side of the road and without hesitation Meirs slows our car and turns across the road into this dirt and leaf-covered path to follow close behind Radwell's truck. I saw no other vehicles on the road when we did this, which is good. We bounce down this path quickly, watching the truck dance before us on the uneven coarse ground. We're glad, as we look back, that the ground is moist and packing and not kicking up clouds of lingering dust to alert the law. The road disappears from sight, but Cal and I still stare at what lay behind us for several moments, before turning to see what is ahead.

The path winds this way and that as we make good speed even as the woods grow thick and close in. There are signs of recent use by other vehicles in the pliable gray clay and we eagerly follow them. For many minutes the truck ahead shudders and accelerates and decelerates through the ups and downs and twists of the darkened path as the path splits many times. Our pace and the path are brutal to the car we're in. If we keep this pace up it won't be long before the car breaks down.

We stop our vehicles in clear open sunlight, gazing at a golden brown field of tall grass, brush, and isolated young gray leafless trees all spread in front of us on both sides of the road. The grasses and brush wave from gentle breezes and this scene stretches out wide and open until the fields reach the distant woods roughly a half-mile away. There is nothing of human origin in sight, except for the road we are on, so, before we can call to him, Radwell stomps heavily on the truck's accelerator and shoots away from us.

"He's goin' too fast," Perez says. "Don't you go tryin' ta keep up. We'll find him."

"Yeah-man," I say.

"Oh man," Cal speaks out against Perez and I, "I dunno 'bout that."

"I'm gonna keep up," replies Meirs as he stomps on the gas pedal and off we go in chase of Radwell.

"Meirs don't go so damn fast," Perez demands, "We'll pop a tire, miss a bend or another path. Slow down ... Franklin?"

"You askin' me somethin'?" I respond in surprise. "What for? Meirs slow down. Dis car breaks down Rad might not stop for us, ya know. Dis car's ta only way we got, man."

Meirs reluctantly slows the car while murmuring, cussing something under his breath.

Minutes later the path turns and we leave these golden fields behind. The road takes a steady rise through the woods and crosses other paths before we come out into a more open area like we did minutes ago, but where our attentions go to this time is not to the horizon of what is around us but to what we are driving on; stones and pebbles, instead of the natural clay mix. Why this in the middle of the woods? The stones and pebbles are a deliberate human touch, and for what? This road has ended in a large semicircle heavy with this gravel. Meirs has us stopped at its entrance. Radwell is a bit further in with his truck.

There have been many cars or trucks here, as shown by the numerous paths cut through the thick layer of stones and pebbles, mounding the gravel into little curb-like hills. There is, however, nothing else human to see beyond this, only overgrown fields running like a sea between islands of timbers.

Someone has to be out here, but where are they? Another thought; this is not the place to try and hide our truck. We have to go back, or go cross-country, and only Radwell's truck can do that well. We all sense this. A quick talk later we're on the move again, only slowly; searching.

"Go along the edge, try ta follow ta tracks. The cop won't know if any are ours," Perez instructs Meirs. "Go slow so our tracks look the same. We can't go back far without coming face to face with that cop. You guys remember anyplace near in which we can hide this thing?"

"Hey, man, dat's even if ta cop comes here—no, man," I reply.

"There ain't nothin' back there that ain't ahead a us, too—I don't want ta do anything takin' us back anywheres, man," Cal rasps.

As Meirs slowly drives the car along I quietly study what lies around us. The edges of the stone-pebble semicircle blend into the grass and brush which I frequently look beyond. I find we are on something like a ridge, for all the land around this semicircle gently sweeps away below us about seven feet or more. The drop off is deceptive, because of the heights of the grass, the ground falls further than first appears. The field slants away before rising again, remaining open to the edges of various woods which stand at varying distances of between two to three hundred yards from us. A few young trees and many saplings litter this openness—three trees are grouped below us at the bottom of this hill's slope. Driving straight out into these fields will leave a noticeable path.

"I don't wanna go back any either, man," Meirs protests. "I'd rather take my chance somewhere out here."

"None a us want ta go back, man, I hear what ya say," I respond as something slight catches my eye. Following the sight back I see an entrance to a grass-covered path, where a large vehicle has recently gone, or several, over the edge, and this unexpected path quickly leaves my sight as it declines away from the slope.

"Stop the car Meirs."

"You see somethin'?" he asks me.

"Yeah, I do. You guys see it?" I question.

"What're ya talkin' 'bout?" Meirs asks.

"How can I—I'm on ta other side from ya," Cal protests.

"Shit head, I looked at your side a the car, stupid," I reply as I point to the path. "Meirs, turn dis thing around, don't make no deep marks in ta stones okay? Dis is ta answer to your prayers, Meirs, do as I say."

We would have easily discovered this recently used path if we had been turning the opposite way about this circle, but none of the others noticed it in the way we did come—and neither will the law, I reason.

Hurried moments later Meirs slowly takes the car down the hill, following Radwell's truck and the pathway of bent grass, until he reaches the covering of the next woods where he will wait for us. Tollin is walking along the semicircle's edge and is talking to himself again. Even rode over twice more this path is hard to see from the semicircle, the waviness of the grasses and the angle it makes as this path runs away from us hides it well. Tollin, after a wink of his eye towards me, hurries to where the vehicles are and guides Meirs and Radwell deeper into the woods, disappearing from our sight, while Drew and I finish moving the pebbles and stones back into rough shape to hide our tire marks.

"What's that?" Drew asks, moments later, lifting his head and peering back into the woods from where we came as we hear the noise of an approaching vehicle. "Car comin'."

"Down," I say as we both hurry and drop into the cover of the grassy slope.

The vehicle nears. Drew and I hide almost within touch of each other, but I can only see Drew if I raise my head. I don't like the thought of not seeing what this car may be doing. Against quiet protests from Drew, who somehow does see me, I slowly crawl on my stomach up the slope until my eyes barely peer over the edge of the stones. Through the tall blades of brown grass I can see the cop, a lone cop arriving at the circles' entrance, stopping there, looking around carefully, like we had. Drew quietly calls for me to slide back down the slope but I have to see which way this cop will go around. I have to know. I tell Drew to shut up. I know it'll be natural for the cop to circle the way we did, but he will have a better line of sight on us if he chooses the opposite way, and if he does he will see the path we took.

He is on the radio with someone for a time and when he finishes he takes another long look around. He comes back and seems to look straight at me and for many seconds his look freezes me in place. I wear no hat or colorful clothing and my black skin on my bald head either blends in with the background behind me or stands out for what I am. While there is enough grass between us to blur my image—does he see me? I can't tell.

He continues to stare in my direction as he begins his drive. He follows our route, to my relief. His car crawls along. He looks towards his right searching the edges of the circle. I still don't move, not sure if this is all he is doing, for his eyes refuse to wander far from my position. If we have been found out I need to kill him, but how? How can I get to him—there is too much distance to cross in too long a time. I don't have a chance. Now he looks the other way, across the circle, but the moment I lose contact with his eyes I push myself down the slope just once, just as far down as my arms can extend above me. I can't see him or the car anymore, can't see the edge of the circle. I lay my head down and press it tight against the earth and wait.

For a second time in just hours I hear the roll of tires slowly moving forward, this time crunching stones and pebbles under their weight; of an engine idling fast, like all cop cars seem to do, and the cackle of a radio ... and I can only wait.

The ground is cold yet the grass my head presses against has been warmed from the sun. I smell the sweet mustiness of the ground while I listen to the car's movements. The slight scratchiness of the grass against my face doesn't lessen its invite to be a pillow. I'm physically fatigued. The warmth of the sun against my back tempts me to sleep, despite this situation. This is like the time, as a kid, when I hid from the cops in an open vacant lot, after being chased on foot for six blocks. The very openness of the lot saved me that day. The few mounds of grass littering the lot couldn't possibly hide someone my size, or so the cops must have thought. They moved on with just a look from their distance; did no searching. That was then. Now, however, the squad moves on by above me and I wait long enough before I carefully lift myself to see it head back out onto the logging road and into the woods much quicker than it had arrived. The officer must be going through the simple routine of checking out every logging road he comes to. He probably hadn't seen any sign of us at all. I wait until I'm certain the squad is not coming back before I move on down the slope to meet Drew.

"You can get shot that way asshole," Drew comments as he stands up as I near.

"Didn't n why do you care?" I answer.

"I don't, except that if they're shootin' at you, I'll be next, and I don't want that, so don't do that again, hear me?"

"Yes-masser," I reply in as much of a black slave to white owner manner as I can muster—a double insult with Drew being black. He doesn't like it. He likes less the glare I give him to follow up my words, but he says nothing more.

41

"What's up?" Rick asks.

"Before all of us split. I've always meant to ask ya. Sebetic once told me you got into a bunch of fights in Italy. That he had to drag your limp body home one night after some guys beat the crap out of ya. That you kept fighting them until you couldn't stand no more—true?"

"Ah," Rick answers, his voice and his body adjusting with an uncomfortable memory, "No, not exactly."

"Well, now, just what does 'not exactly' mean, Smitty?" Doug challenges, "Since you don't back away from a good fight. There's somethin' to this. Out with it."

"Ah—well," Rick replies in willing resignation; "Ron and I were out on the town one night, in Italy. I got drunk and ended up arguing with this one guy slightly shorter than me in this bar. We moved it into the street and began to fight. Sebetic watched my back. This guy and me went at it, but I was drunk. He got the better of me, beat me until I couldn't stand."

"Holy shit—and you skipped the blow by blow details—all amazing to me," Doug breathes out emphatically and his surprise reflects both my own and Mark's. Rick, next to Bill, is the largest, strongest man among us, though Mark comes close. Anyone can get beat … yet none of us ever heard of Rick losing to anyone, except from what Sebetic said. None of us expected to hear Rick admit this; that not only did he lose, he got beat to a pulp.

"Wow, how'd that happen, Turk?" Mark asks. Rick was waiting for one of us to ask.

"Turns out the guy was a black belt in something. Which brand of karate, I don't know, and it don't matter. He came at me in ways no one else ever did. When I got better and ready I went looking for him again," Rick tells us.

We are all ears now, forgetting anything else we're doing. Getting beat once would've been enough for any of us. We certainly would not search the guy out a second time like Rick just claimed.

"Found him, too," Rick continues, "Thought now that I wasn't drunk on my ass he wouldn't get so lucky. I got several good shots in at him this time, until his foot found my nose. Then he beat me down to the ground again, and he enjoyed it, too. Fucker. I was beat good. Only guy, only fight I ever lost. Yeah, Sebetic had to drag my ass back to base."

"Dang!" Mark and Doug chorus.

"Didn't you say I had a death wish, Rick?" I say. "Ah, you need to correct that."

Roy, Tom, and Bill nod their heads in agreement with me, and shake them in disbelief over Rick.

"Heck no," he replies laughingly. "No death wish, just wanted the fight on even terms. Didn't want no guy boasting he could beat me when I was drunk when he did it, you know?"

"Shit … I knew I was hanging around crazy guys back then," Doug states. "Didn't know how crazy."

"Because you were crazy, too. Remember, you already admitted to driving on top of a snow bank," Rick answers.

"Shit," Doug discounts, "That was more circumstance and plain luck. Heck, I felt great when I could show my dad up when he told me I couldn't make a decent weld bead in my life and he watched me lay down a perfect one out in the field to fix his tractor. That's more me, you know?"

I jump in. "I remember challenging my dad out in our driveway and him picking me up clear off the ground and holding me easily up there, teasing me, asking me if I really wanted to challenge him—and he was lifting me with one arm ..." I stop as I realize the others are looking at me as if I came out of left field. I probably did. "This ain't the same thing Doug was talkin' about, is it?"

Mark and Rick shake their heads and sigh while Doug looks at me kind of strange, as if questioning my sanity.

Rick agrees, smiling wide, "It ain't, but I remember both—Doug doin' the weld and you challenging your dad, I was there. And you," Rick looks at me, "Payback is hell—ya got me just now."

I shake my fist in celebration, along with a smile. "Yes. That'll teach ya …having them ask me 'bout my divorce."

Rick smiles back. "Sure."

"Wild good times back then," Doug says introspectively. "But what's up for this afternoon? Before anyone starts wandering off again?"

"Well, wait—what about Roy and Tom? You guys got anything to share?" I ask.

Both shake their heads no.

"I ain't got a wild hair on my body," Roy admits.

"I ain't had one either, can't seem ta grow one, eat a lot a spinach though—ain't that supposed ta help?" Tom says, "Is there a way of gettin' one? A hair, ya know? Like do I still got time for shit like that? I want ta pass some outlandish memory on to my grandchildren, ya know."

"It would look a little crazy now," Bill replies. "Sorry, age is a factor, ya know."

"Ah-shit," Tom answers, "I ain't got a chance then."

Rick points to me, "He is going to chop up a birch tree with Tom. Roy, you can get some firewood. Doug, you and Mark can finish up securing the trailer and maybe show the women how to work the guns…."

"I can help Gay and Mary with the guns," Paula asserts.

"Okay," Rick nods, "Bill and I will dig, at least until the power line people show up. That should be enough for a couple of hours, don't you think?"

"I believe they're coming now, Rick," Paula said. "I think I hear them."

"Wow, that's quick."

Two vehicles soon appear following our trail, both trucks showing their company logos. I watch Rick direct them to park parallel and left of Bill's camper. I politely and briefly meet Mason and Terrance from the Power Company, and a youthful Jason, from the septic system company, before Tom and I leave for the birch tree—and, before Tom and I do that, I walk over to Mary.

"Don't work too hard," she says.

"Oh, you know I will. I know you will be."

"Yeah, but take care, be careful around that saw and that axe—whatever you're going to be doing. Paula and I have talked already about dinner. I think you'll like it."

"Anything you two cook is good, if not great. I love you."

"Love you, too," she answers as we kiss.

42

I turn hoping to see Mary and she does not disappoint. She stands there at the path's start, waving to me as I hoped; waiting and knowing I will look back for her. I smile broadly and return a wave by lifting the long armed axe high into the air, swinging it side to side above me. I turn off the path and into the field to the west and north, hurrying to catch Tom.

"I love that woman," I say to myself just before I reach Tom as we begin to follow the trail of damaged grass we crushed during our excursion before lunch. She is a good-hearted and resilient person. Life would be hard without her.

"Oh, no kiddin?" Tom replies.

"What?" I ask, then realize I had spoken aloud—how much did I say?

"Pretty obvious you love that woman with all the kissy-kissy, touchy-touchy, purring, and eye contact you two do."

"Uh ... are ya sarcastic, 'cause I'm pretty gullible too?"

Tom turns his head and gives me a long gaze, followed by a smile.

I shrug my shoulders, resigned to whatever fate he is thinking of for me.

"Well it could be worse, ya know," he finally says.

"What could?"

"Marriage."

"Oh yeah—I know—I definitely know."

"Aw-yeah … I guess you do from what you said back there at lunch. How'd ya meet her?" he asks as we enter the grove of oaks, maples, and hickory trees, which tower above us all around. There is scant ground brush about below, making it harder to follow our faint trail.

"Mary, or my first wife?"

"Mary."

"Mary and I met through the personal ads. She responded to mine."

"Really? You put the ad in—and it worked?"

"Well don't make it sound so surprising, geez. The usual routes didn't get me nowhere."

"Now that's expected."

"Ah, what is it about me that makes people feel they can ridicule me?"

"Um—you're gullible. And you accept that you're the comic relief in our group."

"I was hoping that was you."

"Oh, I might be, but situation-wise—you are."

We make fast time through this grove and are about to leave it behind and enter into the heavy brush when I stop to look back, to make sure I can find my way back.

"You get any others?" Tom asks.

"What?"

"Responses from your ad?"

"Yeah."

"Well?"

"Mary was six of eight."

"Really? What're the others like?"

"One said she was curvy like an hour glass but looked like a beach ball when we met."

"Huh," Tom says with a smile.

"It wasn't her looks, man. It was her misrepresentation that killed that."

"Sure. I think that would be enough for me, too."

"Well ... whatever."

"Any crazies?"

"One. Another said she didn't smoke and she lit four cigarettes in the first twenty minutes we met over coffee."

"That was the crazy one?"

"No. The crazy one thought I was playing games when I suggested we meet over coffee."

"Really, wow, and why Mary?"

"Oh, something about the way we talked in the five weeks preceding our first meeting kept me interested. I liked who I saw when we did meet. No misrepresentation of what she looked like and she looked fine, a nice brown-eyed brunette with a ready and bright smile. She was easy on my eyes ..."

"She is. What else? I mean, she had kids, that didn't scare ya off?"

"Didn't care, don't care—she told the truth—that mattered. And I like kids. She worked two jobs, and that said a lot to me right there."

"It does to me, too. What else?"

"Well ... she values much the same things as me. By the time that first hour over coffee was done, I knew she was the one, or darn well could be. We married three years later on the day we met, and have been married four years now—four very good years."

Tom shakes his head, holding a slight smile that quickly disappears. "My future wife and I met while drunk at a party—both of us drunk, and we conceived a kid. Didn't know her before, and twelve years later I don't think I know her yet."

"Wow, didn't know that, Tom. You didn't have ta tell me, to marry her ..."

"Didn't have to have the child, didn't have to do the act, didn't have to stand and be responsible, but I'm glad I did. My in-laws, she may be a little crazy, and I'm wantin' ta avoid them this Thanksgiving, but, overall, I love her, and more each day—but don't let her know that—she's mad at me for goin' on this huntin' trip, and things seem to work out best when we have an attitude to each other—don't know why. A man's gotta do what a man's gotta do, though, ya know."

"Playing with her emotions?"

"Naw, naw, I don't want ta mess with her any, just assert some independence. Get a little life of my own. We got two other kids. Love them, too, just never gettin' a time for anything much that I want ta do, ya know? Gotta get a little space to let things shake out a bit."

I stare into his eyes a fleeting moment before I smile. "I've felt that a time or two."

We enter an open overgrown area filled with young saplings and brush, bright with sunlight from the clear blue sky. My eyes squint as I look up; there's no hint of the expected storm. The brush is dense. The ground gently rises and falls beneath us as we make our way forward. Tiny branches constantly grab at our clothes. This won't be good on a return trip carrying heavy logs so we use the axe often to help open the path. The further we go the taller the brush grows. By the time we come out of the now taller than head high brush and onto the ledge overlooking the fallen tree, both of us are soaked in sweat. A long sigh of relief comes from us as we survey this small ledge of grass and seedlings, the creek bed, and the fallen birch.

There is room to move about between the three other birches and I take advantage by taking my jacket off and hanging it on one of the stubs sticking out from the one birch a few steps to my right. I take a seat at the base of that tree, leaning my back against it. Tom watches me, likes what he sees, and does the same over at his pair of trees. We rest until we're cooled off.

It is nice, sitting there with the sunshine hitting the open spaces around us, the blue skies, the gentle breezes, the sounds of leaves rustling, birds calling. Solitude sometimes gives great rewards. Peace of mind. Only Tom is here to share this with me. He is being quiet, holding onto the power saw and the rifle, which he leans against one of the trees—it had been his turn to carry those, while I have the axe laying across my lap.

"And the fun is about to begin whenever you say," I say.

Tom nods, glancing my way. "That tree looks a lot bigger now than before. How'd that happen?"

I chuckle. "It grew, wants to intimidate us, fight us to the end."

Tom stops his rise from the ground, his eyes move side to side, then he looks at me and asks; "You played with dolls when you were a kid, didn't ya?"

I return a look of disbelief.

Tom points a finger toward the tree. "Ya just gave that tree character. What's ya doin'—it's dead?"

I think it over. "And, you didn't play superhero *not once* as a kid?"

Tom's eyebrows raise and a moment later he nods his head. "Okay, ya got me. Ready?"

I stretch my legs and arms, roll up my sleeves, before I jump down onto the creek bed and look the tree over. I feel myself focusing in as Tom moves to the top of the fallen tree.

In the past, my soul often found relief through hard physical work. The work would not relieve all the emotional or mental stress, the pain, I was under but it gave my body a needed form of expression, and an eventual positive reward. I used to do a lot more of this in a regular routine of running, push-ups, sit-ups and, what I liked most; pull-ups. I stayed in excellent condition for many years, more than ten, actually stopping serious workouts only a year and a half ago when my nephew, Craig, finally showed me up by whipping me in one of those serious workouts. Just as convincing was my body simply hurting too much every time I exercised, and for too long afterwards. Age … I was proud, though, for at several different points in those years I could do up to one hundred total pull-ups, push-ups and sit-ups during the workout routine, after typically running three miles. I gained fifty pounds of solid body weight over those first seven years and maintained that weight since. At age forty-three, I thought this was just fine, as I watch Tom start the saw to work the upper branches, as I ready to chop the trunk. Five foot nine and a half inches tall and one-hundred-ninety-five pounds ... I considered myself stout.

Several of the trimmings fly from my axe. One was a short one-inch thick branch broken when the tree fell, leaving a sharp ragged finger of wood pointing out at the break. I used both hands to bring the axe against it and it flew away to land somewhere on the ledge beside me; another, similar to that first bolt, falls into the creek bed, and a third flies off somewhere else. Many of the trimmings are tiny and I move through them with ease.

I began my workouts in earnest after my first wife and I separated. I had stayed in shape during that marriage and the raising of our four children by often doing my running and light workouts after we put the children to bed. These workouts were not a high priority; they were more for relief, as our marriage became strained over time. Then, after our marriage fell apart, it was for every reason; as well as to beat back anger and frustration. My ex-wife never wavered in her determination to deny a relationship with my children. It was clear she was always claiming I had no interest in our children, to our children. Our children did not suspect the behind-the-scene efforts of denial she continuously worked for, nor did they completely comprehend their mother's actions when she acted out in front of them—they were still too young.

I felt the axe hit harder against the weakening tree.

Time after time she would deny visitation, right in front of our children, after I traveled six hours to see them—many times during the year, and year after frustrating year this would happen—too frequently.

The court absurdly only slapped her hand and she laughed at them in return with her actions, making her further efforts of denial more visible.

The muscles in my arms and shoulders are swelling as I find a rhythm in my work.

The first section of the tree gives way and I begin work on the second without pause.

I worked out to stay in shape for my children, so I would be able to practice soccer with them, baseball, basketball—whatever they may have wanted me to do with them. I looked forward to that. Part of being a father is to play with one's children.

I hear the sounds of only my ax-cutting echo back from the woods about me.

The time came when I knew I had enough—no, more; a preponderance of evidence to take her back to court in a second try for custody. I pleaded with her beforehand such an action was not necessary, if only she would allow easy and legitimate visitations to happen—why take the kids from their schools, neighborhood, and friends they knew? She laughed at me.

The second section of trunk falls and I start on the third, again without pause.

"Hey man?"

She said she would turn my children against me, make them hate me, before any court trial came about, and that she would get them back no matter what any court said. What a witch! What for? Why do this to our children? Because, she claimed, without acknowledging she was doing anything towards our children, that I had abused her. Nothing I did warranted this; wasn't she emotionally and mentally abusing our children now? Didn't she gamble away much of our children's futures by playing the casinos to incredible losses and by delving into their trust fund accounts—

almost totally done behind my back while we were married and after, or under false pretenses? Damn!

"Hey man!"

The axe slams through the wood snapping what remains in two and continues through. The blade head half buries itself into the ground just inches from my feet, splattering moist dirt and fine pebbles all about. I let go of the axe and step back, realizing just how angry I have become. I take in several deep breaths as I stare at the axe and the results of my work, trying to relax. I have not been this angry for well over a year and thought I would never feel this way again. Damn. I love my children so very much and know they will never know this, never trust those words from me, and never bother to know me, because of her. Damn. I step forward to pick up the axe to begin trimming the remnants.

"HEY!"

Tom is staring at me from a few feet away, holding the saw. Holy shit, I forgot he was here. "Yeah?"

"You okay? I mean I'm supposed to be the one cutting through this tree, you're supposed to be trimmin' it—or do I got the wrong tree? Nope, this is the only tree layin' across the water, so, yep, that's what I'm supposed ta be doin'—so what the heck have you been doin'? Somethin' get inta ya brain—I had ta shout like three times."

"Uh ... uh, yeah," I answer, "Somethin' definitely got inta me. Sorry. Go ahead and cut the rest."

"Yeah, yeah, sure," he hesitantly replies, looking at me carefully. "Just drop the axe and step back a bit. Go up on the ledge and rest awhile. Just don't get out of my sight, okay?"

I smirk as I look at him.

"No, man, I'm serious," he explains, "I watched you. Man, you got one ugly lookin' face when you're mad or whatever you were feelin' there. Scary somethin'. I wanna know you're okay—stay in my sight, don't scare me no more."

"You serious?"

"Yes!"

Mary always understood my reactions over these issues and these emotions strike whenever they please but she always gets upset when she learns I feel this way. She says my ex-wife smiles whenever I react like this. It is what my ex would want my life to be like—to be feeling miserable and in emotional pain. Mary is right, of course; this is what the creature would want.

The witch was right too; my children already hated me by the time I received custody. The creature was right in that the court did not know how to handle her contemptuous actions, or was unwilling to harshly treat her because she is female, and she was hiding behind our children. What to do about them? Any action against her would make her look like a martyr to them ... It became clear if I had done a fraction of what she had I would be looking at a good part of my life behind steel bars.

Basically, because of their minimal reactions, the courts, both criminal and civil, stood by and watched her as she stole our kids back, and that was at the point where I had exhausted every financial resource. I was then many thousands of dollars in debt. I could only watch her take them back. My attorney said the District Attorney, and the police, refused to do anything further, stating the children have made their choice. It was time to give up. Damn! Damn! Damn! I did everything I could except give up though, technically, I did, but not in my heart ... not in my soul.

Tom just finished all the large branches, and he trimmed them, too.

Mary could not keep me from this anger, but she could help me with it. She stood by me throughout that troubled time and helped me gain custody of my children, and watched me get robbed of them. She saw me through everything—who else would do that except an angel? Mary had nothing to gain by staying by my side. From my first face to face meeting with her I thought I would be marrying her—these actions by her were tremendous icings on the cake to convince me to do so and to hope I could spend the rest of my life with her, if she would say yes.

I am still sweating profusely as I jump off the ledge to help Tom move the pieces of the tree.

"You safe ta be around now?" he asks as he tosses the axe up on my side of the ledge, then looks at me as he bends over to gather and grip the logs we are about to carry.

I give him an annoyed look as I do the same. "Not if you keep questioning me like that."

"Uh-huh, well, you got your end?"

"Yeah."

"On the count of three."

"What about the saw, the rifle, and stuff?"

"Nobody's gonna be here, man, and we're comin' back."

"Okay, just thought I'd ask."

"Uh-huh … three," he says with a smile as he suddenly lifts.

"What happened to one and two you moron …"

43
(Franklin)

"Bitch—no knives or screwdrivers in this truck," Drew exclaims as he searches behind the back seat.

"Shit, we gotta find somethin'," replies Radwell, standing outside the driver's door.

"Any wire or rope?" Tollin asks Drew as he searches the glove compartment.

"No."

"So we got nothin' ta hunt with?" I say. No one answers as I look underneath the passenger's seat.

"Unless someone can figure on how ta hunt with nothin', we're gonna be very hungry two days from now," Drew states.

"Well, what about goin' back?" Meirs asks. "We only got so much gas—can't waste it wandering out here for no reason."

"You sure changed ya mind," Perez states as he stares at Meirs. "A minute back you weren't goin' back fer nothin'."

"We ain't at the end of this path yet. We go until then," Radwell declares. "No goin' back until then."

"What a we meet someone?" Cal asks.

Radwell pauses and looks around at us as we all stand about our vehicles in the middle of this nowhere land. "Well, depends on lots a shit, I guess. If we outnumber 'em we overwhelm 'em. If not, match up the best ya can size-wise. Somehow we gotta get their guns."

"We can't talk long with 'em—they'll smell us out," Tollin says.

"They'll smell you out," Radwell replies. "Yeah. Good point. That makes Meirs, Drew, and me the front men. You guys hang back unless ya can't."

"So whatever happens, happens fast?" Cal asks.

"Yeah Cal, you're swift. A short talk to get position then we gotta move, unless we see some other way, but look at us—there's no other way. One long look they'll figure who we are," Drew adds. "So we gotta act fast."

"We gotta get guns—how we gonna get guns?" Cal ups his concern.

Drew sighs.

"We beat ta shit outta 'em, man," I say.

Radwell scoffs. Tollin shakes his head.

"They might have those outside," Perez offers.

"What? They might have what outside?" Radwell asks.

"Guns," Perez answers.

"Now why d'ya think they might do somethin' as foolish as that?" Meirs asks.

"Ain't foolish, man. My grandpapa farmed, took me huntin' and campin', tryin' ta straighten me out. My pop, though, he was too bad for me, so I didn't listen to my grandpapa."

"What's that got to do with guns?" Tollin asks.

"Kept ta guns out overnight when we camped in cold weather like this. Below dew point—know what that is? Too cold for water ta form on a gun when its this cold, but if ya take the gun inside with ya, it will get wet inside and out because the gun itself is cold and inside the cabin has warm moist air. Then ya have ta clean it whether ya shot it or not. So maybe they got them guns outside already," Perez says.

"Can't be much chance a that, man," I say. "Guns get wet anyway."

"True," Perez agrees, surprising me. "Guns still get wet, depends what kinda weather, but sure to if taken inside. Good chance they're out, man. A good chance," Perez insists.

"If we don't find nobody?" Cal asks.

"Then we stay out here a day or so. We have ta. We ain't got much choice," Drew answers, shaking his head, rolling his eyes.

"Drew's got it, man. No choice. C'mon, no more talk," Radwell says, "Let's find out where this trail goes."

We climb back into our vehicles and start moving again.

We don't go far, maybe a minute passes, but the trail is already endless. The rough bouncing vehicle pounds my insides into resignation—despair; we'll be out here exposed and hungry for what'll be too long a time to stay, well, … sane.

Then, around a stand of brush, comes a glimpse of their camp. My heart jumps. Someone is out here. There is a place to hide. There will be food. This camp gives every chance in the world to avoid the law, to gain freedom to Canada. I can hardly believe my eyes. We'll make it … we can make it. A new life … soon … and it'll be wonderful—meant to be.

Radwell's truck rumbles away from the woods into the final clearing letting us here in the car see the layout of the camp; a large main trailer forms the border farthest from us almost straight ahead and slightly to our right. Further away—immediately ahead of this main trailer is the first of four trucks. The first one had pulled the trailer but is detached from it, is the farthest truck from us, and makes a corner to their camp, and its front end points back at the trailer. The second truck, to the left of this first truck, stands closer, holds a sleeper camper on its bed and points the opposite way the first truck does. To the left of this emerald green camper truck stand two more trucks, both of these have company logos printed on their sides. These four trucks plus the main trailer form a rough-shaped ell. A slight rise of ground, its length about the same and laying opposite the trailer, holds two young evergreens standing off-center of its length, these trees being nearer to where the trucks are parked and stand across from the trailer's door, to complete the general U-shape of the campsite with us approaching the opened end of this U.

Two women can be seen, and five men.

"Holy … will you look at that!" exclaims Cal, referring to the women.

"Never imagined some sweet thing would be out here," adds Meirs, with anticipating pleasure in his voice. "Blessed—and we got two. O-oh, my groin hurts."

We laugh briefly, suppressing our glee because those in the camp have noticed us.

"Jerk-off somewhere else, Meirs," I joke. "Let's get ta game plan goin', man."

"Watch out," cautions Perez. "These women will make things hard for us..."

"Ha, sure will, man, what'yas think they'd do—make your dick go soft?" Meirs scoffs.

"Don't touch them," Perez warns.

"Perez, were you somebody's bitch back at the prison—jealous already?" scoffs Cal.

"No one touched me," growls Perez. "Say that again, I cut your dick off. These women can divide us—we can't let that happen."

"Don't let that happen. Oh, don't let *that* happen!" Cal replies. "You're a momma."

"Shuddup, Cal," I say. I'm surprised I'm defending Perez, putting a hand towards him to calm him. Perez reluctantly accepts my stance with suspicious eyes.

"Cal," says Meirs, "Perez oft that woman back at the station right in front of ya, so he ain't sayin' what ya think."

"Oh what's he sayin' then?"

"We don't kill 'em. We keep 'em for days."

"Oh, yeah ... yeah, that be better, ain't it?"

"You have eyes in the back a yer head Cal?" Perez threatens while looking at me in a questioning way. He has not stopped looking at me since I extended my hand towards him.

"We'll just have our fun with them—they ain't gonna do nothing," Meirs interrupts, stopping Cal from replying. "Heck, I think we're freakin' lucky to come upon women. They're usually very willing to do whatever it takes to save their own sweet asses—know what I mean?"

We smirk at this and agree, even Perez smirks before he sternly warns us again not to do anything to the women; "Touching them will enrage their men, cause conflicts among us. We don't want either to happen."

"We kill 'em," Cal exclaims.

Perez remains stern, "No. We'll need them."

"For what?" Meirs challenges.

"Don't know yet, but it's not wise to kill off everyone here just to kill—don't do it. We need to survive days here, man. Don't know if we can do that without them yet."

"You're a..."

"Cal," I snap, stopping him. "We killed at ta station 'cause they could snitch. These people can't, man. Makes sense ta hold off killin' 'em—just go with it, man, just go with it."

The people stand their ground as they watch us approach, puzzled to why we're here, and who we could be. The two women are attractive brunettes, one lighter haired, and the other nearly black in color. They wear heavy flannel shirts but no coats, no gloves. The day isn't warm enough to wear just those shirts casually. The four campers had been working hard before we interrupted them. The two women stand apart from each other, but both are at the center of the small clearing formed by the ell. Both women wear tight fitting jeans and their body curves show. Their flannel shirts hint at their breast size. I have to get in one of these women. I've been denied sex twice this week, man; the Sunday prison fight, today at the station. I ain't going to be denied three times, not in one week.

One of the five men is by the two evergreens, holding a shovel with gloved hands, both hands on the top of it, leaning lightly on it. My eyes come back to study him. He, like the women, wears a flannel shirt and blue jeans. He has gray hair at his temples and streaks of gray accent the rest of his brown hair. With a strong tall stature, he holds the gaze of a confident tested man—a hunter, a fighter, a true threat to us. The three company men are behind this hunter, further away. One glance tells me to give them no regard. Across from them the other camper man is near the entrance to the trailer. This man wears just a dark blue T-shirt and blue jeans. He is a large man, rotund, but one not afraid to work as shown by the stains of his sweat soaking his shirt. I have met men like him before, while usually easily winded from their size sometimes they can fight longer than expected, and they're always surprisingly strong. His gaze is different than the hunter's. He looks at us with his balding head tilted forward just a bit as if to confront and challenge us like a bull defending his ground. No doubt he will hold his ground. No doubt he will be hard to put down without a weapon, but it is this first man, the hunter, who worries me more. I don't like the hunter's piercing eyes. They speak loud of a tested past with many fights. He carries himself. I know I'll have to be the one to fight him.

The main trailer is large enough to sleep six, maybe eight—large enough for more people to be here than the seven now seen; four are campers, three are company men, there could be more campers. Beyond this people concern, what we really want is now seen like unwrapped Christmas presents leaning against the driver's side rear quarter-panel, the near corner, of the emerald green truck—the second truck, the one with the camper.

"Guns!" Meirs suddenly announces in a whisper.

"Where?" Perez asks.

"By the green truck."

"Oh yeah—sweet, man."

We count eight weapons; two semiautomatic and five bolt action rifles, and a shotgun, all in a row … waiting to be taken by us, except for a barrier of propane tanks lined like a fence a few yards ahead of those guns, keeping us from going right to them. There are too many weapons for just two men. Too many even if the two women hunt. Where are the others?

"Cal, you and Perez take the big guy by ta trailer. Meirs, ya ta fastest of us, ya know it's ya job ta get ta guns. The others know this too."

"Yeah, I know. I'll get 'em."

"Go for the semi-autos, they're closest," I tell Meirs as we watch Radwell boldly and suddenly accelerate his truck straight into the center of the camp, grass being ripped from the ground and getting flung high in the air by his tires. He's going for the weapons, forgetting about any talk, but those six propane tanks stand as a barrier, and will force him to stop short of the guns, giving these damn campers a chance.

Meirs spins the tires of our car as he, too, speeds up and heads to the right side of Radwell, scattering the now frightened and stunned campers on our side further from the guns, who run or dive out of the way of our vehicles, but who now know what we're doing, as we slam on our brakes, fling open our doors, and jump out.

44
(Franklin)

Pumped to fight, to seize control, we jump out of our vehicles into this deliberate confusion we caused. Meirs leaves the car motor running as he runs for the guns. I see Radwell doing the same out of his truck. Perez and Cal head for the bull-man. The others look for position to block any of them who try to interfere with us.

A blond-haired man appears from the far side of the first truck and comes to the nearest corner and, while he lets me see he holds nothing in his hands as he hesitates there, he reacts fast and gets in Meir's way. They begin to fight.

My eyes catch quick sight of yet another man, tall and slender, with a rugged worn cowboy look, possessing dark hair with streaks of gray and a heavy dark mustache, appearing at the doorway of the trailer. He holds a dishrag in his hands and is using it to dry them off; his sleeves rolled up beyond his elbows, his forearms greasy dirty. His eyes widen as he throws the dishrag away and jumps off the trailer steps, heading into action. I search for the hunter. He's coming fast. He knows he has to go through me to protect the guns, as I brace for him.

His shoulders come in low and barrel into my chest as I step forward to meet him. He impacts hard against me, lifts me clear off the ground, carries and slams me back against our truck, as my arms manage to grab hold around him. His fists and elbows pound my chest, shoulders, but miss my jaw as we fight tightly entangled with one another. He hits damn hard and I got to get him off me as I struggle to land hard elbows and fists on him. I manage to grab his left ear with my right hand and try to tear it off while I push his right shoulder away with my left hand. My pull on his ear moves him. As he pulls away and frees his ear, I move with him, bend down, and my arms clamp around his legs to lift him, and drive him, as he falls backwards, into the ground. I jump to stand above him as his legs kick free of my hold. I kick his side three times; his arms swing at my legs but fail to protect his side from my blows, before he manages to stand again. We go at each other with heavy punches, trying to grip, to find advantage over the other, before I sweep a leg out from under him and he falls against me. Still standing I feel the impacts of his fists trying to find my kidneys as I drive him forward before he finds his footing again. Our fight takes us across everything; into the two evergreen trees, both of us struggling with each other as the pine branches sweep us both off our feet and we find the ground again. He twists; his fist cracks against my skull twice and blurs my vision. His strikes force my arm to rise and block, and that sets him free again. His knee slams my chest as I rise and I gasp for breath. I fight to retain control of one of his arms but another kick breaks my hold and I stagger and stumble back, breathless.

I expected his power. I expected his experience, but his stamina is more than I'm used to. I land a hard blow to his lower groin, but miss his crotch. Out of nowhere his other fist finds my nose to shock me, coming across his body yet lacks strength to break my bone. In swift action I catch his withdrawing arm and wrench him over as my body twists to throw him, clamping this arm in both of mine as his body sweeps by my own, enabling me to follow through and kick him while he is down. He tries to pull his arm free but *he* has not expected *my* quickness or *my* strength and is out of position to deal with the hold I'm applying so effectively. I hear him call out in pain as I wrestle his arm up across my leg, as I kneel with one knee on his back, my other leg held straight out to the side, applying force, his arm held across and getting bent back at his elbow over my straightened leg and I have full intent to break his arm as I push down on it. Most men would stop here and plea, fearful of a broken arm, but this hunter man isn't about to resign himself. He is strong enough to resist a few moments more.

Being in such commanding control, I glance quickly around the camp. The three company men did react and quickly, bringing Radwell down and fighting both him and Tollin. I can't see what else is going on.

My self-distraction enables the hunter to shift his body, turn his arm, to cancel out the grip I hold, even if he can't get out of it completely. He is strong, determined. He has slipped his arm back almost off my knee—he is breaking my hold!

A gun blast stops everyone. A woman shrieks as warning shouts are made by Drew, twice repeated. Drew commands a handgun to the head of one of the women.

Taking advantage of everybody else holding still, I hit the hunter man in the mouth before he resists me again as blood flows from his lips. I move quickly off his chest, move down, and grab his struggling legs tight.

"You fight I tell them ta kill," I warn him. His eyes are recovering quickly from my hit to his face and fill with flame. It is in him to keep on battling despite my threat but he chooses to heed my words—this time. His defiance, his willingness to take a great loss, is too big a part of his character—he finds a way to get things done. He will have to be the first I kill, if we have to kill, or he will become big time trouble later.

My mouth bleeds. My nose bleeds. My chest feels shaken and bruised. My muscles shake from this rush and from the past hours of hard use, from lack of food, but I will be okay as I look about and scoff, smile, at the fearful expressions displayed across every camper's face.

I see Cal quickly lost his struggle with the big man, being sprawled on the ground face down and bloodied, but he interfered enough to keep the big bull from reaching the guns. Tollin has quickly grabbed a semi auto rifle and is now pointing this gun just inches away from the big man's belly. The big man breathes like the enraged bull I thought he would be, but he is settling down, his eyes looking over the scene, taking in the state of things, the conditions of his friends. He realizes there ain't much he can do with a rifle aimed at his belly and another gun aimed at his women friend's head.

I watch Meirs cuss at and kick the blond haired man, who'd given him a whipping, directing this man and the darker haired brunette, who is raising herself off the ground, her right hand clamped to the lower area of her chest as she gasps for breath, to stand in the center of the clearing, away from all the vehicles, back near where the trail begins. The blond haired man is lucky, Meirs does not have a gun yet but badly wants to kill him. Radwell tells Meirs to forget it. Meirs hisses back at Radwell, yet he listens.

I work to drag the hunter man by his legs over and closer to this point, to join these others at the center clearing. It would be just his style, this hunter man's, to give further trouble at any opportunity and I'm not allowing that.

As these things go on Drew commands the ones inside the trailer to come out. Only a blond woman comes forward, for the cowboy now stands above the rising and angry Perez, who is still on all fours, the cowboy having jumped from the trailer to pounce on him. Perez is again clutching his right hand and is in quiet agony.

The blond woman's eyes are wide with fear, as is the dark haired brunette's that Drew holds his gun to. The third woman's eyes, the lighter haired brunette, though fearful, also searches, assesses, and seems calmer than the other two. While she doesn't have a gun pointed at her head and she ain't being ordered to do anything, she still looks in more control of herself than I want her to be. She, too, is raising herself off the ground, looking as if she attempted to tackle Meirs as he went for the guns, or perhaps Drew, but didn't have the wind knocked from her as the dark haired brunette did.

The slender cowboy, his stoic looking silent stance adding to the western image I quickly had of him, looks intently toward my supine hunter man for a lead as to what he might do, now or later. He is plainly Meirs' counterpart; this cowboy is physically very quick, probably the quickest of all of them to have come off the trailer to stop Perez as he did.

"Hey!" I bark at him, for I sense a connection of long-term friendship and teamwork between this cowboy and the hunter. I don't want such a thing to be at work against us, "Put your hands on ta back of this big guy n look toward ta trailer," I order.

"And do it now," Tollin sternly reinforces my order with a quick point of his gun.

I throw the legs of the hunter man off and away from my side as I walk for the guns.

"Get up," Tollin orders the hunter, "Get up slowly and put your hands on the back of this guy here. What're we call this blond guy?"

"Blondie," I snap over my shoulder.

"Put your hands on blondie's shoulders," Tollin commands the hunter.

"Aw, man," I say, as Cal grabs a semi-automatic and checks it for ammunition, after handing me a bolt action—both rifles are loaded. "I'm glad you slinky white people loaded up dese guns here. Big relief, man, like really," I say as Meirs chuckles in the background. "Awful considerate of ya," I continue, "ta do us dat favor."

I wipe my hand across my mouth and again see my own blood, feel the sting of the wounds as the salt of my sweat from the back of my dirty hand slips into my opened flesh. I feel the many suddenly tender areas of my body pulse with pain from the hunter's heavy blows. My eyes narrow as I look at him. He will pay for this. He will pay.

Our attentions suddenly turn to the sounds and sight of the youngest company man bolting out of our camp into the fields heading for the nearby south woods. None of us seemed inclined to shoot this bastard, or none of us have a good shot to take.

Damn.

45

(Franklin)

"Tollin," Radwell calmly says as he watches the young company man run and begin to disappear from view, and the intent is clear—get the man.

"Too old, man," Tollin lazily responds, rejecting the order while adding; "And to bring him back alive."

"Meirs," Radwell states, now looking at Meirs, repeating the same tone he used before.

Meirs shakes his head no. "Man, can't ya see I'm busy? Just shoot 'em while ya still can. Do it yourself."

Radwell ignores Meirs and turns to me. I give Tollin my rifle and start running off after the man, before I lose complete sight of him.

The young man is desperate with fear, uncertain of what to do. He stays in the fields bordering the woods too long—lets me keep him in sight, lets me gain ground. He breaks the grass down for me as I follow his path. He looks back too often, slowing himself. He only runs, but runs as hard and as fast as his feet will take him, yet without direction—without thought. When he finally starts trying to lose me by going into the woods I'm already too close. We've covered a lot of ground by then, maybe a minute of hard running, jumping, dodging the obstacles in the woods and each other, but it is only a matter of time. My rush from fighting the hunter has not worn off and coupled with the rush I'm having now I feel none of the weariness my body does hold.

As if in a movie I watch him stumble over a small fallen branch and drop face first into the hard weedy ground, unable to get up before I close the remaining distance. Terror fills his eyes as he rises up on his arms and looks back at me. He reacts slowly. His strength is no match for mine as I pounce. I intend to subdue him, bring him back alive, until an open pocketknife suddenly appears in his hand and its blade slices through my shirt to cut part of my chest. The pain seems like nothing. It takes only seconds wrestling with him before I'm in control. His back is against my chest, and he is above me as my back sets against a trunk of a tree in much like a half-sitting position. I take that hand of his which still clasps the knife, my larger hand clamping over his to make him unable to release the blade. His struggles change from trying to escape to that of solely resisting me as I make him draw the knife up to his chest—with purposeful slowness. He resists with both arms but he cannot stop me. I laugh as I hear his pleas begin, hear his cries, feel his body shudder, as the knife bit by bit … gradually enters his heart.

I pivot the knife back and forth to make sure, cutting through the toughness that had been his heart. This has been so much like being in a movie—detached, watching someone else do the deed. I don't even feel like I actually lived the part, but I know I did. I know I did this deed … and it's such a thrill.

46
(Franklin)

My five cellmates stare at me as I stroll into camp. “What?” I ask.

Radwell takes a hand off his gun and makes a quick movement to ask with this free hand where the man is. Tollin scowls at me until I silently point to my slashed clothing, the bloody gash in my chest that will need a few stitches, and show the knife. Nobody says nothing more. Radwell momentarily hangs and shakes his head.

“Seven rifles and a shotgun, guys,” starts Radwell, turning to us all as he stands next to the line-up of our captives placed in the center of the camp, near the beginning of the trail. The round faced blond woman from inside the trailer is first, to my left, facing the parked trucks, then comes the lighter-haired brunette, the darker-haired brunette, the big bull man, the cowboy, the blonde-haired man, the hunter, a man named Mason—an old company man who dared to help in the fight, and finally a middle-aged utility man named Terrance. “And we’re lookin’ at three women and four men. What do you guys make of that?”

“Six men,” Cal corrects. “Seven … countin’ the dead one.”

“The utility men don’t count, stupid,” Radwell snaps back, “Especially the dead one—they’re not part of the hunting party.”

“Oh.”

Radwell and Drew roll their eyes in reaction to Cal’s word.

“I make it like they might have other guns inside that trailer or in their trucks,” Meirs answers. “Hey, where’d ya get that handgun, Drew, we didn’t reach the guns before you had it?”

“Back at the station. Pulled it out when I realized we weren’t gonna make the guns here.”

Radwell cocks his head back just a little, observing Drew, scrutinizing him. I can’t help but do the same. Somehow we forgot about that gun, so ... so when would Drew reveal he had it, why didn’t he show it before, remind us of it—what else was he planning on doing with it? Not good he didn’t let us know, but no matter, though, we all got guns now, control, ‘cause of him.

Perez too, scrutinizes Drew while Tollin seems not to mind. Cal is oblivious as he unloads the ammo from the two remaining weapons of these people. We all watch as he tosses these two rifles on top of the camper’s roof to get them out of easy reach. "Free pussy," he chuckles to himself, smirks, and turns back to face us as he does, to realize we heard him.

"Cut that out Cal," Radwell replies mildly and with a touch of a smile, "Let's not scare some of our hosts so early as to what's expected of them later on." These words visibly makes the women squirm, for our enjoyment, which is what Radwell wanted.

"I'd say we might be missin' somebody or bodies," offers Tollin to Radwell, "'Cause there's seven of them campers here and eight main guns. Shotguns are used for those beginin' or those who don't want ta hunt seriously like—the way I know it, and women don't usually hunt."

I say nothing as I take back my rifle from Tollin, walk over to their line and begin to poke the barrel of my rifle into the sides of each woman, near their breasts, to bug them—and this should bug their men, which is something I want to do—get them—keep them emotional, irritated, to loosen their tongues.

"Each of these fine ladies don't look like they have it in them at all to do any such huntin', so I suspect there's a man or two we haven't found yet—am I right?" Tollin asks.

We watch each of our newfound friends closely, hoping they'll say something or show a telling change in their face to confirm Tollin's question. They're all stressed and nervous—too scared to respond, I figure, but they're not terrorized to a paralyzing submissive fear like I hoped. I see nothing in their faces telling me anything whether others are about.

Tollin purposely coughs to gain Radwell's attention and to draw him next to me, 'cause I stand several feet away from the captives now, as Tollin himself comes close and whispers to us two; "Eight guns total, seven rifles and a shotgun ta spare for seven people makes real sense guys, there could be nobody else—I'm just having fun here tauntin' them about there bein' more. I could easily be wrong—makes sense that I'm wrong. Want me to keep going?"

I look to Radwell, who appears deep in thought.

"Yeah, well," he whispers in response, "Three more of them showed up after we started for the guns. Chances are a chance there could be more. An unlikely chance, but let's play with 'em a bit, one never knows what may fall out of their mouths—right?"

We agree with a silent nod of our heads.

"That's what I've been thinkin'," replies Radwell in a raised voice as he makes his way back beside our quiet captives. "And I cannot expect these upstandin' people to tell us straight, so Franklin, Meirs, do your thing. Meirs, check for a handgun or any other kind of weapon. Franklin, see if there's other people. Meirs be real thorough. We don't want them to surprise us—at all."

"Yes boss!" Meirs eagerly responds as he makes his way over to the first truck.

I take a step towards the main trailer but then stop and look at the hands of each woman out of curiosity; to find each wears a wedding ring. I notice Radwell watches me do this before I leave to go inside the trailer. Is he curious about them, or about me? And why do I wonder? Something in my mind is disturbed over Radwell. A tiny warning buzzer rings in my head but I can't figure out what it's trying to tell me. Or am I simply being nuts again? Drew and Tollin also watched but I'm not bothered by them doing so—why? 'Cause I killed the young man? I had no choice and Radwell sent me … the worst has happened and we're not worse for it. I don't understand why I worry here. Ah, just forget it.

The main trailer is as large on the inside as it appears from the outside. The lofted sleeping area at the front, the part of the trailer overhanging where the truck would be, is the second bedroom and can sleep two on one twin bed. The lower living area in the central part of the trailer holds two twin sized sleeper sofas, each set within the pushed out alternating portions of the trailer and diagonally opposite the other, but now folded up as sofas for the daytime needs of space. The one sofa by the lofted area sits against the wall on the center side of the camp. Between the lofted bedroom and the center side sofa is a small kitchenette. The opposite sofa, the one nearest the trailer door, sits away from the door, on the side away from the center of the camp. Both sofa backs are set next to windows. There are two double sets of sleeping bags and nightwear stored nearby to match these bedding needs. The rear of the trailer holds the secluded main bedroom and evidence shows two people sleeping there. A bathroom, with a door that opens to the main living area, is located between the main bed and the rest of the trailer.

A woman and her husband, a woman and her husband, as I survey each place again; two, four, six ... and two: eight all together. We have seven. I look again into the main bedroom. It looks like two slept there, but there is a cot folded up beside the main bed. Who'd want a cot when they have a bed to sleep on? Who'd accept this odd man out sleeping scene? They'd sleep somewhere else, but where? I wouldn't tolerate another man in my bedroom when I'm with my wife, and a second woman sleeping on the cot makes no sense at all. Seven people, though, with eight places to sleep means we could be looking for one for sure.

"One," I announce as I exit the trailer. "Dere's a bed in the back made real tight and a cot. So I think one."

"One," Radwell echoes with a nod of his head.

"There's sleepin' stuff laid out here in the cab of this first truck, too," calls out Meirs, as he returns. "Nothing in the cab of the green truck;

the green camper and its cab are stuffed full of supplies everywhere, man. Don't look like ain't nobody sleepin' in there."

"So," Radwell drawls long with delight, "We do have two—at least two. But that don't make sense, now, does it?" he asks, as he glances at me. "If you say a cot in the back and he says one … that don't make sense—one sleepin' alone in a truck all by himself, one sleepin' with ... well, that could be interesting ... three gay men—two women and a man, two men and a woman, or just one person alone, the other choosing the truck? Huh, interesting, confusing. Last night was all right to be out in the truck. We were runnin' around in it last night—but to sleep out in a truck more than a night? Durin' a huntin' season over the next week? It's cold out here, colder at night. Well it *could* make sense since that would make from five to seven men and three women for eight guns, with the women not hunting, but I just don't believe it. Just what do we got here? … Why do we need to guess? What makes sense is we're looking for somebody. How many is not clear. Are there two we're looking for or just the one I suspect—or three?"

Radwell's long-winded rambling got me confused. "Ya mixed me up, man. How many?"

Radwell scoffs, though his mouth does not open while his cheeks and lips expand briefly, before he speaks to me, as he and I watch Meirs leave the trucks and walk over to enter the trailer. "Fuck, Franklin," he starts, "Get past second grade?"

"Huh?" I answer.

"Ahh, the numbers don't add up, Frank. Somebody's missing—at least one," he explains, "And why do I got to think 'bout that this time? Let's ask them how many they are."

Radwell moves over to the front of the captives, near the women, and points his rifle at them; "All of you answer at the same...." Both the hunter and the big man answer together, before Radwell finishes, before the other captives react.

"One!" the hunter quickly calls out.

"Two!" the big man says in harmony.

Radwell and I react in surprise and then anger. Now we know someone is missing and we *have* to know how many there are, where they are. We're surprised the number two was said, and angry just because they interrupted us. Radwell slowly, ominously, draws his words in response.

"How delightful," he leisurely says to them. "Answerin' me before I even ask the question. Now, is it one ... or two, or three? I can safely gather it ain't three. There aren't ten of you here, maybe nine. You would have said so—stupidly said so. Then you would've needed to explain—very exactly, the curious sleepin' arrangement a number like ten would've caused. I suspect I would've caught you lyin' to me with ten. Lyin' gets me angry.

One of you lied to me just now. Understand—you all, we're trying *not* to kill you, so don't get me angry. Don't lie to me again. Understand? So does lip—if either of you care for your lives, you will not give me lip again, understand—you'll answer correctly."

For emphasis Radwell places the point of his gun to the blond haired man's head. The man instantly becomes rigid from the gun's touch, and as the moments begin to tick by he begins to shake faintly, his face flushes red and beads of sweat appear on his forehead, staying there through a stiff cold breeze that blows through the camp, for Radwell is purposely slow to continue.

"Now," Radwell states as he lightly begins to tap the tip of the gun against the side of this man's face. "Would anyone care to answer me just how many men there are?"

"Seven," resigns the hunter.

"Seven," the big man sadly agrees.

But during their answers the blond man with the gun to his head meekly says; "Eight."

"Found a nine millimeter! The place is clean otherwise," Meirs announces loudly from the entrance to the trailer. The hunter's shoulder slumps just a little, almost without notice. In fact, neither Radwell nor I are quite sure we've seen him do it. We react off each other to confirm the hunter man had moved so.

I lean toward the hunter to catch his attention and whisper; "Too bad, asshole, we got ya gun." His jaw clenches tight in response.

"Meirs," chides Radwell, "Sometimes your timing is just impeccable. Good you found the gun. Keep checking."

"Alright," answers Meirs as he slips the large handgun under his pants waistline as he moves off.

"Two said seven, blondie said eight," I remind Radwell.

Radwell is staring down the hunter while my words cause the blond man to speak his answer again and yet again, his voice cracking in fear; "There are eight of us here," he almost whimpers, as Radwell renews his tapping the gun's tip against his head. "Eight. *Eight,*" blondie says as he tilts his head away from the guns painful tapping.

"Well, well," slowly words Radwell, "We have a liar in our midst. Let's see, which one could that be?" he ponders, still staring at the hunter. "I wonder who." Radwell turns his eyes towards me and I look expectantly back. Radwell then looks at Cal who returns a similar questioning face. "Should we find out who these people are before we start killing them?"

"Fine with me," Cal replies, "But keep one of the women alive, you know, for a while at least."

Radwell grunts. “You don’t stop thinkin’ ‘bout your cock, do ya Cal?”

“Not when you got one as big as mine,” flatly declares Cal, which makes Radwell chuckle, Tollin sneer, and me smile.

“Franklin?” Radwell asks.

“Not me. If I don’t know their names I can’t confess ta killin’ ‘em, can I man?” Radwell is worrying me again but I believe what we’re doing is just show. We have agreed to avoid useless killing, but killing them could be useful.

“Chicken-shit,” Radwell says to me.

“We agreed to hole up a few days and get out of here. That’s what we should do. And tie ‘em up when we leave. No killin’—we agreed,” Tollin asserts firmly from where he stands a few feet away—ah, so they, in Radwell’s truck, thought the same way we did approaching the camp.

Radwell turns and scowls at him. “Yeah, like Franklin here really listened to that shit.”

“Hey,” I assert, “The man tried ta kill me, man. Had no choice, man. Shut-up.”

Radwell only laughs. “I know you, Franklin, you’re a fuckin’ liar—you enjoyed it.”

I set hard angry eyes on him, yet I can’t do or say anything—the truth prevents me.

47
(Franklin)

"Nothin' in either truck," Meirs says as he walks up, interrupting us. "Nothin' else in ta trailer. The kitchen gots some metal knives and stuff, but mostly plastic shit. What you want me to do?"

"I don't," answers Radwell gruffly, "I want Cal. Cal, you go, take this ... no, wait a minute. What's your name—you each tell me your name," Radwell commands as he takes the gun away from blondie's head and gently pokes the first woman's breast with it. "Starting with you. Don't make me wait," he warns.

"Paula," she answers quickly.

"Paula what?" he questions.

"Paula Morris," she replies, her lips and face showing signs of trembling and of wanting to pull her body away from the gun. She sets her jaw, attempting to become resolute.

"Can you prove it?" Radwell asks, suspicious of her answer, "After all we may have more than one liar here. Are you saying if I find your purse the credit cards and driver's license I find in it will say Morris?"

Paula's head drops and her eyes tear. "No," she confesses, "Paula, Paula Smith."

"Smith! Oh. Smith. How convenient to give a name like Smith. How about Anderson, Johnson, Jackson, or Miller? You lyin'?" Radwell mocks. Her lips tremble so much I doubt she can say a word as Radwell raises his gun to her head. "I said are you lyin'—*bitch*?"

"She's my wife," the hunter interrupts firmly, watching the gun move from her to himself, as he watches Radwell's eyes.

"*Did I tell you to speak?*" Radwell growls, glaring at the hunter with widened eyes. The hunter does not respond. "Your wife takes after you, you lyin' piece of dog shit." Radwell quick steps over and bellows at the next captive; "You! What's your name?"

"Gay," she spits out just before Radwell roughly pokes the gun barrel stiffly into her side. She winces from its force and a short high-pitched whimper escapes her. She forces herself to be as undisturbed as she can after that, staring straight ahead into the back of Paula, but sweat runs from her forehead and down the sides of her cheeks, her eyes staying wet with tears.

"Did someone accuse me of being gay?" Radwell taunts. He carries a slight smile as he glances first at Cal, at Meirs, and then to me.

I pull a smile onto my face. "No," I say, "I think she was sayin' her name's Gay."

"You really think so?" Radwell asks, straightening his body and cocking his head to one side, glancing again at Cal, Meirs and I, before leaning forward and getting close to her ear; "Who ... your parents really loved you, didn't they?" he says and laughs. "And who are you married to?"

"Bill," she answers. Her voice quivers as she still refuses to look sideways at Radwell, or to any of us.

"And who's he?"

"Me," the big bull man says.

"You people don't get it, do you?" Radwell snarls. "I'll tell you when to speak." Radwell mumbles to himself, cussing. "Which one of you women cook?"

A moment passes before we hear the answer.

"I do," Paula declares with resignation.

"Cal," he says as another cold breeze chills us, "Take this Paula inside. Get her cookin' somethin' hot. Watch her close. Make sure she eats what she cooks—and you pick out the pieces. Go! ... Meirs?"

"Yeah."

"Did you find any duct tape or rope when you were lookin' 'round?"

"Yeah, plenty, why? You want me ta tie 'em up?"

"Start with this big guy—your name again?" Radwell orders the bull.

"Bill", he answers.

"Start with Billy-boy here," Radwell says to Meirs.

"Be back," Meirs replies.

"Your turn, missy," Radwell announces as he shoves the point of his gun into the left breast of the dark haired brunette.

"M-Mary," she answers.

"M-Mary," Radwell mocks, "You scared?"

"Y-Yes," she answers as her voice cracks and her lips tremble. She, like Gay, keeps herself looking straight ahead.

"You 'fraid of dyin' Mary?"

"Y-Yes."

"Y-You think you're gonna die now, M-Mary?" Radwell sneers as he plays with her emotions.

"I-I...."

"I like hearing you say 'Y-Yes', it's so cute," Radwell says as he cocks his head one way and then the other as he stares at her, "C-Can I hear you say y-yes again?"

Mary opens her mouth but hesitates to say the word, tears stream from her eyes as her face flushes like blondie man had, believing if she says yes Radwell will kill her. Radwell pokes the tip of the gun into the side of her face, leaving a red circular mark. “C’mon,” he demands, poking her again, “C’mon, I want to hear you say it again.”

Enough, I think, Rad’ enough. You senseless behind a gun, or do ya got a point? “I think they’re plenty scared, yo. No need ta scare further, man.”

“Shut your face, Franklin,” Radwell growls, looking to me. “We ain’t gonna be playin’ good bad guy—bad bad guy here. They’re gonna know to do what we tell them when we tell ‘em and I wanna make damn sure of that happening—got it?”

I can’t go no further. “Got it.”

“I think they got that, too,” Tollin adds sternly. “We agreed not to kill.”

Radwell scowls at Tollin but gives no response as he again carries that unsettled look in his eye that troubled me before. His attentions turn back to the woman beside him, reaching to her, caressing her face with the backs of his fingers of his free hand. She pulls her face away from his touch. Radwell caustically sighs as he takes his hand back, resenting her action. “What’s the matter? Don’t like my touch, huh? Don’t like my touch … you will.”

Meirs comes out of the trailer and draws near to pull the bull man, Bill, out of the line up. Meirs gives me his rifle and begins wrapping Bill’s hands behind his back with duct tape. He works quickly and wraps the man securely. Does much the same with his legs, though giving enough length to let him move, making Bill look like he has prison ankle cuffs on and a chain strung between them. He shuffles Bill over and sits him down against the outside of the trailer.

“Ah, Meirs and his timing again, so wonderful,” Radwell comments out loud, as he once more pokes the tip of his gun into Mary’s cheekbone. “Franklin, too,” he spits out resentfully in afterthought. “Almost makes me forget where I was at. Bet you wish I did, don’t ya?” he asks the woman.

“Y-Ye...” Mary stops short of finishing the word.

Radwell forces a breath from himself to try and laugh at her as Meirs reclaims his gun from me.

The hunter, Smith, is studying us intently.

“I don’t like dis man,” I say as I raise my own gun and point it directly at this Smith.

Radwell sighs, his shoulders slumping just a bit, taking a glance at Smith. “Yeah, he’s an asshole.” Then Radwell turns back to Mary and addresses her; “Looks like I keep getting rudely interrupted by the well intentioned men of mine. Good for you, I've lost my desire to play around with you because of it—for now. Franklin?"

"Yeah?"

"Tie these two women up. Put them over by Billy-boy," Radwell instructs me.

"Yeah," I answer, stepping away and exchanging my rifle for the duct tape Meirs hands me before pulling the two women from the line. I take each of them over to the trailer to stand facing Bill the bull. I move behind the women and let my hands pass heavily across the breasts of one woman and linger there on the other. Each of them squirms and shakes, and each dares to try to pull my hands off them, before I draw their arms back behind them. I laugh quietly in their ears as I tape their arms, before making them move backwards over against the trailer, directing each of them this time with one of my hands in their crotch and the other feeling, squeezing, a breast. I delight in their squirming, the rage in their eyes, the high pitch whines of fear, and their tones of intense anger which escape their clenched un-taped mouths. I smile at Gay's husband, Bill, and give her an extra feel, just for him.

"How you doin' in dere, Cal?" I call inside from where I crouch as I tape the women's legs like Meirs had done with Bill.

"Doin' just fine," he answers.

"She actually cookin' us up somethin' in dere or is she cookin' you up some?"

"She's actually cookin' us up some. I'm too hungry for food right now, man, but she is kind of cold, bein' she's half dressed and all."

I hear Meirs and Radwell chuckle behind me and I smile while making sure each woman and Bill are far enough away from each other so they can't help the other with their bindings. I move back to join Radwell and Meirs, standing near the line of remaining captives.

Drew stands off away from us by the open U corner of the main trailer, watching the entire scene, being quiet. I take him as standing guard for us as we do our thing. He will make sure no surprises come our way from the outside. Perez has been quietly doing the same but at the near corner of the first truck.

"Well," Radwell says in a more relaxed tone, "We have five left to question, here. Let's find out who and where the missing man is—or is it men? Why this man, or men, aren't here right now—stuff like that."

"Maybe it's a woman?" offers Meirs.

"Seriously," berates Radwell as he looks at Meirs. "Meirs, get a brain."

48
(Franklin)

"Seriously," berates Radwell as he looks at Meirs. "Meirs, get a brain."

Radwell steps back as he says this, as much in reaction to yet another stiff cold breeze sweeping in as to watch over the five captive men better.

This breeze causes me to glance skyward to see tall, thick, and gray wall of clouds fully stretching across the horizon, moving in from the north and west. I can't see the bottom of the front, it hangs so low to the ground the trees hide it. The storm's height disappears into the dull grayness of the sky above it. A half an hour, if that, the storm will be here. It's coming in fast and looks bad ... real bad.

"I'm not interested in jerkin' ya around this time, guys," Radwell says to the five, "I want the answers now. How many are missing?"

"One!" the blond haired man quickly replies. Smith reluctantly acknowledges. The cowboy is just as reluctant in his agreement. The two utility men are silent, and we did not expect them to speak.

"Ya know," I say, as I consider what I just witnessed, "I noticed a tight thing between dis cowboy here n dis guy Smith before. You notice dey agreed after blondie said one? Like whatever said first dey know dey'd betta go along with? As if dey know dere's two out dere and know when dey'd be coming back, man? Ya notice dat, Rad?"

He tilts his head, glances at me, as he ponders. "What's your name, cowboy?"

No one answers until Radwell swings his gun to the man of his choice. "You know I mean you. Do you want to risk your life being stupid?"

"Doug," he answers slow in a deep clear voice.

Radwell bobs his head indicating he wants a great deal more said by this man. "Do-oug," he pries, as the gun waves in the man's face.

"Sorensen," the cowboy replies, as he tries hard to look unperturbed by the gun barrel floating by his face.

Radwell sighs; "Damn cowboys sure know how to say a lot, don't they? ... Well, cowboy Doug, is the man right? Is there only one?"

"You got it," Doug clearly answers, his voice firm and steady. He shows little fear, except for a single quiver in his lip that appears briefly on the left side of his mouth.

Radwell seems amused.

I'm annoyed—at both men; Doug and Radwell—Doug is not cooperative and Radwell is still playing games. Meirs, who now stands guard near the evergreens yet can hear us easily, is going along with whatever is happening. He doesn't care. Tollin is again silent. I feel the urge to hurry on and get settled with a storm approaching, as more cold breezes rush by.

"Okay Smithy boy," Radwell says as he turns his attentions to the hunter man, "I say there's still two of you out there. You prove me wrong."

A pause before Smith concedes; "There's two out there."

Meirs, Radwell, and I straighten our stances and look at each other. We all react this way because we can't tell whether Smith is lying or telling the truth in resignation.

Radwell asks him, slowly; "Do you think you answered my question, Smithy-boy?"

"You … you say there's two out there … there's two." Smith is hesitant, realizing his precarious position and that Radwell must be looking for an excuse to abuse, which I think he is.

"You ain't saying much to me, liar-boy," Radwell responds, "Except saying stuff that will let me believe what I want to believe. You a yes man in real life, Smithy?"

Smith hesitates again as Radwell waves the end of his gun barrel at him. Smith doesn't always watch the gun; he also watches Radwell's eyes and body language. He's trouble, for sure, for not many got the mind to watch a gunman's eyes while under the point of a gun.

"You got the bunk in the trailer and the stuff in the truck to prove it," Smith finally answers, the smallest cracking in his voice giving evidence to the stress he feels within. "Plus, if you don't know the area, goin' out alone in these woods is a bad idea."

"I didn't say anything 'bout goin' out there."

Smith shakes his head slightly, hesitant to correct Radwell, but he does; "Not you … I mean for any one to go out alone without already knowing the place very well."

"You're a fool, too, to correct me—you think I didn't realize that—huh?"

"Don't know what you realize, man. I was just clarifying to make sure we understood each other, that's all."

"That's all, huh? Well, one thing I can say 'bout you, Smithy boy," Radwell taunts, "Is that you lie good."

"I'm not ly..." Smith begins as Radwell lowers his gun towards Smith's legs and pulls the trigger. The loud crack of the shotgun and the spray of dirt behind the far side of Smith make us jump as we watch Smith go to the ground landing stiffly on his right side, holding the back of his left thigh up off the dirt and grass, cussing like a crazy man from the sudden intense pain. Radwell laughs at Smith's utterances as he butts the end of the hot gun barrel against Smith's head, while Smith grabs it in automatic response with his bloodied left hand.

"Stay put!" Radwell orders all of us as he peers down along the gun to enjoy the defiant stare on Smith's face. "I can pull the trigger a whole lot faster than you can push the gun away from your face, asshole, so try it. I want you to," Radwell says quickly with enjoyment, and with a measure of alarming calmness. Smith acknowledges and slowly removes his hand from Radwell's gun. "Franklin," Radwell says to me, "Tie Smith up. He talks and lies too damn much. See how hurt he is, too, just for laughs."

"Yo, what he said made freakin' sense to me Rad—why'd ya shoot him?"

"Made sense to me, too, Franky, too much so. That was the problem, man. It was too logical …." Radwell replies.

"Too logical not to consider two men bein' out there?" questions Tollin.

"Franklin, Tollin, my gut says he is lyin' and while it seems good *logic* to have two men out there I just somehow believe we are not searching for two, just one."

"Rad?" I say, bewildered.

"Franklin, I told you to do somethin', now go do it."

I resent being ordered to do this sort of thing a second time, like an errand boy, since I did the women. I'm confused, worried too, over why he shot Smith. There can so easily be two men out there. I don't get it. Radwell is getting too big for his pants but I'm going to do what he says anyway, because Smith is the macho hunter man, because I got an easy excuse to weaken Smith further, because he is trouble, because he defied us, because he *damaged me*.

After Smith took his hand off Radwell's gun barrel he put it to his wound in hopes of stopping his bleeding. Now that I'm over him I pull this bloody hand away from his body by grabbing his forearm, not wanting to get bloody myself, to give a quick look at his wound. I ignore his subdued cussing and his angry pain-driven threats, because they mean nothing.

He's lucky. His wound is shallow. The slug missed major flesh or arteries, just shredded and wrinkled his skin back some, his muscle is barely touched, all blood red with some dull yellow fat mixed in. The wound crudely forms a shallow cupped shape on the backside of his lower thigh, about two knuckles of my index finger in width, about that long in length, half a knuckle in depth. There is some scorching of his clothes and skin by the powder burns from the closeness of the gun's blast—nothing to get a medal over. I don't know medical stuff, but this seems a clean wound, for what it is. He'll live. It'll just bleed good for awhile. He is real lucky because a tiny bit of distance more into his flesh and the slug surely would've grabbed enough to make a horrific wound. He's lucky, too, that it was a slug, I think pellets would show differently and grab more flesh. If Radwell had wanted to take his leg off, he's a poor shot. He sure didn't want him dead, or to die quick. Why did Radwell do this? If I was going to shoot someone, I'd kill them—don't let loose ends stay loose, cut them off.

I stand Smith up and push him towards the trailer. He hobbles and hops over to it without resisting. He's too concerned about his wound to bother giving me lip. I tie him up good and tight and kick him in the crotch for good measure—after I have him kneeling on the ground. I give him a knee to his head, too, banging it against the trailer's wall, just because I want to. I'm disappointed though—no new blood comes running from his nose or mouth, but kicking him again will make me look weak.

Cal showed himself quickly at the doorway to the main trailer, using the blonde woman as a shield, soon after hearing the blast from Radwell's gun. He still stands there with his gun at the ready as I finish with Smith. Cal had cussed us after finding out what happened. He stopped to watch me, but cusses us again as he pulls the crying woman back inside by the back strap of her bra as I start moving away from the trailer, but I'm slow to leave as I look over the two brunettes and Bill, the big man. He is showing a face of manly fear, one of being helpless and wishing he'd die attacking us than the way he now thought he would, dying while being all tied up. The two women are both quietly emotional—not crying, but show fear and confusion, questions to what has happened and why, what will happen, all seem to flash across their expressive faces, but what catches me is that they both can meet my eyes with theirs, though with forced effort. This bothers me enough for me to step up and cup one of the women's jaws in my hand as I push her head against the trailer wall.

Gay gives out a restrained one-syllable yelp before she glares defiantly through her teary eyes. How this look turns me on. I look down at her as I stand there over her and think of other things to do with her mouth. I start to smile when she speaks up.

"Assholes," she hisses and I mentally laugh.

"Yo—baby," I reply, "I like your style, gets me on—want ta get away from dis crowd?"

"Fuck you," she hisses again, keeping her voice down so Radwell won't be drawn to us. She's a smart one, I realize.

"Later, you and me, we can do dat, but now I want ta know what ya do for a livin'," I state, "And I don't want no freakin' lies."

She draws in a deep breath and glances at her friends and husband, who nod for her to answer. "I'm a nurse," she answers. Her breath frosts heavily, as the air has gotten colder over the last few minutes, "I ... take care of elderly people."

"Ah," I exclaim, "Dat explains ta calmer, heartless look in ya eyes. Ya used ta seeing people die. I'll get ya later—baby. I'll get ya ta fix dis slice in my chest, too, later. Bet your man would want dis cut cared right away, like a good wimp. I can wait. I'm real and your man ain't. You're gonna know what a real man is like real soon—and you'll enjoy it." I finish by pushing her head back against the trailer wall once more and feel a breast, squeezing it painfully tight as she tries to turn away from me while I look towards her husband and smile, enjoying his reaction, before leaving them and returning to stand near Radwell and Meirs.

49
(Franklin)

"And you, what's your name?" Radwell is doing the asking.

Blondie instantly responds; "Mark. Mark Schultz."

"Ta gun really has a affect on ya, don't it white boy?" I taunt Mark.

He remains silent, then realizes I take him as a coward and he cautiously straightens himself up.

"Ah, I like defiance," I jeer through my teeth on seeing this. Radwell smirks in pleasure.

"Meirs, Franklin," Radwell announces, "The last shot might bring in whoever is out there now. Post yourselves somewhere where you can still see me and the entrance to the trailer while we wait for him—or them—got it? And someone get the ones by the trailer inside for Cal to watch. We don't want the sight of tied up friends so clearly alerting the ones, or one, coming in that somethin's wrong here. Drew—you see anything happenin' out there?"

"No. You know I would have said something."

"Perez?"

"Nothing, man."

I silently point to the line up of the four remaining men. Radwell replies; "I got a plan going on here, don't you worry. I'll take care of them in a minute. Now go do what I said."

Meirs starts moving the people inside. That'll take a few moments. I move away, though staying within easy hearing of Radwell, posting myself off the front of the farthest utility truck. Perez is by the first truck and Drew stands in the opposite corner from me by the rear of the main trailer. I give a quick search over the line of the south woods which stand so close to us here on this side, and to the east, but I keep glancing back to watch what is going on.

Tollin keeps his gun on the remaining captive men as he stands watch and Radwell keeps that unresolved disturbed look as he rocks impatiently back and forth in his stance beside the captives as stiff cold breezes, carrying flakes of snow, sweep through the camp. What plan does he got in his head and why ain't he sharing it with us?

"That third woman there," Radwell points to the dark haired woman named Mary as she is being brought inside the trailer, the last to be put inside, "Which one of you four belong to her?" Radwell demands, as he studies Mark and Doug's responses, and ignoring the two utility men. Doug and Mark both hesitate before Mark answers he is. The hesitation ain't much but is all Radwell, or I, need.

"Franklin, you're moving about back there—you can hear us, can't you?" Radwell asks.

I nod my head as I rotate back around the corner of the truck for them to see me better. "Yeah, I can hear ya."

"You see them react?"

"Yeah."

"Well, what do you think?"

"Ain't dem," I answer, as I watch Meirs hurry out of the trailer and move past the center group of captives, Radwell and Tollin, to go behind the evergreens where I first saw Smith, and disappear from my sight, to take his post at the fourth corner of the camp.

"How about you, Tollin? What do you think?" Radwell asks.

"Neither of 'em," he agrees.

"Neither of you," sigh's Radwell after he's done watching Meirs, "Ah—so, it is her husband who is out in these woods, or out somewhere. Must be … must be. I understand. Yes I do, blondie, your attempt tries ta deny us leverage over her husband when he does return, but you decide to become heroic and ta lie ta me like your friend Smith over there in the trailer…"

"No sir! She is my wife!" Mark responds desperately.

Drew speaks up from his post; "Can he prove it?"

Radwell pauses. "Well, yeah, blondie-boy—can you prove it?"

A strained expression comes across Mark's face. His mind races for an answer.

Radwell signals for me to hurry near. "Answer quietly blondie-boy, I'm going to have Franklin check on you."

As I come to stand next to them Mark has yet to answer.

"Any day now," Radwell calmly reminds the man.

"Her … her middle name is her maiden name," he offers.

Radwell nods his head and almost smiles. "That is pretty unique. That is. I think I need a couple more things like how long you been married, how'd you meet? That should be enough."

Mark is sweating again. The cowboy shows signs of answering for him but Radwell sweeps the gun to the cowboy's face and shakes his head in silent reminder not to say a thing.

"Jus … just about ten years. We … we just kind of met one night."

"Oh, a few more questions … second marriage for both of you, then?"

Mark shakes his head in agreement.

"She older or younger?"

"Older."

"Where was she born?"

"Illinois."

"Brothers and sisters—how many?"

Mark hesitates. "Uh, I've answered enough…"

"How many?" insists Radwell.

Mark squirms. "You can just, just ask her our last name."

"Too easy. How many?" insists Radwell again.

Mark squirms again.

"How many?" Radwell commands.

"Three," Mark's voice trembles; "Three sisters, two brothers."

"Go find out," Radwell instructs me.

I hurry inside the trailer. Mary is sitting on the floor against the wall near the entrance to the lofted bedroom, her feet and hands taped.

"Been told ta ask ya questions. Answer quick, truthful," I tell her.

"Why? Why do I have to?" she asks, her eyes wide in apprehension.

"Because I tell ya to."

"I-I'm not answering anything."

"Someone's going ta get hurt bad out dere if dese questions ain't answered. We can make it you who hurts—or also, if ya like." Clearly she doesn't want anyone hurt off her answers nor does she want to get hurt herself. She is confused as to what to do. "What is special about your name?"

She returns a puzzled look. "Special? My name is Mary?"

"Your middle name."

No hesitation. "It's my maiden name."

I'm relieved. Though I don't care whether Mark told the truth or not, the truth can end Radwell's games and determine the number of men missing. "How long you and Mark been married?"

Again she looks perplexed, her eyes widen once more as she ponders the question. She composes herself quickly and answers slowly; "About four years—he won't know the exact time—he's odd, he doesn't keep track that way."

"Number a years ain't dat hard, woman."

"Listen … please. We've been married actually a little over four but we met years before and dated no one else. We sometimes consider those years as being married, too, you know?"

"So, how many?"

"Many what?"

"Ya stupid—years."

"Um-ah, since we met?"

"Keep bein' stupid woman," I reply as I nod my head impatiently. I recognize she is wisely keeping her replies open-ended, but I also know women think of these things differently than men and that she intends for me to think her way. That doesn't matter, her answers match close enough for me. "He older or younger?"

"Younger." She doesn't look at ease with her answer and she reads my face before she asserts; "I am older."

"Where were you born?"

"Waukegan."

"Where's dat?"

"Illinois."

"How'd you meet?"

"Personal ads."

"What?"

"We met one night after personal ads."

"Personal ads … what's dat?"

"What?"

"What are they?"

"You put a notice in the newspaper and someone responds."

I tilt my head in surprise. "Mmm. Didn't know dat. Why'd dya pick him?"

"I-I answered his—no beer gut and with hair on his head."

I scoff. Again, women think different, I accept the answer. Personal ads, however, is something a man will remember.

"Last question. How many brothers n sisters ya have?"

She hesitates long on this one. "You can't expect him to know this," she pleads.

"Why not, bitch?" I sternly ask.

She draws herself back against the wall; "Be-because the … the …."

She is thinking fast, searching. "How many?" I growl, leaning toward her face.

"I-I'm one of ten," she blurts out.

I rise, turn, and begin walking away.

"But-but the situation is confusing," she says calling after me. "Family situation, you know? He can give a different answer and be right."

I hear but ignore her as I exit the trailer.

Mark's expression is of a man looking inward on himself in a resigned sort of way.

Radwell looks expectantly at me as I near.

"Said all correctly except for how many brothers and sisters," I state as I see Radwell's face brighten with gleeful anticipation over this error between their answers, so I quickly add; "But she said whatever number he gave could be correct 'cause while she is one a ten, man, dere is some sort a situation of family dat confuses people."

Radwell's gleeful expression leaves him for one of consternation. "What's that supposed to mean?"

"Don't know. Didn't care. All ta answers basically match, man. Got one more thing though … blondie—how'd you come to meet her dat one night?"

Mark looks at me with fear. "What?" he softly asks.

"Ya two met one night."

"Y-yeah."

"Dere was something special dat brought ya two together—what was it?"

"I … I don't understand. Why do I need to answer more …"

"Better reply, blondie," threatens Radwell.

"We just met, that's all."

"What brought you together?" I ask.

"We just met!"

"According ta her you didn't just meet on accident, man. Now tell us. Dis is something you should know. How did ya arranged meeting with her come about?" I demand.

"I-I don't know what to say!" Mark blurts out, almost in tears. "What do you want from me—I answered all your questions."

Drew speaks up from his distance behind us; "How many out there?"

"Three," Mark answers before thinking.

All of us pause and fall silent, watch as Mark comes to realize his error. The moment he does, Radwell continues; "Well, Smithy was lucky for whatever reason there was at the time, just getting his leg shot, but I said I didn't want no more lies from any of you. You ain't agreeing with what you said earlier; one out there, two out there, now you say three. Disturbing. Really disturbing. Three really don't make sense ta me. Now blondie, how did you meet your wife?"

Mark's mouth opens then closes as he breathes quiet sighs, quickening in pace, as he closes his eyes briefly. His pallor is making him a really white guy, for a white guy. "It can be three," he daringly protests, "One guy has business in town, man…"

"I don't care…"

"…and he'd be going back instead of comin'…"

"I don't care—how did you meet your wife?"

"I-I can't answer with a gun to my face. Shit, if I say something you take as wrong you'll kill me!"

"That's right Blondie—you got that right," Radwell coolly replies. "Now you answer me or you *are* dead."

"Please?"

"Blondie don't beg. It makes ya look ugly."

Mark hesitates, breathing rapidly and shallow, sweat breaking out all over him.

"Blondie?"

"A … a blind date maybe—I can't remember—please don't shoot me!"

Radwell looks to me to confirm Mark's answer. I shrug my shoulders; "Personal ad."

"That's like a blind date!" Mark pleads.

I first don't think of it that way yet I'm about to agree with Mark when I see the edges of Radwell's mouth curl up into a slight smile of anticipation.

"Lies, lies, lies. So, good-bye, Blondie." And with that Radwell puts his shotgun to Mark's head and pulls the trigger before I can protest.

The sound and act happens so fast, so unexpected, everyone except Radwell jumps. As Mark's body falls sideways into a heap, Tollin reacts the most wildly, turning and jumping, cussing at Radwell for killing the man for such petty reasons, and Cal once again very quickly reappears at the trailer's entrance cursing behind the shield of the horror-stricken blonde woman. Meirs bursts through the evergreens to this sight and he glances my way before he also cusses Radwell, joining the rest of us. We had not wanted to kill anyone here—certainly not execute someone! This is not what we agreed to earlier. We wanted our breakout to remain free from this notoriety. If, when the law learns we killed in such a sadistic way, their efforts will double. They'll shoot first and ask questions never.

"Damn it, Radwell, you fool," I shout.

"Damn Franklin," Radwell muses, in a striking calmness of tone, "You just killed for fun. Killed twice today. You ain't convincing me with your sissy-like wounds you got. I wanted some fun, too."

"I did not execute dem!" I shout back.

Radwell smirks with a slow shrug of his shoulders. "Yours still dead ain't they?"

He tells Meirs to get back to his post, but as Meirs turns he suddenly stops his angry cussing and draws our attentions with him towards the sight of an unknown pair of men standing off a distance into the field.

The men had been approaching us along the vehicle trail, but now stand motionless in shocked silence within clear sight of the camp. The two men carry several logs between them, logs long and strong enough to be used for almost anything. They had either carried this load a while or have hurried here after hearing the earlier shots, for they look strained and soaked with sweat despite the cold. They have seen the effects of blondie's shot and are stunned by his death, now drop their load of wood as they notice Meirs point them out.

My attention diverts to the quick movements of Radwell, who jams his shotgun into the side of Terrance and pulls the trigger—another blast, another spray of flesh, another body falls.

Radwell's intended distraction keeps the approaching men paused on the path as Meirs raises his gun and takes aim at them, as Drew also does, but the men now jump with fear on seeing this second man fall and are running by the time Meirs and Drew pull their triggers.

"Go after them!" snarls Radwell to Meirs, who begins chasing the men. Drew, however, stays.

"Fuck it Radwell!" I shout viciously as I start towards him, "Why'd ta fuck ya have ta do this, god-dammit! We said we weren't going ta oft nobody! What if ta fuckin' law heard those shots, huh? Damn you!"

"Shut up," Radwell answers firmly, without raising his voice, as he carefully watches me approach. "As soon as you killed that first man this path was set, so don't go cryin' away here, nigger."

"Soon as ta woman and station man you killed, nigger," I retort. "My guy tried ta run. You did. You started this," I respond as I stop in my tracks. Radwell has swung the tip of his gun into my projected path. He does not point it at me, but he is ready to, the intent is clear. My blood boils but my emotions haven't taken full command of me yet. I stand my ground and go no further.

It is Doug who speaks next and with such inherent authority I know we can't say no, as he dares to lean over his fallen friend and, with tenderness, examines his dead body. "I will cover Mark up," Doug states, "Treat him decent. There's a pair a plastic parkas in the trailer. I'm getting them, to cover both men up," Doug finishes, as he rises to a stand in front of us, his eyes burning through ours. Without waiting for our answer he turns and heads towards the trailer.

Cal, not hearing any of this because of the squirming and loud fretting from the woman he holds, and from those within the trailer itself, points his rifle at Doug, using one arm, and orders him to stop before Radwell waves Cal off and tells him to let Doug cover his fallen friends.

50

My shoulders, hands, and forearms are tight and sore from the strain of chopping and trimming the logs, but now carrying them, constantly pulling them through the heavy underbrush, even with Tom's help, brings such exertion that I am winded, all but exhausted—and Tom is, too. This time, as we free the lengths of wood from an entangling finger-like branch of the thicket growth, they slip out of our hands and we jump back, letting the lengths of wood drop on each other and onto the ground with rapid clunks.

The sounds of them hitting, however, come across strange; there are echoes across the woods—echoes that had not come from the logs—the timing was not right. Tom heard these sounds, too.

"What was that? That ain't from these logs," Tom states.

"I know—I don't think so. Gunshot?"

Tom and I ponder. "Has to be," Tom answers and, with a shrug of his shoulders says; "Must be the women practicin'."

"Hey ... hope they're not aiming this way," I reply as I lean over to place my hands on my knees, to catch my breath. "I need a rest, Tom."

"Me too."

A minute or so later I shake my arms and legs to loosen my muscles and get ready to pick up the logs with a reluctance of knowing I will have to make this trip several times more. My back will hurt after this day is done. "Definitely getting Mark or Doug to help us."

"Or? Or? No OR about it, man, they're both comin' ta help."

I smile, nod my head at Tom. "You got the better idea."

"Well, yeah, Mr. Engineer, you're not that smart."

"Thanks. My ex used to tell that to me, too. Mary disagrees, though, she says I'm smart."

"Yeah—smart-ass."

We soon enter the open grove of oaks, maples, and hickory trees—no thickets here, yet carrying the logs seems just as hard to do. What a relief, however, not to fight the underbrush any more, I think any more of that would do me in. Those thickets had not come to an end soon enough.

Brisk cool breezes greet us as we leave these mature woods and enter the open field on the hill across from and above our camp and we make the turn to our left to follow the tree line down towards the truck trail. While the sky remains bright to the east there are storm clouds sweeping in from the west and northwestern horizon behind us. From what we can see the clouds are menacingly dark with no definition to their heights. It is not a good sight and this storm seems to be moving in fast. Already some flakes of snow are being carried in by the wind.

Over the tall grass and the bit of a rise that is between us and the camp we can just see the tops of the heads of our friends from where we walk. They all appear to be standing around the center of our camp. "What is that all about?" I wonder.

"Got me, man. I need to put these down again," Tom replies. "Don't think no one's seen us yet. I wanta rest, don't want them teasing us, ya know—we gotta carry these all the way in or they'll make fun of us, ya know."

I nod my head, and while I wouldn't care if they teased us, I don't mind resting some more. "Sure."

We carefully place the logs down on the ground and sit on them. There is no way our friends can see us from the camp, the grass is too tall, and we don't bother looking their way, either. We just look over the north woods and watch the approaching storm.

"We had to leave our coats back at the site, didn't we?" I say.

"Yeah, it's gonna be tough carrying the next load with this storm coming."

"Borrow somebody else's jackets."

"Borrow some *bodies*. The load we got ain't enough."

I look at the approaching storm again. "One more load is all we might get. This storm's coming in fast."

"Maybe they're telling jokes," Tom says, changing the subject as he nods his head to acknowledge me.

"Mm, maybe, I can never remember many jokes," I admit. "I do got one though, wanna hear?"

"Sure," Tom answers without excitement.

"Mary has a couple of nieces, Sarah and Kelly Warner ..."

Tom shrugs his shoulders. "I don't know 'em."

"Yeah, well, they told us this a few weeks ago when they visited. How does a blond pierce her ears? She glues a needle to each of her shoulders and bounces her head once from side to side saying as her head is to one side; 'Oh!' In the middle she says; "My." And to the other side she says; "God!" And when the blond double pierces her ears she bounces twice as she says: 'Oh!' My god!' 'It' 'Really' 'Hurts'."

I watch Tom for a reaction. He finally catches the cue.

"Oh—oh, I get it. That's cute, but don't quit your day job. I was expectin' somethin' a whole lot more vulgar, ya know. Ready?" Tom stands up, causing me to do the same, and we pick up the logs once more.

"Yeah, well, it had been fun to watch their heads bounce side to side, their expressions, and hear their voices changing pitch as they told this joke. Only girls can do it right, I guess."

"Yeah, I guess. Let's get movin'."

"Sure."

The girl's joke still holds a smile on my face as I look up toward camp as we come onto the truck path to hear the shot, see the spray of the shot flying through the air, and Mark's limp body collapsing to the ground.

51

My eyes … see … what … bloody flesh blowing through the air, from a friend who is dropping with a peculiar limpness towards the ground. My body throbs from the sudden pounding of my heart, from the intense shock that strikes me. I am outside myself—not myself. My eyes squint closed and open again to see the remnants of the same scene. My arms and hands go weak as the logs drop free. They hit the ground and one bounces painfully against my shin—yet I hardly notice. Any nightmare of my past cannot match this real horror I see in front of me.

I watch, immobilized, stunned to silence as Mark's body continues to convulse in his death throes as he lay beside Doug, who oddly stands slightly bent over above him, clearly rigid in his own fear, but Doug now looks at someone else. My eyes pull away from Mark to follow Doug's lead to the sight of the man who had just pulled the trigger. This man is stepping back from them with obvious pride in what he has done, delighting in the moment with the immense but sickening powers the gun has given him.

I notice another man standing nearer to the evergreens pointing us out. The man who shot Mark, on seeing us, quickly steps forward and jams his gun into the side of a utility man and blood and flesh spew out the far side of this man as the sounds of another shot announce.

The man, who discovered me, is aiming his rifle at us! What is going on? "*RUN!*"

We turn and run as bullets zip through the grass near us, accompanied by the sounds of the rifle blasts so near, shocking me into wild reactions as I jerk myself to one side in a stumbling manner and spin myself around to crudely follow our trail back towards the nearby woods. Tom is ahead of me.

My body strains for maximum speed as my mind replays the sight of Mark's body collapsing to the ground, the spewing of flesh exploding from the other man's side, the point of a rifle towards us; all surge my body to higher levels of exertion.

The sound of the last rifle blast barely fades when I dare a glance back to see the first man who fired at us coming hard on a run pursuing. The fear I felt a moment ago—my panic, strengthens its restricting grip, heightens my adrenaline rush, as I see this man and hear a voice—my voice, giving out whimpers of fearful desperation as I run. "They're comin'!"

Tom returns a grunt as he runs ahead of me. “How many?”

Why doesn’t he look? I do. “One.” I cannot take deep breaths. I gulp air rapidly. *God—What is happening?* My body tightens in a frightful slowly paralyzing grip as I struggle to maintain my efforts through my fear. My sprint falters across the last of the field, slows me in my confusion, but my legs somehow keep moving and I enter into the grove of woods. Tom is gaining distance from me. I don’t want to lose him. I regain some speed. I look back and cannot see, look back and see; the man is closing on me—fast—*I don’t want to die!*

Crossing the grove of woods with little awareness of doing so I face the first wall of thickets that Tom has already disappeared into and hurl myself into them without hesitation. Tiny branches and thorns grab me, tear and pull my clothing, slap and scratch my face, as I try barreling through, but the increasingly tall thicket draws me down to stumble and fall.

I look back in terror. I am near enough to the open grove behind me to see the often-shadowed image of the pursuing man. He runs like the wind as he begins crossing these woods, his arms and legs pumping hard, his rifle accenting his moves.

He is aware I am down.

I roll and come to my feet, staying low as if moving off sprinter’s blocks in a track race. *Think*; my mind screams emphatically to me—*think!* The word resonates as another wave of fright scorches through my being. I cannot let panic take me like this! Like it had twenty years ago in this same forest—*not again!* Please. Dear God, I have to think. Let me think!

I run with leaps through a knee-high slope of thorny brush, barely keeping my balance as my legs feel their lack of recent conditioning, my feet hardly able to stay in front of me as they fight the snagging undergrowth. My legs are scarcely capable as they bring me up the next slope. I pant painfully, nausea and dizziness start to fill my senses, a taste of bloody sputum rises in my mouth, burning lungs, yet this fear drives me along the vague path and into taller brush and keeps me alert. The tiny branches and thorns of this higher thicket continue to slap and tear at my face, my hands unable to protect enough of me as I bull my way through.

The final thicket is full and compact bordering the opening to the ledge—I know that—he does not. I need to get through it and—the axe—my one chance! Grab the axe and ambush him! The thicket is substantial enough to hide me.

A loud crack—a slap across the right side of my face. What—a bullet? Did it hit me? Yes! I am bleeding! No, a branch tore me. No, he hit me! I am alive. Keep going.

A sound of laughter or cursing arises behind me. He had taken a shot. I’m just enough ahead of him to do what I am thinking. Not much farther, I tell myself. Don't slow before you break through—leave nothing, show nothing, in which to tip him off. *I have to get that axe—it's my only chance!*

52

The wall of brush breaks open before me to the sight of the ledge and the creek bed below and of Tom heading and starting to reach for the rifle we had left here by the two birch trees, as I dive to the ground to my right toward the single birch and roll through the grass and tiny saplings to reach the axe. I grab it and come back onto my feet squatting, breathing heavily, but trying not to make any sound, crouching in readiness as I move up tight against the wall of thickets to the path's opening for the arrival of the man intent on killing us.

Rapid rustling of the thickets sound first then come his footsteps and his own heavy breathing, all within seconds of my grabbing the axe. He comes fast.

Through the undergrowth I see his feet as I swing the axe out from well behind my body, swinging long and hard to where the man should exit the hedge but he senses something and reacts before he appears—I miss! As my arms swing by him I watch the man's eyes look ahead and widen as he sees Tom and our rifle.

The rifle Tom holds doesn't fire!

I continue to turn in a quick circle completely around, pulled by the axe's momentum as I keep it clear of the brush and drive it forward back towards the man I missed.

The man shoots him, shoots Tom, and reloads his bolt action quickly as he begins his turn to face me while stepping away from me at the same time. I hear Tom yelp and catch sight of his body thrust back by the bullets impact. Before this man can bring his gun to bear or step far enough away, my axe comes to where his chest should be. I watch his face as he follows the swing of my axe, until his eyes set to the sight of me, as his own body pulls away, as the axe impacts against his right arm. I see his face wince in sudden pain and his mouth opens to scream as I feel the axe handle jerk loose in my hands from its contact with him. His rifle fires into the ground beside my feet as his right arm gets pulled back and up by the impacting axe. The axe frees completely from my grip and flies out of sight. His rifle has also come free and falls, spinning through the air, the barrel coming down and digging into the ground yet bouncing enough to take that gun out of our reach.

I lurch towards the man as he attempts to turn away from my recovering, reaching grasp. He goes for the handgun in his belt as my hands and shoulder slam into his injured shoulder, both of us tumble over the other to the earth, sprawling and separating from each other. I find myself on the opposite side of him and facing him as I rise to go at him again.

He attempts to pick himself up but the axe did its work; his arm visibly buckles in two with a loud snap. He screams in terrible pain and anger as he drops uncontrollably on this damaged right side, the side furthest from me.

His left hand reaches underneath towards his belt line and the handgun tucked within again as he draws his right knee up below him and begins to rise. He has the handgun free and turns it towards me when blood spurts out from his chest and he stops, looks down to the wound, coughs, looks up toward Tom, before his eyes roll back and he falls face first to the ground. I wait until the gurgling sounds cease in his throat and his body stops jerking before I do anything. I move away from him—to collapse onto the ground myself in a sitting fetal position only steps away, as flurries of snow sweep by in curling descents to the ground, snow that is quickly covering everything about me; the ground, the brush, the trees, this man.

Tom coughs and I jump back into awareness and hurry to him. "Oh-God-Oh-God. What are we doing? Oh-shit, Tom. Tom. Thanks Tom. I owe you my life."

Tom coughs again. "I, I owe you mine, too. I forgot the freaking safety—can ya believe that, the freaking safety."

"Yeah but you got him. You killed him. Thanks, man. Thanks." I see blood soaking his jeans just above his left hip at his waist line. His left hand is covering most of the wound area. I have little medical knowledge but I know what I see is bad. Tom winces in pain and his eyes tell of an inner worry one instinctively understands. "How bad, Tom?"

His jaw shakes as he answers. "Bad, man, getting worse. I need medical help or I ain't gonna make it."

"You're gonna make it, man, you're gonna make it. We'll find help. I don't know where out here, but we're gonna find it ... what're we gonna do? I can't do nothing for you, Tom—I don't know nothing medical. God, why is this all happening? Why are they after us? Why did they kill us? Jesus Christ what can I do? ..."

"Don't ... freak out on me, mister, I need you—understand?" Tom moves, trying to stand, as I make my pleas, but he falls back against the two birch trees and his whole body shudders, his face turns deep red, his arms stiffen in their hold pressing against his wound. He is crying silently as he lays there sideways on the ground below me.

"Tom?"

"It hurts ... it hurts bad, man, shit, it hurts bad," Tom replies, as tears run down his cheeks.

"What can I do—what can I do?"

"Man, ah-man, I don't know—ya gotta put me on ya back and, and carry me outta here. My only chance, man, can ya do it?"

"Um ... um, yeah, Tom, yeah, I'm gonna do that. What do we do?"

"Ah, shit, I don't know ... get the guys rifle. We'll put both guns on my back—this one has a sling. Attach the other. I'll carry both on my back. You carry me, okay?"

"Yeah-yeah, okay," I answer as I hurry over, grab the dead man's rifle, suddenly remember his handgun, stop, and reluctantly, disgustingly, turn his body up to grab the handgun that fell underneath it and put it in my beltline. Then I realize I am not wearing my glasses. In a hurry I luckily find them in the gathering snow. Both lenses are still in and I am able to bend back the twisted frame enough to use them again. I rush back to Tom and attach the two rifles together. "But where do we go?"

"Mother-fucker," Tom exhales with a clenched jaw, sweat shows on his neck and face, "I'm the one who's shot and I'm telling you what to do? Fuck, I'm in pain, man, and the wound hasn't really said much yet, my adrenaline won't keep that away long. Clear thinking, you lucky bastard, you better start doin' that quick."

"Gotcha, gotcha, Tom. I-I think we go for the semi-circle and get out one of the logging roads, huh?"

Tom only nods as he rolls his eyes, clenches his jaw again, and offers his arms up, reaching for my shoulders as I turn around, bend down, and brace myself to lift him. He wails in pain as I do so and I can tell he is near, if not in, unconsciousness, but he holds on, somehow. I'm glad his mind is numbed for I had unthinkingly reached around and grabbed his left buttocks with my left hand, as I had done likewise with his right side. I feel the bloody, gooey, warmth, and smell the stink that flows from his left-sided wound, and feel a crunching, a bending of his bone—all horrifying to me, but I somehow do not let go as I carry him piggy-back.

I carry him as gently as I can down the embankment and head east, following the waters as steadily and as fast as I can. The snow falls harder, the breezes become gusts, and I feel Tom's body heat because neither of us are dressed for this kind of weather as I realize I left my coat hanging on the one birch tree—we are not going back for it even though I know our outlook, already dim, is bleak. Tom is right. I'm the one who has to think. I'm the one who has to make choices—the right ones, but going back, moving him about, putting him down, picking him up, losing that time when time is so against him—I can't do it, and I pray I am making the correct decision.

53
(Franklin)

I pull the keys from the utility men, both the dead one here, Terrance, and the remaining living one, Mason, and check their trucks over for something useful. There ain't nothing I can find, other than their money. This takes me about a minute to do, as Tollin finishes driving our vehicles out of sight into the south forest.

"When you get the chance," begins Radwell, talking from the entrance of the main trailer to me, "Move the propane tanks into that camper."

"Why?"

"We're gonna need them. The snow that's fallin' here will cover them up. We might miss one if it's buried."

"Ya think we're gonna be here dat long?"

Radwell shakes his head. "Don't think so, but let's not make things too hard on ourselves if we do have to stay. Then make sure the trucks are all locked up, too."

"Yeah. Okay."

All goes well until I get to the first truck, the one that pulled the trailer. Beside its cab wall beyond the single post hitch that the trailer attaches to, is a diamond treaded aluminum tool box stretching from one side rail across the truck bed to the other rail. I can't lock it, but it looks closed and sounds like it latches the very last time I try to close it, so I forget about it. What I saw inside, though, was a blanket or parka, some tire changing tools, some rope, a heavy chain with hooks, and a large roadside emergency kit. There might be some other things inside but it don't matter—I can't put any of this stuff into the cabs of any truck—I already locked them, and I'm too tired to carry this stuff into the trailer—what for?

#

I stand inside the trailer watching the women shake with fear, or from the increasing cold, for Radwell left the door open that I'm standing near, keeping it open with the tip of my rifle with my arm extended. I want to hear the outside, since Meirs isn't back yet, and want to know what's going on inside. The captured men are the same way the women are, either scared or shaking from the increasing cold.

Outside the falling snow steadily increases. My arm tires and I bring the rifle down as I move to the door's threshold. From there I watch the flakes of snow hit then melt off the parka's wrapping each dead man's warm body—Blondie and whoever.

Though busy for us here at the camp, it's been only three or four minutes since Meirs ran after the two men. I had heard one shot earlier, but knew Meirs still had to kill the second man. As if answering my unspoken question another, more distant and muffled shot, announces in the snowy air. A second or so later another, then a fourth, shot announce. These sounds are encouraging.

"Hey," Radwell says with pleasure as we hear that fourth shot, "Meirs got 'em."

I smile. I hear Cal and Perez praise Meirs.

"I hope he can find his way back, man," Cal states.

I wonder, too, for the day is getting dark fast with cloud cover and the steadily increasing snowfall and blowing wind—all cut down our range of vision and the storm is just beginning.

"Well, Radwell," I state as I let the door close behind me and move inside, "You gonna slit ta throat of these, ah, people, or are ya gonna shoot 'em, man?"

My words rivet the attentions of our captives on Radwell, and myself, for I made sure I spoke loud enough for all to hear.

"Now why would I do that, Franklin?"

"What're we gonna do with 'em?"

"Don't know yet, but I want Meirs back here before I decide anything."

While I know Drew has heard us talk, he keeps looking intently out the trailer's back window facing away from the center of the camp, leaning on the far corner of the closest sofa from me, standing over the seated nurse, as he has since I came in the trailer. He looks to the nurse, slaps her shoulder lightly, and asks as he points out the window; "Which way is this?"

She answers; "West."

"And this way?" Drew is pointing in the same direction as the open end of the camp, and also towards me, the way Meirs ran after the two men.

"North," she replies.

"Franklin come here," Drew asks with an urgent wave of his hand as he continues to stare out the window. When I'm next to him he points; "See?"

I lean down to look out the window and follow his point up to the crest of the west ridge. The snow has yet to obscure its line completely so what I see is plain enough to see though I don't see much of the man running north across the ridge. The man soon disappears from sight.

“We gotta go Rad,” I say.

“What?” he says. “We ain’t leavin’.”

“Not dat. Drew and me we’re gonna bring Meirs back in. Think we seen him runnin’ back ta the north woods again. Think he didn’t see us. Lost his way.”

“Don’t ya get yerselves lost, man, hurry back.”

“Yo wait ‘bout slittin’ their throats for us ta get back, okay?”

“Nobody’s goin’ nowhere, man. I told ya I ain’t killing them. Hurry back. Use their huntin’ jackets. Make sure ya got enough ammo, case somethin’ goes wrong.”

54
(Franklin)

Mark's hunting coat fits me well, snug in the shoulders but nothing bad to stop my movements. The coat is warm, too. I grab a handful of bullets that fit my rifle. Drew does the same for his. We are out the trailer's door in less than a minute after we last saw the man crossing the ridge.

"I-I don't think that was Meirs, man," Drew says as we jog our way up the slope. "Somebody else."

"Yeah," I answer.

"Yeah? Ya mean ya know it ain't Meirs?"

"Think it ain't—I know if it ain't, we gotta kill him."

Drew nods.

The snow now sticks to the blades of grass, comes down hard and steady. I'm thankful we can still see a good distance and, while this storm gives us a wet-cold, and its breezes are often stiff, nothing worries me. Things are looking up. We got ourselves shelter, food, vehicles, guns, and women. All this is better than it was just hours ago.

We arrive at the crest and the man's trail can be seen. The snow he knocks loose from the tall grass shows his way and we quickly follow his trail.

Drew looks at me and shakes his head. "Don't wanna shout for Meirs just in case ..."

"No," I quickly agree. "We be quiet."

The trail enters the north woods but the man has stayed on the outskirts of the trees, going in and out of the edge of these woods, or this opening in the woods, for the trees begin again about twenty to thirty yards to our left. His staying on the outskirts lets us follow him quickly and his path becomes clearer, fresher—we're gaining on him. Another minute and we know we're close. We come upon a creek, a small waterway, and its stony banks remain clear of the snow from the waters warmth up ahead. The ribbon of water runs west to east, left to right as we look at it, and its waters look dark in contrast to the falling white. No trail shows from across its banks. Drew and I are puffing clouds of frost from our hurry as we stop.

"Don't see no tracks, man, but I got a feelin' he went right," Drew whispers.

I look east, then west. “I say so, too, man, but we be sure. You go right a ways. I go left. No more than a minute. Don’t lose sight of me, man. Don’t want ta shoot each other as we come back.”

Drew nods his head and we split up, walking carefully and as quietly as we can along the stony bank. It doesn’t take long for Drew to find something and catch my attention. I hurry back to him.

“I think those are his tracks, man, what you think?” Drew whispers as he points to vague curved arrangements in the stones and edges in the underlying clay—the snow is beginning to claim these stones, but these are shoe prints.

“Yeah,” I answer. “Dat be him.”

Maybe a minute later, as we follow these tracks down this creek, the creek does a gentle S-bend, first bending southward then back north. Ahead of us we see scattered branches and trimmings of wood not yet hidden by the falling snow lying scattered over the first S-bend bank and these things sometimes reach into the water as they trace a fallen tree that has been worked, cut up, extensively. I put my hand on Drew’s shoulder to stop him as I point this area out. It is about a hundred yards away, about the limit of good sight.

“He’s there?” Drew states quietly.

I nod my head as I whisper. “Has ta be—on this side of ta water. He has ta be. If he ain’t he’s really runnin’. Everything we see is done on this side of ta water. Stay on this side. Wait till I go across. I might get better sight. Then we go for him.”

“Ain’t Meirs?”

I shake my head. “Ain’t Meirs, man, quit wishin’.”

My way across the stones and water goes well until my last step noisily crunches and pops a stone out from under my foot. Drew stops moving, glances quickly at me, searches out ahead as he readies his rifle quickly.

The noise alerts the man we hunt as my eyes catch rapid movement between two white barked trees up ahead about fifty yards, on a ledge above and just to the right of all the fallen wood, above the first bend of water. In sudden fear I realize he has clear sight of me from there and I race up my side of the bank to the cover of a small tree as the first blast from his gun is heard.

What catches my ear is a follow up sound, a rather strange set of sounds—like a handful of pebbles falling on stones ... he has a shotgun and does not have the range on me, but I do on him. I can see Drew taking aim as I do and we blast the trees in two places as he fires back again. That’s two. I cannot see him well enough and I race for the next tree east as he fires at me yet again. That’s three, and once more the pellets fall short. Drew draws nearer, too. Both Drew and the man do not have good lines of sight on each other and while Drew shoots at the trees, hoping to hit the man, the man does not fire back at him.

"Give up, man. Give up now n we might not kill ya," I taunt loudly to the man we are going to kill.

"Kiss my ass! I saw what ya did at the camp. I'm taking ya with me."

His voice is full of fear. He has to be looking to run, but seems too frightened to move. That's okay. That's alright. Just stay there a little bit longer and nothing will matter no more for you in just another minute. Drew has moved up the bank and onto the ledge about thirty yards away from you, man, and I can tell he does see some part of you now. I run to the next tree and quickly to the next after that. My second run draws a fourth blast from his gun. He realizes I am out of his range and, increasing his fear, he realizes he is not out of mine, or Drew's, and it's too late to run, yet he has no choice now but to run. I think he reloads.

Drew fires on him. I fire on him. Bark blasts off the birch. I see him cringe, crouch, then spring into a run toward the bushes behind him, showing himself square in my sights.

The shotgun goes flying from his grasp as my bullet enters his back and he falls forward. I watch him crawl towards his gun as Drew and I race toward him. I splash across the thin line of water and jump onto the ledge, my rifle set on him all the while. He knows we're next to him and he slowly turns himself to see us, a trickle of blood streams from his mouth, as he gives up going for his gun.

"Where's the others?" I ask the man.

"Fuck you," he garbles.

"Tell me and I'll help ya live," I offer as I squat down next to him.

He looks at me with pained eyes as a tremor rolls through his body. He answers weakly and with distant eyes; "Fuck you."

I put the tip of my gun to his head and pull the trigger.

Drew says nothing about this but points to the body of Meirs a few feet away, covered with just a sprinkling of snow, his body warm to our touch as we examine him. It seems this man we killed had been looking at Meirs, too.

"Rifle shot," Drew says about Meirs wound. "One shot to the chest, seems just above the heart. Meirs went fast."

"Good for him," I answer, "But this man had a shotgun ..."

"Man ... what happened to Meirs arm?" Drew exclaims as he lifts Meirs right arm up and it folds almost in two with sounds of crunching and cracking coming from within it, coagulating blood seeping out from its wound. "Looks like something ..."

"An axe—over there. It's bloody," I say as I point out the tool, its handle partially snow covered but its blade is fully exposed laying about three yards away from Meirs.

"They have Meirs rifle as well as a shotgun, then?" Drew asks.

"Well they don't have no shotgun no more, man. I don't see Meirs gun. We gotta look for it. We gotta find dis other guy who has it, too."

"You think Meirs might have got 'im—the other guy?"

"Don't look like it now, does it? Unless he fell somewhere else, has to be near from the sounds of ta shots we heard before if he did."

"This guy was running for that crease in them bushes, Frank. Why don't ya go through that a bit and see what ya can while I look around here?"

I nod my head and carefully go through the bushes. I move about thirty yards back on their trail but find no sign and I figure there's no sense in going any further. As I get back to the ledge Drew points out blood splatter and smears, and a small pool of blood by the base of the two birch trees that the snow has yet to find.

"That ain't his," Drew says, pointing to the man I killed, "That ain't Meirs. This comes from somebody else. Meirs did get one," Drew surmises, "But where'd he go? If Meirs got him, then how did Meirs get killed?"

"Dere two of them now—was," I reply. "Ta broken arm and ta axe tells a lot ... dey somehow got the better of Meirs. We got some more searching ta do—dat second man could not have gone far, man, not with bleedin' like dat."

55

They killed Mark. I saw that. I saw my old friend fall. I saw the sides of the utility man get gruesomely blown apart. Another shudder of nervousness runs through me. Who else have they killed? Mary? Gay—all of them? *Mary!?* I don't know how to live if Mary is not around. What am I to do? Will they be coming after us when their man does not return? Will I want that? How can I avoid them if they do? What can I do? How can I do it? Why has this happened? Who are they? Why us? Why Mark? What am I to do? Who are they? I need to get Tom out of here and get him medical help, but in which direction? Yes the highway, can it really be three miles away, and which of the several logging trails is the correct one? I've always run for help in the past … always, only to be disappointed. Will this time be any different?

Gunshots announce from not too far away. I turn us around, peering about with fear but we see nothing among the gathering snows and the blowing wind. We hear more shots.

"Hurry," Tom weakly says.

"Who are they shooting at?" I softly ask as I start moving again, but I do not run, do not jostle Tom any more than before, yet I do go faster. My shoulders and arms strain from this odd positioning and prolonged use in my carrying of him, but I will not let go, not stop. What I feel is nothing compared to what he is going through.

Tom's answer is to lay his head on the back of my shoulder. I can hear his labored breath come and go rapidly, feel his chest rise and fall against my back, the tremors in his arms as they hold onto me. He does not answer me. I can feel where his blood has soaked my jeans. It is both warm and cold from his blood—warm when my leg goes back up against him, cold when my leg goes forward, exposed to the wind.

I assume the shots come from the trailer site but, as more sound off, they seem to come from where we were, the tree cut site, which makes no sense at all.

We hurry on and another minute goes by. The semicircle has come into sight and is about fifty yards away. We are getting there—to the way out, for help—a positive thing. I wondered if this increasing storm would play games on us and have us lose our way, but we've made it here. We're going to make it.

A pain begins at the base and back of my neck and shoulder muscle. Tom is biting me, weakly biting me.

"Tom?"

I feel his bite release and his head comes to rest against me again.

"Tom?"

"At circle, stop," Tom exhales the words.

"Stop, at the circle, Tom?"

An effort to give me a soft bite comes again on my shoulder and I feel his head give a slight nod as my flesh moves under his teeth.

"Yeah, okay," I say, and in another ten seconds we are there.

"Down … put me down," Tom softly says.

"Tom? I can go further."

"No … not me," he answers with a small shake of his head and a brief but prolonged closing of his eyes as I strain to look sideways back at him, still holding him.

"Tom?"

"Down."

Where the path and the semicircle meet is where I squat down and gently drop him onto the pebbles. I am scared as I see his eyes. They are sorrowful, looking within, teary. Tom does not look good. His right elbow props him up off the ground as he sits there, or lays there, almost sideways below me. His left hand once again holding tight to his wound.

"Walk this side," he weakly says, looking up to me after pointing with a small thrust of his head, "Stay on stones protected by grass … don't touch the grass."

I glance along the edge of the circle and see the snow has not covered everything yet. The tall grasses have kept a thin margin of pebbles free from a telling amount of snow and Tom wants me to use that, but I do not want to go on without him. "Tom we gotta keep going."

Tom weakly and slightly shakes his head and gathers a deeper breath. "Tell my crazy wife and kids I love them."

"Tom?"

He returns a stern silent look. I have been avoiding the issue. He is dying. I am so scared, I am so scared—what am I going to do? I have to answer him. I have to start making the choices now. I ... have to. "I will, Tom. I will tell them all you've done," I manage to say but with trembling lips and words.

Tom weakly nods his head and takes another deep labored breath. "Give me the guys rifle, get out of here. Save us."

"Tom, I ..."

"No time. Get."

56

(Franklin)

So the snow covers the ground an inch, maybe twice that. So what, it doesn't hurt our tracking none, but helps show the way. The bloody stains and the man's heavy foot prints are plain to see. It only took us three-four minutes to find these tracks leading us to the east end of these north woods. The man is not in sight across the open fields, obscured by the falling snows, falling ever harder, cutting our range of vision to half what it was before I killed his friend, but this time it don't matter as much—where this man is headed is known. He's going for the pebbled semi-circle and the logging road that'll lead him out of here—where else could he be going?

"Ya know," begins Drew, "That guy back there wasn't dressed for this kind of stuff, this storm. He'd a died in it over the night, ya know."

"Yeah-yeah, you're right, and dis guy can't be any better dressed. Ya saw ta sweaty t-shirts dey be wearing before?"

"Yeah but, but that guy ya killed back there had more than a t-shirt on, man."

"Not much more and if they had coats he woulda been wearin' one. This guy can't be havin' one either. Pretty clear they didn't think they'd have ta worry 'bout this storm comin' on 'em."

"I saw a coat hanging on a tree back there—had to be the guy's we killed. If this guy's wearing a coat like that, ah, he still ain't got a chance. Then this wind and cold, his wound, should be pushin' him ta crazy soon, don't ya think, Frank?"

I take a moment to answer Drew, to consider things in my mind. A bell is ringing somewhere in my brain as I look at the man's tracks but, like with Radwell earlier, I just can't draw its warning out clear in my head. The ringing has nothing to do with Drew—that I know, but with the man we hunt, something obscure, something, maybe, out of place? "Not dis soon, crazy later, yeah, he's wounded. Looks like he's wounded bad. Dat'll make things happen fast. We ain't havin' ta go too far ta find him is what I think. I think, too, dat he heard our shots, be lookin' for us over his back. We better not stand so close ta each other from here on, Drew."

The circle can be seen now up ahead and the man's trail runs right up to its level but no man is in sight, and I take a long time looking around for any sign. While there's a good three inches of snow or more on the ground now, the tall grasses that hid me just hours ago from the law still stand tall through it. I'm wary, though a wounded man won't lie in wait if he thinks he can make it to safety. He won't lie in wait unless he's sure he cannot make it, is sure we follow too close. "Drew."

"Yeah Frank."

"I used dese grasses to hide from ta law before."

Drew understands; his answer is to crouch down and move further away from me.

The snowfall increases—unbelievable how much is coming down. The day turns to evening. The wind gusts more often. We take our time approaching this hill. I'm only fifteen feet away from the circle, following the path. Drew is off to my right and is about to reach the three trees below. I can see the snow covered level of pebbles and I look hard and long around its perimeter, but don't see anything to help me find the man we seek.

"Frank," Drew calls out in a normal voice from below, by the trees. "I found him."

I look to Drew. He is standing relaxed, looking from me to what lays hidden to me below him on the ground and back up to me again.

"He's dead," Drew confirms for me.

I look around to see how the man got down there without my seeing his path. I soon find it. He reached the pebbles then slid down to where he died. I follow his trail to Drew.

"He's got the gun Meirs took. I recognize it. Smell that—see that?" Drew asks.

It is a blood and shit mix of a smell. "Yeah, stinks."

"His gut got opened. I hear that's painful," Drew states.

The bell rings in my head again, rings louder this time. I still don't catch its meaning as I look over the dead man and his wound. I start looking around once more, searching, but I don't know why.

"What's ya thinkin', Frank?"

"Don't know, I don't know."

"What's ya suspicious about?"

"Said I don't know."

"We saw two guys run. We see two dead guys. The storm's coming in harder every minute we wait out here, Frank. I'm willing to look around if you think there's something more to look for, but I'm getting cold, too. We ain't exactly right dressed for this either, and I don't want to lose my way back to the trailer, you know?"

"Understand ya. I don't know, man. It's like a bell is ringin' in my ear, tellin' me somethin' is wrong."

"Like what?"

"I tell ya, I just don't know."

"Well, nothing is ringing my ear. C'mon, Frank, let's go before this storm gets worse and we can't find our way back," Drew says as he picks up Meirs rifle and checks the man over, takes the money from his wallet.

I stand there, listening to those ringing bells in my head, looking about, trying to understand why I feel unsettled on finding this man, but I can't place the why.

"Frank, ya comin'?"

"Yeah ... yeah, I'm comin'."

57

I'm not going to make it. I'm not. I'm not whining. I'm just ... just facing the truth as I study the diverging paths in front of me. My body shivers as I rub my hands up and down my arms, trying to gain warmth. I miss Tom's body heat. The extra effort I made in carrying him kept me almost warm. My teeth chatter. My nose runs like a small stream. My ears hurt. My fingertips hurt. Only my toes do not hurt. Those ten lucky digits are in boots made for this weather, the rest of my clothing is not. This weather will take me if I don't know which way to go, I know. These two logging trails mark an 'x' in the middle of nowhere, and I do not recognize either path. For all I know either choice in front of me could be the one to take me east to the highway—either one could circle around to bring me deeper into this forest. I just don't know which one. I just ... don't know. What I do know is, if I choose wrong, I'm dead. And I realize that if I choose correctly I still may be dead. I'm dead! I'm dead no matter what I choose—I'm dead! *Dead!*

Tom's dead ... Tom is dead. It's been long enough, but I can't believe that. He still lives. He was—he is a smoker. So? Well, damn it, it's cold, I'm cold, it means he carries that butane lighter in his pocket. I could start a fire. That means going back. I can't do that. I can't choose which path to take here, either—I can't make a decision. I'm damned if I do go back, damned if I go forward. Damned if I do, damned if I don't—then you get damned for doing ... but what will I be doing? I don't understand what the heck is happening.

I could take Tom's clothes.

You can't because he is alive.

I can use his lighter for a fire to warm us.

You will kill him with the time you lose in going back instead of going to the highway for help. What are you thinking?

I could save Tom by giving him the warmth of that fire.

You go back, you cannot come back here—you're choosing your death.

I'm dead either way.

The others only chance is for you to go to the highway and get help.

Yeah, like Rick and Doug ran and rescued their bicycles by themselves while I went to get just this kind of help—I helped no one. They helped themselves. I should do it their way—Rick's way.

You're a fool.

Yeah, I always end up a fool. What's new?

Your risking other people's lives, people you love, people you care about—that is critical here, you moron.

They may be alive.

We do hope they are alive, stupid—that's why you are going to the highway. If you go back then just what do you think you can do anyway, mister moron?

Free them, give them a chance, is what I hope I can do.

You have no idea how to do that. You're no Marine, no Special Force's man, not even regular Army—what if they're already dead?

Avenge them.

Ha-ha-ha-ha! It's not in you to kill.

I'll get used to it.

It's not in you. Go for the highway.

Rick fought for his watch. Rick went after those trying to steal John's car. Rick fought and fought again against the man who beat him. Rick knows how ....

Exactly, Rick knows how—you do not. This talk is ridiculous, this coldness is driving you mad—end this stupid argument with me—me, the other and sane side of you, and get to that highway—now!

58

(Franklin)

A couple of hours have passed since finding Meirs. Since then the wind has grown strong and constant, buffeting the trailer, whipping heavy moist snow into high drifts and packing them hard against the structure. Every twenty minutes or so Drew steps out to clean the three black metallic steps that fold out from just below the trailer's door, then two, then one, until he can only clean the top step. The snow's coming down that heavy, that fast.

Forced together by the winds to cluster into tiny balls, this snow is non-stop in its splatter against the trailer, coming in waves of muffled thumps. It clings to some windows, not sliding or melting off, to further limit our vision to the outside world. The inside window surfaces frequently fog over with moisture making us wipe the wetness off every time we try peering outside. On some windows this inside moisture cools enough to frost over. We have a habit of looking out but why we do in a storm like this—in a place like this, seems foolish. It's clear we ain't going anywhere, even if we want to, and why would we want to? Everything to keep us happy for several days is here; shelter, food, warmth, three women. What else could we want?

Meirs' death bothers us, bothers me and Drew more than it worries Cal or Radwell. I know Tollin don't like it. Perez doesn't care. His hand, even with the nurse being forced to care for it, is his center of attention. His hand looks bad, too; deep red in color, swollen, and this condition now reaches up his arm. Perez is right-handed, too, but I've given him as much respect as he'll get, I ain't giving him more, certainly no pity.

I don't like the numbers game Meirs loss gives; six of us now against seven of them. There are just too many people in just too small a place and just too many of them campers. Those numbers will change before too long. Is this not ironic? We being the jailers and them campers the inmates ... and how much better it feels being the jailer.

When we first got back, Smith and Bill watched Drew and me intently, listened to us intently, as we told Radwell, Cal, Tollin, and Perez about what happened out there. They listened better when we came back than when they had guns pointed at them earlier, and I don't know what to make of that. It makes another bell ring. What is this one about? I will figure this out, I will figure all the bells out, but I want some more food before I do.

"We gonna let them eat?" I ask.

They are still taped up and sitting on or beside the two sofas, except for the blonde woman named Paula. She remains employed as our cook and has been doing her 'thing' not so well at first, and she only got going after emotionally leaving the blonde haired man's death, and that of the second utility man's, behind. Then she repeated her emotions after learning of the two dead in the forest. We had enough of her and were ready to take her outside when she gathered herself together and started cooking again. Women; this emotional woman, for sure, is worthless to me if not for her cooking. The others reacted badly to the news of their friend's deaths, even the men, but Paula took the cake, as I put it. It's amusing to me—did they expect anything else when they do the things they do? They force their deaths on us; give us no choice ... fools.

The food looks ready to serve. I hope so. Its smells have made my mouth water for a long time now. The earlier amount of food she made wasn't enough after a day of us going without anything substantial. I glance at Radwell to see if we are going to feed our captives.

"No," Radwell answers with a slight tightening of his eye as he catches my look.

"Yes," Tollin corrects him, making me turn towards Tollin, who is looking straight at Radwell. "We'll have the cook give a bite of food that we select to each of them first, before we eat. I want to be careful."

Radwell growls each word with increasing anger; "I don't want to feed them."

"I don't care," firmly answers Tollin. "We won't be feeding them enough to keep 'em strong and we'll know the food is safe to eat—unless you want to be the guinea pig?"

"We already have the cook tasting her food."

"She might poison herself if she knows she's doin' it only to us. She won't do it to everybody she cares for."

"What poison can she use?" Cal asks.

"Anything you don't know is food, Cal—you been watching her close enough to know everything she cooked with?" challenges Perez.

Cal remains quiet as he looks back at Perez, Tollin, then at us, before stepping closer to Paula and looking her over intently, watching her with almost a stare.

Radwell acts resistive but says nothing before he reluctantly nods his head in acceptance. "Yeah, feed them the bits."

"You gonna let us relieve ourselves too?" Bill asks.

"Uhh," sighs Radwell. "Heck if I care—go in your stinkin' pants—no."

"Yes," Tollin corrects again, giving Radwell a determined look, who returns a likewise stare. "We're gonna be here for days. I ain't staying in no barn. I don't think you want to either," Tollin pauses to see if anyone else will speak, no one shows they will, before he continues. "After they eat and we eat we'll have the men shuffle to the can and have this cook woman pull their pants down. I don't want to untie the men at all—understand?"

"Just kill them and throw them out in the snow," Cal tells us, "Save on food."

"I've been thinkin' about it, Cal," Radwell answers. "Think about it a lot.."

"Enough killing for today," Drew says authoritatively. "Enough … understand me? We have no need to kill anyone else here, no one at all—at least not yet. Five-six men are dead from here, not counting the ones we did earlier. These campers here have got the message real clear like, no need to do more … anyone disagree?"

Radwell seethes. "What's the point in keepin' 'em alive—won't make no difference to the law, won't make no difference on how they come after us—not after Franklin…"

"Kiss my …," I begin.

"Shut-up," Tollin demands. "The difference remains … Franklin defended himself. It don't help him much—or us, but your executing the two others hurts you more. None of it we helped in. None of it we could've stopped. You two are going down …"

"Not without you," Radwell spits back. "And Franklin went out and killed two more."

Drew interrupts, stops me from speaking; "We keep these ones alive because we all got a better chance at everything. Realize that, hostages to bargain with. Better chances of getting out in public, over the borders, with females among us … c'mon, think a little … *think a little* …they're better for us alive then dead, at least as far as we can see right now, okay?"

Drew is backing Tollin. Sides are not so quietly being drawn. What side do I need to be on? The silence of Perez is disturbing.

"What you say, Perez?" I ask. Perez caresses his injured hand and arm—his pain is all his world. "Perez?" I ask again.

He looks at me, sneering. "I want ta kill 'em. Kill them all. Maybe a woman lives. Maybe two, for us to enjoy and take over the border like Drew suggests, but kill the rest. Any trouble they cause me and that's what I do, kill them."

So it's Radwell, Cal, and Perez against Drew, Tollin, and … me. I trust Drew more than Radwell, Drew thinks more than Radwell, and killing them is easy enough when the time comes. "I say keep 'em alive. Dey might be useful."

"Changing your tune, Franklin?" Radwell accusingly asks. "You wanted ta slit their throats before."

"Changed my mind, yeah man."

"I still say kill them," Cal says.

"You know how to work a generator?" Drew asks Cal as he faces him.

"What?" Cal answers.

"Neither do I but, if you haven't noticed, the lights in the trailer here are slowly going dim," Drew answers, "We on battery power? Who owns this trailer?"

"I do," Smith replies.

"Am I right?"

"Yeah."

"See Rad, we need them for shit like that," Drew states, then turns to Smith. "What do we do—where is the generator?"

"You think I'm going to help you?" Smith asserts.

"Make a bad choice," Drew snaps.

Smith understands and quickly answers; "We keep on just the lights we need. The battery will last to morning that way. After the storm we can reach the generator."

"No, we get the generator now," Radwell spits out.

"Rad, we can watch them better in the daylight, and I'm tired. We do it in the morning as Smith here says," Drew states.

"You questioning my authority?" Radwell growls. "What I say goes."

"We need sleep, Rad," Tollin calmly interjects. "Let's argue tomorrow. You can take the first watch, Radwell. Wake me up a couple of hours from now. No one's going nowhere."

"Hey," Doug speaks out and directly to Radwell, "About the bathroom?"

Radwell sighs and nods his head yes. "Have the cook do it, keep the men tied up."

Drew sneers and says; "No, not the cook. Not the nurse either—the stutterer—what's her name—Mary. She'll do it."

One at a time we make them shuffle to the bathroom and back with the help of the women, who we partially untie. We watch it all with our guns pointed at them.

59

*What **are** you thinking?*

With no reluctance, I pull the dead man's shoes off and look at his socks. Tom's socks have helped warm my forearms and hands, these will help more as I carefully open the toe end of the socks by poking and ripping it with a small and rough length of a broken off tree branch. The cold readily bites at my skin and the weather will only grow colder tonight. These socks will help me, as will Roy's. Their pants, too, after some likewise trimming. I pull whatever clothes I can use off their bodies. I tear a sleeve off Roy's shirt to use as a scarf. The jacket he wore I wrap around my lower body, securing it with the use of his belt. I take all things worthwhile to take off him—the dead man, off Roy, as I did with Tom, and I do not feel the least bit strange in taking them—especially so in taking from the dead man, swearing often at him as I plan to make use of each piece of his clothing. I do not care that he cannot hear me. I do not care that he is dead. I do, though, want him to hear me. I want him to know I insult him. I hate him. I hope his soul is not allowed to wail, his pain not allowed any release, as he agonizes in the deep recesses of Hell.

I was wrong. Tom did not smoke. There was no lighter in his pockets. I came back here only for my lightweight coat—anything to help me more against this cold and snowy wet. Roy was the smoker. The fire that is warming and drying these snow drenched clothes of Tom, Roy, and the dead man I started with his butane lighter. I'm sorry you're dead, Roy, but thanks for being a smoker, thanks for leaving me your lighter. Another shiver runs through my body.

My hands and fingers have amazed me. They had felt swollen and numb, tingly, clumsy, when I first got back here to the tree cut site to find Roy and the man Tom had killed, but my hands built a fire, growing hot, for the fallen tree offered easy and a lot of good firewood, and, as the fire first took hold, sheltered from the direct wind and snow as I built it by and underneath the two birch trees, its flames gave me my first sense of vague comfort since all this violence began. I saw remnants of other tracks—not mine, but others. I believe they think Roy was me, and they had found Tom, so they may also believe no one else is out here alive. They saw two, killed two. Somehow I know that must be and is to my advantage, but I am not sure how I can use it. I'm too cold yet to think clear enough. At least I'm warm enough to realize I'm too cold to think clear enough yet—ugh, I'm too cold still to know what I'm saying.

The fire is roaring hot. The four sets of jeans laying over makeshift poles are steaming themselves dry, as are all the rest of the clothing I will be using as I stand shivering next to this fire naked except for my underwear and boots. Sometimes it seems futile to be doing this as flakes of snow batter against me, but the fire is so hot I consider myself dry as I turn around as I stand in place. It is time to dress and start my plan.

The snow continues to fall heavy. There is over a foot of this white stuff on the ground now, away from the fire. And away from the fire it is dark, almost too dark to move about, but I must. My boots are warm and dry inside and I'm getting myself well bundled up. Whatever I next choose, this is the best I can do.

There are four rounds left in Tom's rifle, and it is a semi-auto, but we carried no extra ammunition with us, a disappointment, for I feel far more comfortable firing a rifle than a handgun. Four shots may only be enough if I ambush.

*What **are** you thinking?* You are crazy thinking this—I understand the fire, the clothing bit, but the guns—ambush? Go for help, you moron, do something smart.

By the time I zip up my own wool and camel colored leather jacket and slip on my own gloves over the ragged socks that are on my hands and forearms, pull my thermal cap out of my jacket pocket and onto my head, I feel my composure has nearly fully returned, as I review the actions I plan to take against them.

Against them? *Really?* Are you *INSANE*—go for help!

I am glad for the additional warmth the dead man's clothing gives me, for Roy's, for Tom's, for the snow is driving hard and blowing everywhere. The day is dark from this storm and the setting of the sun, which I feel must have set about the time I came back upon Tom, but there is just enough light for me to move about—even when there isn't, I still will have to. None of the dead men carried a watch for me to know what the time actually is and I don't carry one, either, but my guess is it's near six-thirty at night. Tom and I went to cut the tree shortly before two o'clock, worked there about an hour, maybe an hour and a half—two hours when we got onto the truck path? Another two hours or so for me to be where I am at here. That would make the time closer to seven at night, but not eight. What's the point? Why know the time?

Once again the right side of my face feels like it is burning as I wrap the crude scarf around my head, causing me to reach up and touch it with bared fingers. Pain follows my fingers as they trace a long gouge in my skin where my cheek had been sliced open but this tracing only gets my mind into sharper focus for what I now want to do. The tracks of the other men are everything but gone, covered by the heavy snowfall. Time enough for them to forget about the possibility of me existing, making it prime time for me to hit back.

Just what do you think you're doing, moron, besides being stupid—go for help! Just go for help. *You are not the man for this.*

I hear you, voice. You come from somewhere inside me. You mean me well but, you know what—shut up.

But you don't have a plan ....

Shut ... up.

60

Flakes of snow splatter against and drench the lenses of my battered eyeglasses before they slide down to drip off onto my cheeks as icy fingers of wetness from which I cannot hide. I'm moving east as I walk alongside the thin ribbon of ink black slush that defines the creek bed from the carpet of white. I chose this way because I have no desire to make my way back through the thickets in this storm, if ever again, and I know this way, the way I carried Tom, even in this darkness I know where I am. This creek bed will help me circle these woods to get near enough to our camp to find out if they are still there, if anyone else is left alive—if any of my plan is possible. I peer into the whipping snow, a flurry of white against the deep murky blue darkness of the night. It falls over the blurry background of an open field, which I have no choice but to enter. I can see maybe thirty feet in front of me—not very far. I look back, out of the wind. The storm came from the west and I cannot explain why this wind sometimes blows from the east. Getting lost out here is much too easy, is what I fear, but I know where I am—I know where I am and I know I say this to myself to keep me from panicking.

The snow packs beneath my feet softly, surprisingly quiet as it compresses—noiseless. The grasses and brush below the snow make the sounds I hear. The temperature, so cold a while ago when I was not dressed properly, now feels relatively warm, probably just below freezing, but I expect this to change with the night, to become much colder and these clothes I wear will not help me much then. This snow will become much harder and louder to move around in as the temperature falls, the time passes, as the land freezes.

There are no city lights to bounce off the clouds and make things brighter out here. It is scary dark. This weather forces me to take my time and I'm careful in tracing my path—finding the truck path of yesterday, obscured but just recognizable in this mess, even in this snowy darkness I know I'm again where I was hours ago when I saw Mark killed. I don't need to see the path or all the landmarks. I know I'm here even though I cannot see the camp.

Large clusters of flakes driven together by the incessant, strong, howling gusts of winds smack against my face and jackets in a constant barrage that often comes so hard I can feel these tiny snowballs hit through the jacket linings. This snow sticks to my clothing, already having turned one side of me into a mottled wall of walking whiteness. So much snow slaps my face and so wickedly I cannot feel anything else but those cold impacts against my skin and the cold gives me a painful headache. A hard shiver sweeps through my body on the side where the snow has caked onto my jacket and pants. It seemed futile, at first, to scrape this snow away, but then I fear having moisture soak through to my skin—certain death, so I stop and clean myself off. I turn my head away from the wind and hear myself sigh as a feeling, which I believe is warmth, comes rushing back into my cheeks and forehead. Damn, my nose drips like a faucet and I can barely feel my gloved hand press against my chin and nose. The tears constantly run and blur my vision when I'm slow to blink, and give a burning sensation to my cheeks where they trickle.

It is odd to view our trailer from the perspective of that place being my warm home—of which I cannot enter. The lights are on inside the trailer. The curtains are closed. Shadows move across the windows from time to time, but nothing is helpful to understand what, or whom, I'm up against. I set my sights and release the rifle's safety. I will kill the person, whoever it is, when they walk back again, but then I realize I don't know who that person would be. There are images of people sitting up tight against many of the windows. I recognize one silhouette as being Bill. He is on the sofa against the window on the same side but farthest from the trailer's door. Something, or someone else, blocks the other windows. Bill's sight gives me hope—with him being alive there is a good chance the others are, too. I pull my rifle back down and reset the safety. I have to think about this.

The trailer's yellowish light penetrates the falling snow enough to cast itself dimly over the center of our camp. There is a shallow depression in the snow near where I imagine Mark and the utility man fell dead, at least that is my guess why a depression is there, caused by their once warm bodies, but I cannot see them.

I strain my eyes to see and then clean my glasses the best I can and peer again, but I find no trace of any recent tracks in the snow from the trailer's door or elsewhere. They have holed up inside, confident by virtue of this weather they are safe for the time being—but who are they?

Are they bothering to post a lookout? I scan the trailer and the trucks for an answer. Seems no one is inside either truck, or posting inside the trailer.

I move closer, much closer, a few steps at a time, until I'm behind the twin young evergreens. Suddenly I slide waist deep into the snow, my legs stretching painfully apart. I realize right away what has happened; I have one leg down inside the pit which Bill and Rick had begun to dig, mostly hidden in the carpet of snow. I look with alarm toward the trailer but no one is watching. I feel confident enough to shift my body and get out of this pit when my movement and pressure makes something roll under my foot. My weight is just enough to bring the top of the shovel pole up to break the surface of the snow a little distance from me. I quickly look over the trailer again to see if anyone discovered my presence, but it seems no one has. I shift back to my original hiding position and watch the windows once more as ideas flow into my brain as my body shivers. My mind races with thought.

I cannot shoot through the windows hoping to get them. I can't imagine a scenario where I successfully enter and kill all the bad guys inside the trailer. I have to draw them out for a sure kill. How can I do that? What could I do, can do, to lay bait strong enough for them to come out?

The answer comes to me as I back away from the evergreens until I'm better hidden from the trailer and begin to swing around to approach the trucks. Treasures may be inside these trucks and I need whatever help can be found within as I consider the answer; my plan.

The two utility trucks offer nothing—they are locked. Bill's camper substantially blocks the view to and from the trailer in the way I approach, so I peer at the trucks more carefully than the trailer, just in case, but no one is in either truck. Standing alongside Bill's truck I brush the sticky snow off his driver's window with trepidation—fearful someone might yet be inside, but, again, no one is. These doors are locked. None of the camper's windows are large enough for me to crawl in if I broke them. The propane tanks are not here. The guns are not here. I am out of luck at this truck.

Rick's truck has also been locked. I look around once more, long and careful, because I will have to climb into the bed of his truck to lift the tool box's cover, leaving tracks exposed that they will be able to see from the lofted bedroom windows of the trailer and they will easily see me standing on the bed of the truck from there, too—if they bother to look. I want to peer into the trailer to see whatever I can; how many of my friends live, how many enemies I face, but Rick's truck is not parked quite close enough and I do not want to be found out, so I bring my attention back to Rick's tool box set across the bed of his truck. He said it does not lock. The cover cracks open as I lift it slowly. The weight of the snow on top of the cover makes it heavy and for some reason it will not open all the way, so I reach in with one bared hand and search blindly as I strain to keep the cover open with my other arm. My concern on being seen, on being quiet, equals my desire to find something helpful. My hand searches the side panels, the center, and everywhere else within reach. Mostly all I feel are cold steel tools. None of those are helpful. A few other things are; a rope, a parka, a flashlight, three road flares, and a pair of work gloves. Nothing else—I'm getting too nervous, too long in one exposed place. I take these things, and the shovel, all quietly away.

61

This flashlight has been my savior, guiding me back through the darkness as this storm reaches what I hope is its peak. Wind whips into me. Snow smacks at me. I'm losing body heat too fast. The ledge offers some shelter from these elements. I must get back there and hope the fire is still going. Somehow get out of this direct wind and cold and warm up again.

Crackling embers glow where fire used to be. The carpet of snow isn't as thick as in more open areas of the woods. Even so, the body of the man Tom killed is not easy to see, nor Roy's, as I arrive at the ledge, except an opossum, investigating their bodies, gives their positions away.

"Can't have them yet," I say to the hissing desperate varmint as it tries to stand its ground and protect the huge meal prize these bodies represent. It must be famished to search for food in this weather and to stand its ground, defend its prize, be so near a fire. I had not known opossum's to be anything but timid before. The thought of it being rabid crosses my mind.

"Get out of here," I yell as I extend my arms suddenly upward and lurch quickly at the good-sized animal. It runs off reluctantly and only after I keep shining the flashlight in its eyes.

Yet the flashlight's beam is fading. Its batteries are old or worn down, but its light lasts long enough for me to find the ax under the carpet of snow. I swipe the snow off the arm and start swinging at the thin branches of the lone standing birch, clipping them off and tossing them towards the base of the two standing birch trees up on the left side of this ledge. I chop enough to bring a minimal body heat back to me and enough wood up from the cut tree to maintain heat in the fire.

A strong gust of wind comes and sends burning embers flying onto me as I jump away and the fire starts to fade. This forces me to use two of the flares to help the fire burn the wet brush and wood to get the heat of the fire up again. I feed the reviving flames until they are roaring hot once more. I manage to dry my pants and most of my other clothes before the fire begins to ebb away. This time I will let the fire go. I am not coming back. I know I cannot stay the night here. My plan will not work if I do and I'd be just wasting time and become indecisive if I stay. This time the woolen parka will keep me warm enough, dry enough, to do all the things I hope to do—I hope.

I roll the dead man up to rest on top of his broken arm to look over his stiffened body. There is nothing else his clothing can give me, but there is one more thing that he can as I let him fall over onto his back. I reach for the axe as I take a final long hateful look at him.

62
(Franklin)

The small television they have ain't working. The radio gets bad reception but we hear ourselves described well enough, often enough. We smile over that, but don't like it.

We're described yet again as Radwell and I stand in the kitchen area dressing in our captives' warmer clothes. I find I fit into the dead man's clothes quite well—Mark's, and realize he picked his winter wear knowing what's truly needed to survive out in this kind of weather. Good man. Thank you. Glad you're dead. You would've been trouble. We took our turns taking showers, Smith telling us how without using too much water. Getting rid of that swamp smell, that grime, felt good. We listened to Smith, but it was hard not to let the warm water run and keep running as it removed the stink from my body.

The interior lights seem duller than before. I turn the radio and one light off and the other lights become a bit brighter. I look at Radwell, who looks back at me.

"Smith," I say, "What's with the lights?"

"Told you, don't turn on anything more than necessary."

"Where is this generator?" Radwell asks. Tollin, Cal, and Perez are sleeping. Drew has been standing guard while Radwell and I took turns in the shower.

"Outside under the trailer. We did not finish getting it set up. It will need to be moved."

"Great," Radwell replies.

"You want, I can go out there and get it runnin'."

"You wish, Smith. We know you ain't thinkin' 'bout just fixin' a generator. If we get somebody out there it sure ain't gonna be you until the morning," Radwell says.

"You guys don't really know what you're doing, do ya?" remarks Smith, suddenly regretting saying those words, as he should.

Radwell, Drew, and I exchange glances. Drew is the first to respond. He raises his hand to stop our responses. "What movie did that come from, Smith, thinking you're a hero? And seeing that you're tied up, we're in control, and you got a leg wound we let the nurse tend to, insulting us ain't very smart. We're not idiots."

"But you are, Smitty," Cal caustically adds as he woke up from hearing our talk. "You're the idiot. No one knows we're here. No one knows we're here with you. No one knows where you are and if they did, they can't reach you. We have your clothes, your weapons, your food—*and we don't need you.*"

Radwell laughs on hearing Cal's words. I enjoyed them. Drew shows a look of knowing the truth to Cal's words, but we know Cal wants to kill them—again, and that don't do us well, right now. Tollin and Perez remain sleeping through this. Drew, however, does something more; he moves over to Smith and checks his bindings, then checks the rest of the men's bindings. All the bindings remain tight as Drew looks at us and nods his head; "They're good."

Drew has done his turn at guard and walks off to the main bedroom and I see him go and peer out its rear facing windows. Those windows face the path we took driving into camp and face the direction to where Meirs chased the men. Drew comes back, nods once more just at me, turns and closes the door.

I watched Smith's expression change when Cal spoke before. Smith knows he encouraged the worst on himself and his friends. I don't care, really, but care some; to keep them alive after we leave ... maybe. No. It's true the law goes for those who kill more than those who don't. I've killed too many, won't matter how many more I do, but this is a matter that can wait.

Cal pauses a moment after Drew closes the door to speak again. "Why don't we just kill 'em. The men, I mean. What are we waiting for?" Cal is impatient, as he looks over the women wantonly. Two of the women are fitfully sleeping—we didn't do anything with Paula, just sat her on the floor next to the women's sofa. She's managing to just stay awake. Their men are fighting sleep, trying to stay alert during this conversation.

I snarl my answer; "Dey hostages, Cal. Better livin' than dead, man." It is the best answer I can quickly think of.

"I'd rather kill 'em," Cal responds. "Less chance of 'em messin' us up later."

"Give it up, man, you'll get your chance, it ain't happenin' tonight," I sigh. "If ya ain't gonna take your whole turn ta sleep, I want ta."

63

I'm doing the only thing I believe possible, and I think I am insane. Does an insane person know they are insane, or is their insanity the only sense of reality they have so, therefore, they know they are just as sane as the sane person knows they are not sane? Whatever it is that comes from this, I know I am committed to it … like an insane person.

Packets of snow smack against me as more fly by, rushing away to disappear back into the darkness. Nothing has changed. I shiver. My jaw trembles. I hurry to maintain warmth. My earlier tracks are almost completely covered over. The storm has added yet another inch, possibly two—maybe even more, since I passed here before. I have not witnessed a storm like this since I was a child.

Finally, in the darkness ahead, glow the lights from the trailer.

This is the sickest thing I can think of doing with what I have. I just could be as insane as that one voice in my mind says. Yet this is also the most effective single act I can imagine for drawing them out of the trailer to get an idea as to their numbers, of giving a chance for my friends within to react, to escape, to attack their attackers. This certain distraction will provide that chance, provide me assurance whoever I shoot will not be anyone I know, for my friends will not be the ones, should not be the ones, coming out of the trailer first ... I hope.

A great chance is getting caught doing this. I depend heavily on their apathetic watch, depend on them leaving the trailer out of curiosity. I do not know what to do if they don't come out or if they come out using someone I know as a shield. That would make it extremely difficult to kill one of them but, then, I would have gotten the answers to most of what I want to know. Hopefully these sick men do not think like I do.

My left upper arm strains to keep my rifle between it and my chest as my left forearm cradles the gun for balance. My left hand holds onto my prize. With my right hand I quietly insert the blade of the shovel into the snow, guiding the pole between my right arm and my chest as my right foot plants the blade firmly through the snow into the ground. I stand about two strides away from where I remember Mark's body lays, the snow covers his corpse completely, gives no indication at all now that two men lie underneath. I carefully watch the trailer windows for any sign of them, which is only a few yards away, as I do this. I have planted the shovel across from the trailer's door, beyond where the light from the trailer is bright on the snow yet still in its cast strong enough to stand out for something strange, and my tracks will be visible to show this something strange is also new.

The running of my nose drives me nuts as I sniffle twice, wipe my nose with my right sleeve.

The dead man's head, the head of the one Tom killed, slips over the end of the shovel's pole with bloody ease, the teeth of his upper jaw catching the rounded end of the shovel as the shaft comes up through what is left of his throat, while the ragged chopped remnants of his neck provide a wedge against the shovel's pole, tenuously locking the head in place, much as I hoped.

Taking one last look at the trailer's windows, I grab hold of my rifle with both hands and turn to hurry off. I plan to quickly circle around to get back to the pair of evergreens I hid behind earlier, not going directly to them—they will see my path if I do, to set my ambush complete.

64
(Franklin)

I'm groggy but realize Tollin wakes me as I feel a cold rush of wind and a burst of moisture fall across me. Our captives stir. Snow billows in from the darkness through the open trailer door directly across from the chair we placed in that short hallway-like area that first Cal, then Tollin, and then I chose to sleep on. Radwell found something outside.

"Yo, what ta heck you got ta door open for, man?" I complain as I shiver and sit up, tossing the throw blanket off as I see the disappearing silhouette of Radwell moving away outside. Tollin stands replying something next to me as I start pulling my boots on while peering out the trailer's door into the murkiness beyond, not really hearing Tollin's first words.

"C'mon," Tollin insists, not answering my complaint as he tugs at my shoulder like an excited kid, something very unlike him. Whatever it is Radwell found it sure has unsettled Tollin.

"Get ta f—get yo freakin' hands off me, man," I protest as I knock his insistent hand off my shoulder then turn my eyes to look at our awakened captives, visually checking from my chair that their bindings still hold secure.

I finish with my boots, grab my coat and gun, and rise to follow him outside as Cal comes in half asleep from the second bedroom holding his gun between his arm and side while his hands pull his belt tight in his pants. His appearance momentarily stops us and I take that moment to finish wrapping my coat around me.

"What's goin' on?" he asks.

"Don't know," I answer.

"Radwell found something—and it ain't good," Tollin replies as he looks Cal over. "You're not dressed. Stay here. Watch them."

Cal glances out the door and then to the captives as he nods yes to Tollin's order. Drew comes out awakening from the master bedroom with no shirt on, yawning but aware. He is carrying his rifle and motions for us to go ahead and go.

From the dim lights of the trailer casting out over the deep snow I follow Radwell's, Perez's, and Tollin's tracks as I move off the trailer's steps. The snow packs down from my weight with each of the two strides I take before I stop suddenly still. There, before me, between Radwell and Tollin, as their movements part enough for me to see, stands a polished piece of wood standing upright a few yards in front of them in the snow, shiny in the trailer's dim light and streaked with dark ribbons of ... blood. It is a shovel, and on top of this shovel's pole is perched Meirs' bloody head.

65
(Franklin)

Meirs' mouth is stretched open to expose his teeth, his face slanted back, staring with fixed eyes towards the sky as flakes of snow trickle down over his lifeless face. I make out ragged chopped edges of flesh and bone defining the back of his neck wedging his head to the pole. His brutal sight stuns me. I drop into the snow as nausea fills me. I'm going to puke.

As my knees fold flashes of gunfire break the darkness nearby. Impacts sound as thuds against the trailer behind me. Blood sprays out from two places in Perez's back as he begins to fall without a word just feet from me as the rest of us scatter and dive into the cold deep snow.

Muffled curses come from Radwell and Tollin. I hear myself curse. I hesitate to lift my head but when they begin firing back I raise enough to join them to fire madly away toward where the points of light sparked. We fire there and to each side leading off into the surrounding darkness until each of us needs to reload. No shots are returned. We fire nervously a few more times, then wait a long minute straining to hear, to see, any sign of our enemy.

"How many are there?" I softly call out.

"Don't freakin' know," Tollin answers in an equally soft tone.

"It ain't the cops," Radwell states in a roughened voice, also softly said.

"You sure?" I ask.

"They'd announce themselves, stupid. Who the fuck is this—you killed the two Meirs chased," Radwell replies, his voice still rough, his words becoming louder.

"How the fuck do I know," I return sharply.

"Blondie said three," Tollin reminds us.

"How can that be?" Radwell questions with angry disbelief. "He would've gone for the cops by now—this ain't the cops."

"Can't be," I assert, no sense in being quiet after Radwell's louder words, "Dey'd come with a bunch a them, man. We'd be still fightin'."

"Then who is this?"

"Maybe we killed 'em?" Tollin wonders.

"Maybe—want ta go look?" Radwell replies.

"Hell no," Tollin returns.

"Who else could it be?" I ask.

"Do you not see Meirs head dipshit?" Radwell yells at me in frustration as he realizes the truth, as I now do. "The cops don't do this shit. Has to be someone from here—no one else would know."

A moment of pause as that recognition sinks in, before Tollin exclaims; "Damn."

We fall silent.

66

Sounds of the trailer's door opening and excited men's voices declaring back and forth behind me cause me to jump off my trail, spin to face the trailer quickly, as I dive into the snow. The parka drapes down over my body and I hear it settle across the snow, blending me, hopefully, into the dark landscape. This is too soon! I'm in the darkness but I did not make the evergreens, yet I do find I have a decent line of sight.

One man is already well out of the trailer, stepping toward the perched head. Two more appear at the doorway—no three, and two more behind them busy themselves dressing for the outside. They have not seen me. This is as good as it will get.

I pull the rifle to my shoulder but snow has covered the barrel by my dive and I have to wipe it off to aim, take my glove off to use my trigger finger. By then four of them have moved out into the snow, the first man already is beyond the pole as he traces my steps cautiously, checking to see how fresh my tracks are and realizing they are just made. The second man hurries quickly towards the first. The third is slow, off to the side and I have the best line of sight on him. The fourth and last man looks shaky as he sees the severed head and is dropping to his knees, yet stays in line with the first two as they closely follow one another's path. I take aim at the third man—my best sight, as the first turns to warn the others I am near, but he is too late. My rifle punches my shoulder as I fire-fire at the third man, quickly sight the first two and fire-fire again.

I grab my glove but leave the now useless rifle behind. The extra jacket I wrapped around my waist is roughly stripped away from its securing second belt by something catching it within the snow as I rise and run but I do not dare go back for it as these men return fire and bullets sing through the snows and the air around me. I'm scared, but this gunfire puts no panic into me as those first earlier shots did in the afternoon. These men cannot see me and are scattering their bullets. I quickly clear the area where they continue to search for a target no longer there.

I have done it! I feel that thrill of success as I dangerously and almost blindly run in this darkness. Damn I'm good. That'll show them. That will not let them rest easy. Everyone will know I'm out here. That I survived, that I can bring the law.

That will ... make them strike back against my wife, unprotected friends and sister. Retribution. Jesus, what have I done? Lord forgive me, I'm so stupid ... so stupid. Oh, God .... four shots and I saw not one of them fall. I wonder if I even wounded one. What was I thinking? Why didn't I think of this possibility? I did not want this. Why did I want to be a hero? I feel the fool … a damn stupid fool.

Darkness and the difficulty of the land stops my run a little ways within the east side of the south woods. I peer back into the gloom towards the field to see if someone has followed but see no one, nothing but the falling and wind blown snow, not even distant reflected lights from the trailer. I did my running mostly from memory of the lay of the land from our walk-around Rick gave us, so I know this place, but I also realize I can see further in front of me now than before—why? Looking into the trailers lights, especially the opened door, should have taken away whatever good night vision my eyes had. I look around and then up to the night sky. The storm is breaking. The moon's light is piercing the clouds.

In the pit of my stomach comes a turning. A flush of heat arrives within my cold numb cheeks as real tears begin to form in my eyes. I feel like a scolded child who innocently, but purposely, caused some unforeseen yet immeasurable irreparable wrong. Did I just guarantee the death of everyone I hold close and dear? Oh God, what a fool I am.

What do I do now?

67
(Franklin)

We don't speak—we listen, but hear nothing of our attacker amid the howling winds and clashing of trees from the nearby woods. Minutes pass before we dare to move or speak again. Moonlight pokes through the clouds. The storm must be breaking, or there is a break in it, though the snow still falls heavy. This waiting time is too much for those inside the trailer.

"You guys still out there?" Drew calls out.

"Yeah, Drew, we're fine," Tollin answers. "Just don't come out. Don't show yourselves."

"Holy shit," I exclaim now that our silence is broken.

"We didn't get him?" asks Tollin.

"Stop wishin'," says Radwell in a forced voice. "Is Perez saying anything over there—Perez, you hurt?"

"He's dead, yo, I saw two go through him, man," I answer. Funny, I can watch a man die with no problem, but a severed head makes me want to puke.

Radwell cusses over Perez's loss. Tollin cusses too. I'm kind of glad.

"How many shots ya count?" I ask. "I think four."

"Four," replies Tollin. "I think four."

"Four," Radwell confirms.

"There's just one of 'em out there—right?" Tollin asks.

"I believe so, man," I answer. "Dere woulda been more a somethin' if dere were, man—what ya think, Rad?"

"I think he's alone—and it is a man—this sure ain't the work of a woman."

"I-I don't know, Rad, I knew this one ..." Tollin begins.

"Don't joke," Radwell snaps back. "This changes everything worse for us—don't joke."

"This man is, is crazy then," Tollin states, though we are all sure of that already.

"The man is also smart," Radwell replies, again in a strained voice.

We three cautiously begin to rise and look about. If he is around, now is the time he should shoot, but nothing happens, no sound is heard other than the wind, the trees being pushed by it, and the sporadic whimpering, at least I'll call it that, from the women inside the trailer which seems to now have stopped. I reject the thought of going back inside the trailer. There'd be no good way to get the man out here if we hole up inside that place too soon. It's clear Radwell and Tollin think the same.

"Why aren't we being shot at?" Tollin wonders.

"Because there is only one of them," Radwell answers caustically. "Don't you get it yet? How many times do I have to say it?"

"I know, man, I know, it can't be ta cops," I answer for both Tollin and myself, realizing so many of those bells that rung in my head earlier all pointed to this now oh-so obvious fact. I'm angry I hadn't listened better to their warnings, as we move carefully to the place in the snow where the man shot at us, though we stand well apart from each other and we keep our eyes searching the dark landscape.

"He waited here. Look at the trailer; see how well he could see us coming out that door? He couldn't see all the way inside but, damn, how'd he miss killing more of us?" Radwell ponders. Tollin and I glance that way.

"Why only four shots?" Tollin wonders as he steps on something hard. "Since he wanted to kill us, he just missed his best chance—and he left his rifle behind." Tollin leans over and picks it up out of the snow. He checks it for bullets. He looks at us and shakes his head to let us know the gun is empty.

"No shit. Maybe we did hit him," I offer. "Why'd he leave his gun behind? Why didn't he keep shootin', man?"

Radwell shakes his head. "Can't see enough in this dark whether there is blood, but seems like we had to hit him for him to drop his gun. If he's wounded, well, that's good."

"You think he maybe has another gun?" Tollin asks.

"I would know?" Radwell growls.

We peer into the murkiness around us, visually tracing the man's paths to and from this point over the short distances we can see.

"What if four were all the bullets he had?" Tollin asks.

"Is he dat crazy, man? Why be out here, den do this, man, when enough time has gone by dat he could of done get ta cops, man—I don't understand."

"Why this now? Why Meirs head? Yeah, Rad, why?" Tollin asks.

Radwell is slow enough to answer to cause Tollin and I turn to look at him. "My guess is he wants us to know, guys, that we're not alone," Radwell says. "To unsettle us. To let his friends know."

"How's dat gonna help him?" I scoff. "How's leaving his rifle behind going ta help?"

"Ah," Radwell slowly speaks, "Well, I think he believes we'll keep his friends alive—to bargain with him, maybe … hard to say. He's playin' a dangerous game with us if that's how he is thinkin'. Why he did not go get the cops is what troubles me. Why didn't he do that?"

"Cal's gonna want ta start shootin' 'em right away," Tollin warns.

"Can't. Can't let him. We weren't thinking of killing them yet. I see no reason to now," Radwell replies, "Maybe one. I'll agree with this crazy man to keep his friends alive—for now, but I think we can play this hostage game against him. Let's play along a bit. We might be able to draw him out to show himself on our terms because I don't think he would've run too far."

Radwell's last words make Tollin and I crouch down and look around in the darkness.

"You gotta plan for dat?" I ask.

"Thinkin' up one, yeah."

"How'd ya know he was out here?" Tollin asks.

"Heard sniffles."

"What?"

"Heard someone suck the boogers back into their nose, man—what did you think I said?"

"Strange way to call us out."

"Ya got a point. We might a come out before he was ready."

"What kinda guy is he to cut off Meirs head?"

"A crazy idiot … maybe."

"Well he's gotta be an idiot to think we don't realize he's out of bullets—because we got his gun. Good thing he wasn't a better shot," Tollin says.

"He was good enough," Radwell responds. "He put a bullet through my right shoulder. And there's no way we know for sure he's got no more bullets, no other gun. He's crazy. I don't think he's stupid—not yet. We should expect more crazy shit."

68
(Franklin)

The bullet went through Radwell right near the base of his neck, about an inch over, and he believes it busted his right collarbone. Whether from this bullet, or from one of the others, there is a window shattered in place as we come back to the trailer, its glass cracked in dozens of ways, some of the glass missing from its pane but most still held within it, set above where the second sofa sits, where the men campers are kept. I see no marks on the trailer—can't find where the bullets that went through Perez ended up. We leave Perez lay where he is. There ain't no point in doing anything with his body right now.

Radwell cusses as he is forced to use his right arm to enter the trailer. He goes immediately for the chair I had been sleeping on before.

I slam the trailer's door closed behind us and squat down alongside Cal—inside the main living area, away from the doorway's path to that chair Radwell is sitting in. If a bullet comes through that door I want Radwell to receive it, not me. We four stare at Radwell; Cal, Drew, Tollin, and myself—Drew is now dressed for the outside. Cal is not, his blistered bloodied feet were bound up in gauze by the nurse just before he went off to sleep a couple of hours ago. He is in no shape to go anywhere far.

"My collar bone feels busted," Radwell says again, gasping, "I can't barely use my right arm." And he cusses once more.

"You're gonna look at him, nurse," I state as move towards her, "I'll untie ya. Is dere going ta be enough bandages ta fix him?"

She returns a resentful look, but knows she has no choice. "There's a third—and last, medical kit in the bathroom. Maybe it will be enough," she replies.

"What happened out there?" Cal questions us, looking first at Radwell and then follows my eyes as I look back at him while I move the few steps to the nurse. "Is it the law?"

"No," I answer, "Someone from here—what ta heck, Cal, does ta law stick a man's head on ta end of a shovel? Shit no!" I answer, becoming quickly angry from rising frustrations over these new events as I move away from Radwell. "Ta law would've blasted us to ta lowest places in hell if dey were out dere just now, man. Dere's one crazy bastard out dere who thinks he can whip our butts," I yell, pointing with a raised arm towards a trailer window, "We got trouble, dammit."

"Well I didn't ...," Cal begins to offer.

"Well you what, Cal? Didn't think? Freakin' right you didn't think. When ta heck do ya, man? Yo sooner start thinkin' ta freakin' better," I reply, as I lead and shove the nurse towards Radwell. "Dat man out dere shot four times—just four. He's goin' for ta law now, if we didn't or don't get him."

"Oh Jesus!" Cal exclaims, "Let's get the truck and get the heck out of here. Whose head was it?"

"Meirs head idiot!" I shout as Tollin and Radwell add silent stares to answer him. In the background Drew's shoulders drop and his face turns as he briefly looks down to the floor.

"The lunatic placed it right, right on the borders of the shadows of the trailer's lights," Radwell explains. "I wasn't sure what it was, then I didn't think, after seeing it, until it was too late. Set me up but good, that asshole."

"Where's Perez?" Drew asks.

"Dead," I answer. Drew sighs as this time he looks up and shakes his head.

"Dead? Dead?" Cal exclaims. "Let's kill these people, kill them now."

"No," Radwell replies. "No. We use them as bait. Use them as shields. We'll use them then kill them. And, Cal, the trucks are freakin' useless in this snow."

"Who is out dere?" I demand, then realize I can get that answer as I swing my rifle into the nearest camper to me. My gun's tip comes to rest on Bill's belly. "Who?"

Bill's red face fills with the fear that I may pull the trigger, and I just might. The right side of his face is all bloody and cut because of many shards of glass that are embedded in his flesh. I glance behind him. It was his luck to sit there when the crazy man's bullet went through the window. Too bad the bullet didn't kill him.

"I ain't sure, man, I didn't see the two you killed," Bill replies.

"I should kill ya just 'cause ya lied earlier—one, two, or three, shit head. Who were ta three—and there were three, you hear me Rad—who were ta three out dere—tell me their names."

Bill does not hesitate; "Roy, Tom, and my brother-in-law."

"Brother-in-law?" I am surprised.

"Brother-in-law," Drew repeats. "To who? Who is his … the stutterer—Mary. Blondie tried to act as her husband so we wouldn't think more people were out there. Check her purse—we'll find out what this guy looks like, see if it's him."

Mary's eyes are wide with fear, but she stays silent.

"I don't get it," Cal remarks, "Why it got ta be her husband out there. If Blondie weren't then why not this cowboy guy?"

I'm about to snap at Cal, as the others are, but he has made a point. If not Blondie, why not the cowboy, and these campers were just being quiet about it. "Give me a purse," I say to Tollin, who is already looking through Gay's. The purse he gives me turns out to be Paula's and I toss it across the room in disgust. Drew hands me the last purse, Mary's purse. I flip it open and scramble through the things she has inside it until I find where she has pictures of her family ....

"God-damn," I remark as I stare at a picture of her and who must be her husband. "God-damn."

"What?" Radwell asks for all the others.

A smile pulls slow and wide across my face. "Meant ta be, man. Us getting outta prison and going for a new life. Meant ta be. Ain't one a those we killed. Ha, her husband is ta guy who pitifully tried ta fight me last Sunday ..."

"Oh, no kidding?" Radwell erupts in near laughter cut short by a stab of pain.

A big smile crosses Drew's face; "Oh, fate is kind. Now we know why the guy is crazy—because he is—and we got his wife—ha-ha-haa. It can't get better than this, Frank, it just can't. Revenge handed to ya, just handed to ya—ain't it great?"

I slowly nod my head. "Yeah. Oh yeah. Any of ya take this woman yet?"

All shake their heads no. I smile as I look at Mary.

"You ain't either," she screeches, and to that I laugh.

69
(Franklin)

"Alright now," Radwell begins, in pain, as Gay hesitantly finishes pulling his coat and shirt off, "That man out there ain't going nowhere far. He's gonna freeze to death or get shot by us. We have to deal with him, Franklin. Nurse, what are you waiting for?"

"I need a first aid kit," Gay quietly answers.

"Wha—why you sayin' that?" Cal asks Radwell, puzzled over the reason or reasons.

"Where is it you say again?" Radwell asks her in reply, ignoring Cal.

"In the towel shelf in the bathroom."

"Go get it, Cal," he orders, and then answers Cal's question; "Because he can't see any better than us in this blizzard. He ain't goin' nowhere 'till it's over or it's daylight."

"B-but he found his way back here," Cal points out, speaking from within the bathroom, "He knows the way out, too."

"He's seeing good enough to shoot you, Rad," I jeer as I watch Cal return and hand the kit to Gay, as I take the fear-stricken Mary from her sofa by putting my hand down inside her jeans at her waistline and pulling her up to stand next to me, intent on getting her to a bedroom. She erupts with emotion.

"Get away from me!" she screams as she kicks and hits me. "Get away you asshole! Get-way!"

Her kicks land painfully against my shin while her fists have little power, yet I'm enraged. I let go of her with my left hand then bring it up then down, the side of my hand impacting hard against the left side of her jaw, breaking open her left lower lip as she falls back into the couch. She still kicks and swings until my fist finds her right cheek and knocks her back again into the couch. Now stunned, I pull her up once more. Again she kicks and hits, until the mid-stock of my rifle finds her face as my right arm swings into her. This time she weakly grabs hold of my arm as she keeps from falling back, fighting to stay conscious, but not fighting me anymore, as she sways around, her eyes barely coherent. I do it for her—I push her down into the sofa again, and there she stays in a daze. She breathes rapidly, her eyes filled with a curious mix of incoherence, fear and rage, but she says nothing, and while she may still want to, she wisely doesn't resist further. Her face already shows bruising and swelling from the guns impact.

"Maybe," Radwell now replies, after watching what happened between me and Mary, jerking from the intrusive cleaning Gay gives his wound as she prepares to bandage him. "But I think he got here by luck. If he had been a good shot, I'd be dead. I suspect he ain't gonna wander far from the lights. AH! Watch it!" he yells at the nurse.

She looks at him briefly; "Do you want me to do this or not?"

"Yes," he snaps, then continues; "Anyway, he thinks he can take us on, the fool, instead of going for the cops. So he must not know how to do that, where to go."

"Or, since he has let us know he's here, now he's going to get help. Making us chase him," Tollin offers.

"So one a us can go out n get him while it's still dark," I say hesitantly, almost in question, "Is dat what you're thinkin', man?"

Radwell nods his head and grabs the nurse's arm with his blood soaked left hand to look at the time on her watch as she cringes from his touch. "He's bought time for his friends here—successfully … for a short time," Radwell adds as he stares into the nurse's eyes. "We've got … maybe four hours, probably more with this heavy storm, before the sun shines the place up enough to help him out there—help the man get out of here. He don't know his way. He just can't. Why else would he be here? I can't get over why he didn't go for the cops first if he did know his way out. That's our advantage. For the next four hours or so he is as trapped here as we are. He's got to be. Why did he show up so late? To me, to me that says he tried to leave but couldn't. We have to get him before then—before morning, or he'll be able to find his way out to the cops. What's the verdict, nurse, my collar bone busted?"

Gay looks at him straight in the eyes as she pulls her arm away from his hand.

I should be dragging Mary into the bedroom, should've done so already, but I'm conflicted. I know what Radwell is saying, leading to, it's simple enough, and it's just enough to keep me standing here. I got my revenge on this man, for sure. I can take his wife now, or later, or I can go after him myself now and kill him, but I'm not sure what I want to do first. My groin tells me her. My other head tells me him, for he is more risk. I'm stuck standing here, though I coming to realize if I do her first my mind will be on him, but if I kill him first, I have no worries about what I'll do with her.

"No," Gay reluctantly begins, snarling the single word at him before answering in a more flowing habitually professional tone that turns into another snarl; "Your clavicle is intact. You're not going to be able to lift your arm much, probably ever again, like you used to. Some good amount of muscle is gone. I could stick two fingers into you from the back. I'm a bit surprised you can hold your head up so well. I'm really surprised this isn't bleeding more. I was really hoping the bullet hit an artery and you'd bleed to death or pierced your lung and you'd drown in your own blood—that there'd be nothing I could do, but none of that is going to happen," she purposely pauses to let her words sink in. "This is the last of the big bandages, mister. This is the last first-aid kit we have, nothing more. The bandages will need changing in a few hours to prevent infection. You need a doctor, then, not me, or infection will set in deep."

"We don't need a bitch like you," Cal growls as he takes a small threatening step toward her, stopping only upon Radwell's words and upraised left hand.

"Ah, lots of words lady, so you try to imply my time is limited," Radwell states with scarcely any emotion. "This really changes things, doesn't it? Not a chance. Put my shirt and coat back on," he orders her. "Tollin, Franklin, Drew, I need you three to go back outside …," he says and, as she finishes slipping his jacket on; "…Drew, you've been pretty damn quiet. Let's hear you now."

Drew takes a breath while his head sways in a slight agreeing nod. "The man counts on drawing us out. We need to go now while his path is still in the snow."

"What's with the backpack, mister?"

"Yeah, he figures it's a good time to leave, cross the border," the cowboy adds.

It was Bill who first spoke. I quickly move to put the tip of my gun back onto his belly, which also quiets the cowboy. Bill's eyes meet mine as he carefully points with his head toward Drew. All eyes fall on Drew. Bill daringly, cautiously, adds; "He packed it well and quick while you guys were out in the snow."

With Drew's heavy garb the large backpack actually looks small. I hadn't noticed it, but I do notice Smith smiling.

Drew becomes uncomfortable, momentarily glares at Bill and the cowboy, and feels compelled to explain; "Since that man found his way back here in a storm like this, even with telling tracks in the snow, he won't make it easy for someone to track him down. I figure I'll be out there a long time—I don't want to come back until I get him."

"If you're planning on coming back at all …" Radwell is hostile. "Take the pack off—I want to make sure you do come back here."

Drew appears properly insulted. "Do you want this man dead …?"

"Dead and you back here so we all manage to get out-a-here. Get rid of it."

Drew glares silently a moment first at Radwell, then at Bill, then again at the cowboy, before turning toward the main bedroom, slamming the bedroom door behind him.

"You can't go out there," Cal says to Radwell. "Us four will go get the bastard."

"Cal, face it, man, you're stupid," Tollin responds. "Radwell can't watch these people alone. You stay—look at your feet, dipshit."

"Tollin's right," Radwell states. "You can't go nowhere and I need you here."

"I ain't stupid. My feet can ...."

"Shut-up Cal," snaps Radwell.

Drew returns. "So what's the plan … sir?" His tone is sarcastic as he says this to Radwell, but Radwell doesn't care.

"I'm sending you three out. Drew, you'll go north along the man's path—I don't know whether he came or went that way, Frank will show you where. Tollin, I want you to follow the man's tracks south. Franklin, I want you to go east a good ways, splittin' the two. I believe that guy don't know the area good at all, so he'll swing around one way or the other to come back to what he knows, but he won't back-track, so you're the cutoff man. Go about five maybe six hundred steps. If ya don't find nothing, come back and go the other way—got it all of ya?"

"He's closin' in on a good thirty minute head start now by the time we go," mentions Drew, "If we don't go now."

"Long enough for him to start feeling secure about not being followed," Radwell replies, who seems to have all the answers. "Get dressed for it Frank, Tollin. Hurry that, too."

#

"So let's do it," Drew says about three minutes later. "Turn the lights off so we can't be seen and let's go. Franklin, you first."

"Me—no," I quickly respond. "You can do dat, man. He might be nearby."

"Thought you were a brave man, Franklin."

"Stop it," Radwell commands. "Change a plans. Tollin, you show Drew the path. Franklin, you take Mary out with ya, use her as a shield. She's this guy's wife, I want him to see her—we'll turn the lights back on thirty seconds after you two leave—Drew, Tollin. Then Frank, make sure you point the gun, have it firmly planted against her head. Anything happens that we don't want—shoot her. I want Mason. You guys got it?"

"Hey, I thought I was goin' ta do her—I'm going ta do her first ..."

"Later, the man out there is more important, ya know that."

I notice Drew and Tollin nod their heads in agreement. I don't like it, but I nod my head, too. I guess I just wanted to restate my claim on her.

"Yeah," Tollin answers. "Plan is Drew and I first. Thirty seconds to reach the paths in this darkness—thanks, man, then you'll turn the lights back on and go out yourselves with Mary and Mason as your shields—what ya gonna do then, Rad?"

"Send Frank as before. Don't stick around to see but if you hear more than two shots, come back to help."

Moments later the lights are turned off inside the trailer and the door is quietly opened. Drew and Tollin hurry out into the darkness. We can hear them move away. Thirty seconds later the lights inside—and outside, come on again just bright enough to do the job we need them to do, the drain on the battery is telling.

"Cal, here we go. We'll be right outside. Step ahead of me here old man—you're goin' out first," Radwell says to Mason, "Let's do it."

Radwell kicks open the trailer's door, hoping the sound is loud enough to catch the attention of the man if he is still nearby. I follow him, forcing the stiffly moving and frightened, resistant, Mary along ahead of me in the snows. Radwell pushes Mason out in front of him about ten feet from me to my right.

"You out there!" Radwell yells, as he pulls on Mason's collar, turning his eyes toward the hideous sight of Meirs' head then around to Perez's body and back again; "You got five minutes to show yourself before we blast the life out of one of these hostages here. Your wife! You see your wife you mother-fucker? We know she's your wife. We know you ain't the law. You're cold. Wet. You come in we'll take care of ya … you hear me … and your wife and this man will live … you hear me? I'll say this again …"

Radwell continues his speech for another minute but there is no response.

"…We're waitin' for ya," Radwell shouts, finishing, as he turns the frightened Mason, along with himself, first one way and then another one last time, as he peers into the falling snows, "We won't kill anybody if ya come in. You want your friends all to die? You want your wife to die? We'll do that. Be glad to. Won't kill anybody if you come in. Do the right thing. Your friends are all scared of dyin'. They think you're foolish for doin' what ya did. Ya got five minutes—five minutes. Hear me—five minutes."

70

The adrenaline rush from shooting and running, rather my plowing, through the snow, should have given my body sustainable warmth, but any given is drained by thoughts of consequences my actions may bring. My lower jaw chatters against my upper teeth as shivers run through my body, shivers that do not only come from the cold. I don't want to know those consequences. I don't want to know.

I pull the handgun out of my belt and hold it close to my eyes, pulling my wet and dirtied glasses off to see, as well as feel, the safety slide to its firing position in this murky darkness.

The storm clouds are thinning again allowing the moonlight to come through. As scant as this light is, it allows me to perceive what is ahead of me a reasonable distance. What I see surprises me. Mostly buried in snow is a truck and a car some yards away, their forms unmistakable. I hurry over to the nearest one and try its door—locked. The other is locked, too. Why are these vehicles here? I search the darkness for anyone following me as I come to realize these must be stolen vehicles the convicts used. There'll be nothing useful found inside them. Wasted time. Wasted hope. Wasted energy. With the moonlight showing again I take a strong pace to go further into these woods, intent to go west, then north, to circle the camp.

I once watched a movie of a wanted man being hunted through the Alaskan winter wilderness. He was heading for the safety of the Yukon Canadian border. This man moved at a tenacious pace to stay warm; so will I. This man kept that pace for days, all but exhausting his trackers and making them respect him, though they killed him by the movie's finish. Well, I want to and will survive. If they do kill me, I hope to make them work hard for that pleasure and extract a heavy toll from them before I die … and, and if I am the idiot I now fear I am, and have forced them to kill those I came to help, then there is nothing left to live for anyway; no choice but to try to kill those men I've seen. Striking soon, from a different direction, is best.

The wind is weakened by these woods, though it blows the dark treetops together often with loud clunks and scraping sounds. Twigs or other small branches snap and fall frequently from the heights, adding a certain chatter of noise to what is around me. This winter turmoil does not stop the snow from sticking to the trees where the wind and the tree's movements lack enough force to shake the stubborn white off. When I was a child the wetness of true ice storms would glaze over everything. Trees split not only from the freezing of their internal sap, but from ice forming at the junctions of branches and inside the crevices of their bark—how that kind of cold reached in and stole heat from you to claim it viciously, more than this storm does, but I am in trouble; most everything but my toes complain as I hurry along. My lower body feels the loss in protection that extra jacket had given. The parka isn't enough to keep me warm.

The rustling of the trees covers the sounds of my rapid movements as I work to build warmth, and nothing comes to mind as I struggle to think about what I can do next. It is too hard for me to move away, for long, from the thoughts that I did some immense harm instead of good. That I failed. Oh God, if they die because of what I have done … there'll be hell on earth for the rest of my days.…

Maybe I should have used the handgun to try and finish those outside the trailer, but I'm not sure of the handgun's range and have no confidence in shooting this gun at that distance *and* I did not think of it, though I wish I had.

As the clouds again cover the moon I stop and lean against a good-sized oak and look back into the murky darkness that cannot hide my obvious path through the snow as I regain my breath. Damn, what should I have done back there—anything different than what I did? I need to make a decision and stick to it; no regrets, no doubts. Questions, okay, they'll make one think ... they cannot leave—they cannot anymore than I can. The drifts, the cold, the snow, that have intimidated me from leaving have become much too deep for them to leave, too. They are certainly not desperate enough to go off on foot—not yet. They are as stuck here as I am, and they must know this. Will they keep my people alive because of this? Oh, I hope, I truly prayerfully hope, that they need Mary, my sister, and my friends for some reason—to dig out, maybe, or for bargaining chips or protection if the law finds them, but these reasons don't seem strong enough. They will not need them all. They will keep the women, the three of them, the six men I counted will pair themselves with the three women. Bill, Rick, Doug, and whoever else will be killed because they are extra and dangerous baggage—but are these men alive now? If only to promote a reluctant but willing response in the women … maybe so, yet Bill's silhouette had not moved in that window ....

I'm deep into the south woods and probably a good ways above the trailer on the slope rising to the west away from our camp, and I'm still leaning against this oak as my breath returns, when I hear a shot ring out and my heart falls heavy. They have killed someone. Why else would the shot sound? Who was it—Bill, Rick, Doug, or someone else? Both my hands come up, with the handgun in one, to squeeze each side of my head as I wallow in frustration, trying to make this headache go away. I should have been there. Should have gone back to fight with this handgun the moment thoughts of their killing my friends came to mind. Now another of my friends, possibly my wife, is dead … my wife … Mary … God, my head hurts, make this nightmare go away, make it go away.

Should I do that now—go back and shoot it out? Should I run for the law even though I don't know how? What should I do? My knees weaken and I find myself kneeling in the snow, trying to sob … trying to cry … trying to pray … yet unable to.

71
(Franklin)

Five minutes pass. Then probably ten more. We've been silent, turning our shivering captives one way, then the other, as we peer into the surrounding landscape but we hear and see nothing of the man. I notice Radwell is looking at me and once he has caught my attention he places the tip of his shotgun to the back of Mason's head. Radwell gives a nod of his head toward me. I place the tip of my rifle against the back of Mary's head and whisper to her; "You make a sound n I pull ta trigger—understand?"

She gives a slight nod and a quiet one syllable response of fear as her breathing becomes rapid and shallow. Both her and Mason shiver constantly from the cold—we have coats on, they don't, but she also shakes from fear of my gun, as she should.

"Cal," Radwell calls out.

"Yeah," he answers as he carefully cracks open the trailer door.

"Turn off all the lights."

"What for?"

"Do it, Cal."

The flash and sound of gunfire shatters the darkness around us seconds after the lights go out. I hear Mason's body collapse into the snow. Mary jerks and does make a sound, but it is not a loud one. She cries, but these sounds won't carry far. I can feel her tremble and cower from my hold on her. Radwell comes and takes her.

"She's mine," I remind him in a whisper.

"I know," he reassures. "You'll have her."

The darkness is striking as I make my clumsy way through the heavy snows. I imagine the man out there, if he watched, wasn't fooled by what we did. I feel sure, however, that he carries no gun. He would've used it considering the opportunities just handed him. How could he resist trying to defend and save Mason's life? He can't possibly be hesitant about saving his wife's life after what he did with Meirs' head. He would've attacked us somehow, had he been near—her life wouldn't have stopped me—I wouldn't have revealed myself for her, but I would avenge her death. If that is the crazy man's plan ... well, I can respect that.

How can this crazy man be dressed right? If he was dressed anything like the two we saw run from us earlier, in this cold and wet ... I'm surprised to find he survived this long—the thought, the fact he has disturbs me. I'll savor the opportunity to kill him after his defiance at the prison. He ... what kind of sadistic creep is he to cut off Meirs' head? Then stick it on a shovel pole? Did he do time at one time, or what? He must be one fanatical bastard—insane enough not to know he should be curling up and dying in this freaking freezing blizzard. Damn him for making me come out here in this freaking cold.

While the soft deepness of this new snow smothers the sounds of my movements the stiff long grasses lying underneath still seem loud as my weight crushes them and stops me in my tracks often, despite the louder sounds of the howling winds and the clattering collisions of the treetops in these eastern woods I now enter as I make step number four-hundred-fifty-three.

The depth of this snow often reaches over the height of my knees as I step among the brush and small sapling trees, the older evergreens, on the edge of these woods. The snow rises almost to my breast line in many of the drifts I pass. Do I really have to be out here? We only got to protect what we got, man; the trailer and trucks, ourselves, and to leave him be, out here, to shiver, freeze, and die. Why risk my life? What for—what could this guy do to us now? What would he do? He no longer has a weapon. But I want him ... dead, but slowly dead. Maybe take his fingers off first, take out his crotch—he should remain conscious for that, then maybe I'll finish him ... mmm, maybe.

The clouds break again to allow the moon light to brighten the landscape.

The crazy bastard got this far—got us to do all this. The cold and snow drove him crazy enough to make a mess of our plans. Who knows what he'll try to do next? Set the whole trailer on fire? Actually go get the cops? Whatever he next does we have to stop. We can't ignore him. It's not wise to. Yeah, yeah, yeah, I know that.

He'll have to keep moving to stay warm, unless he can hole-up somewhere, but then he'll be wet—how could he dry off? Hypothermia will creep in, seduce him to sleep. He'll drift off to death. Then we will have to find his body. This can't be as hard as Joey, my first kill, or the two Mexicans. Damn crow, if I just stepped on it to keep its squawking from giving me away. That surprised bird caught itself on a garbage can—I had my chance, but let it squawk. I let it get loose and fly away, but it knew I wanted to kill it. I hesitated. I won't with this man. I'll kill this man, unless Drew or Tollin kill him first. This trail of death we make is what we got to do for our freedom and will only grow. We can't do nothing else—so why worry? Find this bastard and be done with him.

He'll be foolish to return, desperate, or simply the crazy bastard we think he is. Without his rifle what does he have left to kill us with—a power saw—an axe? Only if he went to the place where we found Meirs and he must have, to cut off Meirs' head. He is one crazy bastard. Maybe he believes if he didn't stake Meirs' head on that pole we'd kill them sooner, once we felt they were useless to us—a kind of insurance policy granting extra time, as Radwell said. A chance worth taking? Maybe. That has some logic, though I'd like him simply being crazy.

I'm taking step number four hundred ninety six—well into the woods, when I hear muffled shots. Two-three, very quick, distant and to my right—in the south woods well up the rise. These sounds drop me into a crouch once more, searching everywhere for signs.

Tollin found him.

Minutes roll by as I wait and listen for more but nothing comes, just the sounds of the slowly dying storm. Now what? Did Tollin just plug the guy three times—must have. Is there any sense staying out here? I'd better take one more look around, in case Tollin missed and the guy is running towards me.

I don't know. It's been minutes—I don't want to wait and look no more. I'm going back to the trailer. It's time to hear how Tollin got the man. This hasn't taken too long … maybe somewhat more than an hour by the time I get back.

72

My thoughts slowly become clear as I stay crouched against this tree and stare at the black trunks of the surrounding trees, white on only one side and thick in numbers, and notice how they meld quickly into the dark background of the night. Here, around me, the snow falls as gently as I have ever seen it and in contrast to the howling wind and the scraping treetops above—a scene recalling a childhood memory of calmly watching out our front window, with the house lights off behind me, the differing faces of winter's cold beauty, as shown by our lone shining porch light. I shake the pleasant thought off as my eyes grow heavy again and I come to lean against this oak once more, out of the wind to continue to rest, depressed in my thoughts.

Several moments flow by before I hear the rustle and lift my sight to scan the woods about me. The moonlight comes and goes more often. The noise was out of place somehow and now comes a second time—from around the back of this tree, along the trail of my path. Someone is coming. Someone is speaking.

Speaking?

I quietly slip off my gloves and grip cold gunmetal, realizing there is nowhere to run, the wooded area around me is too perilous for that with these sounds so near. I will have to face them before they see my path ending here.

Oh God.

The hesitant sound grows louder. I gulp a deep breath before I turn round along the edge of my tree to see an image drawing out of the shadows—one image. The man is cursing, blurting his words out quietly. I pull back behind the tree.

He does a poor job if he hunts me. I'm confused. I gulp a deep breath again and turn round along the edge of my tree. "Freeze," I call firmly, not yelling the word but making sure the man who stands silhouetted in my sights about thirty feet from me clearly hears it.

His silhouette stiffens. He is out in the open, in my path, close enough for me to see his image but not close enough for me to see all he can do with certainty. He carefully glances from side to side, searching the woods to find where my voice came from, before returning to look straight up my path.

"And who says that I should?" he asks, matching the level of my voice. The outline of his head turns from side to side, waiting for my response, trying to hear, to find, my location.

I begin to pull the gun's slider back to the cocked position, trying to be quiet in doing this, but its noise still focuses him towards me—and the bullet already chambered ejects ... shit! But another has been loaded.

"I see," he says, his voice constricting a bit as he studies the tree I hide behind. "You needn't worry," he continues, stopping me from speaking, "I heard shots out here and came out to investigate."

He pauses for my response, but I keep silent, sensing he will speak again.

"I can help you," he begins again, pausing to see if I will answer.

I do not.

"Why are you here?" he asks, yet again pausing for an answer.

Again I do not give one.

"C'mon, man, I can't do anything for you if you don't answer me," he states, still searching for my exact location.

I remain silent. The more he talks the more I learn?

"Look. I don't know what's goin' on out here but if you're poaching you picked a bad night for it. Can't drag a deer anywhere far in this stuff and you should know that…" again he pauses. "You there? Anybody here? Or did I just imagine someone calling out to me? I'm gonna start movin' again in a moment if…."

"Drop your gun," I order. His stance goes rigid and he is focused on my tree.

"Okay—okay—don't shoot. You got all the advantage. I'm not sure yet where you are so I cannot shoot you if I wanted to—and I don't, so don't shoot. I'm gonna put my gun down now—see?" After a moment's hesitation he leans slowly over and places his rifle down in the snow directly beneath him before carefully standing up straight again.

"How many are you?" I ask.

"W-What do you mean?" he asks back. "I'm the only one. Can't you see that?"

"I mean how many are you? You're one of those who got control of our trailer, so don't give me no shit, understand?" I demand.

"Oh-god!" he exclaims with relief. "What trailer? I thought you were either a poacher or, or one of those who escaped from a prison last night. The news said they're likely in the area. Oh thank god you're not one of them. I'm the county sheriff. I live south of here a ways. I heard shots. My wife said she heard some earlier, too. She pestered me into coming on out here. You know how women are—nag, nag, nag. She got me to wondering if someone was in trouble though, or if it were poaching. What's going on, man?"

I hold my heart back from leaping for joy. The man is a sheriff and here to help! I feel myself relax as relief sweeps through me. Why does he have to be someone hunting me from the trailer—I had seen no one following before? He can be someone else coming to investigate, just as he says. Man, I hope so—I really hope so.

I answer; "I'm one of those from a trailer a little distance from here where a number of men took my wife and friends captive. We have to get help—call the law. Your place far from here?"

"Don't have to call for help," he answers, "I said I am the law, but we will. My place is some ways south of here. A number of men? Do you know how many?"

"Not sure. I'm pretty sure I saw six. I have seen them kill. They … they killed."

"Shit. Sorry. And six is too many for us. We got to go to my place to call for more help. Come on. The sooner we get back to my place the better."

"They tried to kill me too."

"Ah … wow, man, I really don't know how to answer ya better. You're lucky to be alive. But as you say, though, means just the two of us won't be enough. We got to get back to my cabin and give a call. We'll get lots of help."

"Don't know who you are yet," I reply.

"Well yeah you do. I said I was the Law before. You think I can pick my gun off the snow now?"

"Yeah, go ahead," I answer as I ready to leave the protection of the tree. He quickly picks his weapon up as I innocently ask; "What force you on again?"

A slight hesitation before he answers; "Said I'm a sheriff, didn't say what county—what force."

"What county then?"

"Why the grillin', man?"

"What county?"

"I work for Nicolet County. C'mon, the weather's bad. You must be freezin'—I'm freezin'. It'll be warm at my place, get more help, get you thawed, then we'll come back and get your people out of here."

I stop and draw back for the protection of the tree before too much of my body is exposed. Something is not right and I'm not sure I remember correctly. "I did not quite hear ya. What force you say you on?"

The man is slow to answer. "I said I'm a sheriff."

"Know that—what county?"

"Nicolet."

No ... Oh no. No. No. We are in Forest or maybe Florence County, maybe if he said Oneida county, but I know there is no Nicolet county—I trust what Rick said; Nicolet Forest but no Nicolet County ... damn, and my heart begins to race. “Drop your rifle. You ain’t no sheriff. Drop your rifle.” But my mind pleads with me; come on, mister, give me a reason to keep on believing you—*please*.

The man shifts nervously, but holds onto his rifle. “Now wait a minute, man, I already dropped my rifle once. That should prove to you I’m okay. Don’t go off doin’ somethin’ crazy. The State’s on strike—I know it. That don’t mean I can’t come out here lookin’ to see what’s goin’ on. Just don’t get trigger happy—don’t pull that trigger. Let me show you my badge.”

I mull this over. I want to believe him.

“Alright,” I answer as I take aim at the middle of his upper torso as I tuck myself behind the tree as far as I can manage. “Go ahead, step forward some and show me your badge, toss it my way and make it a good toss, not one I have to reach for—do you understand me?”

“Yes I do, but you’re pretty far away.”

“Come closer, slowly, until I tell you to stop.”

The silhouette takes several slow steps forward but I stop him before I can see his face. If I can see his face, he can see mine, and I think that gets him too close for my safety.

“Still too far, mister,” he says.

“Make it a damn good throw then. You ain’t comin’ closer.”

I watch as he slowly transfers his rifle to his left hand, his hand possibly holding onto the stock just below the trigger as his right hand looks to be partially unzipping and reaching into his bulky coat, all done in a slow deliberate manner.

His hand pulls out something square, like a wallet.

“Can you see this?” he asks.

“Not really.”

“It’s my wallet ...”

“Strange place to have it—in your jacket not your pants.”

“Man, don’t get too damn picky when you put on snow wear—okay? You’re searching for things that don’t mean nothing. Don’t get yourself going over it.”

“You’re talking too much.”

“Alright-alright but I don’t want to toss it to ya, ‘fraid I’ll be losing it in the snow if I do. I know I got to, I heard you before—just, just keep a good eye on it, don’t lose it the snow, alright?”

“Toss it, I’m not saying it again.”

"Yeah, you should apply for a job in my department. I'd hire ya within a minute you stubborn cuss, you're doin' better making sure a things than most of my staff do."

"Toss the damn wallet."

"Just don't lose sight of it, okay? I'd hate losing it and tryin' ta find it out here—okay?"

"Yeah, get on with it. Toss it."

He throws it well and the wallet lands close by, a single step away from my tree, but it does go hidden in the snow. I could not want for a better throw.

I am cold. I so want to believe him. I want this nightmare to be over. I take that step away from the protection of the tree without pause. Out of the corner of my eye I see him quickly respond to the sight of me.

No thought—only reaction as I pull the trigger repeatedly an instant before his rifle flashes bright in the darkness and bark sprays out around me as his bullet hits my tree, just missing my side.

The man reels back as he falls into the shadows. I hit him! I hear his body pushing the snow, crunching the brush underneath, and a secondary sound like his arm stretched out and slapped something.

I see his darkened image slink away through the cover of the trees, not giving me good sight to shoot again.

He had not been the law. He couldn't have been the law. I did the right thing—I'm sure I did. I'm sure. Find the wallet to be sure.

Did something fall away from him as he reeled back? What was that other sound?

A broken branch? His arm?

No. No, I don't believe it was either of those; something heavy, more substantial, fell.

73
(Franklin)

“I’m coming in!” I shout as I near the dimly lit trailer. Cal gives reply and I approach.

“How’d he get him?” I eagerly ask. Cal stands nervously at the door holding it open only so far as to see me and to allow me in, as if the door would shield him from some outside attack. “What’s wrong?” I ask.

“Didn’t get him—we don’t think,” Cal answers. “Tollin’s inside. A few minutes ahead of ya. He’s got a bullet in his belly, upper right. Don’t look good. We got the nurse looking at him.”

“No … no,” I lament, frustration fills me as I hurry inside to the sights of our captives, whose eyes speak of both fear and delight in the dim light. “Where are they?” I ask, not seeing either Tollin or Radwell.

“In the master,” answers Cal. “Nurse said there’s internal bleedin’, says some hepacratic artery or somethin’ might’ve been cut—his stomach’s swellin’. He’s looking bad, man.”

Tollin is laid out on the bed as Gay works nervously, hurriedly, at his side. She is beyond her training and tries to hide this, unconvincingly, but works hard at tending to him. He anguishes in pain both from the wound and her efforts. Blood coats a large circle across his bared chest and belly. The small round entrance to the wound pulses blood, is plain to see as the nurse continues to work him. I feel a chill, but not from his sight. There’s a breeze coming through a crack in one of the windows, a section of its screen flaps in the wind. Tollin is sweating so I think they opened the window for that. His face turns to me.

“Creep has handgun,” Tollin rasps.

“How’d he?…” I begin.

“Meirs’ must’ve kept the one he found in the trucks,” interjects Radwell from behind me. “Come here,” Radwell orders as he leaves the room. “We need to talk.”

“Tollin?” I ask in respect. Tollin nods acceptance.

“You hang in dere, man, I’ll be right back.” But I see Tollin shake his head slightly and his eyes reinforce his quiet negative response. He doesn’t believe he will be all right. He doesn’t look right. I don’t know what else to say.

"We've got to get this asshole right now, before daylight, before he can see to get somewhere—you understand?" Radwell forcefully says in a hushed manner, as we stand near the trailer's door. I nod my head as I look around the short partition separating the doorway from the rest of the trailer and the captives. They watch us with concern, and it is apparent the nearest ones can hear us in spite of our lowered tones.

"We got to get him so we got time to think about what we gotta do next. Whatever that is, it's gotta be on our terms—not his. Understand?" Radwell asks.

I nod yes again.

"I can't send Cal out there, ya know that. I gotta have him here. You gotta do this. Take what you need and go quickly. Find him. Destroy this bastard."

I nod agreement again as I look over the captives. Too many things are suddenly not going right—too many. And when things do not go right for too long a time they add up to nothing going right. I have not risked my life for failure. And now I'm the only one able to change this feeling, this path. I'm not going to let that bastard out there destroy my chance for a new life. He is going to die. "Wait … what about Drew? He come back yet?" I ask. "We can do dis better if he knows."

"Naw," answers Radwell over his shoulder as he starts back to Tollin. "It's too early. He could still be on his way."

I stand there a moment considering what I'd need to take along with me. First though, I need the bathroom.

I stare at the toilet paper roll as I sit and consider how glad that I don't need to do this in the wild. I should … take … some … along … in a backpack. I flush, dress, and enter into the main bedroom….

"Rad?" I ask from the doorway watching the busied nurse. Radwell has his back to me.

"Yeah Franklin why ain't you gone yet?" he replies, while trying to help the nurse. Tollin's face is pale with cold sweats beading his forehead as he lays there. One moment he appears to want to say something, the next moment he is too involved with the pain he feels, the strain his body is under, to have a coherent thought to say. The sight of him makes me uneasy.

"Drew hasn't come back?" I ask.

"Stupid question."

"Den he ain't comin' back."

This makes Radwell turn toward me, looking as if my words just drove a nail into his coffin. "Now why you sayin' that?"

"Did you guys open dat window?"

Cal stands in the doorway and shakes his head. Gay shakes her head. Radwell replies; "No, man, none of us—what you getting' at?"

"Den I think, man, he shoved ta backpack out dat window dere—you were right with ya thinkin' ta way ya did."

Radwell doesn't respond as he briefly stares at the window that is not fully closed and with the torn screen. I point out there's no backpack in the room. Radwell is disgusted as he turns to face Tollin, but speaks to me; "Get out of here, Franklin … and come back. Get the bastard."

Cal comes up beside me. He stays silent as our eyes meet then speaks to me as he looks at Tollin laying on the bed. "Now ya got two to hunt down. Show no mercy."

I find a couple of boxes of ammunition for my rifle on a shelf in one of the kitchen's cabinets and I grab one of them. This box is not full but holds what should be plenty of shells and I stuff them into my pocket before heading to the trailer door.

Radwell passes on more information before I leave, from Tollin. He had slanted west up the south woods hill. I would think Mr. Crazy will continue that way—to the west after the exchange of gunfire with Tollin. He won't dare head back east the way Tollin came. Even a crazy man will know that was crazy … going south won't help him attack us again, only going west then north to circle us will. This is the way I am going—straight up the field behind the trailer while keeping the south woods to my left. I will see if I can cross his path.

Tollin's rifle fell free when he had been hit. He had fired only one round out of five from the semi-automatic, less than I thought I heard, and has no idea if he hit the crazy man. Radwell says to assume the crazy man found Tollin's rifle. I do. This crazy man is having an unbelievable run of luck.

"I'll get him, Tollin," I promise from the doorway of the bedroom. He nods his head. The nurse pauses to give me a pained hateful look.

"How many bullets *he* fire?" I ask Tollin.

"One?" he ekes out through his pain but he is also shaking his head a little. He doesn't know for sure.

"How many bullets in him, nurse?" I ask her.

She hesitates, knowing why I'm asking. She again gives me that pained hate filled look. "One, that's done a lot of damage. I think it's cut the hepatic artery."

"What's dat?"

"The main blood line to the liver."

"Fix it," demands Radwell.

"I can't," she asserts as she looks at him before more calmly repeating; "I can't. See his stomach swell—that's internal bleeding that I cannot stop."

Tollin's face fills with anguish.

"I get him," I promise Tollin, hesitate, wanting to say more but I don't have the words, before I turn and leave.

74
(Franklin)

I peer into the darkness of the south woods searching for sign of him, as I shake my trigger glove off and stuff it into my pocket, but there's nothing to see and nothing to hear between the heavy flurries of snow and the blowing wind. I creep forward going straight up this rising field behind our trailer and I'll do so until I cross his path. He has to leave these woods on my left. If I don't cross his path—he'll be in those woods. I'll go well past the hill's crest, to make sure. He can't see the trailer from beyond that range, not even half that—I lost sight of it a minute into my climb. He'll come out because he has to. He seems to have logic behind his actions but I still don't want to give him smarts. He might be only lucky and nothing else.

This snow works you. It's so deep and the grass that stands among it and lies underneath it catches your feet. There is eeriness above in this mottled dark sky with the moon behind it and the changes in noise sends shivers down my back whenever the wind stops blowing.

Why did Drew run—and the bastard did that without me, asshole, and I do feel like I have to kill him. Why did he leave without me—that's the only question I'll have for him. I checked that side of the trailer as I came out this time and it showed signs of him returning and something heavy being in the snow—he came back for the backpack—*that bastard.*

Three hundred twenty-one strides. I don't know why I'm counting. Most of the time I can't see but an arm's toss around me. When the moon breaks through the clouds I can see maybe seventy feet. The crazy man can be anywhere. If I can't find his path in the snow how will I find him? Maybe he did go east—toward the road.

What's that?

That sound? It's gone.

Am I hearing my own footstep again? *There—that image!*

BOOM-BOOM-BOOM!!

75

I find his wallet but I can't see or read anything useful from it in this darkness, while I keep a watch on my surroundings. I stuff it within the inside chest pocket of my coat. I take my time, not wanting to move away from here too quickly. If others are near hunting me I will hear them first—and I realize I'm taking a chance on that—I can't stay too long ....

He got hit. He reeled back and something heavy dropped from him as he grabbed his side. It was not an act I saw and heard. He continued his retreat without care of the noise he made. He did not try to shoot me again … I hit him, so he is not around here to ambush me. He is off somewhere else to care for his wound or wounds ... so, what did he drop—if anything? I need to find out and do it quickly, before I lose sense of where that something may have dropped in this dim light …

… Gracious God thank you! He dropped his rifle and it's a semi-automatic. The sheriff … no … no, he was not a sheriff. I know I'll be in deep trouble if he is, but he isn't. He can't be. He'd know what county this is; I pray that I recall what Rick said about the counties correctly.

I begin to high-step away from this place yet the varying darkness and the difficult land only allows me to move like before, a few careful effort-filled steps and stopping, several more and then looking and listening again, but I feel I move quick, fearing the other men who could be out here hunting me. I keep pushing on up the slope through the woods until I believe it's safe to move out of the timber and into the field well above the trailer, beyond the crest where this western field begins to slope down again. I can't see the trailer as I move into the field's openness, nor do I feel I have to. With trackers trying to find me in the woods, this has to be a good time to half-circle and approach the trailer again from its other side.

It is colder in the open than within the woods. The heavy snow is giving sound now, a soft crunch, as I step through it and head down the slope in a wide curve away from the woods. Three steps and wait, three more and then I continue on with a steady gait as I feel the pressure of time. The wind comes gentle against my face, not anywhere near as strong as it was earlier. Yet the snow keeps falling. The dark sky yields only to a changing patchwork of varying glows from the moon behind the passing of these dense clouds, sights of a lessening storm.

The snow smears my glasses to the point of making them useless again and the glass frame again feels frozen to my nose. Wearing them is not doing me much good and, while I'm handicapped without them, I stop moving and take them off to jam the glasses inside my coat pocket alongside that man's wallet. Almost at the same time the wind stops blowing.

As I bring my hand back out from under the parka I stiffen from a sound. I am not sure of it. I do not want to believe it. I certainly fear it as it comes again, closer this time. The sound comes in like the way a deer would move, but it is too heavy and plodding for deer. The man is back? I twist my body and turn my head around as I stand there and my eyes strain to see into the darkness from where I came. It is remarkable how much and how little this carpet of white aids sight on a dark night as this, on whether the moon shows or not. The sound comes again, closer than before—not from behind me, but from somewhere down the hill.

They have tracked me—found me, much quicker than I thought they could. I ready the rifle in front of me as I hold onto it with both hands. I dare not give alerting movement beyond this, not even to crouch down. The sound comes too near this time and to the right of me, almost directly to the east. A shadowy image emerges and stops some sixty feet away as the moonlight breaks through the clouds. My eyes squint hard to give it more definition as I aim and fire; ***BLAM! BLAM! BLAM!***

Flashes of light ignite in front me with loud cracks, each near a second apart, as I hear him work a rifle's bolt, as I race to a different position, different place; to get away. A fourth flash ignites my voice—I shriek as my lower left leg jerks out from under me, pulls and turns me forcefully to that side, yet the leg somehow plants itself in the snow and keeps me upright as searing, crippling, jolts of pain blaze through my body, but I voice no more as I strain to keep this horror inside, and hobble away as silently and as best and as fast as I can to the north, across the open field, away from the trailer and this assailant.

76

(Franklin)

Five shots burst from my rifle—*one* at a time—*damn this bolt action*—I can't work it fast enough, but the magazine empties before my mind counts five, and before I dive left side down into the snow to go more than right shoulder deep in it. This white powder is now moist enough to hold rigid walls, to hold a mold of my shape, as I hesitate to listen for him. *He scared the hell out of me.*

My heart pounds, my body throbs from its beat. Quickly, quietly, I reload the rifle as the cold snow stings and wets my bared hands that work by feel alone to place more bullets into the magazine and the magazine back into the receiver. My eyes and ears search for any sign of him in this murky darkness as I bring myself up to just peer over the snowy edges of this rut before hiding again, realizing something warm trickles down along my shoulder and around my neck while the pain of a wound in my right shoulder grows. My coat has been torn open along the outside of my upper right arm and its linings are dark with my blood. I flex my arm just enough to know this wound can't be too serious.

I hit him—he cried out—didn't he? With the noise of my shots and dive into the snow, I don't know. Long minutes pass as my whole left side grows cold and a wetness seeps in on my left arm, whether from my blood or from the snow melting through my coat. And snow is beginning to cover me as time goes by yet I still hear nothing, see nothing. Is he waiting, like me, for a sign to give advantage? One of us has to move. He needs to be the one.

That handgun Meirs found was large and can hold what—twelve rounds—fifteen—leaving him how many bullets? Tollin believed crazy man shot twice. I believe he fired three times at me here, or did he use Tollin's rifle? It don't matter—he remains dangerous, and I doubt I killed him—I doubt if I hit him; the man has the lives of a cat. I will have to see him dead.

The wind grows again, particles of snow careen over the surfaces that surround me and pour over this rut's edges to fill the spaces between my body and these walls of snow. Time has passed with no further sign of him and I can't wait. He has outlasted me, the bastard. I rise slowly, listening, searching the graying darkness and the gentle white slope of the land but see nothing of him as I come to a careful, cold, trembling, crouching stand.

Then, slowly, I go and find his tracks. They show he had run off immediately.

I crouch again as I see something under the new layer of snow within his tracks and carefully brush it aside to find the stains of his blood. I like what I see; not only did I hit him, I hit him bad. Looks like the hit was on his left side, probably the left leg, as the amount of blood shows, as does his tracks, which are odd and dragging on that side as I begin to follow them. My wound doesn't disable me, my wound barely hurts, but his, well, his looks like it does both.

The growing morning shows through the thick dark clouds and these clouds promise to remain heavy for hours to come to keep this day gray and easy on the eyes. The winds again slow. The snow lightly falls as the worst of this storm is over. His advantage of daylight that we feared would let him run for help I put a stop to—his wound is serious, enough to bed him down and attend it. He can't run. He can't be far away. My being slow here to follow him has likely helped me—he will not move for fear of doing more damage to himself. It *feels* better to stay put but staying is the wrong thing for him to do, but he will do it, for a time, and time will stiffen him. Time enough for me to get to him—no doubt. When he does see me, he may not be able to move much, or at all. Things that have been adding up and looking so bad now have turned for the better. I can make things go right again. I just need to kill him.

There is one in the chamber, four in the magazine, seventeen more in my pocket—twenty-two bullets should be enough, though I thought the box I grabbed carried more. He has to be bedded down by now, caring for that wound. With any luck, I can kill him from a distance. I hope this doesn't take long—those back at the trailer will get anxious to leave as the day grows … damn Drew running off … and Tollin—I have to believe he's dead.

77

I curse, plead, pray under my breaths, as this pain voices itself. I hurry along the best I can. I need to tend this wound soon while this retreating darkness still protects me, but not out here in this field—not in the open. Keep moving. Oh God, how much of my leg do I have left? I fear to look—I will not look, until I can find a place to hide.

Electrifying pain shocks me with every step. My left foot feels like a dead weight flopping around inside and carried by my boot. Oh God ... I blew out my left knee playing basketball one night when I was thirty-eight, torn a tendon, ripped cartilage, resulting in surgery. This pain is every bit as debilitating right now as that whole injury had been through days of time, and this injury I fear far more. I fear I am bleeding to death yet I have to keep moving for my life—adrenaline is keeping me alive, like a deer that runs after the mortal shot. The only thing I feel sure of is the bullet had not struck bone or I could not support myself, but every step feels like it tears further at the wound. Oh God, what a blood trail I'm leaving. Did I hear Rick say wild dogs? He said there are bear. Oh, Jesus Lord, I had not feared a bullet because I thought it would strike me dead. I didn't consider this—a slow death. This is not something I expected.

The day is becoming grey as I enter the north woods, but further west than the timber I had been in most of yesterday. The gain of morning light is reveals a stand of tall and full evergreens in the distance, beyond some young sparse growth of deciduous and other, younger, evergreens that stand well within a break, a pocket, in the long running tree line that define these woods. I make my way toward and into this timbered pocket before reaching a sufficient number of evergreens both close enough to each other and broad enough to hide myself under. I circle around to the far side of the one I opt for and crawl under its lowest boughs, careful not to unduly disturb the snow laden tree. I can see the path I made from inside here, and see it a good distance back, as hoped, while the other evergreens give a small measure of protection and confusion to anyone who follows me.

The smell of pine is strong. While there's snow by the tree's base, it's light; fallen brown pine needles show through the snow everywhere. I hurry to clear the tiny nuisance branches immediately around me before I sit back against the tree trunk, place the rifle and the handgun beside me, take off my gloves, and gingerly pull my left leg up close to see the damage done.

I heard stories telling if one takes their boot off they will never get their foot back in because it will swell from the trauma of the injury, so I leave the boot on. I also heard if one does not take the boot off they could lose their foot due to loss of blood circulation ... with the blood trail I've made, however, I might not live long enough to care.

The wound is over midway up my lower leg, just above the boot's edge, and blood amply pulses and flows out from it, both in front and from the back and from around the rim of the boot itself. The front of the wound is just a hole as big as the tip of my pinky finger. The back is a jagged mess of open red flesh, a rough oblong opening about an inch wide at its greatest width and the oval runs almost vertical on my leg. A reddish-purple color exists all around the wound, under my swollen skin, and I know this is anything but good. I carefully test my toes and ankle through my boot. I have feeling in them but they are numb and pin-pricking tingly, and not due to the cold and I'm not sure I'm moving all the toes. I do suspect the bullet sang through my flesh too quickly—before the slug expanded fully. I only hope the bullet missed major arteries and veins and that I am not bleeding to death.

I lean forward and deftly pull my coat and shirts off within the confines of this tree until my chest is bare. I compare the shirts to one another as the cold air grips me. Though the undershirt is moist and stinking from my sweat, I use it instead of the outer flannel shirt, thinking its closer cotton weave will be a better dressing to my wound. I tear it in long lengths, taking the material from around the shirt's waist and wrap the lengths tight in three layers over my wound, grimacing from the immediate pain, but finding relief from the compressing of the wound afterwards. The wrappings become crimson in color at the places where the bullet entered and exited my body and blood drips to the ground well before I have my clothes on again. I slip the second belt off, the one that once held the other man's coat around my waist, and wrap it tight against my leg, just above the knee, to help slow the flow of blood. I wait, watching, feeling fatigued, watching the blood drip from the wrappings as I count one ... two ... three ... four ... five seconds between each drop. The flow of blood slows. The pain closes my eyes. I grimace with them closed for a long time, my hands clutching the top of my wounded leg, until the pain seems bearable—but only if I do not move my now straightened leg.

The temperature inside this snow-laden tree is forgiving, almost comfortable. My mind considers the exchanges of gunfire and thoughts of how long I can exist with a wound such as this; Mary, Gay, the others; my life's path. I take a glance back along my trail before I close my eyes again to deal with the pain but open them quickly as I feel the tug of sleep come over me.

No, I cannot do that—I may not wake up.

The snow still falls outside, but the winds have turned gentle and whisper to me. My eyelids droop.

I jerk awake.

My body aches. I'm exhausted, but I try to move—it hurts too much. I'll stay here just a little while longer, just a little while.

I jerk awake again. Get up—I need to get up, but I am too exhausted. I need the rest—what's the harm ... what's the harm, for a little while?

I cannot rest. Blood drain—have to care for that—it's fixed, let the leg be still, let the wound heal. I cannot fall asleep ... shock …have not slept in so long … I cannot ... must … fight this ... must....

78
(Franklin)

His tracks lead into a stand of trees on a slight hill far ahead that sticks out like a stubby finger within a pocket-like opening, denting the otherwise straight running wood line of this north timber—the same broad deep woods where Meirs chased them two men. We're on the western side of it, however, over the ridge, out of sight of the camp, well away from the point where I believe Meirs ran yesterday. Crazy man chose this place well—he can look down at me, see me coming—has cover. He has the main woods to disappear further into if he can't kill me first. He is a crazy smart dude, man, quite a challenge, considering what he's been through—especially if he can give me any kind of a fight here. If he can, it makes for a better kill. The better he fights, the better I'll like it. I want to kill him slow, because I want him to feel his life slipping away for all the damn trouble he's caused.

I can see more snow coming in the distance, like rain falling far away in summertime. I've had enough of this white shit.

I move twenty paces off from his tracks to the left of his trail to gain some cover while I follow them carefully in parallel toward that finger of trees, searching every bush, every tree I can see, as I slowly push forward through this often thigh deep snow along the left edge of this dent in the woods. There's better cover on this wooded side than the more open-spaced right, and I expect him to set up somewhere within this left side. He will hope I'll follow his path, actually use his exposed path, or that I'll choose the side opposite him, in a simple hope to get a better shot at me. Keep hoping; I ain't that easy, though he probably sees every move I make.

His trail don't wander much. No turns around the first trees that tip the finger, no wandering around stands of brush from which he can hide behind and shoot from as I approach. He no longer gives attempt to cover his tracks or to delay me in my search—not that he did that before—he didn't do any, because he hurts too much. Since this snow is rough to move through for me, it has to be double so for him—he can't afford the blood or time loss—which means I've got him.

I tracked a man down a long time ago, in the city—a different sort of tracking. Beat him bad. Beat him because he molested my girl's sister. He was a member of our gang. He knew I was coming for him. It took a few days, but I found him and pushed him around before beating him bloody. He killed my girl in return. I didn't expect that, so I killed him; Joey—my first kill. I was seventeen. Nobody knew this, outside our gang, and nobody said nothing. I loved Rosalene—my girl. I loved her all the way to jail for her murder. It took three years to get there. They pinned her murder on me—they didn't know about Joey. They didn't care. They thought I made him up until there came proof of his death. They arrested me four days after a year from Rosalene's murder. I hated the world by then, had killed again—more than once, had just enough twisted parental upbringing to figure the world was doing right—why fight it, as the world put me away for her murder, though I hadn't killed her. It was supposed to be a short sentence. I was under age at the time she died. They tricked me—lied to me. They made me as an adult and put me away for many years; all these years. The world took away my love, my future ... my life. Nothing I did deserved that … nothing at all—not even killing Sheila's lover, my bitch who comes to the prison for fear of her life. One word from me and my gang would take care of her. She and they may use her looks and body, but two-timing means betrayal, and that punishment is death if she ever strays again. She is … now owned by us. Back then she offered herself just to me days after Rosalene died, but she two-timed me. She saw me kill her lover—I made her watch—a justified kill. The world had no right to put me away for that—and they didn't—they didn't know. Sheila stayed quiet, like a good bitch. I deserved none of the prison time for nothing I did. I don't see how they say I do. I don't understand their sense of honor, their sense of justice—their world is all screwed up.

I got something in return though—a prison education, nine full years of it. I'm smarter than those damn lawyers and smarter than them damn head doctors. I read the books, plenty of books—got a bull-shitting degree that don't change me much. I'm having me a life soon even if I have to kill a dozen times more to get it. This bastard I track stands in my way, but he won't for long. Then, a few years from now, I'll knock on those damn head doctor's and lawyer's doors … but I'll start with the judge first … maybe his wife.

He made a straight run for that thick stand of evergreens more than mid-way up the finger. He's making this too easy. I'm a good hundred feet away from those evergreens as I move beside a tree to search about, long and careful. Myself, I'd go on by them evergreens to set the ambush. I'd make it look like I hide underneath one of them front trees so that, when my tracker approached, I could pick him off as he searched there. What else can he do? It's only the unknown of when and where he does that's the problem for me, man.

I've lost sight of his trail. As I search for it only the sights and sounds of the forest I find. The low hanging thick gray clouds push air as they pass on by above. Once in a while a tree splits open with a loud but usually distant blast from its sap freezing. Here and there snow falls off a tree and piles with a cascading muffled thump into the carpet of snow on the forest floor. Yet there are no direct sights or sounds of him, but I've re-found his trail.

More and more over time, as the sky brightens, come sporadic and distant pops of gunfire, scattered over the land, from insane hunters who just have to be out in this weather to claim a deer, in order to consider themselves men. A snowbound deer most likely, I sneer, but just as well; their shots will mix with mine. After all, who is to tell what happens after hunting season begins—accidents happen. I can read the newspapers now; man found dead in woods—five rifle shots to the head, ruled suicide. Makes you laugh, don't it? Like when someone accidentally falls down a closed elevator shaft—a *closed* elevator shaft. I actually read that in the news once … too funny.

The snow is too deep to move around in quickly, impossible to do quietly, even though the snow, still soft, quiets everything. All I do seems to favor him, but what else can I do?

I'm about seventy feet away as I study them evergreens and the area between them and myself. The depth of the snow looks to be less beside those trees than in front of them and he would welcome that. The snow's height here barely reaches my knees. The wind starts to pick up and with it more snow, that which I saw in the distance before, now begins to fall around me as I continue on.

The signs of his trail lead to one tall wide based evergreen. It turns to the backside of this tree, something I couldn't see if I had followed his trail directly, but there appears no trail leading away that I can find. No other trail at all. Can he be that stupid as to hide under this tree? It sure'd be good luck to me if he did. Some twelve-fifteen feet beyond this tree there's some sort of drop off, but the snow along its edge—that which I can see, is clean, and it makes no sense for him to hide down there, below what he'd need to see. Now is as good a time as ever to drive him out of hiding. He has to be there. He just has to be. I check things over again to be sure. He has to be there, within this tree.

I begin raising my rifle when I hear and see some snow fall from the branches on the far side of this evergreen, which stops me with concern. The snow will cause him to look about and behind him—where I am—or has he seen me already and he is moving?

I take one quick sidestep to gain the protection of a maple, and its trunk is large enough to hide my body. I lean against it as I peer around to search the snow-covered evergreen forty-fifty-some feet away from me, hoping to see a sign of him. Did the falling snow set him running or just a shifting of his position inside? I would hear more, see more, if either of those are true. No, this must just be the snow coming off the branches. He *has* to be under this tree. It makes too much sense. This is his ambush, simple and direct, and a fairly good one—just not good enough for someone like me—otherwise he would've shot at me already.

I search yet again for other tracks leading away, but find none.

Satisfied, I quietly raise my rifle and take aim to where the base of his tree would be through the covering of snow weighing down its branches as my finger finds the trigger.

79

Mary, I tell you, I can remember a time … so vividly …

Rick, Doug, and I chose to ride our bikes across town to the high school we will attend for the first time this fall, to sign up for classes and to pay the sports fees for the sophomore football team that will start practice next week.

The ride is Rick's idea. He thought biking would be a good way to get our legs into shape, though the three of us are in excellent physical shape. Our constant competition between ourselves and other friends in running, baseball, football, weightlifting, and basketball, keep us in a high state of physical condition. Sometimes we hunt with pellet and BB guns. Sometimes we box, agreeing we cannot hit above the shoulders—to keep our friendships. From early morning into the darkness of night we would do these things; some of the best times young teenage boys can ask for.

We store our bikes in a bike rack at the school, enter its commons area, and search for the offices to pay our fees. All mundane things to do, but life delivers an unexpected lesson as we leave.

"Shit!" Rick yells.

"Damn!" adds Doug.

I am speechless.

Rick clenches his fists. "Shit! I earned the money to buy that bike. Damn-it!"

Doug, watching Rick as I was, is less reactive but no less angry. I am stunned and unbelieving as to what I see, or rather do not see, for their bikes are the ones missing—not mine.

"We should call the cops," I say nervously as our eyes search the area for the thieves. We stand there dumbfounded, next to the bike rack.

"Shit," Doug says, "I want—I got to do something. Who the fuck did this? I want to go punch their heads in! Damn that'd be nice."

Rick replies, "The cops ain't going to do anything."

"What else can we do?" I question, and then see him straighten his stance. He realizes something.

"There's a place off the bike path about two-thirds of the way to my cousin Joe's. I've seen rusting bike parts tossed around there, in the brush. There is a wooded rise above the path. I'm sure they'll pull our bikes apart there."

"I'll go inside and get the cops," I tell him.

"The cops ain't goin' to do nothing," he firmly repeats.

"I remember the place," I say, "It's almost two miles away; we can't run fast enough to get there in time. The cops can."

They both look at me, briefly, with some puzzlement in their faces.

"I'll run with ya, Rick. I gotta do somethin'," Doug announces.

As the cop is telling me for the second time that he cannot help us Rick and Doug ride up on their bikes, exhausted and proud. A sudden new bond exists between them, one I know I cannot share in and immediately envy. The cop soon goes away. In our excitement none of us thought about using my bike to get there, instead of having them run.

Rick and Doug say they are glad I called the police, but they say so in passing. They are rightly filled with their heroic rescue and efforts concerning their bikes. The thieves took their bikes to the place Rick described and were still there when Rick and Doug came running up to do battle with them, but instead ended up chasing those kids off without a fist being landed.

A pattern of life was cast that day. Rick would take decisive action; damn the system. Doug would assess both ways, but always chose quick action. Somehow my choice that day of calling the police, though not wrong, was not right. This inaction, of seeking help from others rather than taking action myself, still haunts me, and it repeats itself time and again. It all happened so fast, so seemingly fast.

...Did I talk too much? Mary, do you understand I need your counsel? I sense I am dreaming, yet I feel a cold wind, as if I am sleeping while awake and speaking to you. I'm confused. Help me, before my mind drifts again ...

One Saturday night in the summer after we graduated from high school, Rick, John Stancato, and I came out of St. Mary's gym after playing basketball.

Rick, who was waiting for us at the back corner of the rectory garage, suddenly stiffens and yells at someone unseen. He gives us a quick glance and blurts; "John's car is being broken into!"

We round the corner of the building in time to see the accused man diving into a waiting car and this car races off, its tires squealing as it turns away onto the street. Rick hurries into his step-dad's car and drives off after them, yelling at us to follow.

The pursuit is short–the two cars ahead of us race around a corner, turning right. Rick takes the corner far better than the other driver, who corners so badly he panics himself to a stop against a curb. Rick gets his car alongside them. We pull to a stop behind them so they cannot back out. The thieving driver gets out quickly to meet the approaching Rick. John and I jump out of our car, too, as Rick and the driver begin angrily exchanging words. When the driver hesitantly moves his right fist off his side Rick strikes first–like lightning, landing hard knuckles into the man's jaw. We watch the man's body slither to the ground after he slumps against the driver's door of his car, blood streaming from the corner of his mouth, his eyes incoherent.

The other thief, the one who actually tried to break into John's car, is standing on the far side of their car, holding his hands up and open. He wants nothing to do with us and rapidly spews out apologies and requests to have us leave them both alone. This is enough to appease Rick, and if Rick is we are too. The three of us leave to discuss this excitement elsewhere.

Again, Rick took immediate decisive action. John and I really only followed. I wonder if this has to do with our stricter and schooled Catholic upbringing of which Rick, though also Catholic, does not share. Turn the other cheek. Those who are sinless can cast the first stone–instilled teachings which make one hesitate without knowing why one is doing so–and sometimes hesitation is a deadly thing, but Rick does not hesitate.

Tell me why I am recalling these things, Mary, reliving the past? I feel a strange cold wet wind. I'm not sure where I am ... dreaming. I need your help. I sense imminent danger, but don't know what it is, or why. All I know is a feeling I must do something, but have no idea what that can be. Where do I go for help—can you help me?

Around a year after this car incident John and I have entered the Army National Guard together, placing us in Colombia, South Carolina for basic training. And Rick is there, too, after joining the regular Army with his best friend, our friend, Ron Sebetic. Ron, however, is already overseas in Italy where Rick will also be stationed. Rick has another month or so to stay. I go to visit Rick in his barracks. We are upstairs walking along the hallway going to see someone or to get something. It is a hallway with many open doorways without doors, unlike most barracks I had been in or stayed in. As we walk a group of black soldiers, six or seven of them, approach from the other way. I move in front of Rick to form a single line of myself and him to pass by alongside this group. I pass by just fine but Rick does not. Rick calls my name. During the brief time it takes me to turn and see, Rick is already furiously fighting at least three of the soldiers as I come to face two of them blocking my path. I see fists flying everywhere in the background of my vision. I am going to get seriously hurt but cannot let Rick down. I pick the man on my left to attack, hoping to keep things one on one for as long as I can. I start my suicidal move when suddenly and as quickly as it began the fighting stops. The man I chose to fight disappears, his friend having grabbed and jerked him back by his collar, leaving me to lurch forward into emptiness, my fists looking uneducated and silly as they find only air.

"One of them took my watch," Rick states angrily to a huge black man, rock hard in physical shape who stands authoritatively in the doorway next to and looking down at Rick, in the middle of this crowd of men. This huge man is wearing only a green T-shirt and white briefs. He had ordered the fight to stop. "They ripped it from my arm while we were walkin' by," Rick explains.

"Give Rick his watch back," the huge black man orders.

A voice begins to protest: "Ain't got no watch, man..."

"Bull-shit!" bellows the huge man. "Give it now or we'll start this again–and I'll be after you!"

The watch is quickly given back. I am awed by the other soldier's fast and silent responses to this huge man's orders, for he holds no rank. They also out-number him–us. Many of them possess size near enough, especially taken together, to challenge him, but not one dares to.

It turns out the huge black man is Rick's friend, having played basketball with him frequently on the base. He heard us coming up the hallway and was leisurely coming to his door to greet us when the action started right in front of him.

Again Rick reacted correctly and against huge odds, without hesitation. I did not. When am I?

You see Mary? Rick is telling me to do something—screaming at me to do something, but what is it? I can't be who I normally am. I can't, but I don't know what to do—help me. I know … I know I can't believe in the cops this time. I have to do this, whatever this is—isn't this so, Mary, isn't this so? To find courage I have never had and act, no matter what the cost ... no matter what the cost—but do what? What do I do? Why—why am I covered in cold white bed sheets? Mary? What kind of dream is this? This is not how I talk, not how I think—is it? Why am I so cold? Mary ....

My body jerks awake and my eyes open.

The bough of the evergreen rebounds to its normal place above me, after dumping a layer of heavy wet snow on my lap and legs. Automatically I slowly begin to brush this snow off in stunned silence, first not realizing where I am and why, then remembering as the wind gusts through the woods and falling snow hurries past my sight beyond this evergreen I huddle under. The sharp pains within my left calf muscles tell what happened earlier. I still slowly bleed from that wound. I feel cold—as cold as I have ever been. I feel stiff. I console myself but feel foolish, again. I have unthinkingly bedded down—like a wounded and hunted deer, except I am the one wounded and I am the one being hunted and I do not fully know why.

Bedding down is a technique used to trick a deer into thinking it can rest, that the hunt is off, so its body will stiffen, get colder, weaker, like mine is becoming, so the deer cannot run so far away again, if at all ... *but I ... am not...a deer!*

In sleeping I know I have stayed in one place too long … and it is too late. My ears perk to the sounds around me as the hairs on the back of my neck rise. I slowly move my hand to find the handgun by my side and draw it near and then the rifle.

They, or he, are here, somewhere close.

I hear more unnatural noises—movements of adjustment and not of travel, that come from behind me. My heart works hard inside my chest as I quietly turn my stiff and pained body to lay down and line up better with the trunk of the tree and peer through its snow-laden branches towards the source of the sounds as I ready my rifle. Do they know this is where I hide? They must. I should have—could have seen them coming, but I fell asleep instead ... damn.

My body jolts in reaction to the shot as light powders of snow, with scatterings of pine dust and chips, fall across me, but I do not react further. Their first shot clipped the trunk of the evergreen just inches above my head. Where did that shot come from? The blast sounded so near and seems straight ahead, but only one shot came. Where are they? What are they doing? *How can I get out of here!*

I wait because I have to, not moving, listening for any sound that will help me focus in on any one of them. Seconds drift by—why only one shot? Eventually they will have to come here to investigate if I am dead. They will come and I hope to take at least one of them with me. Please, let me do that, let me know that. Don't let me bleed to death like they want me to. Please give me this compensation before I go because the throbbing of my leg tells me I am losing my life, slowly but surely.

Oh shit—quiet adjustments sound again; the material of a jacket rubbing against itself as arms move to aim the gun they hold. The sounds come from straight before me, somewhere well within my gun's range. I fire the rifle's one last round.

80
(Franklin)

Am I wrong?

He there?

He already dead?

There's no movement, no sound, except the cascading echoes from my shot returning from the woods. I search for sign of him, but see none, hear none. My eyes return to this tree. He's got to be there, but nothing happened—why, he really dead so soon? He can't be. He plays dead, hoping I'll show myself for an easy kill—no way, man. Take a deep breath in, consider things—another round should get him out from there.

A bright flash of gunfire from within that tree startles me, and its shockwave pops a falling cloud of powdery snow off that tree, just before I pull my trigger. His gunshot comes nowhere near. I smile as I center my aim to where the flash showed.

"Hey—I'm sorry, man—I'm sorry," I shout, **"Thought dere was a deer in dere. Sorry, man—what's ya doin' in dere—you crazy? Yo, come on out—it's safe. I ain't gonna shoot ya."**

I wait for his answer. Seconds tick by. He is not going to answer and I got no patience to play the game further. I fire three rounds; one to where his gun flashed, one slightly to the right, and one to the left. I pull the magazine clip from my gun, put it in my pocket, and begin reloading it using only one hand. I have a round in the chamber to use if I gain sight of him. I smile proudly; I knew he was there—I never want to doubt myself again. His firing that one shot doesn't even get my blood going. This is going to be fun.

He hasn't fired back again, though—did I hit him this time?

"Hey, twink, ya dere?" I call out. He gives no reply. I don't expect one. **"Ya pain in ta ass bitch, answer me. Meirs was his name, ta man's head ya cut off, ya stinkin' asshole. Spooked us good it did, seein' his bloody head dere stuck on a stick. Good work, white shit. Have you done time before?"**

Calling him out won't work—he will see through this game, but I enjoy it just the same, as I restore the magazine clip into the rifle. We both know he is wounded; know he can't go far. He knows I play with him—it should irritate him, even knowing why. **"You, ah, have ta be stiffened up by now, feelin' death in ya leg, man, ya left one—yeah, man, I know I'd**

hit ya dere—bad, too. Ya die today man, today. How's dat feel, man? How's dat feel? Ya feelin' dizzy, weak, light headed—sound like ya twink? Got ta shakes, man? Huh—sound like ya? Ya dyin' slow, asshole, and I can wait all day ta make sure."

Maybe I can get him to use more of his bullets.

"Ya know, if ya come on out right now, stand before me like a *real* man, I can take ya back for some medical attention. No harm done, ya know. I ain't holding dis against ya. We just don't want ya shootin' at us, ya know—cause a white shit like you don't know what ya doin'—ya think ya know what ya doin—sure done stupid if ya think dat. Come on out, man, come back ta ya wife."

He ain't going to respond—and I wait a good half minute hoping. I roll my head, sigh, as impatience drives me to aim towards the trunk of the tree again and let go three more rounds—one to each side and one to the center of the tree, as before, feeling that slight smile curl the corners of my lips after firing the last shot.

81

"Hey—I'm sorry, man—I'm sorry. Thought there was a deer in there. Sorry, man—what's ya doin' in there—you crazy? Yo, come on out—it's safe. I ain't gonna shoot ya."

His voice throws me off focus. He has fired once—I have fired once. I don't believe a word he's saying. He calls out to distract and taunt me to do something he can use to help kill me. It's so obvious, but this must mean a second man is moving into position somewhere near and he wants to cover those sounds. I hope his talk will also keep him from hearing my own movements as I ready to run.

Mixes of snow, wood, and dirt explode into the air as three shots land so close their impacts shake the earth and the one rattles the tree. Quickly I slip my hand inside my jacket and pull out my much needed glasses. As soiled as the glasses are they drastically improve how well I can see now that it's morning. Snow cascades down off the branches above. If any more powder falls they will certainly be able to see me through the branches. So far the bullets come from only one gun, one direction, but that doesn't mean there is not another man nearby. This is my one and only chance to run, while this other man is not yet in position.

"Hey, twink, ya there?"

Just keep talking, mister, give me time.

"Ya pain in ta ass bitch, answer me. Meirs was his name, ta man's head ya cut off, ya stinkin' asshole. Spooked us good it did, seein' his bloody head there stuck on a stick. Good work, white shit. Have you done time before?"

He gives me another chance to answer—forget that! I've turned myself around, searching where to run, taking the safety off and quietly pulling the slider back on the handgun—and another bullet ejects. I don't learn well. I pick the bullet up and put it in my pocket. This large gun overwhelms my hands. Just a short distance away is an edge to a ravine—my only good choice.

"You, ah, have ta be stiffened up by now, feelin' death in ya leg, man, ya left one—yeah, man, I know I'd hit ya dere—bad, too. Ya die today man, today. How's dat feel, man? How's dat feel? Ya feelin' dizzy, weak, light headed—sound like ya twink? Got ta shakes, man? Huh—

sound like ya? Ya dyin' slow, asshole, and I can wait all day ta make sure."

His talk is too stupid to be for anything other than cover for the second man to move.

"Ya know, if ya come on out right now, stand before me like a *real* man, I can take ya back for some medical attention. No harm done, ya know. I ain't holding dis against ya. We just don't want ya shootin' at us, ya know—cause a white shit like you don't know what ya doin'—ya think ya know what ya doin'—sure done stupid if ya think dat. Come on out, man, come back ta ya wife."

To my wife—what does he mean? I'm on my knees and with the handgun at the ready I part the branches before me with my left hand as the next three shots come, scaring me into a hobbling run directly away from the tree. Frantically I search for the second man as I strain to make distance in the heavy snow. He is nowhere to be seen. I glance back, knowing the man in front must now be aware I run.

I struggle on the slope for the snow drifts high—I cannot move fast enough. My left leg shudders with quickening cramps from the wound and shocks me with pain, and my body inhibits from the lingering stiffness of rest. The snow grows deeper nearer the edge—and I need just a little more distance to get over and out of sight to gain precious time; time to find other cover in which to make a stand, or to hide—to make a better stance. I think too much—move—move—*move!*

Looking back an image appears from beyond the evergreen. A black man moves into the open and he raises his rifle as he smiles but I am quicker. Twisting back to take aim my left leg gives way and I begin to fall backwards into the snow. I watch the smile come off the familiar black man's face as my gun sets during my fall, before he has readied his own, causing him to hesitate—flinch at the sound of my first shot as he begins turning himself away from me. The first bullet rips through his jacket below his left armpit and he loses balance. He goes to his knees in the snow then smoothly turns back around towards me, swinging his rifle up to his right shoulder, as I shove myself backwards through the snow towards the slope's edge, kicking and pulling myself back. He smiles as he takes aim. I fire wildly at him, the second bullet going uselessly into the snow before me, the next two towards the man as his shot explodes the snow next to my face. I hear myself whimpering as I struggle to stay on top of the snow and keep moving for the edge.

A double jolt of pain hits me like hot knives slicing through the skin of my upper left thigh and my upper left arm as this bullet finds flesh. I fire two more rounds at him before I feel myself sliding down into the ravine and out of his sight. One more shot sings out uselessly from his gun above me as

I disappear and my body gains momentum in my tumbling slide before I get embedded in the snow fifteen to twenty feet down, halfway to the bottom of this ravine. I stop face up towards the edge and ready myself for my end. The snow is too new to keep me, but I know trying to run is useless. I have little strength for that. If there are any rounds left, I will make them count ... if I can—I have lost my glasses, as I watch my breath crystallize and the sparkling flakes my fall stirred up flutter down over me as I search quickly back and forth for him along the snow encrusted edge above. The low, dark, and heavy gray clouds move swiftly by above the treetops seem a fitting cold backdrop for the last moments of my life.

"Thanks, Lord," I whisper, "for letting me live today and all the days of my life. You didn't have to give me life, but you did. I'm grateful for it. I hope I lived it in a way you can accept. Thanks."

"Hey twink—ya survive ya tumble?"

His words ring out from above. I say nothing. Something sounds familiar in them, too—why is that, why would I know him?

"Damn, ya lucky!"

Forget him—I will not give him evidence to where I am.

"Ya dere, white shit? Ya dere ghost man? 'Fraid ta answer me twink? Think I'm tryin' ta fool ya here? Well maybe I am n maybe I ain't. Tell me you're dere white boy ... Come on! Ain't got ta guts ta answer me? Ya ain't got the guts for much. Ya look n lust but ya ain't got the guts ta take."

I look and lust but don't have the guts to take—what the hell is he talking about? But something sounds familiar in it—his voice, a situation, something that's meant to distract me, to remember him—to distract me. This is not the place where I want to die. Look around, there has to be a better place to hide—to fight. His voice sounds as if he is moving but I cannot tell where.

"Mister—ya fuckin' wastin' my time. Stand like a man ya chicken-shit."

I still ignore him as I look about. There is not much the ravine offers for protection.

"I know you—you're stupid. You are a stupid white shit. Thinkin' yerself a hero—I got yer woman, honky."

I need time. There is a fallen tree pointing down the hill about ten yards away above my shoulders. I cannot see any better cover. It does look like I am going to die—and where is that second man? I should be dead already if he were here. I think I am dead anyway. I want to know some answers before then; **"You hunted me alone, didn't ya?"**

There is a time of silence one can count before the man answers; **"I'll just keep ya worryin' 'bout dat. I know you, man—you're lucky but you're stupid."**

"Did you kill the others?" I just have to know … I just have to—to have my efforts be in vain will waste my life so completely. Please, mister, be honest—let the truth sneak past you—tell me they are alive—and what does he mean he's got my woman?

"Like I said, you're stupid—don't you know you're stupid, man? You're stupider than I thought, man."

The man's non-answer gives me hope that he contemplates telling me, as I get ready to run again—the wound in my leg is holding up better than I thought it could, and the other wounds are just painful. The man feels very confident he will kill me if he does lets me know—I'm not going that easily, though—hopefully.

"We meant not ta kill nobody, but people are crazy, like you, ask ta git killed. It don't matter much now, though. Now we got ta do what we got ta do, ya know? I suppose I should say I'm sorry 'bout your friends, but I didn't know 'em. The others, too … Sorry ya gotta die—oh shit no, I'm just lyin'—you know me, I'm gonna enjoy ya dyin'. You're bleedin' rather bad. Means a slow death ta ya. Ya know I'll be finding ya dead by tonight—why not make it quick?"

Emotions swell and I have to respond; **"Only way you'll know I'm dead is if you kill me, bastard, but you're scared I'll take you with me—aren't you nigger? I'll take you with me."** Two can play this insult game. How many bullets do I have—do I have any? The magazine slides free into my hand and it shows six bullets. Another will be in the chamber for a total of seven. I thought I had none … I have a chance—I must've been counting the rifle's bullets, too.

"Ah, ya make me laugh—ain't done dat since I was ten. Ya ain't realizin' who I am yet, do ya dumb-ass? While you die, think about dat n think about how much I'll enjoy what's between ya wife's legs today. Mary's her name. Dat's right asshole. We figured out who she be. You think we stupid like you, honky? Mary likes bein' sweet ta me. She saw what I got n it's a lot more than you n she liked it. Licked it right up. I like her a lot. I'm goin' back for more."

My emotions knot my stomach—I don't believe him—Mary would struggle—refuse, but a man like this would rape her, viciously. My emotions swell again and I cannot contain them. **"Damn you—DAMN YOU! You lyin' ... touch her and I'll freakin' rip your balls off—you hear me!"** His words make me slow my travel to yell back at him as I move for the tree. **"You fuckin' hear me!"** Shit! I yelled those last words out unthinkingly, while facing away from the ridge—he will know I'm on the move.

"Oh ya such a big bad white boy! Ya scarin' me, honky. Die on ta thought a your wife pleasin' me while ya fade away asshole—and you still don't know who I am?"

Since he knows I'm moving maybe I can distract him and get some answers; **"Why you doing this to us?"**

He does not answer. My time is short. The distance to the tree is short. I have to get there; **"What did we do to you? Why? Who are you? ... Who are you?"**

82

(Franklin)

He's bolting.

My legs plow the snow as I move forward and left, away from the maple, to see him clear of the large evergreen he runs from. He is substantially clothed—more than I thought he could be, but his left leg carries the expected dark shine of blood. He frantically looks about, searching for an escape, searching for me. I smile as I raise my rifle to take aim just as he finds me.

He quickly turns—his gun comes up fast—freezing my stance. Instead of diving into the snow, I twist myself away from the anticipated blows from his gun; the sounds are terrifying, the blasts so near. A strong sudden tug on my left side whips me around and down to my knees before I rise to face him again. Pain comes sharp along that side of my chest, making my eyes water. I gasp for breath as I set my rifle onto my right shoulder.

Snow flies over his face. My shot missed. His frantic moves to avoid me has him down on his back like a snow angel and he struggles to gain a fall over the ridge behind him. I fire again, this time seeing cloth part and blood spurt from both his left leg and upper arm, but this still doesn't stop the damn cat man. I fire quickly once more as I see him disappear over the edge. I got no idea if I hit him with that last shot ....

... Damn! Damn! Damn! Damn! Damn! … I thought I was dead! And how can I miss him so often when he's so open to see—*so close!* You can't ask for better shots than to find your target sprawled, crawling, backwards in the snow. It's daylight, you idiot, and you're thirty-some feet away—and you can't kill him? I choked! I choked! I choked!

Damn.

But now he's over the edge. I don't like the set-up. How many times did he shoot? Aw-man, I don't know—three there ... two more ... aw-man, how many were there after that? I don't know—just glad to be alive. He froze me—he froze me! He's made me dance. He's had my life in his sights three freaking times now—Meir's head at the trailer, the open field last night, and here. I'm lucky—lucky to be alive. I'm meant for the life I want to live. Fate is on my side, clearly. I'm justified in what I do here. Freedom is my future, man, and mine to take.

Seven shots under the tree—and I miss him. How? Him scrambling in the snow, three more shots—and I miss him? How? Crazy cat man lost two more lives to keep on living. He's down to three. The weather, the exchange at the camp, Tollin, me earlier, this now under the tree and then seeing him clear. This sucker is unbelievably lucky, but fate *is* on my side.

His shot nicked my chest, sliced the side of it open but it's just a flesh wound, as they famously say. No big deal, just like the right arm. The bullet had tugged my coat, pulled me around. *Fate is on my side!*

I search my pockets for more bullets to load as I crouch in the snow, thinking, searching the edge of that slope ahead of me, listening for him. I release my magazine; it holds one bullet, with one still in the rifle's chamber. I fill the magazine with three more bullets. Five shots in the rifle, but I only find four more bullets in my pocket. Did I count them right? The other pockets are empty. I quickly search the snow and find only one more.

Ten shots will still be more than enough, even after seeing how many can be fired without hitting anything. Damn, I never thought it would be this hard to hit a moving target—why is this so hard, but then I've never been shot at before while trying to do this. I ambushed my other kills. Why didn't I just grab that whole other box of ammo back then—why?

My eyes return to search the snowy ridge before me. He will wait there below this ridge. The fall, his wounds, his fear—I doubt he is on the move. He can't move far if he does. He can't risk it, not yet. Or he risks it for some protected place, but that will be nearby. I have no reason to hurry here. I can take my time.

There stands a large oak to my left near the edge of this ridge. Farther left I can see the ravine continuing into the forest, getting steeper and narrower. To my right the ravine grows shallow and wide as I lose sight of it passing into the forest. At most this ravine is only twenty yards across. He will not dare try for the other side—too much of my view will control that area. He will stay close to me, on this side of the ravine—if he is thinking.

Now is the time to finish him. He is much too alive, man, to let be, to let his wounds bring him down. My chance at freedom has to be certain.

"Hey twink—ya survive ya tumble?" I call out, not expecting an answer, but I wait a moment anyway.

"Damn, ya lucky!" I shout towards where the man went over. **"Ya dere, white shit? Ya dere ghost man? 'Fraid ta answer me twink? Think I'm tryin' ta fool ya here? Well maybe I am n maybe I ain't. Tell me you're dere white boy ... Come on! Ain't got ta guts ta answer me? Ya ain't got the guts for much. Ya look n lust but ya ain't got the guts ta take."**

I wait and listen as the falling snow stops again and the wind becomes gentle. I know he has to be there and I know he is alive. **"Mister—**

ya fuckin' wastin' my time. Stand like a man ya chicken-shit," I say loud. **"I know you—you're stupid. You are a stupid white shit. Thinkin' yerself a hero—I got yer woman, honky."**

I pause a long moment as I think of what next to do or say, for I don't expect an answer, but then I hear his voice; **"You hunted me alone, didn't ya?"**

I'm struck by his question and the clear disciplined annunciation of each word as he spoke through his pain. My advantages of giving him the impression two men hunted him hadn't occurred to me. I wonder if I should try that now—no, he knows enough already to believe there is only one and, despite him being an asshole, he has earned this much respect—but I ain't giving that to him. **"I'll just keep ya worryin' 'bout dat. I know you, man—you're lucky but you're stupid."**

"Did you kill the others?"

"Like I said, you're stupid—don't you know you're stupid, man? You're stupider than I thought, man." I consider his question but a moment. Radwell, that white bastard, pissed me off, angered me, by executing, not killing, but executing that blond haired man and then the utility man—I had reasons for my kill. This man here greatly angers me over Meirs death and wounding Tollin—if Tollin is alive—no, Tollin is dead. I could really mess up this man's mind if I want to, but three times he had me dead in his sights, the chances he has taken … no, I will allow that begrudged feeling of respect for him to begin my answer … **"We meant not ta kill nobody, but people are crazy, like you, ask ta git killed. It don't matter much now, though. Now we got ta do what we got ta do, ya know? I suppose I should say I'm sorry 'bout your friends, but I didn't know 'em. The others, too … Sorry ya gotta die—oh shit no, I'm just lyin'—you know me, I'm gonna enjoy ya dyin'. You're bleedin' rather bad. Means a slow death ta ya. Ya know I'll be finding ya dead by tonight—why not make it quick?"**

I hear his annoying response; **"Only way you'll know I'm dead is if you kill me, bastard, but you're scared I'll take you with me—aren't you nigger? I'll take you with me."**

Well, he sure ain't lost his knack to insult me at the wrong time, and I find myself breathing out a one syllable laugh before I reply. **"Ah, ya make me laugh—ain't done dat since I was ten. Ya ain't realizin' who I am yet, do ya dumb-ass? While you die, think about dat n think about how much I'll enjoy what's between ya wife's legs today. Mary's her name. Dat's right asshole. We figured out who she be. You think we stupid like you, honky? Mary likes bein' sweet ta me. She saw what I got n it's a lot more than you n she liked it. Licked it right up. I like her a lot. I'm goin' back for more."**

"Damn you—DAMN YOU! You lyin' ... touch her and I'll freakin' rip your balls off—you hear me!" His response causes a smile and I clench a fist rejoicing, knowing my words got to him. His physical needs are becoming too demanding for him to shout, though, because his next words I barely hear: **"You fuckin' hear me!"**

I laugh loud to taunt him. **"Oh ya such a big bad white boy! Ya scarin' me, honky. Die on ta thought of your wife pleasin' me while ya fade away asshole—and you still don't know who I am?"** I fall silent, hoping he will show himself, but he doesn't.

I quietly—as quietly as I can through this snow, move back and away from the ridge's approach, near where he fell, to move by the large oak on my left. Ten bullets I remind myself, five in the rifle, more than enough if I choose carefully.

"Why you doing this to us?" he calls out.

I'm not going to answer him. He will call out again before his mind suspects I can be moving, time I'll take advantage of.

"What did we do to you? Why? Who are you?" he calls out again, **"Who are you?"**

By then I'm twenty yards up from where he went over. I look to my right, searching along the edge for him and down alongside the ragged snowy slope of the ravine. He has gone quiet with suspicion. The carpet of snow lays thick and undisturbed on the floor of the ravine fifteen feet or so below. Snow clings to the steep sides of the ravine wall I'm over as it juts in and out along its length, making my viewing difficult. There is a large fallen tree about halfway between where he fell and where I am now. Its branches block most of my view but there he is, hiding among it. I can see the path he took to get there. I can see a part of his right shoulder and some of the side of his head. He has placed himself expecting me to come from the other side, not knowing the tree protects him well from this side, too. Still, I think I see enough of him.

83

The distance to the tree is short. I have to get there—say something to distract him; **"What did we do to you? Why? Who are you? ... Who are you?"**

No response … he's moving, but I don't see him and can't hear anything of him while I'm moving. I reach the tree and clumsily dive over a protecting archway of a large branch stemming off the main trunk and it gives me good protection as I look back the way I came, searching for him. The archway of this branch curves before me and it connects to the trunk about two feet to my right. It's hard for me to see anything beyond the trunk as I rapidly search the snowy edges of the ravine as the roots of the tree are above me, the tree's top points towards the bottom of the ravine.

Ground debris blasts into the air inches from my head, stinging my face and neck as the echoes of this gunshot ring through the forest. The shot came from my right, not from where I had been, not from where I had expected him to be.

I hear him cursing for missing me; **"Ya *could* just stand up n die like a man. Ya know I'm gonna getcha."**

This time I won't answer. Another shot hits wood two feet from my head. I cower, but without panic, as I roll over to gain more of the trunk's protection. His shots came closer together in bunches before, as fast as he could turn that bolt. He surely would've killed me had he done so here. Maybe he's just being more careful with his shots, I don't know.

"I'm gonna move 'round till I get ta shot I want, man. Nothin' ya can do 'bout dat. Dat tree ain't gonna protect ya for long. Might as well stand up n take it like a man, but you ain't man enough, are ya?"

He is still to my right, but he does sound closer. He is moving again. I ready myself to shoot back.

"Ya know what ya wife said? Wanna know what ya wife said?" he taunts from somewhere over the ridge, **"She said, when I told her what I was going out here ta do—ta you, she said 'Oh poor baby, don't let him hurt too long, n come right back ta me in a hurry, I'm wantin' you. Yeah, man, what do ya think a dat, honky-shit? What do ya think a dat?"**

A response flows to the tip of my tongue, but I catch it, do not speak it. That is what he wants. His next words come from my left, back along the ridge near where I fell. I scoot over once to lie tight beside the large branch that arches off the dead tree which is just large enough to give adequate protection from this direction.

"Ya know nothin' ya did changed nothin'. Everything is going our way. Ya can see dat by me having ta time ta mess around with ya here—don't have ta do dat, ya know. I can finish ya quick. Stand up—make it quick. Ah—dat's right, you're not *man* enough. Dat's what she said, too, after she had me. She'll dream about me ta rest of her life. You know dat, don't ya?"

He is becoming easy to ignore, being ridiculous, though Mary's dreams will be nightmares if he has touched her.

Slowly sliding out from the edge, perched on the snow, comes the sight of the tip of his rifle barrel being directed towards me—he believes I cannot see this. I squeeze myself down into the snow. Bark slaps hard against my face as the bullet tears through the top of the thick branch just over my head and some of the snow that rested on the branch flies everywhere, followed by another. I fight the urge to fire back as a nervous fear rumbles through me, shaking my hands, making me tremble—pain shoots up my leg as I push myself down the hill away from where the shot landed. I don't know what to do! I can't hold my mind together much longer.

"Who are you!" I scream in a voice that seems detached as I remain cowered down behind the branch.

Laughter. Joyous laughter comes from above. **"What makes ya think ya can survive this?"** he mocks.

"'Cause I can," I respond before I think of what to say. My words settle me, taking some of that nervousness away.

I try moving down along the branch's length some more but I cannot go far—the branch thins out and I might need the archway for protection soon. I hear faint sounds of his magazine being inserted back into his gun before bark and snow burst from under the branch at the point where I had just been. Another shot splinters through the branch beside me, but misses me.

"Who are we?" he mocks, incredulous that I do not already know, **"We all over ta news, stupid. Know who we are now twinky-lady?"**

There is like a dull moment of stillness in my brain before his words make me feel as stupid as he claims me to be, as I realize he is one of the escaped convicts the man, posing as a sheriff in the south forest, mentioned, before I shot him. Oh Lord, I have been so dumb not putting this together, I knew it but I didn't think of it, didn't connect it ... my stomach sinks, my pallor changes ... I realize who he is, his voice ... something inside me sinks further with dreadful weight as that truth comes to bear and, if it were possible for me to feel more apprehension than what I already have, then that is what I do feel ... **"Franklin?"**

"AH-ha-ha-ha-haa! Three times? Ya make me laugh so many in one day, man. Ya tryin' hard ta make me like you, man. Ain't gonna work, though, man. I keep my promises. Ya die, man. Ya die today, man. See though, man, how stupid ya be? Took ya dis long ta know me? Not been a week, man, and my promise is coming true ta ya. Franklin keeps his promises."

Holy Mother of God, pray for me. Franklin has been playing me, and I had my chance up by the tree, had my chance in the field. What can I do? … He is on the move again.

"You dere twerp?" he calls out moments later. He is back by the oak tree on the ledge above, probably the best place for him to be. I sense, from his position there, that I cannot hide enough of myself from his sight.

"I'm here," I answer, unable to disguise my tone of resignation, and he picks up on this.

"Ya getting ready ta stand up man? We can make dis quick—promise ya dat."

I close my eyes to imagine my body being punctured by his bullet and to crumble and collapse to the ground. **"Let me think about it."**

Laughter and agreement; he gives me a minute, without giving a reason why.

This terror of knowing my end is coming makes the thought of standing up hold a certain, yet strange, mystic appeal—of standing up and taking it like a man … or a fool—I might not live much longer but the longer I do, the longer I keep him here, the better.

"You can give me more than a minute—I ain't goin' nowhere," I call out.

"I'm getting' impatient," he returns.

"Well, then, go ahead. You ain't too good a shot."

Laughter. **"I like playin' with my prey, lady. Like ta see 'em squirm like you, ya know. Adds ta the fun. Besides, ya make me laugh and I ain't ta one leaving a trail o'blood so bad a hibernatin' bear could follow it in its sleep."**

He *is* one who enjoys his kill, like a cat with a mouse.

"How melodramatic," I answer. I can see him now. He is not looking towards me but over the surroundings about him on the ridge almost directly above, nearer to me than the oak tree. He is certain he can take me anytime, and he now probably can. Though I can just see him, I do not have a good shot, not without giving him a better one on me.

"I try," he answers.

"You and your pretty boyfriends never came lookin' for the man we killed yesterday—what makes you think they're gonna care if you come back?" I ask.

"We found him, asshole. Ya shot him once in ta chest, busted his arm with a axe. Ya ain't got nothin' right yet, man. Go down ya list, honky. Just what ya think ya got right? I know ya stupid. Wonder if you know how stupid ya are."

I think for just a second. **"Yeah, obviously we killed a man important to ya—but how important are you to them? I saw your tracks in the snow—there were two of ya yesterday. No one's gonna come looking for you."**

"Dey don't need ta. I want dis fun for myself, twink. I ain't the one gonna die here—you are."

He's got an answer for everything, and everything does make me feel stupid, but I got to keep trying. I judge the arm-length distance over the main trunk of my fallen tree to the other side, which would force him to move again—hopefully there is more protection on the other side of this tree than the side I'm on now. His gaze begins to return to me as I begin to move for that other side but I stop *for he is falling—the snow is collapsing under him!*

I see his gun flash and hear the shot hit my tree as I come to a stand beside it and fire at his scrambling body while he frantically reacts to stop himself in his fall. He catches himself but he cannot work his rifle's bolt to shoot at me a second time. My wrist hurt from being slammed back by the first shot I took so now with both hands on my gun I pull the trigger again and again—*but the gun does not fire!* He disappears from my sight up and over the ridge as I drop for the protection of my tree. *What just happened?* The gun jammed—there's a spent shell stuck in the slider—how do you un-jam it? Watch for him, keep your head low! How do you get this thing working again?

Damn. I need my glasses.

Bluff him. Bluff him good.

"Who is chicken now asshole?" I yell after him, as I rise to just look over the tree and aim my useless gun to where he was.

"Kiss my ass honky," he replies, unseen, from over the ridge.

"I can keep this up all day," I shout to him.

"You … ya were tellin' me dat I can't shoot straight—whitey, aw-man whitey—ya don't know how ta even work a gun. Can't give ya a prettier picture ta shoot at can I?"

"A black man turned white kinda picture—sure, do it again. You're scared of me. C'mon, let's finish this. You got all the advantages. You're incompetent. C'mon black boy. Come and get me."

"Ya fuckin' dead whitey."

He is cursing again as I scramble to the other side of the tree, and it is the more protected side, my moving, stretching, making me wince in pain. I have to work this gun, get it un-jammed quickly.

84

(Franklin)

Debris blasts into the air inches from his head.

I missed again. Shit. How can I not hit him—this gun ain't sighted? Oh-shit—he just gave me another chance … I wasn't ready—I was cussing myself. He's found better cover. Add insult to injury crazy cat man—two lives—two more lives you just gave up. Two. Got that? You got only one left. You die now—hear me? You die now.

"Ya *could* just stand up n die like a man. Ya know I'm gonna getcha." I call out. I'm angry with myself. I pull the trigger—not caring to aim, I'm so frustrated. The shot bores itself into the tree an arm's length away from the crazy man's head. **"I'm gonna move 'round till I get ta shot I want, man. Nothin' ya can do 'bout dat. Dat tree ain't gonna protect ya for long. Might as well stand up n take it like a man, but you ain't man enough, are ya?"**

The crazy man doesn't reply, doesn't want to talk … imagine that.

"Ya know what ya wife said? Wanna know what ya wife said?" I taunt, **"She said, when I told her what I was going out here ta do—ta you, she said 'Oh poor baby, don't let him hurt too long, n come right back ta me in a hurry, I'm wantin' you. Yeah, man, what do ya think a dat, honky-shit? What do ya think a dat?"**

Crazy man gives no response. I don't care. I move quickly to my right, seeing a possible place along the snowy ridge from which to get a better shot.

"Ya know nothin' ya did changed nothin'. Everything is going our way. Ya can see dat by me having ta time ta mess around with ya here—don't have ta do dat, ya know. I can finish ya quick. Stand up—make it quick. Ah—dat's right, you're not *man* enough. Dat's what she said, too, after she had me. She'll dream about me ta rest of her life. You know dat, don't ya?"

I can see him again, enough for a good careful shot. I place the barrel of my rifle in the snow to steady it, slide it slowly forward and take aim. Bark scatters from the branch just above his head ... I'm too annoyed to get angry. Another shot and miss—this rifle cannot be sighted.

"Who are you?" He screams.

He makes me laugh. At least I'm good at working his head, keeping him crazy. **"What makes ya think ya can survive this?"** I return.

"'Cause I can."

My eyebrows raise—good response, man, but it ain't gonna work. I pull the magazine to reload but reinsert it as I see him moving. Debris spurts out from under the branch where he moves from. Then a second shot at him—both damn *miss!* When I get back I'm getting a different damn rifle.

I decide to answer his question, because he ain't figuring out who I am, because he really is too stupid. **"Who are we?"** I mock, **"We all over ta news, stupid. Know who we are now twinky-lady?"** A moment speeds by as I wait, before he puts another smile on my face.

"Franklin?" he asks.

"AH-ha-ha-ha-haa! Three times? Ya make me laugh so many in one day, man. Ya tryin' hard ta make me like you, man. Ain't gonna work, though, man. I keep my promises. Ya die, man. Ya die today, man. See though, man, how stupid ya be? Took ya dis long ta know me? Not been a week, man, and my promise is coming true ta ya. Franklin keeps his promises."

This suddenly ain't fun no more, I liked it better when he didn't know. Now the fun is over, nothing to play with him about. I can see a better line-of-sight on him from the ridge almost right above him. I saw this before but didn't like it—it'll give him a line-of-sight on me, but I'm getting impatient.

"You dere twerp?" I call out moments later. I'm in the snow on the ledge almost directly above the crazy man. I look around my surroundings, see if anyplace else offers better advantage—none do.

"I'm here," he answers in a resigned tone.

"Ya getting ready ta stand up man? We can make dis quick—promise ya dat."

"Let me think about it," comes his response.

I have to chuckle and agree. Even with an unsighted rifle I have to have him now.

"You can give me more than a minute—I ain't goin' nowhere," he adds.

"I get impatient."

"Well, then, go ahead. You ain't too good a shot."

I chuckle again—he stays amusing; **"I like playin' with my prey, lady. Like ta see 'em squirm like you, ya know. Adds fun. Besides, ya make me laugh and I ain't ta one leaving a trail o'blood so bad a hibernatin' bear could follow it in its sleep."**

"How melodramatic."

"I try."

"You and your pretty boyfriends never came lookin' for the man we killed yesterday—what makes you think they're gonna care if you come back?"

I smile. Just rewards. He tries to put doubt in me. I know Radwell and Cal won't give a shit if I never come back. That thought doesn't sit well but does nothing about making me want to hurry back to camp. **"We found him, asshole. Ya shot him once in ta chest, busted his arm with a axe. Ya ain't got nothin' right yet, man. Go down ya list, honky. Just what ya think ya got right? I know ya stupid. Wonder if you know how stupid ya are."**

He again tries to put doubt into me; **"Yeah, obviously we killed a man important to ya—but how important are you to them? I saw your tracks in the snow—there were two of ya yesterday. No one's gonna come looking for you."**

I smirk but know he is right; no one will come looking for me. **"Dey don't need ta. I want dis fun for myself, twink. I ain't the one gonna die here—you are."**

The ravine's edge is less than an arm's length in front of me. Off to my left stands the oak tree and beyond that I can see down into the ravine. Ahead of me the opposite side is open to see almost to the fallen tree below where the crazy man hides. To my right the ridgeline jaggedly curves in and out and down as the ravine slowly widens. If I stay to wait him out I have him pinned down until nightfall, but that's too long a wait. I want him now. I search my pockets. I search again. I wish I miscounted before … oh, shit, only four bullets left to get this done.

I creep forward, one leg bent under me that I sit on while I push myself slowly and carefully towards the edge with my other leg, helped by my left arm and hand. My right hand carries the rifle at ready, doing this until I can peer over the edge and survey all of the tree below. I see him. He sees me. We both pull back quickly. This is a dangerous game that's gone on too long. I have a sudden sinking feeling—***the snow is giving way!***

The powder rapidly collapses about me as I straighten my body and stretch back for something solid with my left hand, reaching as far as I can while trying to keep my eyes on the man below and my rifle pointed towards him as my body falls.

He quickly stands up, takes aim and fires—I see his gun jerk back in recoil—he did not hold it tight enough and it almost comes out of his hand.

I am helping him—I am not falling! My left hand has caught hold on something. Sometime during this I've already shot at him—and I can't reload with one hand. He's trying to shoot me as I twist and turn and pull myself up and over the edge. I see him aim at me as I panic to find safety. I roll into the white powder on top of the ridge then scramble in fear further away until I feel safe enough to turn around and get ready for him to come up over the ridge.

"Who is chicken now asshole?" he calls.

"Kiss my ass honky," I reply. My body trembles with fright. I have to look myself over to see if I have been shot. It does not seem like I have—that I can tell as yet.

"I can keep this up all day," he says.

"You … ya were tellin' me dat I can't shoot straight—whitey, aw-man whitey—ya don't know how ta even work a gun. Can't give ya a prettier picture ta shoot at can I?"

He answers; **"A black man turned white kinda picture—sure, do it again. You're scared of me. C'mon, let's finish this. You got all the advantages. You're incompetent. C'mon black boy. Come and get me."**

Anger swells inside me; **"You're fuckin' dead whitey."** Only I can't go after him again. I can't, and I find myself just staring out into the woods in disbelief—how lucky can this guy get ... how lucky can I get? Somehow I still have two bullets in my gun. I might need those two back at the trailer, for Radwell and Cal—they ain't worth trusting my life to. I might need to kill them—Rad and Cal. I can't go back unarmed. What if something else happened back there? I can use these bullets to kill this crazy cat man, but I can't—and why should I?

I wait to hear his movements, but it seems he's bedded down among that tree again. He's going to bleed out anyway. I've wounded him more, so why stay ... why stay? I want this man dead ... he almost had me. Fate is on my side. A new life for me is meant to be. I will come back to do just that—to see him dead—after I let him bleed out. I don't need to give him any more chances to kill me—why should I chance unexpected things like snow giving way when time itself will take his life for me. I don't need to do this no more. I need a better rifle, more ammo. I need to see what's going on at the trailer—it's been too long. No telling what they could've decided or done in these hours I've been away. I don't need to risk my life trying to kill a dying man. I don't need to. I need to make sure I'm with Radwell and Cal when they leave here. I've got to go.

I wait only a little longer before I silently move away.

85

Since rolling over the tree and falling face first into this scratchy cold mess of branches and snow, and after somehow getting the gun un-jammed, reloaded, and ready again, I have not moved. I've been waiting a long time after that last exchange, lying still, waiting for him to approach, waiting for him to finish me off, but he has not appeared—yet. I expect to hear him, but I hear nothing of him. In my mind I count again to sixty. I have already counted ten times and that only after waiting an unknown amount of time.

If he can see me lying here he will put a bullet into me and I can't stop him, but he must not be able to see me. Surely he will fire again if I move, if he watches—so I must be protected if I stay right here, he cannot see me, unsure of something. I can only wait for his approach. He thinks; why take any chances? Because I'm a dead man … we only need to wait for that time to arrive. He said as much, too.

I count to sixty, eight more times, slowly.

It's hard to continue this with controlled shallow breaths. I'm in pain. It's hard, to lie on my stomach, to know how much of my breath is seen as it crystallizes in the cold air above me; hard not to swallow or cough, sniffle, or clear my throat—while blood seeps out of me—when all I'm trying to do is hear him. No words from him. No sounds of him. I count four more times.

Nothing.

I suspect he has made a major move and is crossing the ravine to shoot at me from the other side. Decisively I stiffly rise to my knees and look around, expecting that final bullet. He is nowhere to be seen or heard. Could he have left me for dead? That would *not* make sense, not what I would do. My body shakes from the cold, from the trauma I'm living through. I lean against the fallen tree, brace myself as my balance falters, feeling faint from my sudden rise.

Moments pass before I regain strength, enough to hobble over the fallen tree and crawl exhaustively up over the ledge to hide and rest under the same evergreen I hid under before. I'm drained and need to conserve my strength. I rotate my bandages around my wound. I don't know why I do, there's not a dry spot on the crimsoned bandages, the wounds reopened. The constancy of pain tempts me to give up—but how do you do that? Life has to be taken from me—I won't give it up willingly.

There's no sense in redressing these wounds. Without the chance of receiving medical help, I'm slowly dying. I can see it with the pallor of my skin, the chills I feel deeper within, and the increasingly frequent lightheadedness that comes with losing blood. The other wounds, the slice across my left thigh and arm, seem minor, for they are overwhelmed by what I feel in my leg. Another time, another place, these two wounds would be something to write home about, get a medal for; today, though, these wounds are petty. I concede—how I hate to, but know my life won't see another day—I don't see how it can. It's clear he left me for the varmints. I don't want to be their food, but will be if I stay here. His leaving me doesn't make sense—why would he leave—because I can't do anything else? He can't be around or he would've killed me just now. I don't understand his leaving, his leaving me alive.

Then the reason comes. Rick arranged for snowmobiles to come to our camp this morning if the storm was bad—why Roy's car is not at our camp, why Rick's truck now points toward the trailer after he came back and parked it there, all done before he took us on the long walk-around … Franklin went back because somehow he knows the time these snowmobiles are expected. Before the snowmobiles arrive they will have to kill everyone, anyone they don't need ... Oh, shit.

With the safety reset I slip the handgun inside my belt after leaving the tree. Holding the gun ready will be useless energy spent—either I will have time to use it or he will shoot me down before I even hear the shot.

I search for a bare branch to break and use as a walking stick, finding one quickly. It relieves much of the pain and pressure in my wounded leg as I make my way back along my own tracks, the ones made earlier coming here.

There is no plan other than to approach the trailer from its bordering south woods and to get there quickly, but some course of action will present itself and, if not, something else will happen. I made it this far. I'll make it there, too … I have to—in time and soon.

86
(Franklin)

I call as I approach the trailer carefully for, though Radwell won't, Cal is stupid enough to shoot me. Besides, if anything else went wrong while I was away ... well, it's wise to be careful.

I grab the disgusting head of Meirs by one of his ears, because he doesn't have enough hair on his head to grab a hold of, and pull it off the end of the shovel's handle. It doesn't come off easily; its flesh became frozen to the pole during the night and it makes gruesome sounds as it breaks loose. I toss his head across the distance into the snow by the two evergreens and the shovel as well, both get swallowed up by the snow. While there's little chance anyone besides us seeing Meirs' ugly sight, I'm still surprised Radwell hadn't ordered Cal to do this cleanup earlier.

I avoid the place where the two men Radwell shot lay buried under this snow, doing so instinctively—the snow no longer tells where they lay. I glance at Perez, his body is almost completely hidden by the snow that fell since he died. Mason's body is much the same way. We'll need to cover them up more, but later, as I watch Cal open the trailer door. I clear the snow from the top step but the other steps are too buried in this white crap to worry about as I make my climb and start shaking the snow off my clothes just outside the door as Cal studies me. He says nothing while I do this, and I say nothing to him, then I go inside.

The warmth of the trailer is welcomed as I close the door behind me. My body shivers as I undress there beside the door, taking my coat, gloves, and woolen sweatshirt off. My legs, my body, feel the muscle soreness of my efforts through the heavy snows and all else that happened outside. I ache all over and a sudden fatigue tells me how tired I must really be.

I pause my undressing on seeing the blackened and swollen left eye, thickened lips, and the thin trickle of drying blood streaming down her chin, still pulsing out from the nurse's damaged mouth. Gay is not tied up, though she is sitting silently at her assigned place with her head half down and her body bent slightly forward in a pose of despair on the far end of the sofa nearest me, to my right, the west side of the trailer.

"Yo had fun in here, man," I comment as I refuse to answer Radwell's quickly repeated third insistence on knowing whether or not I killed the crazy man since entering the trailer. "What happened?" I ask as I point to Gay.

"Damn it, Franklin," Radwell curses and asks for the fourth time; "Did you get the man?"

"Got each other," I answer, unveiling my damaged arm as I pull my bloodied t-shirt gingerly away from my body. The bullet had cut a gash across my right arm, from near and just above the front of my right elbow up to just underneath my shoulder muscle and slightly behind. This bullet hit me while I was diving into the snow during the first exchange on the hillside. This glazed over wound begins to ooze blood after the clothing pulled off its scabs, and now that I start paying attention to it, and it meeting open air, begins to hurt relentlessly. It takes effort to put the pain aside and it's a wound needing stitches, but it's probably too late for that. The left side of my chest, just inches below my armpit, hit when he froze me in my stance by the tree, is not anywhere near as bad as my arm. It's bruised and cut, but the cut isn't deep, to my surprise, yet the area is tender to my touch. That bullet must have hit only my clothes. Unbelievable—fate is on my side—I don't understand how these bullets could hit me like this and not tear me apart more, unless, yes, unless fate is on my side. "He's still out dere."

"Damn it. Damn it," Radwell responds. He is angry, twisting himself to pound his fist, his good arm, against the wall. "I want that bloody mother fucker's head, perched on a stick like he did with Meirs."

"Well, he's ripe for ta pickin's, dere, out dere, somewhere just for ya. All ya have ta do is go seek 'im out," I calmly reply, knowing my indifference will irritate Radwell.

"Fuck you, Franklin," Radwell spits back. "You had a chance and you blew it. Not man enough to follow up and finish the job like a true man would."

I simply smile from his verbal stab. "What happened here?" I ask as I point towards the nurse again.

Radwell insists; "We need to talk about that man out there."

"Afta ya bring me up ta date."

Cal cuts in to answer as Radwell is about to speak. "Nurse let Tollin die. He bled to death. She's a real bitch. Radwell suggested that we have some fun. So we did."

"Damn," I sigh, taking another look at her. I sense Cal is wrong. It was clear to me Gay was doing all she could to keep Tollin alive, fearful of a result like this if she failed. Tollin knew he would not likely make another day. He gave me that impression, but I also thought he would live a lot longer than he must have. His death makes me wonder. Something in Radwell's eyes, his tone, since my return. I don't know what, but after seeing him work, remembering the rumors about him, a bell rings inside my head and this time, this time, I want to know why right away. I do not trust Radwell now, and never Cal, enough to simply take their words for Tollin's cause of death … I just cannot trust them enough. I start for the bedroom, wanting to see Tollin's body, but I stop and turn to grab a hold of Gay gently by the shoulder as I come by her.

"Come with me," I say to her. "I need ya ta tend ta my wounds … not anythin' else." She jerks back from my touch as her eyes briefly and reluctantly meet mine. I mean what I say, however, and this seems to make her hesitate. After what I witnessed, experienced, over this last day I've lost my urge to take a woman by force. I want what is most important first; to be out of here—*alive*. I want life. I want for a new life. Everything is still added to the wrong side; too many killings, too many problems, too much time without moving toward our goal of freedom, and the crazy man still lives. I got little patience for anything less than gaining my freedom now—and we're not there yet. I hold little interest in having, taking, a woman under these terms. I need, I want, a new life, a real life, not this cesspool.

"Ya handle women well," I say to Cal, as I respectfully help the hesitant and suffering nurse to a stand.

Cal laughs behind me, thinking I complimented him, but quickly stops as he catches sight of my sudden glare. He becomes uncertain whether I fume from his laughter or if I intended to insult him. It's both. I'm as disgusted by the damage done to the nurse's face, all puffy and bruised from several welts, as I am in knowing my so-called partners would've enjoyed doing this damage and more. Not that I care about the people here but such stuff reminds me of Joey, what he did Rosalene's sister, and then to Rosalene herself. Things that made me kill him. I have decency in me. I know respecting others will gain respect back—something of value—that so many people mindlessly reject, but not here. There is no respect in the raping of a woman, at least one who has not betrayed you, and this woman could not have done that.

"Ya had fun with ta cook, too, I s'pose, since ya already did Mary," I say, not questioning, just assuming Cal would not stop with one woman when two others can be taken. That Radwell, as angered and injured as he is, would not bother to stop Cal, but would, instead, join him. The other brunette, Mary, also is not tied up or taped. Her emotional condition looks much like Gay's, but looks physically untouched. The cook, Paula, she looks like they got to her.

"Oh yeah," Cal answers smugly. "Radwell and I both. I must say the other two women were just a bit more cooperative after seeing their nurse friend's looks disappear from the earth so quickly. Don't you agree, Rad?"

"Screw it, Cal. We got more important shit to worry about. Franklin, it's done, so don't you get all heaped up and flustered 'bout it. We saved

Mary for you, undamaged. Take her whenever you want. Let's talk about that man out there. He's trouble. He's killin' us. He's messin' up everything. He should've been stone cold dead by now. You said you hit him?" Radwell asks.

Again I'm reluctant to answer for I'm tired of his insistence, of reporting to this self-appointed great almighty leader Radwell keeps trying to make himself out to be. Tollin may have been a bit odd but he gave a balance to us. I realize, without him or Drew here, my situation is not safe if I stay long with Radwell and Cal. They are not ones I can turn my back to. Yet I got little choice but to stay with them—for now. Drew's going it alone closed the door on my doing so—they'll be watching for any hint that I may follow Drew's path to freedom. Somehow, though, I'll have to figure a way to do just that … somehow.

I glance over our men captives. Bill's pained eyes are steady and firm as he meets my gaze, the side of his face oozing blood like my wounds are, crusting everywhere except around the larger sparkling slivers of glass which remain sticking in his face, keeping those wounds open with any facial movement. Around most of the other tiny cuts and slashes scattered across his head the scabs are hardening. The bloodshot eyes of the hunter, Smith, hold a sleep degraded determination and I ignore him for the moment, on feeling my own sleep needs grabbing at me from the trailer's comforting warmth. The cowboy's likewise tired and bloodshot eyes have stayed cool and penetrating—he found a measure of sleep during the night. I ignore him, too.

"I hit him," I answer Radwell, looking again into each captive man's eyes, searching. "Don't know how bad at first. He ran off right away so ta blood couldn't pool, but I know he can't make it through tonight as I tracked him—too much blood, man. He loses too much blood."

I watch for any subtle change in our captive's eyes in reaction to my words, even one ever so slight that will indicate how they assess their friend. Something they can give me to use against him, who already has given us more than we bargained for. Their poker player looks fall short of answering me so I challenge them; "Ya guys look like ya want ta say somethin'? 'Bout ya friend? About dat asshole out dere—ya *friend* who wanted ta play hero but is dyin' as I speak? Ya know he don't give no shit 'bout ya or he would've gone for ta cops? Now you're here with us all *a-lone.* Or maybe ya want ta cry 'bout how we are treatin' you? Want ta threaten us fer what we've done ta ya—your women? No? Look what he's done ta ya. Your friend out dere has made ya death sure. Ya lives are up ta us. He's made sure ya die—unless he dies first. Ya understand, he dies first you stay alive, or are ya three just pussies? … speak up."

Smith needs no further encouragement; "You'd be a dead mother-fucker if I was out there."

"But ya not—he is. Where did he go wrong—huh?"

Smith is silent. His eyes search mine.

"C'mon, man, what's he made of? Nothing like what ya can do—I agree. Dat guy out dere I can't call a man—not like you. I know you woulda killed me if ya were out dere … why can't he?"

Smith opens his mouth to answer but hesitates with suspicion. He debates whether to show how he would have killed me, how his ego can challenge mine and beat me head to head, or to tell me what I want to know, whether he knows that or not. If I can draw him out he will tell me what the man out there may do next. The crazy cat man is bothersome and crudely effective and so damned lucky, but there is no doubt in my mind Smith would have been more able … Radwell would be dead now, for sure. "C'mon, Smith, dat guy out dere is done n over with. He has done his best. He's beaten. Just gotta kill him or we gotta kill you—dat's ta choice, man. Dat's ta choice. No harm in tellin' me his faults. Make me respect him."

Smith is thinking it over. He has all my attention. He is going to answer …

"You play chess?" he asks.

I hate his answer, but I got to see where it goes. "I've played."

"I would've beat you from the start. You had your chance with him. To beat him you got to immediately, psych him out from the start, make him doubt himself. You don't, he recovers and becomes someone you've not bargained for—and you have only one chance to call for a peace between you—and you missed that chance, too. He will not give up now until he is dead, or you are. He will punish you. Take your pieces away one by one as he already has done—four of you are gone, and you will feel the pain as he closes your world in on you and begins to play with you like a cat before the kill."

"He ain't got none a dat goin' on here—he don't know what he done ta us. He just a lucky bastard," I reply as I look away from Smith, not letting him see how his answer irritates me—and Smith, calling the crazy cat man a cat playing with me before the kill—more than bargained for—damn you Smith, using words I have thought of—fuck you. I was the one playing with the crazy man—not him with me. I know what was going on—did the crazy man know—no way. It ain't going to work that way—it ain't. The crazy man don't have nothing on us. I'm killing him—both of them, it don't matter who first; Smith or the crazy man—I don't care.

I look towards Bill, who seems ready to speak next. Smith keeps talking, taunting, but I refuse to hear what he says. His purpose is to provoke me into untying him so we can fight like 'men'; maybe later, maybe never, but not right here and now. What he said is disturbing enough. I wave the gun across Smith's face to shut him up. Then I reflect on the crazy cat man's wounds and hope I'm correct in how grave they are to him. That he is incapable of coming at us again.

"Need the restroom," Bill answers with a slight tilt of his head.

"Oh? No comment about your friend out dere? No threat ta us?" I goad. His request surprised me.

He shakes his head no. "Never much respect for the dork. Just the restroom for me now, hey, and soon," he says in an unperturbed voice.

"Cowboy?" I ask with a touch of impatience.

"If he ain't dead—he ain't dead. If he is, so what? What do you want us to say? I don't know him that well, never did. I hung around with Smith and the others—he just kind of imposed himself on us—I don't know him that well. I need the restroom, too," he answers with irritation in his voice as he catches my questioning stare. "I ain't seen him but twice over three decades. How am I supposed to know him now, huh?"

This was useless. It's as if they don't care about him; what he did or does, whether he lives or dies, or they are on to me and refuse to give a true response, except for Smith's disturbing one. What am I looking for, anyway? The man out there is bleeding to death as we speak. He has too many wounds, his blood loss unstoppable, for me to worry about him. Yet this is what I thought before, worried about before, and the worst came true. The history of him bothers me. I have to go back out and see him dead, bring something of his back here to kill the spirit of these men, his friends, to play with them, before we kill them ... like the crazy man's head.

87
(Franklin)

"Ya get ta restrooms after ta nurse here fixes me up some," I say, pulling the nurse closer towards the main bedroom, as more questions come.

"You didn't track him?" asks Cal. "You were gone long enough to track him."

"Yeah, man," I sigh loudly, impatiently. "I tracked good while. Ta blood marks didn't disappear. Dey didn't get bigger, either."

"If you did all that, why didn't you finish the fuckin' damn job?" Radwell growls.

I glance at Mary, her eyes are sorrowful, of a mind looking within, staring to the floor as if unaware of my closing presence as I move towards her, after I tell Gay to remain where she is. The added news of her husband brings silent tears to her cheeks, and I'm about to say more.

"Didn't ya say," I begin as I gently lift Mary's face by placing two of my fingers under her chin to examine her before turning back to look at Radwell, feeling Mary quickly pull her head away from my touch as I do. "No, it was Cal, dat ta other 'two' women were very willin'? Ya were lyin' ta me, Radwell, when ya said Mary was untouched."

"Damn it, Franklin, I was not," Radwell retorts, and explains with a sigh; "She watched. We felt her up, slapped her some. Nothin' more. Heck, they all watched. She *is* yours to take. We know not to get in the way of such sweet revenge as you got against this guy. She's yours."

Radwell's answer disgusts me, doesn't convince me, and I physically show it, narrowing my eyes as I shake my head with that disbelief while I begin to give him an answer, straightening up away from Mary and stepping back towards the nurse. "With ta mornin' comin' on, I see ta man's tracks running off good distance, disappearin' into heavy woods. His ground, not mine. I was fuckin' wet n freezin'. Time ta come home."

"But all those shots we heard," insists Cal, "wasn't that you?"

"Yeah, dat was me n him shootin'. He's got Meirs' handgun—remember? He's lasted dis long, but his wounds bring him down by night. I see one a my shots go through his upper leg n one a his arms. It looked like I blew a good hole through his lower leg earlier, though he seemed ta fix that pretty good. He got a gash across his face 'bout as bad as I got on my arm. I can't see him livin' long. Ya saw how quick Tollin went down. We ain't got nothing ta worry from dis guy. It-it's ta blood loss, man—it adds up, ya know? A bunch over time. Den ta put a couple more holes in him on top of ta first—naw, man, he is hurtin' bad. Real bad."

"So you did get him," Radwell exclaims.

"Told ya how, man, listen up."

"If you got that close to see him that way—why," Radwell forcefully asks; "didn't you finish him—didn't make sure you saw him dead?"

"Ran out a bullets, Rad, ran out a bullets. I ain't crazy, man. I ain't crazy … I ain't crazy ta go afta him when I can't see him n I ain't got no more bullets—I ain't taking dat chance. He is ta crazy man—not me."

"Just … just," Radwell sighs, throwing a body tantrum of sorts. "We gotta get you back out there and find his dead body."

"I know, but I need some food and ammo—and a better gun. I ain't takin' no bolt action out there—I saw semi-auto's somewhere—where are they?"

Cal answers; "Meirs had one. Tollin the other. I need mine."

"Heck you do," Radwell scoffs to Cal, "You give him yours when he goes."

Cal glares resentfully before he nods silently in agreement.

"Get the stuff and go then, don't wait around," Radwell says to me.

"We promised 'em we'd kill 'em one by one if he didn't come in," interjects Cal, smiling, lusting for the thrill each killing will bring. "And it's been a long five minutes, like, three hours and a half abouts."

"Longer, Cal, it's been much longer than that," Radwell calmly corrects as he sits in that chair, the one opposite the trailer door, like he is on a king's throne passing heavy judgment after casually considering everything involved—as if a wave of his mighty hand can solve anything coming his way. "I suppose we're just gonna have to do some house cleaning. We really ain't got the need to baby-sit all of them."

"Shit," I say in forced calmness, checking my frustration while I look around at the captives and their horrid conditions and, as I do, an irritating and awkward feeling of compassion for them wells up in me. Where that comes from, I don't know—I discard it. "Let me think on dat, while you guys think of ways to get outta here. That's more important."

"Shit," exclaims Cal in disappointment.

"Now just wait a minute Franklin," replies Radwell.

"No, you wait," I hurriedly answer. "I know dat guy out dere has messed with us, but he's dying as we speak. With dose wounds he's likely dead now. Go out n get him if ya want ta. Ya can follow my tracks easy enough. As for dese people—heck, it's like what's ta challenge in killing 'em? A few quick shots—bang, they're gone. We can do dat anytime. So relax, if we need ta do it, we'll do it when we leave—okay? Okay? They ain't gonna hurt us. It's better for us ta leave 'em alive—like Tollin said, at least until I bring that crazy man's head back. Be back." I start again for the bedroom with the nurse.

Cal scoffs while Radwell sighs and looks about the trailer and over the fearful faces of the hostages. I keep a close eye on my two partners.

"I don't know, Franklin, too many of them here. I'd feel a great deal more comfortable if the men weren't alive," Radwell states as I guide the unwilling nurse, who stiffens at his words and stops just feet from the bedroom door. Radwell's following my lead? What a surprise.

"I think 'bout it—okay? Dis nurse fixes me up first."

"Then, ah, then what, Franklin, we lie in wait? Is that what we do now?" Cal asks.

"Why, yes, Cal, wait is a good idea," I caustically answer. "But I think ya oughta do dat lying in wait thing in a funeral home many years from now, shit-head."

"If you believe he is coming, we—you should go out there again, meet the man, drop him in his tracks," Radwell suggests.

My arm pushes Gay into the room, shaking my head in disagreement as I look back to answer: "I said nothing 'bout him coming. He can't. Even alive all he do is crawl." I know I lie. That last sight of him standing up taking aim at me told me he could do more than crawl, but to make it here? I don't think so. "Not me goin', you can. I'm bone cold and hungry. Want me a hot shower, too. Like I said, he's a dead man—too much blood loss ta be a threat ta us now. Said nothing about he making it back here. How you come up with dat? You think so—you go get him. Go on," I go on too much, but can't help it. I want the sarcasm delivered. I ignore anything more they say as I shut the bedroom door behind me and lock it, which causes Gay to step away from me as far as she can go within the tiny confines of this room.

88

Any snow that falls from a tree, any different sound from these woods, makes me react with alarm. I have to tell myself repeatedly this fear of ambush is useless energy spent.

Thoughts of my children come, heartfelt memories; carrying my oldest son on my shoulder while walking through a winter storm, talking, enjoying the winter as we explored several city blocks, just for fun; my oldest girl spinning and dancing in front of me then telling a story of adventure she just had; of my youngest son wrestling, my youngest daughter tumbling with a constant smile in her gymnastics class, and other memories. Images of Mary and my friends at the trailer come to me, too, and how they need my help—now.

I reach the point where his tracks and mine meet, from the night before. His now turn directly for the trailer, which I can't do, so I rest here, feeling weak. The rush of adrenaline from battle and fears of ambush have worn off, to give me a true assessment of my condition—bad.

The sky moves with a mix of shaded grays, the clouds stay thick, heavy, and low. Below, the motionless white of the snows covering the fields underneath and the bordering distant darker tree lines of the south forest, standing rigidly picturesque with their own caps of snow, show in vivid contrast against these sullen clouds. It is a coldly beautiful sight of winter I cannot enjoy, for cold is all I physically feel.

The field is empty. The trailer stands below the roll of the hill and out of sight. I follow my previous tracks; while they are mostly drifted over and filled with snow, they remain visible as a line of depression winding across the field.

Pops of distant gunfire, here and there, sound occasionally and I can't remember when they started, telling me other hunters are in the woods. Ones who have campers like ours and who likely find themselves stranded but are making the best of things at present, who decided to hunt in the morning and dig out during the afternoon. The chance of my meeting any of them, or attracting their attention, is not worth thinking about. My earlier exchanges of gunfire with Franklin will go unnoticed on this opening day of the season. Who would listen? Who would care? Who would think it so strange as to investigate? No one, and none of these hunters will wander far from their camp in snow this deep if they did become curious.

My youngest son likes bugs. Still does, I think. Birds, animals, quiet creativeness seems his thing. He wants to be an architect. My oldest son has varied talents, but I think he wants criminal law. My oldest daughter is a genius and has focused her life on becoming a neurologist-doctor or something like that. She is well on her way. My youngest daughter, the cutest and most charming of the bunch, I hardly knew when her mother and I separated, a mother who at one time wanted to abort her, infuriated at being pregnant again for the fifth time, finding out two weeks after we agreed to stop at three children. The first pregnancy miscarried. After a week of her speaking about it she convinced me she was to abort our child the next day … our child ... my child. No. No, she was not going to do that … and live. It was the only time in my life I threatened anyone on their life … and meant it to my soul. My youngest daughter tumbling with a constant smile in her gymnastics class … she has been worth that threat. Memories—some give a deep bite, a double-edged sword. I know little of my children now. I cannot find reason, but, maybe … maybe I earned this exclusion from their lives off such a death threat to their mother … somehow.

Keep thinking to keep off the pain. I'm making better time across the field than I thought I could, or my mind has lost track of time. They say one's life flashes by before they die. This may be the reason for all these thoughts of my children and such. I sigh with sorrow. Getting spanked for breaking the crystal blue ash tray that my sister actually broke, seeing my mom fall and break her cheek bone, playing catch with my dad, my friends, my children, and my reading and making up stories to and with my children at bedtime, watching their births, holding them, praying beside their beds—all reminiscent thoughts.

You resign yourself to death continuing to think this way. It will fog your mind. Keep moving; keep thinking of Mary and your friends in present time—you must do what you can, here and now ... forget the past, because it is past.

89

(Franklin)

"Relax," I whisper. "Ya safe. I ain't gonna do nothin'. I ain't happy 'bout what happened ta ya and I know dat don't mean much. Tell me what happened ta him," I continue to whisper, as I point to Tollin's body. "And fix my arm. Do both now."

Gay's body shudders momentarily. She's in clear physical and emotional pain but she forces herself to look at Tollin's body and then to me, with her head down, her eyes reluctant to make lasting contact with mine.

"Now," I repeat, as I pick up the tiny first aid kit that lies on the bed near Tollin's feet. She doesn't respond so I take a forceful step towards her. She braces herself and, when I move no closer, she gains enough composure to speak, if only in hopes to stop me from getting nearer.

"Told you before," she begins in a broken voice and with her eyes still down, "the bullet ruptured the liver, tore up major arteries or veins inside him. He didn't have a chance. He died from blood loss about two hours ago, maybe three."

"Ya not sure?" I question.

She shrugs.

"Why ain't ya sure?" I ask in a gentle tone.

She hesitates. Her eyes catch mine briefly.

"I want ta know if he told ya ta tell me something," I say quietly.

She's non-responsive as she opens the now sparse medical kit and tends my wound, as if she is in a trance, while I study the body of Tollin. I whisper; "Were you in here when he died?"

She is understandably slow to know why I had closed the door, why I talk softly, why I have interest in the dead man.

"Yes," she answers, but she is becoming curious. "One time," she realizes, her lips trembling as she speaks his name. "Radwell told me to leave."

"Then Tollin got suddenly worse?" I wonder, pointing to him.

"Yes, he died quickly after h-he left the room and I came back in. Never spoke again."

"Show me his wounds," I tell her.

She shows me the entrance wound, but when she and I roll Tollin up to his side to see the exit wound there is a second wound where a tiny blade entered him near the back and top of his heart, just along the spine on the left side of his body. She looks at me and she is quietly appalled. “This looks like a knife wound going in to where the aorta is. That’s the…”

“I know what ta aorta is, ta big artery of ta body coming from ta heart.”

She nods.

Tollin never wanted to go back to prison. Maybe he asked for a quick death, yet this would not have been quick. Radwell had a perverse pleasure killing him like this if Tollin did ask for death. No … I can’t see it, this is more like Radwell finishing Tollin off so he wouldn’t have to deal with him no longer.

“You’re going to kill all of us, aren’t you?”

I don’t look at her right away. Any promise I make I can’t keep. I don’t know why but I would like to see the rest of them live. We will be long gone before they find help. It won’t hurt to leave them alive, but killing them is so much easier that I doubt I can stop both Cal and Radwell from doing so. “Unfair if I promise ya,” I truthfully answer. “Only way is if ya promise not ta tell on us for, uh, four—no six hours after we leave…”

“Yes,” she quickly replies.

I shake my head. “The other two ain’t gonna let dat happen, ya know dat …”

The knocking on the door ends our stay. She quickly returns Tollin to his position and then stands next to me, her hands on my arm near my wound and quickly, carefully, beginning to cut a corner of my wrapping with a small rounded-tip steel scissors as I reach over in appropriate time to open the lock to the door. “Yeah, yeah, Radwell,” I answer as I do this.

“Don’t you lock a door on me again,” He commands, as he swings the door open rapidly.

“If I choose ta do a woman, asshole, I ain’t gonna be doin’ it in front of you—I’m gonna be lockin’ a door—got it?” I answer firmly.

Radwell glares at me. “You done in here?”

“Yeah, I’m done,” I reply, pulling Gay out in front of me, waving off her efforts to bandage me further, to put her between myself and Radwell, forcing him to step back. He is angry, and he holds his shotgun this time, while I hold no weapon at all. I just had to foolishly place my rifle down by the trailer’s entrance when I came in.

90

I pass the site where we exchanged gunfire on the slope during the night and can see the outline of the snow rut he made to hide in many yards away from the point where I got hit, but I have no time to explore it—I can't afford the curiosity.

I reach the south woods where I came out of them so many long hours ago, and move well enough within to hide from the field yet still see it. The trailer can't be seen, though the crest is only a few yards away. I have to rest here. I'm out of breath. My muscles twitch. Nausea and dizziness flash through me more and more often. I struggle to hold on to my walking stick, to maintain my balance, as pain shudders through my body, causing tears to form in my eyes, as if, now that I have stopped my constant motion, all the pain somehow put off by those movements can come due. I fear I will die uselessly, but I am grateful I'm alive. There is still a chance. I need to stay focused and lose this dizziness, regain my strength.

The branch I use as a crutch keeps me standing as I puke. Dry heaves mostly, having nothing in my stomach, but some dark and disgusting tasting brownish-yellow fluid does leave my mouth. This wrenching shakes me to my core and further drains my energy. My head comes to rest against the back of my cold yet sweaty hand—I've lost that glove somewhere some time ago. I stare down along the length of my crude crutch, gasping, seeing nothing else but the snowy ground and the stain of my puke on the snow, hearing little else for several minutes but the sounds of my labored breaths, until my strength slowly returns, my dizziness disappears. This time, though, my fever does not go away and my strength does not come back with any vigor.

I force myself to start moving again, along and just inside the skirt of the forest, following the field's edge down toward the trailer that is now in sight. I'm not well hidden from the trailer, I'm practically in the field, but I can't expend the energy to be more concealed. My mind is slow to cope with this—that they can see me if they look; that another path is too hard to follow—my brain can't afford to comprehend more than it has to. I feel a different type of time tapping on my shoulder—a limited one … and it's ticking away.

91
(Franklin)

I want out of here.

If sure our captives can't reach help for hours after I leave then I don't care if I leave them alive. Just get me out of here.

I don't believe my partners can take me farther than where I can get alone. I think they think I burden them. I have to be ready to kill them … but it's not clear yet when.

I'm too unsettled. I want to do Mary, but that would take time—and leave me vulnerable to Radwell and Cal to break down the door and kill me. That crazy man out there is still out there, still living, still bothering me that he still could be and I don't like loose ends like him. I don't like the fear he put in me as I fell when the snow gave way. I don't like another man knowing—even a dying man, that he had success against me; wounding me, making me dance, putting fear in me ... I want him dead.

I need to put my mind in order.

As we did hours ago we let each captive go to the bathroom. This time, though, I sense we all wonder why—we won't again—we won't let them again, the time for a final decision nears. I feel this—can read this in Cal's and Radwell's faces—and I welcome it—time to move on.

From my post inside this small crowded bathroom I watch the cowboy shuffle in, finish his business with Mary's help, and shuffle back out with the help of her and then Gay, who stands outside the door. Radwell watches from beyond the doorway and he and Cal make sure everything out there goes the way we want. Smith comes and goes. Mary seems innocent as she stands to block the doorway in front of me as Smith leaves, and she stays there as Bill's turn comes next. This time Gay moves close behind her husband as he moves into the doorway and together they block my view of Radwell, and anything beyond. Mary stands on the same side of Bill that Gay does and she faces her. Mary completely hides his right side from me.

"Keep moving," I say quickly.

Gay looks at me and then at Mary. "He's mine," she says to us.

"No," I command, "No change in ta routine."

"He's my husband," Gay pleads, or protests.

"I don't care woman—she's got him, back off," I answer as I point to Mary, who has turned just enough to see me. "We don't have time for dis."

Both women react slowly and Mary now turns more and to my right, takes a small step, reaches up to a wall cabinet and begins to open it—her body still blocks much of my sight of Bill.

"Stop," I bark as I swing my rifle over to point at her in this tight bathroom. I hear Radwell react quickly in the other room to order Gay away. Before me Mary ignores me as she continues to open the cabinet door and slowly pull a towel from its shelf and only when it falls free into her hand does she move back to where she had been. Space is so tight in this room I could have bent over and reached my arm to the other side of her while she did this, instead I watched her. Everything she did was right in front of me, yet something is wrong. I study her, study Bill, replay the scene in my mind. Warning bells ring, ring loud in my head, but there's nothing obvious to why. I can only wait to see what happens next. Why are we doing this when the crazy man is still out there? Yeah, we still may need you, and I need time to think, but hurry up, people, the reasons to keep you living get fewer by the minute.

Mary guides Bill as he shuffles his duct taped bound legs the three feet it takes him to properly reach the toilet and she places the towel across his hands, which are also duct taped together, set behind his back at his wrists—a painful position stressing his arms at every joint. She leans forward around him, blocking my view, to unzip his pants.

"Get ta towel off him," I command.

"I need it to wipe my hands, thank you," she retorts, keeping her back to me.

"Pull the towel off him," Radwell orders as he puts a foot inside this crowded room. Mary straightens up as I take the half-step needed to lean and reach around her to sweep the towel off Bill's arms, tossing the towel onto the sink. She reacts with restrained concern, looking to the towel, to me, to Radwell, showing a concern that stems from more than just our reprimands and my quick action—warning bells sing and I start to inspect everything I see about her and Bill. I find nothing but my suspicions—and my frustration grows.

Bill begins to relieve himself, trying to look indifferent to our actions, but his head is raised just that little bit and cocked to one side, to listen and see what he can. His bindings look secure. I still don't like it but I begin to think I'm overreacting.

Radwell is not as accepting as he steps inside and squeezes between us to pull on one of Bill's arms, pushes on the other, causing Bill to wince as he looks back. Radwell then looks over Mary, before becoming satisfied. He leaves the room, giving me an impatient glance as he does, as if I wasted his time.

Bill finishes and Mary guides him back to the door and Gay takes over from there, like before, yet, once more, I'm not settled with what just happened. This time I'm not going to let the feeling that something is wrong go. There is something we missed. There has to be. I watch Mary turn the water on in the sink and reach up and open the small-mirrored medicine cabinet above it.

"What'ya think ya doin'?" I ask her.

Without looking back she answers; "No soap—you *mind*?"

"Wait," I command as I step over to her and she pulls her hands down quickly, out of my sight, as I move. She may have clutched the towel I swept from Bill lying on the edge of the sink. Her actions anger me. My right hand slaps and grabs her left shoulder as she still faces away from me and I pull her straight around. My left hand, holding my rifle, comes to rest heavily between her breasts and the rifle barrel almost hits her in the cheek and jaw. The knob of the gun's bolt presses into her chest bone and I realize Cal and I have not exchanged rifles yet. She returns a defiant gaze as we come to stare at each other, so close, face to face. She knows better than to try for the gun. She knows I tempt her, want her to.

My left hand keeps pressing the rifle against her as my right hand grabs hold of the towel and I flail it in the air, but nothing falls free. I study her as I sense a smirk lurking behind her eyes—telling me I'm correct in my suspicions but that doesn't help if I can't prove them. I put fingers down each of her pants pockets and the front rim of her pants, but nothing is there. I feel for her bra then realize she no longer wears one from her takings by Cal and Radwell and my hand pulls back.

"Satisfied?" she asks. She has no trouble looking into my eyes—a change in her I don't like. "Can I wash my hands now?"

Not knowing what else to do I reluctantly nod my head. "Then get back ta ya place."

After she leaves I look over the medicine cabinet; two small bars of packaged soap, an unopened disposable razor package, deodorant—the usual stuff. If she took something from here I can't tell what it could be. As I leave the bathroom, I hear Radwell command Mary to get up.

Bill sits in his place on the men's couch on the east wall. Next to him is Smith. Next to Smith is the cowboy. Next to Doug, however, is Mary, she sits on this sleeper sofa squeezed partly between Doug and the sofa's arm and partly resting on the sofa's arm itself, her right arm hidden behind Doug. She takes a quick glance at me as I appear but her attentions refocus on Radwell, who is coming towards her, for she is slow to rise on his command. As he reaches her he slaps her face with his good hand and she nearly falls yet catches herself by extending her right arm back onto Doug's upper chest. She hesitates after that, as her eyes go to Radwell's shotgun as she considers taking it from his weakened arm, and she probably could if Cal and I were not here. Radwell slaps her again as he realizes her thought and grabs and squeezes her jaw, the fingers of his good hand pressing deep into her cheeks. He breathes on her face as he curses; "Bitch …."

"Feel like a big man pushing her around?" challenges Smith as Radwell continues speaking.

"The asshole isn't a man, Rick," daringly adds Bill.

"… You do what you're told—nothing else," growls Radwell into Mary's ear as he pulls her around with his good hand to push her down onto the women's sofa on the west side of the trailer. He has heard what the men said and turns back to them, and starts to point his shotgun at them.

While all this occurs my eyes catch sight of Paula watching us from across the room in the kitchen area. She also watches Cal, who stands near her, and I see her grab something quietly from one of the kitchen drawers, hidden from my sight. She does not notice me notice her. Instinctively my gun starts to rise toward her as I step forward, and the barrel of my gun by chance comes up under Radwell's shotgun barrel, lifting his weapon up as he pulls the trigger, thwarting his attempt to kill Smith and Bill. His gun emits a stunning roar within the confines of the trailer.

Reactively I reach across and grab a hold of his warmed barrel with my left hand—to keep Rad from pointing it at me, not letting go of my own rifle or its trigger as I maintain my rifles aim on Paula, using my left forearm to balance the stock.

Everyone else jerked from the blast of his gun, deafening within this trailer, brief gasps, screams, and everyone froze in their stances except for Radwell and I. Radwell gives me a wicked stare as he tries pulling his gun out of my grasp but can't.

"Franklin you black bastard—what're you doing?" he snarls.

I nod in the direction of Paula. "Ta cook has something in her hands, man."

Radwell angrily answers then his voice trails off of as he realizes what I mean and looks her way. "So freakin'… what …."

"Cal, take it easy now, man, but yo look what she's got in her hand," I say.

Cal, who froze like all the others from the shotgun's blast, breaks his stare at us to look at Paula and immediately takes a step away from her and swings his rifle towards her as she raises the steel knife and slashes it through the air at him but misses as both Cal and I pull our triggers. My shot misses, I see the hole my bullet puts in the back wall. Cal does not miss, as

Paula collapses back to the floor as does the knife, unseen, on the far side of her.

"Bitch," Cal spits out as he stands above her. "Bleed ta death ya bitch." He kicks her hard twice in the side. The whimpering from Paula quickly stops.

Our attentions return to the cowboy as Smith gives an anguished shout and struggles in his bindings, the other women whimper, and the other two men grimace.

"Doug," I say, "Mary gave ya somethin'. Give it up, man."

But I notice the look on Radwell's face. He is thinking of killing them all.

92

The sound of the blast stops me. It came from inside the trailer and strikes me with fear. Two more blasts come, and my heart sinks. I expect to hear more. I'm not yet halfway down the slope. The trailer and the rest of our camp is in full view. I can't make it there in time to help anyone.

I stand motionless, staring at the trailer below, wondering, by some miracle, hoping, praying, that they had been shooting at me, but reality hits and I get myself moving again, to get down there and finish this, or have them finish me.

93
(Franklin)

There is a hole in the ceiling above where Bill and Smith sit on the sofa from Radwell's shotgun's blast. A light stream of snow falls from there to cover their shoulders and laps, which they both ignore. Bill is silent but Smith surprises me—he taunts us again; angry, distraught, over what happened with his wife, challenging us to free him, to take him on. The cowboy silently looks back at me, and then at Radwell, before shaking his head in resignation. "Mary put something down my pants," he says, "just underneath my belt in the back. I don't know what it is—I really don't—can't reach it."

Radwell's response continues with that same look he carried when he shot each of the three men he killed before. I won't stop him. Like crazed sharks in bloody water, Cal and Radwell want a frenzy of killing, giving me a good time to kill them—Cal first, because Radwell will think I'm killing the women behind him—Rad won't know what hit him. Then everyone will be dead and I'll be free to go for a new life on my own—it'll be safer that way. I just got, man, to let them start the killing.

"Kill them," Cal growls with depravity in his voice, anxious for blood.

Radwell smiles and looks toward me.

"Hey," I say, "What—ya askin' me?"

"Yeah, nigger, I'm asking ya," Radwell replies.

"Yeah, well, go ahead," I answer.

"Naw," Radwell responds, "I think, ah, let's find out what she put down his pants. Then let's kill that guy out dere and bring somethin' of him back here ta kill ta spirit of them before we kill them. More fun."

Radwell disappoints me. I'm ready to kill, as I make slight moves to position myself to kill Cal first. "No, Rad, let's kill dem."

"I live up here," Smith cautiously says as Radwell turns his gun towards him. "Have any of you? …The snow is the deepest it's been in memory."

Smith isn't taunting us. He isn't moaning Paula being shot. I know what he's doing—he is trying to buy time, save his life, maybe save the others. He's a good distraction for me for I don't believe we'll buy into anything he says, and I don't care to listen, now that I chambered another bullet, ready to kill my partners, yet Radwell doesn't pull the trigger.

In the background Cal stops his cussing and prancing back and forth along the length of Paula's body. I see she still breathes, as Cal sees Radwell's gun point at Smith. Cal carries that gleeful look of anticipation on his face. For some reason, I don't like it—maybe it's Cal's job to kill me—who else could he kill from where he stands but me, now that Paula's down. I suddenly find shelter in Smith's words as he continues, as Smith cringes from the point of Radwell's gun, and I'm surprised Radwell still hesitates—hasn't shot him dead already. Radwell wants to play, like he did with Mark, but this gives me time to move and use Radwell's body as a shield from Cal's gun without either man knowing.

"How do you expect to get out of here, alive, without us?" Smith asks.

"As easily as we came in, dickhead," Radwell spits back as he raises the shotgun to his good shoulder.

Smith gives a slow disagreeing shake of his head and ekes out careful words; "Snow has changed that."

Radwell, for the second time, looks to me, shows an impertinent smile, but he will listen, as everyone will, and Smith realizes he is given a chance to explain. I take advantage to move a bit closer to Radwell's body while keeping Cal in sight.

"You try going somewhere on foot out in this snow?" Smith asks, "Try it. Three miles to the nearest road. Five to the nearest place—not as the crow flies but how you'd be forced to get there. Franklin, now, he felt secure out there because he could follow his tracks back here and gave no thought to going further than he had to—where he could lose sense of direction, distance, and time, and what's needed to be done before night falls again—how to do it; how to survive the night—out there. Won't be no tracks showing where you need to go. Franklin knows it's hard just to move out there and when it stops snowing the cold comes 'round to double the danger. Ask him—go on and ask him."

Smith is right, so far. I nod my head in agreement as Radwell gives me an inquiring gaze.

"You three talk about killing us openly—so frequently." Smith is visibly nervous yet calm in his thinking, careful. "Someone says that to you, you wouldn't sit still, would you?"

Radwell straightens and relaxes, his shotgun lowers just a bit. I straighten my stance, too. I am listening to this.

"You kill us now," Smith continues somberly. "I'll know you'll die. You'll get lost in these woods, fight among each other. You will take the wrong logging road and circle around until you die. You can go right by a main road without knowing you did. This snow is so heavy it will take days before they get to clean the roads around here. By some miracle if they do clean quick and you find that road, by the time you go a mile you'll get picked up by the cops. People walking in the road under these conditions are stopped and questioned. If you can't find the road—any road, you might find your way back here to wait for them, the cops, but more likely you'll get lost tryin' another way, then another, hoping each new way is salvation. It ain't gonna be. You are stuck here without us. I have been in this kind of stuff many times. I know where to go, what it takes to get you out of here, to live in this overnight. I can lead you out of here, but if anyone dies, forget it."

A click inside Radwell's gun sounds as he pulls the trigger. Everyone falls silent. Frustrated at not reloading his gun earlier, Radwell places its front tip to the floor and ejects the earlier spent shell and reloads, aims, and hesitates, doing all this with his good arm.

I look at him, puzzled, because Smith's words bother me. "Rad?"

He clenches his teeth and shakes his head as if fighting to let go of a thought that still hangs on. He sighs deeply as he looks at me. "I feel foolish letting them live, nigger. It just seems trouble to me. We need to torment them; get that guy out there, bring a body part back of him, then kill these assholes goodbye, because I don't believe a freaking word Smith says, man—I want to kill him now."

"Aw-man, mother—c'mon Rad then do it. Let's kill them and get out of here," Cal says impatiently. He remains standing beside Paula, who still breathes.

I shake my head and grimace for Radwell to see, to keep him from pulling the trigger—I don't care if we kill them—I care that we can get out of here. "How do we get outta here Cal? Can ya answer me dat? If ya can, we kill dem."

Cal falls silent, his face loses expression. "We walk?"

Radwell scoffs. "To where—you know where?"

Cal shakes his head no in silent resignation.

"Thought so, but I don't either," Radwell states in disgust.

"We get ta men ta dig us to ta stone semi-circle. I think ta trucks can get to ta road from there," I suggest.

"Not doing that," Smith replies quickly, firmly, with a shake of his head.

"Ain't no way," Doug adds.

"To dig ya out just to have ya kill us—not happening, man," Bill says.

Radwell's face lights up with anger as his head cocks to one side. He gives me a glare meant for our captives as he raises his gun once more.

"Ya will," I reply, holding a hand up to stop Radwell, "Ta keep ya women alive."

"Paula's dead," Smith emotionally responds.

"I ain't got no woman here," Doug adds.

Bill has a frightened confused look on his face; uncertain how to take the other two men's responses. "I don't … want Gay to die. Your promises mean nothing. How can we be certain …"

"Certain we keep ya women alive, man?" I finish for him. "Ya dig us out to ta circle n we be more interested in getting' us outta here than goin' back to ta trailer here, man, ta get ya women. Dey stay here alive. We had our fun with dem, anyway—dey did, you assholes," I say as I turn to face Radwell and Cal, my last words meant for them. "What'dya say big man?"

Bill looks pleadingly to Smith and Doug whose faces change in pallor as they slowly nod their heads in agreement.

"Shit," exclaims Cal in disappointment.

"Ya got a better idea, man?" I challenge Cal.

Cal falls silent again and shakes his head no.

"Shuddup den," I say.

94

I'm about five feet above the level of the trailer on the hill when I hear the remote sounds. The snowmobiles are coming and soon two of them appear in the far distance. I look to the trailer and stop my movement as I catch sight of a man looking out the west trailer window by the kitchen area. He looks north across the hillside and glances down along the south wood line where I stand, but his gaze does not go low enough along the hill to see me before he disappears from the window.

The snowmobiler's timing is near perfect, yet the killers have not killed everyone inside the trailer—I can see the backs of Gay's head, and Mary's, as they sit on the west sofa—and they move! Makes sense, to kill the men and take the women. Now they only have to wait for these machines to arrive at their door.

Wait … two men are leaving the camp? They head towards the north patch of woods to hunt me—no, no, not me—they're going out to meet the snowmobilers. I have to keep my mind focused. This fatigue and pain makes my mind wander—stay focused. One of them is Franklin, and his sight sends a shiver down my spine. The other is a white guy. They move quickly along thirty, forty, fifty yards from the camp before my mind realizes this is my chance. I have time, before they discover me, to get to the trailer and free my wife and sister, kill whoever may be guarding them. I start moving, glancing frequently at the two as they place more distance between themselves and the camp. They remain unaware of my presence. Then I lose sight of them as I make it below the trailer's height.

The two snowmobilers are unaware they will forfeit their lives—and none of the ways I think of trying can stop that. Their machines provide what is needed for these men to make their escape, giving these men all the reason they need to kill everyone precious to me, but these snowmobilers do buy time for me. I hope it's enough.

I hope whoever may still be inside the trailer will be watching what is going on between these two riders and their own two men so that I can catch them unaware. They will be babysitting, with no reason to look for someone else like me. That is my chance, my only chance. I have to hurry.

95

(Franklin)

The thirst to kill leaves Radwell's expression as he looks at me, then speaks to us all; "Can't leave on foot—that's the last choice, my shoulder won't let me do that. Don't believe Smith about the roads not gettin' cleaned by the time we reach them—with the trucks. I'd rather chance that then to let you, Smith, guide us to anywhere because, Smith, you're just too much of an asshole to trust and, if what's been done already has not set you to revenge, shooting your wife has—nothing you say can get that out of my mind—and you can't take us anywhere far with that leg of yours anyway, so you're bullshittin' up a storm. You're just a shit ... and you're about to do a lot of digging."

Smith's posture retreats into the sofa, his eyes are downcast and he gives a quiet apprehensive sigh. Radwell finally has said something I like. "Crazy man?" I ask.

"Forget him," Radwell replies. "Don't see how he can do us harm from what you said. He's a dead man."

"Dese men?" I ask.

"Dead after digging—they agreed. We need to stop talking. Get whatever you need together now—get dressed for the outside, Frank, Cal. Then tie the women up ..."

"Hey," Smith protests.

"What?" Radwell snaps back. "We said we'd let them live—we are—you want to complain about that?"

Smith stares at Radwell for a brief moment, then shakes his head no.

"What about staying here—kill 'em, so we got the food, but just stayin'?" Cal asks.

Radwell and I pause before Radwell says; "I'm gonna need medical attention, supplies at least. The nurse is right, my shoulder is starting to pain me." Radwell glances my way; "Franklin looks like he needs some, too."

I do. My wounds are getting loud in their pain, harder to ignore. I will need some kind of medical attention soon.

We tie the two women and we have just finished readying ourselves for the outside when we stop what we are doing to listen. The sounds we hear are remote and more than one machine makes a spirited growl. We look to each other in disbelief. The sounds unmistakably come from snowmobiles. The three of us forget about our captives, forget what we're doing, as each of us find a window instead. Cal looks west, Radwell and I look east. We hear them for awhile before spotting the machines in the distance, probably as far away as can be and still be seen. They have slowed, stopped, as we watch them.

Why are these people out on snowmobiles on opening day, I wonder? They can get shot. They'll certainly anger any hunters in the area, but then the snow reminds me why—joy ride. Whoever these two are, they have what we need to get out of here—and we need to get their attentions before they move on. A burden lifts from my mind. These snowmobiles are the answers to our needs. Fate is on my side. Radwell, and now Cal, who has left the west side window to join us, have to be thinking the same. And I'm right—these riders will get shot.

"Cal, you stay here. Watch these people, keep them quiet. If they don't, kill the one who makes the noise. We'll know to kill the riders if you shoot. Otherwise stay quiet, let us do the talking, the shooting—got it?" Radwell asks.

"Got it," Cal answers.

"C'mon, Frank, let's get the heck out there and get these riders to come here."

Radwell starts waving and I start jumping to gain their attention and we catch it before they move on—somehow they have seen us, or the trailer. They rise up on their machines and wave back. We wave them over. They are coming. We are standing about sixty yards north from the camp now, along what would have been the truck trail, hidden by the snow. We had to move away from the trailer—to better get their attention and to better hide Perez's and Mason's bodies, both discernable under the snow if we stayed closer to the trailer.

"Have your safety off," Radwell murmurs as we watch them approach.

"Got it," I whisper.

"You have the left one. I got the right one. Let's not cross our efforts."

"Understand."

It takes a minute or so for them to get here and I feel tense as they near because both riders are dressed in bright orange hunting garb, one-piece snow suits, and believe they could be armed, but Radwell, I can see, is joyfully relaxed as the men pull their machines to a stop about ten feet before us, bringing their loud engines down to run at idle so we can speak.

"Hey there," Radwell says with an upbeat tone and smile. Radwell moves to raise his hand in greeting and, in doing so, shows no sign of his wound under his own winter garb or the pain he feels. These men have no clue to who we are as yet. I nod my head to them and smile.

"Hey," says the man sitting on the machine to our right. This man wears a bright sparkling metallic blue helmet, like motorcyclist's use, and he has flipped up its darkly shaded but transparent shield to talk with us. "Do we have the right place? We're the guys from Daniel's shop you hired to ride some of you out—where's Smith?"

"Oh," Radwell quickly replies, "Yeah, ya got the right place. We figured you're the guys. Who else would be out using these machines on a day like today, ya know? … Smith's posted himself out in the woods somewhere, but he should be headed in; he knows you would be here about now. He'll be here soon. Is it pretty tough riding those things in this stuff?"

"Not bad, powder's soft for the most part. Fun, but we wouldn't be out yet—got other things to do, except you're paying us good dollar for this ride—understand a few of ya need to get out of here today, not chancing any more of this storm and all."

"Yep. That's true, that's very true. How far can those machines take ya in this?"

"Far enough. Forty miles out and back, maybe, probably more," he pauses as a radio cackles and both men turn off their machines. He answers the call. "Hey, I've been told to ask you about three men who supposed to come out here yesterday. Two work for the power company. The other installs septic systems. Did they find ya?"

"Yeah they did."

"They here with ya?"

"No."

"They'd been missing—when did they leave your place?"

I notice the guy on the left, the one who is not doing the talking, starting to look carefully over our camp as I recall us not moving the utility trucks into the woods, only ours. He'll soon see them. I'm going to kill him, but Radwell cuts my thought as he talks to me.

"Oh, 'bout three," Radwell answers. "What do you say, Frank, three o'clock yesterday?"

"Yeah, about den," I say. "As ta storm began, but dey should've got out a here just fine."

"Hey, how fast can those machines go in stuff like this?" Radwell asks. Smart, I guess, finding out what we can do with these machines, but Radwell is beginning to waste time. The guy on the left squints at something, squints again. I don't like that. He is recognizing the trucks.

His partner continues speaking after he too glances at our camp; "Fast enough. We see you got your trucks and trailer snowed in. You're gonna have a hell of a time getting out of here. You should've parked them up on the logging road ledge. Even there you'd only have half a chance, you know."

"Yeah," answers Radwell, "We should have, we regret it—believe me, but we'll make it out just fine. We got a week to dig out. That is if the weather lets us. You guys come far?"

The man on the right answers slowly, waiting before answering as he studies us. "'Bout ten miles, why?"

"Just wondered. Smith didn't tell us," Radwell replies.

What the heck, Rad, why talk, let's kill them?

The man on the right is about to speak again when we get interrupted a second time by the cackle of the radio. He picks his receiver up and answers; "Yeah ... no, they're not here ... about three yesterday ... yeah, things are fine, see ya in about forty." The man puts the receiver back down then stops his movement to look at Radwell and me, checking us over, maybe beginning to put things together, perhaps he already has. As if to emphasize this, his partner coughs, trying to have him look toward our camp again. He does and I watch their expressions pale as they suddenly realize the danger they are in.

"We want your machines," Radwell calmly but insistently states.

They look to us with apprehension.

"Say again mister?" the man on the left asks.

"They clearin' the main road yet?" Radwell asks.

"They ain't got to your logging road yet, take another two hours—what you say before?"

I notice Radwell casually prepare himself as the man on the left gave his answer. Both men on the machines have begun reaching down for something behind each engine cowl. This is enough for me. Radwell quickly follows my shot as we watch the two men go down with bullet holes in each of their chests. We hurry to their fallen bodies and see that each are still alive. The last thing we want is to fill their helmets up with brain matter, so we quickly pull their helmets off their heads before placing another bullet, this time into their brains, to finish them. That concern also applies to their suits so we quickly pull those off, too, before they get too bloody.

96

By the front of Rick's truck my leg jolts me with a severe pain and I collapse into the snow. I felt internal tearing in my leg. This pain becomes remote. A sense of desperation rushes through me as I get up and keep moving, leaving the walking stick that slipped from my grasp—too much energy and time loss to retrieve it.

Something feels strange in my upper leg, like a slow but sweeping venom crawling up towards the rest of my body and scares me. My left thigh muscles quiver and cramp, that foot I can't feel and its use says my Achilles tendon must be gone, as I make the short distance to the trailer and hide from view of its windows.

Standing there, leaning heavily against the trailer's wall, I feel dizzy, light-headed, and my bloodied right hand quietly slaps itself against the trailer wall to steady my body. I can't tell if I feel the cold anymore, though my body shakes like it does.

The snow has drifted deep against this side of the trailer and it supports my weight—enough for me to climb to the height of the sofa windows where Mary and Gay sit, by folding my right leg under me and using it like a board while my left arm lifts and swings my left leg around and to keep it straight for the only use it has left—balance. The other windows on this side of the trailer are too high for me to see in.

A pain presses inside my chest takes my breath away and forces me to stop halfway to the window, lean my back against the trailer and rest. My breath returns as this pain diminishes and I drop my head for just a moment. As I straighten back up the world spins again.

It's hard for my eyes to focus on anything as two shots sound. Someone joyfully exclaims loudly from within the trailer. The dizziness I feel stays as I realize these sounds mean the two riders are dead, and this pushes me towards the window, but my eyes want to close; it's hard to keep my balance.

Gay is nearest to me, and alive, though her mouth is taped shut and she seems unable to move. She is not aware of me—good; I made it this far unnoticed. I shuffle closer with the gun ready and take a slow careful peek inside.

I see a man with a rifle standing at the opened doorway to the trailer, diagonally across and partially hidden from me, watching something occurring on the other side of the trailer, his back is to me. He's a large white man with white trash written all over him—in his posture and appearance, his movements.

Mary is next to Gay, but I can't see her well, and I don't see Paula. Across the trailer from Gay, and further back in, to my right, sits the men. My eyes set on Doug. I stare at him a moment, perplexed on seeing him alive. He is bound, yet he has been silently trying to gain my attention. He bumps Rick, bound beside him on his right, to look in my direction and away from the man at the door. Rick's eyes light up and winks his eye as he nods his head toward the man at the door then looks the other way and shakes his head no, mouthing words one and … none?

I want to make sure. I raise my hand up showing my gun and point to the man in the doorway, then point the other way. Rick tilts his head towards the man at the door and nods his head yes. He shakes his head no for inside the trailer. Thankfully there's only one man in the trailer—much better odds. I acknowledge.

Rick bumps Bill whose arms are now free! Bill looks at me but quickly returns his eyes towards the man at the door as he blindly reaches back with one arm behind Rick and I catch sight of the tiny pair of rounded-end first aid kit scissors he holds in his hands he will use to free Rick. Bill glances at me again and I try to smile to show him the elation I feel knowing they're breaking free and that everyone I see *live*. Bill drives that out of me by returning a mean scowl to keep me focused on the present. The women are now aware of me.

My mind has become clear again as my heart races with this growing anticipation. Because of the short partition wall Bill cannot completely see the man at the door so he can't free his legs without attracting that man's attention, and he can't attack the man effectively enough with his legs bound. If I shoot now this man will likely fall out of the trailer—with his rifle, and his companions will come before any of my friends can free themselves to grab that rifle. I have to wait, but my friends don't understand this.

Gay can just see me through the corner of her eye. I motion for her to move away from me as far as she can, which isn't much. My efforts concentrate on watching the man at the door.

This won't be easy. The first bullet will likely deflect as it breaks the thick windowpane, which means the next bullet has to find its mark. I can do this, I say to myself, as my head throbs and aches. Not now, I realize, do not shoot now. I must give Bill as much chance to free Rick as can be given. Just be ready and do not hesitate to shoot—do not wait. We don't have much time. Don't shoot now, don't hesitate to shoot when that time comes.

97
(Franklin)

"We need to hide their bodies in the woods, Frank—too open to leave 'em."

"Yo, now or after we get their suits on, man?" I ask as I glance up into the gray overcast skies, then across these barren woodlands, to see nothing but the wild, yet Radwell's point holds; we can't leave these bodies so out in the open.

"After," he says. "I'll need you to put their bodies on the machines—I can't do it."

"Girly-man," I joke as our eyes meet and begin changing clothes. The cold makes that change quick. I grab the nearest body, drag it on top and across the flat at the rear of the nearest machine, then do the same with the other, placing it on top of the second machine. Radwell is busy checking the dead men's bodies for wallets, or for anything useful, while I do this.

"Oh-yeah, man, sweet," I say as I settle into the driver's seat of one of the machines, and look to the other from where I sit, "Handgun in each machine, man—see dat Rad? Sweet. Dey were goin' for dem when we shot dem." I grab the handgun out of the opened glove box—just big enough to hold the pistol, and slip the gun under my open coat within my belt line. There is no extra ammo seen.

"No-ya think," Radwell retorts with a smile concerning the guns, as he goes and grabs the other one. "Come on, let's get these bodies back into those woods behind camp."

We ride the short distance to the trucks before being forced to stop just short of them because the dead man's body on Radwell's snowmobile rolls off the back of his machine. As we rode by the trailer's door Cal was there giving a thumb up sign to congratulate us.

"Get back inside and watch them Cal!" Radwell orders as we stop the machines after the dead man fell. Cal disappears from sight.

I roll the other dead man off my machine near the same place where the first one fell—close enough—neither of us are interested in taking them further, as we turn our machines around and go a ways to park them back on the path we had made, thirty-some feet away along the truck path from the front door of the trailer, pointing north toward the Michigan border, the direction where the snowmobiles first appeared and where we want to go.

As I climb from my machine I stick the butt of my rifle into the snow and lean the barrel over against the cowl, so I can reach it easily when I return. The handgun will be better to use inside the trailer. I have not forgotten that I may need to kill Rad and Cal. I'll just have to make sure I ride alone on my snowmobile if they convince me, by their actions and words, to travel along with them, instead of me killing them.

Things are finally coming around. We got a way to Michigan, to Canada—I got a way for a new life with these machines. Rad and I congratulate each other as we stand beside the snowmobiles.

Cal appears back at the trailer's door again and just watches us as he simply stands there with a broad smile on his face. Radwell flashes a quick smile back to Cal as he murmurs; "We can forget that man out there. If we kill everyone inside, you know, ah, if the crazy man is still alive he'll have a time convincing the law it wasn't him, if we set it up right. You know, leave your gun behind. Wipe the prints from it and put somebody else's on it instead. Ah-so what do you think?"

Radwell, you just signed your death warrant. The only thing keeping me from killing you is Cal holding that gun of his, watching us; "Bullshit. We leave him, yeah. Use my gun—ya outta yo mind? Da rest of it I don't care. We need ta get out a here fast as we can, man."

Radwell smiles; "Ya never could take a joke," as he tips his head in agreement, his eyes studying mine.

Cal remains in the open doorway to the trailer, still smiling at us, and asks if he should ready some food for our trip.

"Cal," I say back, "Check dose people out. Stop starin' at us, will ya?"

Cal disappears briefly before returning to stare at us again.

"Idiot," I whisper as I turn away from Cal and hop on my snowmobile. Radwell laughs under his breath to my word as he hops onto his machine. I can't kill Radwell while Cal watches or keeps so quickly reappearing. Rad's thought of the crazy man getting the blame won't work but it could buy time—to my advantage. "What's the plan, Rad?" I ask as I start my machine.

Radwell nods his head as he starts his machine up. He looks straight ahead a moment before looking to me; "We gotta kill them now."

"Cops'll follow our tracks, Rad."

"We take them back the way these guys came. That'll put a question as when the tracks were made. We still buy time killing them." Radwell waits only a second for me to reply, but I don't. "Kill 'em Cal!" Radwell orders loudly as Cal once again appears at the doorway. "And then bring whatever food you can."

Cal hesitates and comes back to the doorway. "What kind of food?"

"Oh forget it," Radwell impatiently waves Cal off, "Go kill them."

Cal's expression changes to delight as he disappears inside the trailer. I look away to the dash of my machine, turning on its engine and revving it up high and listening to it backfire as it turns down, revving it up again as I argue with myself over whether to kill Radwell. My stomach turns over with what is going to happen to these innocent people, but then I don't really care. What bothers me is that it now bothers me—I never thought it would or could and cannot understand why it does now. Oh, well, I won't lose sleep over it.

The machines are relatively new and well equipped, both having two-way radios and both having cowling heat to warm the driver. An added component to the machine's console is a rather expensive looking compass. I once again wind the revs up till the engine screams at nearly 6,000 rpm's before I adjust the throttle down, before I blow the engine apart. Radwell has been doing what I've done, for fun and with a smile. I reluctantly smile back. The compass will be very useful.

The dream of the life I've wanted for so long is now within reach. After so many years of my life passing by wasted and confined I get to live life again. I did not deserve those prison years ... these people within the trailer don't deserve to die, but their deaths will secure my freedom, enough reason to kill them.

We barely hear the blast of Cal's first shot over the sounds of our screaming engines. Then more muffled blasts.

No! My mind screams! Not the right sounds! I immediately know some of those blasts came from a handgun—the gun of the man I hunted out in the woods! DAMN! I stand up on my machine, letting the engine go to idle and then stop, as I reach for my rifle, becoming rigid in my stance as I do. Out of the corner of my eye I see Radwell, as the sounds of his engine quiets and stops, pointing his gun at me.

"Don't think of it Frank," he warns.

"The man I hunted!" I yell at him as my head points towards the south woods then to the trailer, "Is in there! Cal has been shot!"

Another blast—we see this one go through the base of the trailer's door. Something is wrong! Together Radwell and I hurry to the trailer's door through the path in the heavy snow, rifles in hand.

Radwell is below me on my right as I step up the trailer's stairs and reach for the door handle when I hear a rumbling from inside and Radwell yell; "Lookout!"

The door; meant to open inward, bursts open against me with tremendous force and knocks me clear off the stairs and onto my back into the snow below.

A rifle's blast sounds—but not mine, for my rifle has been knocked free and has fallen somewhere nearby, burying itself in the snow.

The blast came from Radwell's gun, but the shot misses the big man, who came crashing through the door to fling me away. Bill pounces on the retreating back stepping Radwell with terrifying force by launching himself off the steps. His impact tears Radwell's gun from his grip and that gun buries itself in the snow. Radwell tries in vain to guard himself against being crushed by the weight and charging power of the enraged man. Their arms entangle as Bill lands on top of him, burying them both deep into the snow, out of my sight.

I struggle to my feet and begin running for the snowmobiles as I hear the big man grunt fiercely, catch a measure of his violent movements as a frightening backdrop to the sights of Smith jumping out from the trailer's doorway with Cal's rifle—my rifle, in hand, the cowboy following close behind, as I look back in fear. Smith has me in his sights as he stands in the snow and pulls the trigger. I think my life is over, but the gun doesn't fire—the gun's empty! He starts to throw the gun at me.

My eyes catch sight of Doug jumping out into the air from the trailer's steps at that same moment, feet and arms flailing, holding tight to a long kitchen knife in one of his hands and of the trailer door hanging uselessly to the side, pulling at the torn wooden framework that somehow still holds the door to the outside of the building.

I run as hard and as fast as I can. The closest machine is just feet away—I will get to it before they can catch me. Enough so I can start it and take off—I can, before they can grab me, but the timing will be close. Hurry!

An impact against my left shoulder knocks me down as I land face first in the snow at the base of my machine. Smith's rifle throw painfully hit its mark. Get up! Get up! You have a handgun at your waist—use it!

I roll to my back, pull the gun from my belt, as I rise to my knees. I see them—all of them; the cowboy rushing at me on my left; Smith, closer, with fire in his eyes using my path; the big man to my right—his right arm hanging strangely at his side, barreling down on me through the unbroken snow—they will all be dead—I have time to kill them all when more shots bark out very close off to my right—*it's the crazy man*—pointing his gun at me from the north corner of the trailer.

"YOU DIE FIRST!" I scream as I ignore the others. My arm jolts from the three shots I fire. I joyfully see two of them hit the crazy man in the waist and shoulder and he disappears from my sight. I turn the gun against the big man and put a bullet into his side yet feel the gun rip loose from my right hand and the bones in my arm come apart at the elbow, as Bill's falling body impacts mine and slides past. I feel someone else land on my legs and grip them tight, a sharp stab of a knife slicing deep into my left upper leg.

Then there is Smith, my left arm getting pinned under his legs, useless, but he is not looking at me. Smith is looking over the back of Bill, who has turned to hold me down, toward where the crazy man lies and Smith's face, at first full of concern, quickly becomes one of anguish, turning to me with a terrifying scowl.

I watch his hands rapidly reach behind around my head and pull it up to twist it with great force. I yell out. I resist, but I watch Smith's eyes burn into mine as he turns my head and hear his voice as he tells me I am going to Hell.

I feel only the beginnings of the thunderous jolts that snap the bones of my neck—then I don't feel much pain at all, I only hear the rest of the snapping. My head drops into the snow and comes to lay face up to the sky. I cannot move it. The snow is cold against the sides of my face and some falls into my eyes, coming off Smith's withdrawing hands. I blink the snow away to see the heavy gray clouds drift by above and the images of the men's faces as they stand and scornfully look down at me; Bill is clutching his side with his bloody left hand. Shadows pulse around the edges of my sight, growing larger between every quickening but lessening beat of my heart that I can somehow hear. A crow flies across the sky overhead into this covering darkness slowly overwhelming my eyes. The bird caws and mocks me with words I heard it say many times before; I am not going anywhere ... I feel strangely detached from everything, feel no strong emotion. I do not believe this; it is too surreal—there is no time to feel an emotion. I cannot see anymore, only blackness, yet I can hear the men's words and their movements above me, but then these, too, soon fade....

98

There are renewed sounds of the snowmobiles driving near. Then they go quiet again.

My eyes open, with effort, by the man's loud voice inside at the door. He still faces the outside, unaware of what is going on so close to him inside. Rick seems nearly free as Bill works Rick's arm bindings. It is scary to think I almost went to sleep without the slightest realization of its approach. Failure searches me out, trying to find its own success—and I must not let it.

Doug suddenly and purposely moves in a struggling way, enough to distract the man at the door, as this man takes a glance back inside. The man looks right past me and does not notice Bill, who became motionless with one arm behind Rick's back and the man also does not scrutinize Rick. This man at the door just scolds Doug to stay still, before his attentions return to what is going on outside on the other side of the trailer, where more voicing is heard.

A moment of quietness passes before a loud order is given for the man at the door—Cal is his name, to kill the people inside.

Bill stiffens and withdraws the tiny scissors from behind Rick's back to ready himself and his eyes look towards me demandingly, but Rick is not free—Doug is not free. I can hear the muffled exclamations of the women near me as they react to the order. My hand feels the trailer rock slightly from everyone's struggles as some strength returns to me as I ready for what will happen next.

The man at the door begins to turn to come inside but stops as raised voices are heard from the other side of the trailer, so he returns to the door and waits, his hand caressing his rifle's stock and bolt as his foot props open the door, watching whatever is happening outside. I sense he will enjoy the killing and I hate him for that. I glance at Rick as the man at the door suddenly turns, the door slams behind him, his rifle swings naturally to point directly *at me!*

Shards of glass fly everywhere and strike me in the face! Sounds of a struggle come from within the trailer as I point my gun inside. With tied legs Bill had thrown himself at the man as he saw him aim at me, distracting him enough for his shot to shatter the window—and miss me. Bill's right hand clings to the man's waist belt while his left hand reaches and claws for the rifle, but he is unable to dislodge the gun from Cal's grip as Cal turns his body to turn the weapon on Rick, as Rick throws his body at the man, coming down at the feet of Cal—Rick's hands and legs are still tied. Mary manages to kick Cal's leg from where she sits.

I see an opening and fire two rounds. One misses his shoulder; the second finds his chest at the top of his sternum—*dead center* as sounds of snowmobile engines roar outside.

A blotch of red quickly forms on the man's shirt as he buckles from the impact and crumbles backwards onto the floor. His rifle discharges by Bill's head and through the foot of the trailer's door, the flash singeing Bill's clothes at the shoulder as Bill turns away from the blast, deafening him, wracking him with pain, his hands letting go of the man to hold his head and ears before quickly returning to grasp the man. Bill is in agony.

My friend's bodies block any chance for me to take another shot.

Suddenly Paula appears. She moves with uncertainty and in a stagger, carrying a steak knife in her hand. Her face is beaten black and blue, her left side covered in fresh blood. She seems slow to recognize anyone, barely comprehending the fight before her. Doug calls her to cut him free, raises his bound legs in front of her and shakes them repeatedly. She looks at them a moment in a daze, then leans down and cuts them free. Doug immediately jumps up turns around and offers her his hands. She slowly cuts them, too. Free, Doug grabs the knife from her and cuts through Rick's bindings as quick as he can, commanding Paula to go get more knives—but she can't, she barely has control of herself as she crumples down on the floor, holding her side. Doug frees Gay and Mary, while Rick moves up the body of Cal on the floor below him. Bill has gained directional, yet not full, control of the rifle from the failing man. Doug reaches down and over and frees Bill's leg bindings. Gay's face is red with her own blood from the first explosion of glass so near to her, and she is calling out in pain through her taped mouth, the blasts from my gun deafening, perhaps shattering, her eardrum, but she has raced off toward the kitchen as soon as Doug freed her and reappears, this time quickly handing a third steak knife to Mary while holding one of her own.

Mindlessly I try to enter the trailer through the shattered window but stop when my right hand is sliced open gripping the jagged remnants of the window itself. I'm unable to do anything for those inside, so I struggle away from the window, determined to make my way around the north corner to the front of the trailer. I have to help. Maybe I can bring down one more man with the bullets I have left.

I hear the women order the men away from Cal—for the men to get the others outside, as I leave the window behind. I hear Cal's gurgled screams as the women fall on him with their knives. There are other noises and the trailer rocks from the violent movements within but my mind cannot decipher what is going on.

My lungs search for the air that will satisfy as dizzying nausea returns. I balance against the trailer's corner with my right hand after I make the first turn. The gun, also in my right hand, is very heavy, as is my head, shoulders—everything else. As I reach the inner northeast corner of the trailer, central to our camp, my eyes are pulled right to the sight of Bill, in the snow, climbing off the white man underneath him—the man who walked with Franklin and who appears dead. My eyes move left, over to Rick, whose arms swing in violent descent throwing a rifle that is now flipping end over end through the air. Rick begins running in the snow, the best he can. In the same instant I see Doug rising in the snow behind Rick with a knife in his right hand. I hear a heavy thump as the rifle Rick threw hits its target and my eyes slowly turn to find what that is and see the back of Franklin as he is near the snowmobiles, but face down in the snow.

All this motion, all the major body movements are bogged down by the deepness of the snow, making everyone's efforts appear awkward and clumsy. Rick brakes onto the paths made moments earlier by Franklin, and so does Doug, as I stabilize myself against the trailer and begin to find Franklin in my sights; with uncertain legs, I hold the gun before me with both hands.

My friends move rapidly towards Franklin as he rises and pulls a handgun from under his belt and starts to aim at them. Somehow my gun fires though I don't have Franklin in my sights, two bullets fly uselessly away, but their sound makes Franklin turn. He sees me aiming at him. He puts me in his sights. My trigger clicks when.…

99

Unintelligible sounds. A noise announces from one direction and another from somewhere else, and the blackness is total—as if I am buried deep inside a cave.

I can see nothing ... feel nothing.

The sounds come again.

This time I recognize the tones and their variances as being familiar to me yet I still do not understand how they are or what is being revealed. I am confused about being aware that I am confused and understanding that I am confused. Where am I?

Now one sound leaves, replaced by a singular and deeper sound—a voice nearer to me?

The total blackness gets pierced by subtle points of light—tiny, tiny pinpricks flashing so vaguely I believe I imagine or will them to be. The blackened void has been so total, so complete—I can remember nothing about being inside it while there, though I can tell, now, I am coming out of it—but to where?

I recognize my name being gently said.

Something enters my space, then leaves, comes again and leaves again. My senses react as these stimuli play out and my body slowly begins to reestablish itself—I have a body? I do. When this something comes once more I recognize it for what it is—a touch. It nudges my left shoulder as my name is repeated. It's been an insistent touch. I ignore these intrusions the best I can, being so fearfully awed by the blackness I'm leaving behind. Nothing—there's nothing I can remember about it, nothing drawn from being within its dark realm, yet I'm coming out from this blackness and have had to experience something while within. Nothing—an utterly complete void of awareness of any kind, other than awareness of leaving its emptiness, fills my mind.

Have I been unconscious?

Is this a near death experience?

Have I died and being beckoned to join the other side?

The nudge and my name intrudes again as clouds of dull gray light begin bursting through the pinpricks that had broken the once complete darkness, these lights flowing and growing ever brighter and more expansive and very rapidly, colors begin to appear in this light, pulling my thoughts away from the utter void to the awareness of what is developing around me.

The blinking of my eyes startle me as my sight slowly returns.

I become attentive to the rhythmic sound of a machine beeping in chorus with the beating of my heart and again feel that insistent nudge on my shoulder and my name being said.

Images form and take shape quickly; I am in a hospital room.

My senses become more active and assess the condition of my body, rush in on my mind, informing me I'm very weak and sickly with a body chill that'll not go away anytime soon.

I look toward an image moving slightly beside me and recognize the blurry aqua-colored clothed figure as having to be a doctor. He is nudging my arm.

"Welcome back," the balding man says, as he once again states my name.

I so slightly nod my head to acknowledge him while my eyes become focused and clear. I watch him adjust his small wire rimmed glasses with thick chocolate fingers. His black forearms are strong and covered with long dark curled hairs. He looks fatigued, like most doctors do.

"I'm Doctor Davis. I'm your attending doctor and have been since you came into our emergency room—do you understand what I'm saying so far?"

I nod my head.

"Can you answer me verbally?"

I swallow and open my mouth weakly—this simple action is an effort yet I answer him.

"I will be repeating this later, when you feel certain you're not living a dream. You're coming out of heavy medications. Even so, you've been coming out of them for awhile and should quickly come cognizant. Just to give you a little more time to do that I am going to give you a cursory examination while I talk to you. I do encourage you to answer me verbally, though a nod of your head will do fine for the moment—understand?"

I nod my head.

"I'm starting with your left hand. I'm gripping it now. Can you feel me touching you?"

I nod my head.

"Keep nodding as you feel me touch each of your fingers—nod each time a new finger is touched," Davis pauses, and then continues; "You are a fortunate man to have survived what you have. You are very lucky to have a sister who is a nurse. Very lucky to have a wife who has not left your side until I ordered her to do so just now. For the last seven and a half days she has not left this room voluntarily anymore than she's had to, and I think we compelled her to be gone about four hours to examine her, sir—not much time away from your side. And she's been through a lot herself. We did most of her treatment here in this room beside you. Squeeze my hand. Good. Can you feel this?"

I love my wife. I am awed she has been by my side as he has said. Awed more that she is alive ... so glad … so … relieved.

He prods my left shoulder area, pushing with his fingertips. I nod yes to feeling his push.

"You're also very lucky to have friends who can ride snowmobiles and take them through the woods like they're experts flying the latest military fighter planes. Rick? Doug? I think that's their names—the two that rode. Bill? Bill suffered a badly separated shoulder and a bullet to his side, among other injuries, so it had to be the other two. Anyway, they brought you and Paula to the paramedics in quick time—just in time, for both of you, and then brought the rest of you out. Do you remember where you were at?"

It is coming back to me as he speaks. Yes.

"Do you remember what happened to you?"

Yes—some. Anxiety begins to grip my insides as random memories come frighteningly back to me, and I cough with pain as he presses against my right shoulder.

"You were shot here. Missed the joint, but the bullet lodged within the underside of your right scapula—your right shoulder wing bone. I'll try to spare you the medical terms. We went in and retrieved the bullet yesterday. You won't be able to move your right arm, or shoulder, like you used to—at least for awhile. I'm not surprised you're tender here."

Fine, why did you have to press so damn hard against it then, huh?

"I understand you saved the lives of those who are waiting outside here for you."

My heart is passionate to see my wife yet lifts further on hearing that others are here to see me—I did not expect that, yet I shake my head no to his statement. "All?" I rasp.

"Most—all who survived. There are also many family members and those of who died, wanting to speak with you. Paula is in the only other intensive care bed down the hall. She's in better shape than you, though. She'll be moved to a regular room tomorrow. So, what about you saving their lives?"

I can barely shake my head, but I indicate no.

"Oh. You don't feel you saved their lives?"

I shake my head again as he prods my stomach—an awful pain announces itself as he does. I can only see his head, shoulders, and upper arms now. My head lies flat against the bed pillow and I have no strength to lift it up to watch him.

"Another bullet wound here, sir. Why's that—you disagree you saved their lives?"

He forces me to answer; "They break free," I squeak out.

"Ah-yes, I heard that story, too. Yes, they were, but they needed your help."

I shake my head slightly and feebly say; "No."

"Oh, trying to be humble?" he says kindly, with a slight and understanding smile.

"No. They saved their lives … saved mine."

Davis broadly smiles, obviously liking my answer, before he replies; "Accurate—to a point. I would like to talk about that more, but later, no hurry."

He is down by my right foot, squeezing my toes. I nod yes as he squeezes each of those. I can only see his face.

"How about the feeling in these?" he asks, after moving over to my left leg.

"Fine." I say weakly.

"How about here?" he asks again, staring at me. I lock onto his eyes, something suddenly has changed in them and I do not like what I think I see. "I'm going to squeeze hard to make sure you can feel them. Can you?"

I cannot.

The beeping machine increases its speed as fear grips my heart. I recall my wounds as a sledgehammer of feelings crash down on me. Dread. Heat flushes my face. My stomach turns.

Davis waits and watches a moment longer before explaining.

"This is a small local hospital. We could not transfer you out and be certain you would live to finish the trip. I was in consultation by phone with specialists in Milwaukee almost constantly and almost from the moment the paramedics radioed in, and then brought you in…."

"How much," I gasp, "of the leg do I have left?"

"Nothing below the knee. The damage done had become severe; too little blood circulation needing too great a repair; infection, frostbite, and torn and shredded flesh. We had to take it off—I'm sorry."

Tears come to my eyes. I understand why he made Mary leave the room earlier, the indiscernible sounds I heard before. I recall knowing, out in the field, that my leg is lost, but knowing my leg is actually off scares me. I … I want it back. I … I feel like it's there—I want it back. I manage to lift my head enough for my eyes to tell me my leg is gone and my head drops back onto the pillow, tears well in my eyes. I want my leg back. I want it back.

"We put in two inches of stitches in your left arm, five inches in your left thigh wound where something sliced you open. I believe it was a bullet. Those wounds looked worse than they were; though much more so than the one across the right side of your face. The left side of your face doesn't look too pretty either. It was splintered full of tree bark and glass. Your back has the remnants of a large welt across it—actually several, but only one of concern. It will make you feel uncomfortable lying here until it goes completely away. You have a nice spread of bumps and bruises remaining over your body, too, but why worry about the small stuff? Your right hand has a few inches of stitches, and I told you about going into your right shoulder."

He pauses, seeing if I am going to make a response but I'm still stunned over the loss of my leg, before continuing: "That bullet in your side passed through your waist—the fatty area—your love handle." A smile passes across his face before continuing. "Your colon was missed, and for that you are a lucky man. Overall you have been beat up pretty damn good—excuse my language. We put in a lot, and I mean a lot, of blood into you. For a brief time you went back into shock. The first time was during transport. Your critical point was reached that first day about this time. We stood waiting to shock your heart, but didn't have to. We will have to do some heart tests later because of your blood loss and circumstances—we suspect you suffered blood clots to your lungs, and we'll have to run tests to see if you suffered any long term damage from them, or if you had any strokes from them, but, from what I'm observing, you're going to be okay. Clearly, if you didn't have the family and friends you do have, your spirit would have left you out there back in the woods."

He pauses once more, briefly, before continuing; "I think I've impressed you enough of what your condition is like right now. I know it's tough to hear, to comprehend what I've told you, so I'll be coming back. You are going to recover from all this. It will take some time. We will be seeing more of each other in the coming days. We can talk more then. For myself I am, ah, honored to have been involved in the care of and in getting to know your friends—they will all be fine, by the way. Some very tough stuff they've gone through, but they seem to be some very tough people. They should be fine, over time. I am honored to care for and to now talk with you. I am going to let your wife and sister in now. Do you have anything to say?"

I am silent. As if I can have something to say after all he has just said. He offers again to let the others in and I nod my agreement.

"Doc?" I ask weakly, stopping him before he reaches the door, "Can you throw a blanket over me? I'm cold. And, Doc, make sure you cover my leg. The one I … I don't have."

Mary hurries to my side and we kiss long and once more as Gay comes around to the other side of my bed. Gay gives me a hug.

"There are many others waiting outside to see you, too," Gay begins and adds: "Mom and Dad."

"My parents are here, too," Mary says. "And as much of the rest of us as can be."

"Bunch of friends," Gay chimes in. "Didn't think my brother, Mr. Excitement, had so many." She offers up a quick smile.

"Do I?" I ask. "That's good. I like that, want to see them all—find out who they are." I understood her loving jab and return a smile to her.

Mary and Gay each carry a different look of healing wounds, some still look painful.

"What the heck did you do out there in those woods, man?" Gay asks me. "We all want to know—Rick especially."

"Oh he does, huh? You too? I don't know really right now, Gay. Try me later."

"Okay," Gay replies, nodding her head, understanding I'm weak. "Just want to say I am amazed at what I know you did do—we all are." Mary nods agreement.

"Wow," I feebly say and add with a smile; "Then I'll spare you the details."

Gay searches my eyes before a smile comes across her face and she laughs. "Don't want to ruin the image, huh?"

I nod my head—and weakly smile in agreement with her. "The details aren't so awesome … thanks, though. I think … I will be amazed … at what you guys did. And, uh, what happened to you?" I ask them, indicating with a slight point of my head towards their wounds.

Gay points her finger at me: "Bill and I have hearing loss. You sound echo-ey to me. We're gonna talk to you later, dearest and only brother of mine about that. Each of your friends will be saying something to you, taking turns, if we don't do it all together here."

"Oh ... uh-oh, I take it I had something to do with why you two—why all of you, look like you all do?"

"Uh-huh," whispers Mary with a strong nod of her head.

"And, since I can't run from ya, I'm in a lot of trouble," I flatly say. I mean it as a joke but they do not take it that way. I look to each of them as we fall quiet for a moment. "Oh, that was supposed to be a joke."

"A bad one," Mary replies sternly.

"I lost my leg," I almost cry to her.

"I know. That does not make you any less of a man to me. After what we went through, I think I love you more," she replies.

I'm stunned at her words, then give a slight nod and smile to her as I feel tears run down my cheeks and squeeze her hand, "I love you, too." I turn serious. "My memories are coming back fast. Anyone here for Tom or Roy?"

"Yeah," Mary answers. "Both. One stayed from each of their families after they recovered their bodies, hoping to talk with you."

"Good … sort of," I softly say. "I'm getting tired here, but I'm going to stay awake for them. I've got promises to fulfill."

We fall silent for a moment. Mary replies; "They won't let them see you until tomorrow. They won't let you see anyone other than Gay and me until tomorrow and we have orders not to push you much, let you sleep, today."

"Oh," I weakly answer as I consider her words. "Tomorrow, then."

"Rick led the talk with Mark's family," Mary somberly adds. "Damn that wasn't easy. The utility men's, too. I don't know how we did that—it rips you're heart apart—I couldn't stop crying."

"Too much death," Gay adds, with tears in her eyes. "Unnecessary death."

I nod my head to her, to each of them. I want to tell them now how glad I am to see them, so glad that I can, but there are times when you just should not express yourself, I believe, around cherished friends, around the ones you love. Feelings like these are just ones having to be lived and silently understood—words aren't sufficient. My eyes become watery but I blink these tears away.

"Doug told me to tell you that you're about to meet his wife and son," Gay says, breaking the momentary silence. "He said he told you that you never would."

I smile from this, emotion flushing heat on my face, and the tears keep flowing from my eyes, as I nod towards Gay to acknowledge her. "What a liar." I softly ask, my lips trembling; "My children?"

Mary's face turns downcast as she shakes her head no. "We managed to contact them and did let them know—everything, and we were willing to pay for their transportation and stay, but they didn't come. They didn't care."

A moment of deep disappointment and sorrow is all I can give my children … choices have consequences … some good … some bad. I have been given another chance at life. I am not going to use it dwelling on what cannot be. I look at Mary; look lovingly into her eyes as I squeeze her hand. She squeezes back. I have a new life in front of me … and I want to live it.

www.ingramcontent.com/pod-product-compliance
Lightning Source LLC
Chambersburg PA
CBHW062023170626
46813CB00001B/271
9780984874309